The House at Kirtlebeck End

Sarah L King

For Jennifer & Alexander

ACKNOWLEDGMENTS

My heartfelt thanks goes to my family for their love and support, especially my husband David whose help, once again, was so invaluable during the editing and publishing process. This book is my answer to my children's pleas for me to write a 'ghost story'. So here it is, kids, this one's for you (to read when you're much older)!

I would also like to thank my draft readers K.J Farnham, Alexandra King, David King and Diane Robertson for their time, effort and feedback.

Prologue

Eleanor
October 1972

The bus rumbles as it pulls away, spewing out diesel fumes and disturbing the large pools of rain which have gathered at the side of the road. Around me other alighting passengers rush on to their destinations, hoods pulled up, umbrellas flicked open. Unlike them, I don't hurry. Instead, I find myself staring after the bus for a few moments, lost in my thoughts, remembering the last time I got the bus into town. A different bus, a different town. Different business to attend to. That time I wasn't alone, not like I am now.

I fear I will always be alone now.

Cold seeps into the bones of my feet. I look down, shifting away from the murky puddle of water which has penetrated my shoes. I haven't dressed well for the occasion; no hood, no umbrella, no boots. I should have worn boots. I should have realised it would rain. After all, it's done little else for these past few days. My mind wanders over the long hours stood at the window, watching the grey gloom, waiting for something to happen. Asking Anna if she thought the weather was a sign, if she thought God might be crying. She didn't answer, but she did give me a hug. She did tell me that everything would be alright.

But still, it's odd that it's not stopped raining since he went away.

I'm soaked through to the skin now, but still I can't make myself move from this spot. I look up, the heavy droplets chilling me as they saturate my face. I want to feel refreshed, awakened, alive. Instead, I feel like I'm drowning. Too much water. Too many memories. So much dread. I know where I have to go, what I have to do. There is a necessity, an inevitability about it. But it's also terrifying, because once I say those words, that makes it real. Once I say those words, there will be no going back. The burden of it will be shared, but I know deep down that won't really help. It will always lie heavily on Anna and I. After all, we're the ones he left behind.

I force myself down the paved street, one reluctant foot following the other as I squelch along in my sodden shoes. I try hard to empty my mind, to focus on the task at hand. I try to stop the images from creeping in; images of him, of her. Of us. Of what we had, once. Tears prick in the corners of my tired eyes. Self-consciously I rub at them, keeping my chin down to avoid eye contact with passers-by. I'm aware of how terrible I must look; pale, gaunt, my heavy, puffy eyes simultaneously besieged by fits of crying and chronic lack of sleep. Part of me can't believe that this is what he has reduced me to. He betrayed me, he tormented me, he derided me. He ruined my life. But for all the problems we had, for all he did and for all I hated him, I also loved him once.

I wipe away a stray tear. I don't want him back, but I don't want him to be gone, either.

My steps slow as I reach the police station. I look up, drawing an uneven breath as the blue and white sign above the door catches my eye. This is somewhere I never thought I'd have to go. This is something I never thought I'd have to do. And yet, here I am, walking into this red brick building on a miserable autumn afternoon, about to tell a perfect stranger that he has gone. I will start crying again, no doubt, and they will sympathise. They will offer me tissues, perhaps a cup of tea. I will sob out my sorry story, and they will think that they understand how my world has fallen apart, and how badly I need some help. But they won't understand, not really. My world is in pieces, my family is destroyed, but they can't fix it. No one can. They can investigate, they can try to find him, but I already know that it won't be enough. No one can help me now.

I push open the door, ready to tell someone something. Ready to hold back almost everything.

The man behind the counter looks up at me, his expression at once suspicious and inquisitive as I approach. The light inside is yellow and dim, and I know it makes me look as ghastly as I feel. I reach into my pocket, pulling out a damp tissue and wiping my running nose. I shiver, my drenched clothes sticking uncomfortably to my skin. Momentarily I contemplate whether I will catch a chill after today. Maybe I will become so sick and feverish that I will die. Given everything I've been through and everything I must still face I'm tempted to think that would be for the best. Then I remember that I'd be leaving Anna alone, and I can't abandon Anna. All we have is each other now.

I pull my coat tighter around me, teasing the collar up higher around my throat. Hiding scars, erecting defences. My coat is scruffy, well-worn, just like the rest of my clothes. Not for the first time I promise myself a new coat, a new wardrobe. A new me, once all this is over.

The man studies me, his grey eyes growing wider with empathy as he catches proper sight of my grim expression. He's only young, fair-haired and tall but with a slight build. I always imagined policemen to be bigger, but then I haven't met that many in my time. I wonder what he makes of me, standing here, rain-soaked and carrying the weight of the world on my shoulders. I wonder if he's looking for clues, trying to guess what I might have seen, what I might have heard. What I might have done, or what might have been done to me. Oh, the stories I could tell him, if only I had the nerve. Stories he couldn't dream of; stories he couldn't decipher with a mere scrutinising gaze. But I'm not here for any of that. I'm here to say one thing, and nothing more.

"Can I help you, madam?" His voice is heavy with curiosity, and I can see that he hasn't quite made up his mind about me. I could be a victim, a witness, or a perpetrator, poised to confess. I could be all three. It's so hard to tell just from looking at someone. I should know that better than most.

"Yes," I begin, my voice suddenly hoarse. I clear my throat and try again. "Yes, I need to talk to someone."

"Do you wish to report a crime?" He lowers his voice, even though there is no one else around but us.

"I…I…" The words are there in my head, but they won't come. The tears do come, though, hot and fast, as do the sobs, relentless and oppressive in my chest. I stand there for a few moments, unable to do anything but weep. The policeman stands there, watching and waiting. He has seen all this before.

"Take your time, madam. Take your time and we will do our best to help. Just tell me what's happened."

I take a deep breath, forcing myself to be calm. I have to get these words out. I have to say what needs to be said. I have to tell this man that he is gone. I have to do what is right. I have to do what is expected, even though I know it will do no good.

"I'm here about my husband," I say, pausing to pull out my tissue and blow my nose once more.

The policeman raises an eyebrow. He keeps his eyes fixed on me as he grabs his pen and gets ready to commit the dreadful details to paper. "Yes?"

I close my eyes for a moment, steadying myself, trying to hold my nerve. Once these words are out, there will be no going back. Our lives, our family, our story now becomes part of the detail, part of the investigation which must take place to find a man who, I know, will not be found. But what alternative is there? I have to be strong. For Anna, and for myself. Otherwise there is no hope for either of us, no hope at all.

My eyes flicker open and I allow the words to fall from my lips, setting them free before I can think any more about them. They must take on a life of their own now. They must become a story which everyone knows. I can live with that, I think, as long as the rest remains hidden. As long as everything else that happened stays within the walls of our home at Kirtlebeck End. It is the place which bore witness to it all. It is the place where secrets must now be contained.

"I need to report a missing person," I tell him. "My husband, Bert Murray, has disappeared."

1

Harry
January 2018

My car rolls shakily over the uneven driveway, and I have to catch my breath. The house has come into view now, idling there at the end of the gravel road which is having its fair share of fun with my little car's suspension. Even in the bleak January daylight it strikes me that the picture the solicitor showed me simply didn't do it justice, nor did it give any real indication of the sheer size of the place.

"It's late Victorian," he'd said, pointing disinterestedly at a grimy old polaroid. "I believe they call it an arts and crafts house. It needs a bit of work inside – your grandmother was in her eighties when she passed away and hadn't done anything with it in years. Nonetheless, it'll fetch a decent price once you get it on the market, I'm sure."

I'd nodded blandly. He might as well have been speaking another language, for all the sense his words made to me. Now that I can see it for myself, however, I find that I am in awe. I stare in stunned silence, studying its bright white walls, its huge windows, its tall chimneys, its red roof reaching up in dramatic points. For a moment I am reminded of the classic novels I read during my youth, all those stories of young women arriving at grand houses, climbing nervously from their carriages to be greeted by an old aunt, a wealthy acquaintance, and usually somewhere along the line, a handsome gentleman. If I imagine hard enough, I think, I too could be Jane Eyre or Elizabeth Bennett, arriving with curious trepidation at the start of my own adventure.

A pot hole on the driveway jolts me and I laugh at my own absurdity. I've no need of men, however attractive they might be and besides, I know that there's nothing waiting for me here apart from empty rooms, cardboard boxes, and dust. Lots of dust, if the solicitor's words are anything to go by.

I park my car outside the front door, an old wooden affair with flaking red paint, flanked on both sides by slim windows fashioned in stained glass. For a while I sit there quietly, just looking around, absorbing my surroundings and periodically catching sight of myself in the rear view mirror. It's not a pleasing image; my short dark hair is unkempt and my hazel eyes look heavy after such an early start. Not for the first time in the past few weeks, it occurs to me that I look much older than my thirty years. I tell myself that I'm weary from the long drive, that the hours spent concentrating on the motorway have left me feeling dazed, but I know that's not really it. Usually after sitting for so long in a car I am desperate to climb out, to breathe, to explore, but not today. Today I am hesitant. Today I am wondering whether I have made the right decision in coming here. Above all, today I am wondering once again why I am here now, now that she is dead, and why I never knew about this place or about my grandmother before.

My grandmother. The words still feel strange to think, never mind to say. So strange that I couldn't bring myself to visit her grave on the way here, even though the solicitor told me where to find it. I'm such a coward, but then that's nothing new. I've always been better at running away and avoiding things than I have at facing up to them.

"Come on, Harry, pull yourself together," I mutter with an exasperated sigh. There's no use in tormenting myself now. I'm here and that's all that really matters.

I climb out of the car and take my first deep breath of crisp, country air. The day is cold but still, and I am struck immediately by the quietness which surrounds me. I have never experienced rural life before; I have never spent any time in sleepy little villages like Kirtlebeck, tucked away as it is in splendid isolation in southern Scotland. By birth and upbringing, I am a city dweller and this place is certainly a far cry from my home in Manchester with its bustling streets, its air laden with fumes, its incessant traffic which could be heard day and night as it rumbled past my cramped flat. At home I never had space and silence like this, and I find that I am both excited and unnerved by it.

Still reluctant to unlock the door and go inside, I take a few moments to wander around the grounds which are, like the house, unexpectedly large. The front of the house is dominated by the gravel with its torturous caverns and holes, but a peak at the rear garden reveals a long stretch of unkempt grass bordered by mature shrubs, a large sprawling tree placed dramatically at its rear. A small gasp of delight escapes from me before I can stop it. I have never had a garden before, and although this one clearly needs the sort of love and care which is probably beyond me, I can't help but imagine myself sitting out there on a summer's day, a cold drink in my hand as I admire the plants in bloom. The vision lingers for mere seconds, until I remember that I won't be here in the summer, that by then this house and its grounds will belong to someone else. I retreat from the garden, shutting the gate with a short, sharp click. I have a job to do, I remind myself, and nothing more. After all, I have no connection to this place or to the woman who lived here. My family and its many secrets saw to that.

"No time like the present then," I say to myself. I look at the key clutched tightly in my hand, unsure what I'm making such a fuss about. It's just a house, isn't it? It's just bricks and mortar, a fancy roof and some nice windows. I gave up my flat in

Manchester without a second thought and I had lived there for years, ever since Dad passed away and left me on my own for good. If I had felt strange or sentimental it should have been then not now, not standing in front of this house I've never entered which belonged to a woman I never knew.

"Yours isn't such an unusual case, you know," the solicitor had said, clearly moved by my shocked face to offer some words of consolation. "There are lots of people who know nothing of their relatives until they inherit from them. The world is a big place and sometimes people simply lose touch."

I hadn't been able to nod in agreement that time. My family hadn't just lost contact: the disconnect we experienced had been more severe than that. I had a grandmother; my missing, presumed dead mother had a mother who no one had wanted to tell me about. What's more, my grandmother had clearly known of my existence and yet, she had never wanted to reach out even when I was losing everyone around me. Now she had left me a house. Why? Was it because she finally wanted me to know about her, or was it simply because she had no one else to give it to?

Anger and frustration bubble uncomfortably inside me, giving me just enough courage to finally turn the key in the latch. The door sticks fast to the frame, comfortable in its position after months of disuse, and I have to give it a good shove with my shoulder to get it to budge. Feeling more than a little like an intruder I skulk inside, leaving the door slightly ajar behind me. I will have to go back out to my car to gather my belongings in a few moments and besides, closed doors have always unnerved me, especially in unfamiliar places. You never know what you might be walking into, or when you might need to make a swift exit.

"Stop being ridiculous Harry, there's nothing here," I whisper.

The hallway which greets me is large and dark, dominated by mahogany panelling and peach wallpaper. To one side sits the staircase, a carved wooden spectacle meandering grandly to the upper floor. I sniff the air, detecting a smell of dampness mingled with dust. I don't know a great deal about old houses, but I suspect that this place would benefit from a few open windows and the heating being run once in a while. I remind myself that it has been sealed up for well over nine months. The solicitor informed me of my grandmother's death last summer once they had finally tracked me down, and by then she had been deceased for some time. Since then I had quite literally sat on the knowledge of my windfall, trying to decide what on earth I should do. My initial reaction had been to find someone to do all the work, to pay to get the house cleared, marketed and sold. The house had nothing to do with me, I told myself; I had no business rifling through a dead stranger's things. Yet no matter how hard I tried, I couldn't quite bring myself to go through with such a detached approach. Detachment had been the story of my life, and I didn't want any more of it. But I couldn't bring myself to actually come here either, to confront this place and everything it represents, and so I had waited. And waited. Then Christmas arrived and in more ways than one, my life got turned on its head. As the year reached its conclusion, I suddenly found that coming to this place wasn't the worst of the choices facing me anymore.

I wander from room to room, familiarising myself with the layout and taking in the quaint old features. The décor is tired and faded, and the aged furniture is sparsely arranged, but it's not hard to imagine how fine this place would look at its best. I let out small gasps of excitement whenever I spy a cast-iron fireplace or some elaborate cornice. I can't help it - neither are features you see every day, especially when you've spent all of your adult life living in a seventies pre-fab flat.

"I can't believe this place belongs to you, Harry," I whisper, breaking the heavy silence of this empty home with my disbelief.

It's true; I can't believe it. I couldn't believe it when the solicitor told me, and I can't believe it now. I still can't understand how I am related to someone who lived their life in a home like this, with all of this space and tranquillity, and I never knew of her existence. I never knew her; I never knew her story. As I leave the ground floor rooms and walk up the stairs, my footsteps feel heavy with regret. After all, it's too late now; my grandmother is gone and all that is left is this grand, empty shell, its air thick with dust and the memories it held now extinguished. This house is now the only sign that she was ever here at all, and it is my job to dispose of it, to remove its contents, to wipe the slate clean. A harsh laugh catches in my throat. As excited as I might be about period features, I don't think there's any amount of fancy coving that can help me to overlook the bitter irony of it all.

The first floor of the house is just as impressive as the one below, composed of several bedrooms and a bathroom, all joined by a wide, open hallway. Most of the rooms are very bare, containing little more than an unmade bed and a chest of drawers. Even the master bedroom, which I guess must have been my grandmother's room, is quite empty, with only the two perfume bottles and a rather sorry-looking tub of face cream on the dressing table giving any hint that the room was recently inhabited. As I glance at her bed I find that I have to suppress a shudder. She died at home, the solicitor told me. Her illness had been short and quick, and there had been no time for hospital. Standing in her room, surrounded by the remnants of her belongings, I wish now that this was a piece of information he hadn't shared. I glance once more around the room, taking in its lovely dark wood furniture and pale, floral wallpaper. Then I close the door behind me, resolving to sleep in one of the smaller rooms tonight.

Wrapping my arms around myself, I decide to return to my car, to bring in my few possessions and start making myself at home. On my way here I had had the good sense to stop at a shop for some provisions, and my earlier cursory glance at the kitchen had revealed the presence of the necessary mod-cons, all unplugged but hopefully in working order. I decide that I will start in the kitchen and make myself something to eat, before unpacking my things, making up my bed and getting a good night's sleep.

Just deal with the basics, I tell myself. Get some rest and start afresh tomorrow.

I shake my head at my internal monologue. A fresh start. That's what I'm really here for, isn't it? To get closure on a past which isn't my own, to profit from somewhere which probably shouldn't be mine, all so that I can move on with my life.

"I don't understand why she left it to me," I had said to the lawyer. "Didn't she have any friends, any other relatives, anyone else at all?" I didn't name my mother explicitly, but the pained look on my face was no doubt enough to tell him what I really meant.

"As far as we can reasonably know, you're her only living next of kin," the solicitor had replied pointedly. "Your grandmother left everything to you, so if there is anyone else, it would appear that she didn't wish to acknowledge them in her will." He moved his head in an awkward wobble as though he couldn't decide whether he should nod or shake it. "In accordance with her wishes, you are the sole beneficiary of her estate."

"But I never knew her," I'd insisted, my voice little more than a hoarse whisper of disbelief. "I don't even know what she looked like."

"I understand your shock," he'd said in that flat, procedural tone which told me that he didn't understand at all. "Perhaps when you go to the house, when you sort through your grandmother's personal effects – if that's what you decide to do – then you'll find out much more about her. At the very least I'm sure you'll find a photo or two."

As I switch on her fridge and place my meagre meal for one inside, the sting of guilt rises from deep in my gut. I reach into my back pocket and take out the faded photograph of the house, crumpling it with my hands. I'm not sure I want to go looking for more photos. I'm not sure I want to find out what she looked like. I'm not sure I want to take this place apart, to delve into my grandmother's life, her stories and her secrets and to judge what I should keep and what I should throw away. I'm not sure that I even want to cook my dinner on this old-fashioned stove tonight. Even the thought of preparing my food in a dead stranger's kitchen makes me feel quite sick.

"Why did you leave this place to me?" I ask, as though she

might be able to answer from wherever she is now.

I bury my head in my hands, suffocated by the enduring silence and by my sudden, overwhelming urge to leave this house and never return. I shouldn't be here. This place has nothing to do with me. I am only here because I am weak, because I have made bad choices, because things have gone so badly wrong.

I am only here right now because in truth I have nowhere else to go.

My phone vibrates in my pocket, startling me back from the brink of tears. The message which confronts me is blunt and brief, but I would expect nothing less from its sender.

You can't run away from this, Harriet.

It is then that I begin to cry in earnest.

2

Eleanor
July 1972

"This place is an absolute mess."

I stretch out on the sun-scorched lawn, examining my bitten nails as I wait for a response to my statement. Behind me I can hear my daughter Anna shrieking with a couple of local girls as they fling buckets of cold water at one another, partly playing and partly keeping cool in the summer heat. Their childish screams are irritating, but I remind myself that I really ought to relish them. Anna will be thirteen in September; the teenage years are looming large before us and I have no doubt that there will be plenty of silence then.

"Not this again."

My face remains impassive. Only the momentary flicker of a raised eyebrow betrays the feelings simmering within. "Yes, this again."

Bert almost sighs but thinks better of it. "This place has huge potential, Eleanor," he replies, pedalling that familiar line.

"Potential for what, exactly? It's a wreck." I cast a disdainful glance around me, just for good measure.

Bert's dark eyes rest their intent gaze upon me. He scratches his jaw, just as he always does when he's thinking, when he's deciding how best to handle me. My husband's talents are wasted as a mechanic. I often think that he should have joined the diplomatic service and put all that passive-aggressive energy into the national interest instead of expending it on navigating my moods.

"I thought it would be the perfect project, a way to channel all your creative talent," he muses.

I have to suppress a laugh. "Albert," I begin, employing his nickname for maximum effect. After all these years of marriage, the fact that his real name is actually Robert is neither here nor there. Besides, I like the name Albert better; it sounds suave, sophisticated, like something out of a James Bond film. Perhaps instead of a diplomat he could have been a spy, and Albert could have been his code name. "I paint pictures; I'm not an interior decorator. And frankly, the amount of work this place needs, is overwhelming. I really don't know what you were thinking when you dragged us all up here."

"I was thinking about starting again," he replies, his expression turning cold. He hates it when I second-guess his decisions. "I was thinking about a fresh start, for all of us."

You were thinking about putting a safe distance between you and that tart, I think, but I don't say it. I remember my promise to him, the day we packed up the car and drove north. What's done is done, I said. I won't keep raking over old coals. I wish now that I hadn't been so quick to make such a vow, that I had reserved my right to act as the woman scorned for a little while longer.

Bert looks at his watch, a familiar gesture which signals the end of our conversation. "I need to get back to the garage. This place might be less than perfect for you but it still has a mortgage on it which needs to be paid."

I give my nails another cursory examination and refuse to rise to his offhand remark. "Well, perhaps if I manage to sell a few of my paintings we'll be able to afford to pay someone to sort this place out."

"Yes, it's possible," he replies in that voice which lets me know that he doesn't think it's possible at all. He peers over my shoulder at the half-finished sketch sitting beside me. I've been working on it this afternoon; a delicate little chaffinch, perched on a branch, poised and ready to fly. "That's a good one. A few of those would look nice in the hallway."

"Hmm," I reply, "I'm not sure. There's something not quite right with his eyes. I've not captured him well at all."

"I'm sure you'll work it out. He's a cute little fella. You could always give him to Anna for her birthday."

"I'm not sure that Anna finds my doodles as interesting as she used to," I reply, glancing at my daughter. She is sitting at the other end of the garden now, talking in hushed tones with her new friends as they all wring the water out of their hair. "She's not a baby anymore."

"Yeah, perhaps you're right. Anyway, I'd better go." He leans down, giving me a peck on the cheek. "I'll be home for dinner."

I give him my best forced smile and try to ignore the fact that he stinks of engine oil and sweat. "Good. But don't get too excited – I can barely manage to make a sandwich in that excuse for a kitchen."

An exasperated sigh escapes from his lips as he walks away. I know that I should feel bad for being so unkind, that I should try to behave better towards him. I know that I should try to forgive, to forget, to put the past behind us and move on. I know I should embrace this fresh start, that I should throw myself into making this big, old, dilapidated house our home. And I know that by not doing any of these things I am really just hurting myself and my family. The problem is, I just can't quite reconcile myself with the fact that this is my life now. I can't quite bring myself to acknowledge that my husband's answer to his own foibles was to up sticks and run away from our lives in the city and to go into hiding in the back of beyond. Above all, I realise, I can't quite admit to myself that when it came down to it, I didn't have the courage not to follow him.

I pick up my sketchbook, returning my attention to the

chaffinch in an effort to escape from the cyclical destructiveness of my own thoughts. I study those little dark eyes once more as they stare intently into the distance, and I realise then what is wrong with them.

"He looks sad," I whisper as I put my pencil to the paper, lightening his expression with a few careful strokes.

I sit back a little and examine my work. That's better. My diminutive spring bird should be cheerful, optimistic, ready to take flight and embrace whatever's in front of him. He should be a symbol of hope and happiness, especially if he's going to go up on a wall somewhere. No one wants to look at a sad bird; no one wants to be confronted with such a morose expression on a creature and be forced to consider what might be wrong with him. He must hide his anguish, however justified it might be and however keenly it might be felt. No one wants to deal with his sadness.

I close my sketchbook and stretch out my limbs once more, but even the warmth of the summer sun does nothing to soothe me. Poor little bird. It strikes me that no one ever wants to deal with sadness at all.

As the day meanders into the evening, the sticky heat crescendos and a thunderstorm arrives. With dinner time looming and rather predictably, with no sign of Bert, I make Anna and I something to eat. We sit down at the kitchen table, tucking into our food quietly and watching the rain as it batters loudly against the window panes. I realise that this is the first heavy rainfall we have seen since moving here three weeks ago. At least we will find out soon enough if our new home is watertight, or if that will be yet another issue we will need to add to our growing list of renovation works.

"Where's Dad?" Anna asks me, breaking the silence.

"I'm sure he'll be home soon enough," I reply, as though I have the faintest idea when he will grace us with his presence. "He's got a lot to do at work. It's not easy, you know, starting a business all over again," I add, trying to counter the pout which is rapidly forming on my daughter's lips.

"I still don't understand why you did it – why you moved us here," she says, picking disapprovingly at her hastily-prepared sausages and mashed potatoes.

I force myself to suppress a sigh. I don't want to have this conversation again; I don't want to be forced to make excuses, to give half-hearted explanations, to be a damn apologist for my husband's actions to a twelve year-old who knows I'm not telling her the whole truth.

"I've told you, sweetheart, your father and I needed a fresh start. Aren't you happy here? You seem to have made friends already, haven't you? And I'm sure you'll make some more once you start at the school after the summer break."

"Yeah, I have met some nice girls. I suppose it's alright here," she replies, twirling her fork around her plate and avoiding my gaze. "It's a bit quiet though, compared to Manchester."

I nod. "That's true. It's very quiet at night. I think it will take me some getting used to. But I will get used to it, Anna, and so will you. We just have to give it a chance. I promise you that one day soon we will all think of Kirtlebeck as home." Even as I speak I'm not sure who I'm trying to convince, Anna or myself.

"So we're going to stay here, then?"

"Yes, of course we are."

"So, you and Dad aren't going to get divorced?"

I nearly splutter on the water I'm sipping. I have been expecting many questions from my daughter over these past few weeks, but this most certainly was not one of them. "Divorced? No, sweetheart, we're not going to get divorced," I reply in the most even tone I can muster and resume eating my food. Now I'm the one who can't make eye contact. I don't dare – I don't want Anna to see from my expression just how raw that word is for me, and just how many times I have contemplated it and lost my nerve.

"Okay. It's just…you and Dad seem to argue a lot these days. And a couple of my friends back home have parents who are divorced so, you know, it's no big deal." If we weren't talking about something so serious, I would find her nonchalant, I'm-a-grown-up-now attitude amusing.

I give her the most reassuring smile I can manage. "Yeah? Well a lot has changed since I was a girl – parents didn't just get divorced. But your father and I have no plans to separate." I touch her lightly on the hand. "I'm sorry that you've had to listen to us argue. You're old enough to know that things haven't been easy between us for some time now. But that's why we moved here – we want to make things better." I sound so convincing that for a moment I'm almost fooling myself.

Anna returns my smile. "Alright, Mum," she says, taking her last mouthful of food. "Is it okay if I leave the table? I think I'll go to my room and read for a while."

I nod and watch my girl as she heads to her bedroom, marvelling for a moment at the beautiful young lady she is becoming. A few years ago I was still stumbling over her toys and singing nursery rhymes to help her to sleep, now I'm spending my evenings alone while she sprawls out on her bed, pouring over magazines and listening to T-Rex. With a heavy sigh, I get up from the table and begin to clear away the dishes. In a few years she will be a young woman, just as I once was, looking at the years stretching before her, tempting her with their possibilities. I wonder for a moment what she will do; if she will marry, if she will have children, or if she will choose instead to study, to travel, to have adventures and see something of the world. I hope that whatever she does, she fulfils her dreams. I hope that she is happy. More than anything, I hope that she doesn't follow my example, that she doesn't let her dreams slip through her fingers and blow away like grains of sand in the wind.

I finish washing the dishes and pour myself a large glass of red wine as a reward, my mind still firmly fixed on my daughter. If I'm truthful with myself, I know that I never really wanted to be a mother. When marriage to Bert didn't initially make child-bearing the inevitability that I had expected, I admit that I was relieved. I wanted to paint, to draw, to think, not spend my days washing cloth nappies and cleaning up sick. But then Anna came along and changed my life in all the ways that I never imagined. Now I find that she's growing up too fast, that I'd like to keep my little girl for a while longer.

"We could always have another child," Bert said to me a few months ago. "Perhaps it would help, you know, bring us closer together again."

His suggestion caught me by surprise. "Don't be ridiculous – I'm almost forty years old," I replied, and that was the end of the discussion. I should have said more, of course. I should have told him how wrong he was to suggest it, how absurd I found his efforts to heal the rift between us. I should have told him that a child could never be expected to mend the heartbreak his actions have caused. But I didn't. I never do.

I stare out the window as I finish the last few sips of my wine. The rain has stopped now, leaving an eerie silence lingering in the falling dusk. I shiver, feeling suddenly unnerved and I catch myself wishing that Bert was home to keep me company.

"That won't do at all, Eleanor," I mutter to myself as I pour a second glass of my favourite cabernet sauvignon. I need distraction. I need something to soothe me.

One of the first things I unpacked when we arrived here was my record player and vinyl collection, giving both pride of place in the enormous, faded living room at the front of the house. Like the rest of this place the room is in dire need of restoration, but in my more optimistic moments I admit I can see myself sitting in there in the evening, listening to music and drawing until my heart's content. Tonight I decide to give it a try, to relax a little and to see if this house can feel like my home, even if only for a little while.

I flick quickly through my record box and settle on some David Bowie. I bought this album after hearing Space Oddity a few years ago. The song immediately caught my attention, its catchy riff and space age lyrics seeming to capture the mood in a year when the Americans were putting men on the moon and just about everyone seemed to want to go up beyond the stratosphere. In the summer of '69 I played that song repeatedly, so much so that Bert eventually felt moved to comment on it.

"What on earth is that?" he'd asked. "It's very odd."

"I like it," I'd protested. "The words are interesting – it makes me think about getting lost in the vastness of space."

"Well I wish that song would get lost in space," Bert had retorted. "Sounds like the sort of rubbish that all the kids are listening to. Not a patch on Louis Armstrong," he'd added, predictably referencing his favourite jazz musician.

"You can hardly compare the two…" I had begun, before swiftly giving up. I knew then, as I know now, that there is never any point in arguing about these things with Bert. He's a man who knows what he likes, and likes what he knows.

I place the record on the deck and settle into my armchair as it begins to play. I pick up my sketch pad and pencil but I find I can't draw, my mind still distracted by thoughts of my husband. We are so different, Bert and I. We don't share the same tastes or the same interests; we might as well be from different planets. And yet, once upon a time there was something which brought us together, which attracted us to one another…wasn't there? I screw up my face, thinking back to when we first met. I was so much younger then; we both were – it's almost as though we were different people. Is that what happened to us, I wonder; did we change so much that we grew apart? Is that why he betrayed me? Is that why he sought love elsewhere?

The front door clicks open abruptly, mercifully interrupting the darker turn that my thoughts have taken.

"It's just me – I'm home," Bert calls. "What's for supper?"

I let out a weary sigh as I get out of my chair, lifting the needle on my record player and stopping Bowie mid-song. Time for more domestic bliss, I think sourly. Bert might not love me anymore, but he still has his uses for me.

3

Harry
January 2018

I sleep peacefully, waking gradually in the soothing comfort of a warm bedroom. I realise that in grappling with this house's antiquated heating system, I have left it running all night. I chastise myself for the error; after all, this big, old place will not be cheap to keep warm. I might have some money put aside to see me through the next few months, but it's hardly enough to justify extravagance.

After getting up I make a cup of tea and run myself a hot bath. Back at home the most I could manage was a quick shower before work, but with time on my hands and nowhere to go, I decide to be indulgent. I sink down into the water, taking the time to properly examine the bathroom. Like the rest of the house it needs some work, its floral décor faded and the linoleum flooring damaged in places, but the bathing facilities are in good condition. My eyes are particularly drawn to the old radiator in the room, a large cast iron affair which I believe must be from the Victorian era. I nod my head approvingly. My grandmother and I might not have shared the same decorative tastes, but I have to admire how she clearly chose to keep some of the house's original features intact.

Turning my mind to more practical matters, I consider my plans for the day and where I should start in terms of sorting through my grandmother's possessions. Her will left the house and its contents entirely to me, and now that the solicitor has wound up her estate and handed her property over, I am free to do as I wish with it. If I am honest with myself, even after a good night's sleep I still don't feel comfortable with all of this, but I know that I must get on with it. To all intents and purposes this house is now mine, and currently it is filled with a dead woman's possessions. I have to do something about that, sooner or later. It might as well be today.

After emptying the bath and dressing quickly, I decide that the best place to start is in the cupboards. The surfaces and rooms of this property are so empty that I feel certain that I will find all these hidden spaces full to bursting with my grandmother's personal effects. She must have been an 'out of sight, out of mind' sort of woman; perhaps that's where I get the same tendencies from. I have always liked plain, clutter-free surroundings.

"You've always been a bit OCD." The memory of a close friend's voice rings in my ears. A former close friend, I remind myself with a small shake of my head. A former close friend who sent me a text yesterday, a text which sent my head into a spin, which tied my stomach in knots so badly that I barely ate any of my dinner. A text which I still haven't had the guts to respond to.

I leave my room and walk down the hallway, pushing unwanted thoughts of my previous life from my mind. After all, I have chosen to leave it all behind; my flat, my job, my friends, the city I know and until recently, loved very much. I have chosen to come here, I tell myself. I have chosen to make a fresh start. Except, I know deep down that I didn't have very much choice about it at all.

"Come on Harry, mulling over it all won't make any difference. What's done is done." Damn – I'm talking to myself again. I'm really going to have to discipline myself a little better, if I'm going to spend so much time alone in this house.

I decide to start in the master bedroom, partly because I suspect it was my grandmother's room and therefore will contain most of her things, and partly because I know that the longer I leave it to tackle her personal space, the harder it will be to face it. Better to start now, while I still feel sufficiently detached from this place, and for that matter, from her. As hard as I may try to keep a level head about the task at hand, I know full well that it'll only take the discovery of a few family photos of my grandmother as a young woman or my mother as a child to draw me in, to make me feel connected to them. If I am honest with myself, it is a prospect which both excites and terrifies me. I never knew my grandmother, and I barely knew my mother. Mum left my dad and I when I was very small; she never came back for me and there has been no trace of her since. Sometimes I think I can remember her face, that I can remember her sitting next to me in my bed, reading me a bedtime story. I'm not sure whether that is a genuine memory, or merely a recollection of something my dad told me that she used to do. I'll never know, either. All the stories about Mum died with Dad over a decade ago and he told me nothing at all about my grandmother. The reasons for that died with him also.

I open the door of the large mahogany wardrobe, the smell of mothballs and old wood immediately overpowering my senses. One by one, I take out the clothes contained within it, laying them out on the bed for…what? Inspection? Careful folding? I don't even know how to go about this. What I do know, however, is that my grandmother's clothing choices are not what I anticipated. I admit that I went into that cupboard expecting to find a selection of what I'd rather disrespectfully call 'old lady clothes' – tailored trousers, high-necked blouses, perhaps a floral pleated skirt or two. What I find instead is some pretty funky stuff – colourful jeans, pretty tops, shirts and dresses in lovely, flowing materials. Based on the clothes laid before me, I'd say my grandmother was quite the bohemian.

The bottom of the wardrobe yields yet more surprises. Lined up neatly in a row are boxes of my grandmother's shoes. I can't help but gasp as I pull them out and open them up - this woman owned the best shoe collection I have ever seen! Contained within those boxes I find everything from delicate high heels to sturdy, military style boots. I suppress a snigger as an image jumps into my mind of an aged lady tottering around in a great pair of stilettos or marching down to the library in a pair of Dr Martens. These shoes must just have been her favourites from years ago, mustn't they? That must be why she packed them in here and hung on to them, surely. The lawyer told me that she was eighty-five when she died, that she had been unwell, that her sight had been beginning to fail. She couldn't possibly have been wearing these shoes in her final years, could she?

I shake my head in disbelief. "You are certainly full of surprises, Gran-" I stop myself mid-sentence. I know she's not here, and the fact that I know that and yet I'm still talking to her is ridiculous enough, but I'm suddenly struck by the realisation that I've no idea what to call her. If I had known her, I would have known what she wanted to be called, and we would have settled on a name. If Mum hadn't left, or if Dad had told me about my grandmother when I was growing up, then we might have come up with a name for her, one which I could use now. But as it is, my grandmother is gone and so are my parents, and so I must imagine what she would have wanted to be called.

With a heavy sigh I sit down on the bed, staring at her clothes and shoes, the things she used to present herself to the world, to say something about herself, to create her own image. If clothes are a reflection of someone's personality, then this woman was clearly pretty funky and original; she was someone who knew her own mind and wasn't afraid to express herself, to convey her youthfulness even in the face of her advancing years. She doesn't seem like someone who would have liked to be called Gran, or Grandma, or even Nana, certainly not by a grandchild she never knew.

"I think I'll call you Eleanor," I whisper, picking up a handful of her blouses and clutching them to my chest. "Since that was your name, and I think that's what you would have wanted me to call you."

Behind me I think I feel a breeze brush past me and all the hairs on the back of my neck stand on end. I jump to my feet, my moment of sentimentality abruptly ended. My eyes flit around the room, looking for the source of the breeze which is silly, because none of the windows are open and the door to the room is closed. I brush my dark hair back from my face, my mind rationalising feverishly. It must have been a draught from somewhere. Of course there are draughts here. This place is old, there will be cracks and holes and faulty seals everywhere. That's all I felt; a draught and nothing more.

I set about gathering up the clothes and shoes, hurriedly placing them into bags. I will take all this to the charity shop this afternoon, I tell myself. At least then I will have accomplished something today and besides, I think I could do with getting out of the house for a little while. I will stick to my plan, I will keep sorting through things, and I will ignore my wild imagination that is clearly playing tricks on me. After all, there's nothing here – there can't be.

Nonetheless, even while I busy myself packing up her things, I can't shake the weird feeling that the strange breeze has provoked. The feeling that there is someone here, and that they are watching me. And what's more, the feeling that whoever they are, they aren't my grandmother but someone else altogether.

My trip outdoors turns out to be exactly what I need, the crisp January air clearing my head and renewing my resolve to get on with the task at hand. I decide to drive to Annan, feeling sure that as it's the nearest town it will contain one or two shops which will take my bags of donations. Of course in this day and age I could just use the internet and check, but the only internet I have is on my phone and if I'm honest with myself, I'm still reeling from that text message I received yesterday. I don't really want to look at my phone; in fact, I switched it off immediately afterwards and haven't looked at it since. So, in the face of my own determined cowardice, guesswork will have to do.

When I arrive in Annan I find a pretty, charming place, its red buildings lit up by the emerging winter sunlight. I locate a charity shop quite quickly and offload my bags of goods on to a delighted-looking shop assistant.

"These things are immaculate," she gushes as she empties the bags, holding up some of the clothing for examination. "Thank you so very much for thinking of us. So many people prefer to sell things online these days that when we are given quality items, it is that much more appreciated."

"That's okay, I'm just having a big clear-out," I reply as casually as I can manage. "No doubt I'll be dropping by with some more stuff soon – do you take items apart from clothes? You know: books, framed pictures, furniture?"

The lady nods enthusiastically. "Books and framed prints – yes. We don't really take furniture here, but you could try the other place down the street. They deal more with furniture and large items. In fact, I think they will come and collect it from you, if transport is an issue."

"Okay, thank you, that's really helpful."

"You're welcome." She beams at me. "And good luck - it sounds like you're clearing a whole house!"

I give her a weak smile, not really wanting to be drawn into a long discussion about it. I'll only end up telling her the whole story, and then I'll feel embarrassed afterwards for over-sharing. So I stick with a simple response: "Yes, something like that."

The friendly lady looks disappointed, and for a moment I almost regret my evasiveness. Then I remember the promise I made to myself when I came here. In the past I have been too much of an open book; I have let people in and I have let my defences down. The result was pain, heartache and several lives left in ruins. The result is what drove me to come here at all. If I am going to move on, if I am going to have a fresh start then I must learn to keep my own counsel and more importantly, to keep my guard up at all times – starting with seemingly innocuous conversations with nosey shop workers.

By the time I get back to my car, the fresh air has ceased to have its clarifying effect. Instead the drive home is a blur, my mind pre-occupied by a swirl of cyclical thoughts; thoughts about my past, thoughts about the things I have done and the people I have wronged, thoughts which I have tried so hard to suppress. To make matters worse, these familiar thoughts are compounded by new ones as I try to grapple with everything that needs to be done at this house, and the sheer quantity of stuff which must be sorted and removed. As I sweep along the undulating country roads, a sense of being completely overwhelmed creeps over me. What was I thinking, trying to clear a house all by myself? What was I thinking, coming up here, running away, breaking all ties with my old life and leaving all that destruction in my wake?

I am so distracted that I don't notice the man and his truck until it is almost too late. I swerve, hitting my brakes hard as I am forced into the middle of the road by his large red vehicle which he has left stranded far away from the verge. The man stands at the front of the vehicle, his eyes fixed upon me as I manoeuvre past. Thankfully no one is coming the other way, otherwise I would have doubtlessly been involved in a collision. My fear dissolves into anger. Who just leaves a car in the middle of the road like that? Before I can regain control of my emotions, I stop the car and wind my window down.

"What on earth do you think you're doing?" I ask. "You almost caused an accident!"

"No, it was your driving that could have done that," he replies in a gentle Scottish accent. "You were going far too fast for a road like this."

I swallow hard, realising I have no idea what speed I was driving. The man continues to look at me, his pair of bright blue eyes fixed on me. I note with irritation the quizzical, almost amused expression twitching at the corners of his mouth. "Well," I reply stiffly, "my speed is irrelevant. You've basically abandoned your truck in the middle of the road!"

He shrugs at me, seemingly unperturbed by my confrontational tone. "Aye, it's not the best spot. Not much I can do about it though – broke down on my way back from town," he says, tapping the truck's bonnet gently.

"Oh," I reply, feeling suddenly regretful of the way I have handled this conversation. "I'm sorry to hear that. Is there anything I can do? Have you got, you know, a recovery vehicle coming or something like that?"

He chuckles at me, his eyes creasing as his face relaxes into a smile. "No need for that. I'm pretty handy with a tool kit. I was just about to lift the bonnet when you came whizzing down the road. Thank you for the offer, though you know you really shouldn't offer lifts to strangers."

"I wasn't whizzing anywhere," I retort, "and I didn't offer you a lift, either. I merely asked if I could help in any way."

The man laughs again. "I'm just teasing you."

I don't return his smile. "Yes, well, perhaps it's not advisable to tease strangers, either. You never know what sort of day they might have had."

I wind my window up before he has a chance to answer, watching him in my rear-view mirror as I drive away. He just stands there watching me, his hands placed on his hips, that stupid amused expression still fixed on his face. I let out an exasperated sigh. What a cheek! I focus my eyes back on the road, all thoughts of strange breezes and uneasy feelings now completely out of my mind. For the first time, I can't wait to get back to the house, to close the door and to shut myself away. If all that rural southern Scotland can offer me is nosey shop assistants and impertinent men by the roadside, then I'd rather be alone with a dead woman's things. I'd rather be getting on with clearing the house, finding photographs and dealing with the hollow sentimentality which comes from raking through the personal effects of a relative I never knew.

Without warning, a tear slips down my cheek. More than anything, I think, I'd rather be letting go of my past. I'd rather be clearing my head and contemplating how I can possibly move on with my life. But such notions are hopeless, much the same as grappling with my grandmother's big old house, filled with her belongings. All of it is equally daunting and abundant. Quite simply, I realise, I don't know where to start.

4

Eleanor
August 1972

As the summer heat continues unabated, I find myself sinking deeper into malaise. Anna continues to spend most of the long days outside with other children from the village, doing whatever kids do when they spend time together but consider themselves too old to play. Occasionally she shares anecdotes from her adventures with me, telling me about who she has met and where they all rode out to on their bikes. I learn from her that there is a river not far from the village, silt-bottomed and full of fish, and that there is a large area of woodland up the lane, thick with trees and blooming flowers.

"I think you should go up there, Mum," she suggests. "It's really pretty. It might give you an idea for a new painting."

I nod, smiling at her efforts to be helpful, but I know that I won't heed her advice. Since arriving in Kirtlebeck I have confined myself to this house, and as the weeks pass I find myself falling increasingly into a state between listlessness and agitation. I haven't drawn or painted anything since I started sketching the little chaffinch, and I haven't made any attempt at redecoration despite being surrounded by walls which scream about the imperative to do so. Instead I sit, ruminating, staring into space. Sometimes I listen to music and it cheers me for a while, until the record finishes and I remember that all I am left with is emptiness and silence. Sometimes I open a bottle of wine in the middle of the afternoon, draining its contents entirely so that by dinner time I struggle to hide my drunkenness from my husband and child.

Bert doesn't say anything, of course. He just gives me that hard, cold stare, the one which tells me he knows, that he disapproves, and that he despairs of me. I want to scream at him then, to rail at him for what he has brought me to, and to tell him that this is all his fault. I want to tell him that if he hates the drunken recluse his wife has become, then maybe he should stop facilitating her behaviour by doing the shopping or bringing home bottles of wine. Maybe he should try to love her. Maybe he should never have cheated on her.

Instead I say nothing. I just make him his tea and watch him eat while I push my unwanted food around my plate.

Life goes on like this for several weeks, until a knock at my door one Wednesday afternoon disrupts my solitary routine. It is another oppressive, sticky day, too hot to sit outside, and I have sought refuge indoors. With the start of the new school term looming in a little over a fortnight, I have settled upon occupying myself with stitching name labels into Anna's uniform. Although initially dreading the task, I find that once I start sewing it soothes me, carrying me away from my troubles and taking my mind to somewhere more peaceful. When the loud tap on the door breaks the silence it startles me, my heart pounding hard in my chest, and I feel annoyed that my few moments of serenity have been shattered. My irritation, however, is quickly superseded by curiosity and I am shocked to realise, by a strange sort of dread. Who has come to my door, I wonder; who has come to disturb my peace? Who has come to invade my space, to break down the barricades these walls around me have come to represent? Is it her; the tart, the other woman? Has she come to find him? Has she come to take him from me? Do I even mind if she has?

I peer through the stained glass window at the side of the door, trying to get some sense of who is on the other side. I realise quickly that this is stupid; it isn't possible to see anything clearly through that pretty, colourful glass. Presumably that is the point: no one can see out, and no one can see in. Drawing an uneven, nervous breath, I decide that there is nothing else for it: I must open the door. I must let this person in, whoever they are, and whatever they want.

I let the wooden door creak open slowly, taking a final moment to compose myself and fix my face with the most impassive expression I can manage. If it is the tart, the last thing I want to do is let her see me in any way perturbed. I gave her that satisfaction once, on the day that I caught her in my bed with my husband, and that was one time too many. She will never see me look like that again, I tell myself. No one will ever see me look like that again.

I peer around the doorway and breathe an inward sigh of relief. There is a woman at my door, but it's not her. Immediately I realise how ridiculous I've been. Of course it isn't her; she doesn't know where we went. She doesn't know where to find him. Bert promised me that he had left her behind for good. But then, I remind myself, Bert's promises don't mean much, not when he couldn't even find it in himself to honour the ones he made on our wedding day.

"Hello?" says an inquisitive voice, and I realise that I have been staring, lost in my thoughts once again. I shake my head briefly, forcing myself back into the present.

"Hi, sorry. Hi," I reply, a little more awkwardly than I would have liked.

"I'm sorry, have I caught you at a bad time?" the woman asks, her voice laced with the soft Scottish lilt of the local accent.

I shake my head again, trying to soften my expression. I realise that my jaw is set hard. Little wonder, I think, when I constantly allow myself to be plagued by memories of Bert and his dirty little fling. "No, not at all. Can I help you?"

The woman gives me a warm smile. "I just came to say hello.

My name's Meg, I'm one of your neighbours."

Meg extends a hand towards me. I open the door a little wider, taking hold of her hand briefly as I study my neighbour properly for the first time. My initial thought is that she is young, at least younger than me, perhaps ten years or more. She is wearing a full-length sundress fashioned in a floral, floaty material, with a matching bandana just about managing to keep her long dark hair in check. Her friendly demeanour and broad smile are matched by a pair of big, deep brown eyes which stare quizzically at me. I realise that it's my turn to speak, but for a moment nothing comes to mind. Nothing except that I suddenly feel old and plain with my short wedge haircut, my faded t-shirt and shapeless, cut-off jeans.

"I mean, obviously, I'm not right next door," Meg continues in the end, seizing the silence. "But mine is the nearest house to yours, just back down the lane." She points vaguely behind her and I follow her finger, nodding dumbly as though I have the faintest idea where her home is. "I just thought I would come and introduce myself, anyway. I realised this morning that you've been here for a few weeks now and I still hadn't met you." Those large eyes narrow briefly, as though she is trying to weigh me up. "Are you sure I haven't called at a bad time?"

Her question jolts me from speechlessness. "No, no, of course not." I choke out a small laugh, partly trying to put her at ease, but mostly at my own foolishness. "I'm sorry, it's just so hot and I was in the middle of sewing, but it's nothing that can't wait until later. I'm Eleanor, Eleanor Murray. Would you like to come in?"

Meg nods and I stand back from the door, allowing her to walk inside. Having a stranger wander into my hallway makes me feel momentarily ashamed of the state of the place, and of myself for having done nothing about it. If Meg notices, however, she doesn't seem to mind. "This place is even bigger than I thought," she gushes, her arms spread wide to emphasise the size of the space she has found herself in. "What a lovely house. You are so lucky."

"Yes, well, it needs a lot of work," I say, her assertion of my good fortune sticking in my throat. "Come through to the kitchen and I'll make us some tea."

I grimace as I realise that I have just invited this woman into the grottiest room in my house. Then I wonder why I care. After all, I'm not the house-proud type; I never was, even when I lived in Manchester and had my home exactly the way I wanted it. I'm not slovenly, of course; my surroundings have to be clean, which they are, but they don't have to be immaculate. Nonetheless, I can't help but shudder as Meg sits herself down at my faded red wooden table, next to a wall afflicted by flaking paint. It occurs to me then that what bothers me about this place is that it doesn't feel like mine, at least not yet. Perhaps deep down I am harbouring the motivation to decorate, after all.

I make us some tea and sit down opposite her. I notice that her perfume has laced the humid kitchen air with the scent of flowers and I allow myself to breath it in, subtly but deeply, enjoying the reprieve from the stale tinge of old wood. For a moment I wonder when I last wore perfume, then I realise that I can't remember.

"I'm sorry about the state of the place," I begin, "as I said, it needs a lot of work."

"No need to apologise," she replies. "You should see my house some days! Besides, you've just moved in. I'm sure you'll have this house exactly as you want it in no time."

"You're very kind," I say, giving her a small smile. "If I'm honest, it feels like an overwhelming task. I just don't know where to begin. So, I haven't. I haven't begun at all." Inexplicably, tears prick in the corners of my eyes. I feel ridiculous. What on earth is the matter with me?

Meg gives me a measured look, much like the look she gave me on the doorstep, her eyes slightly narrowed but still dark and intense, as though she is looking for whatever lies beyond my expression. A moment's silence follows and I look away, unable to hold her gaze.

"Where do you want to begin?" she asks.

I consider her question. "I don't know..." I reply, feeling stupid. How can I not have an answer to such a simple question?

"Anna's room, I suppose. She's my daughter," I add, reminding myself that this woman doesn't know us at all, that I only met her moments ago. It's odd that I even need to remind myself of that fact. Clearly I have spent too much time in my own company; my social skills are all over the place.

Those eyes remained fixed upon me. "Yes, I've seen your daughter on the lane. She seems lovely."

"Hmm," I muse. "She's reaching that difficult age. I suppose that's another good reason to start with her room, to make it her own. Perhaps we could even work on it together." For a moment I am quite taken with the idea of a mother-daughter collaboration, of feeling close to her, of feeling needed, just like when she was a little girl.

"What a nice idea!" Meg exclaims, her face brightening briefly before growing more serious once more. "But remember, Eleanor, don't forget about yourself. Make sure that the next room you do is for you, won't you?"

A frown creases my brow before I can prevent it. "Why do you say that?"

Meg reaches over and touches my hand. I am surprised by the gesture from someone I barely know, but unusually for me I don't recoil. I look up at her and those eyes bore into my soul once again. "Because you seem like someone who forgot herself some time ago."

A heavy silence descends, smothering any chance of me mustering a response. I sip my tea, tasting the bitter flavour of Meg's accuracy as the hot liquid washes through my mouth.

Meg drains her cup and rises to leave. "I shouldn't keep you chatting any longer," she says, smoothing her skirt. "It sounds like you've got lots to be getting on with."

"Oh, it's okay, honestly," I say, suddenly inexplicably desperate for her not to leave. "I've got nothing to do that can't wait. It's been really nice to meet you," I add, feeling foolish.

"And you," Meg replies with a smile, touching me lightly on the shoulder. "You must come down the lane and visit me at home."

She must see the uncertain look which flashes across my face because she adds: "It really isn't very far away at all, and it's very easy to find. Just look for the little white house with Thistle Cottage written on the gate."

"Thistle Cottage," I repeat. "What a lovely name. Perhaps I should give this house a name."

"But your house already has a name!" Meg retorts with a giggle.

"It does?" Now I feel really very silly indeed.

"Yes. At least, locally it has a name of sorts. It's the House at Kirtlebeck End. You know – because it's the last house on the lane. You would cause all manner of confusion if you renamed it."

"Well, I'd better not do that, then," I say. "I wouldn't want to cause any trouble."

"Why not?" she asks, laughing. "I always think that life's more fun when you can make some mischief."

She breezes towards the front door, her dark hair bouncing behind her, leaving me to wonder just how much trouble my intriguing visitor has caused in her own life. She has certainly turned my afternoon on its head, invading my silent, sombre house with her laughter, her perfume, her inquisitive gaze. Once again I consider that I am no longer desperate to be alone, that I would quite like her to stay a while yet.

"Oh!" she exclaims, jolting me from my thoughts. Before I can intercept her she has gone into my living room, homing in on my chaffinch drawing which sits on top of the sideboard, half-finished and forlorn. She picks him up and studies him, an enormous smile growing across her lips.

"Eleanor, he is just gorgeous. I presume he's yours, that you drew him?"

I nod, feeling my cheeks grow hot. "Yes, he's just a silly little sketch I started a few weeks ago. I've not had time to finish him yet," I add, wincing at my own white lie. Time, I know, has absolutely nothing to do with his current sorry state.

"Well, you must. You must finish him. He's exquisite. What a talent you have!"

"Thank you, but I really don't. He's really very average," I reply meekly, wishing the ground would swallow me whole. I have never mastered the art of accepting a compliment with grace.

Those dark, searching eyes take hold of me once again. "Eleanor, listen to me. You have a great talent. You must nurture it. You must, for your own sake." She pauses for a moment, her expression lightening. "I know! You could create some murals on some of the walls in this house. That way, you'd be making art and decorating at the same time!"

I give her a thin smile. "That's a good idea, actually. I will give it some thought."

"I think it's a wonderful idea. Just think how beautiful they would look," she gushes.

"Do you draw, Meg?" I ask, finally escaping her gaze.

She waves a dismissive hand towards me. "Sometimes."

My interest piques. "Oh, what do you draw?"

"Just this and that." She puts down the chaffinch and glances at the clock on the mantelpiece. "My goodness, is that the time? I must get going."

She heads towards the door once again, with me trailing dumbly behind her. Before she opens the door, she turns and gathers me into her arms, once again drowning my senses in the smell of flowers. "It's been wonderful to meet you," she says. "I do hope that we will see more of each other."

"Yes, I've enjoyed our chat," I reply as casually as I can manage. "You really don't have to rush off. Bert – my husband - won't be home for dinner for ages yet." As soon as I say the words, I realise how odd they sound. Why would it matter to Meg whether Bert was home or not? It occurs to me then that it matters to me, that the last thing I want is for my husband and his roving eye to meet this kind, sweet-natured creature with her captivating gaze.

Meg releases me from her grasp and gives me a final, bright smile. "Honestly, I must dash. I have lots to do and I have enjoyed your tea and company for far longer than I should have. But please, do come down the lane and visit me."

"I will," I promise her. "Now go on, you'd better get going. No doubt you've a husband expecting his dinner on the table."

"No! No husband," she calls as she dashes out of the door. "I've just myself to suit, and to cook for."

How wonderful, I think, but I don't say it.

"Bye, Eleanor," she says with a little wave.

"Bye, Meg," I reply.

And then she is gone. I close the door, and I find myself alone in my sanctuary once again. Except, I realise, I don't want to be left alone for hour after hour with nothing except my thoughts to break the excruciating silence. I don't think I ever did. I just think that right now, I don't know how to be with people, how to enjoy their company, how to interact, how to take an interest without feeling foolish or anxious. I let out a heavy sigh; I never used to be like this. I was never exactly the life and soul of the party, but I was at least outgoing, even adventurous at times. Perhaps Meg is right; perhaps I have forgotten about myself. Perhaps I have forgotten how to be me altogether.

I walk back through to the living room, resuming my sewing as I reflect upon my first encounter with my new neighbour. I try to think about how nice she was, how friendly, but my thoughts insist on taking a murkier turn. Some of the things she said to me were so unnerving, like she knew me, like she knew the pain I've been in. And the way she looked at me, with those eyes…

I prick my finger with the needle and let out a small yelp. "Enough, Eleanor," I say aloud. I force the image of Meg's mesmerising gaze from my mind. She's just a nice lady, very perceptive and a little mysterious, but nice. All the rest of this is just me, reading into things too much as usual. Another sign that I've been spending too much time alone.

I put away my sewing and return to the kitchen, my mind set upon making something nice for dinner. It's time I began to shake off these doldrums I've been living in for the past few weeks, to start making an effort with this house and with myself. If my youthful, fresh-faced visitor has taught me anything, it's that I've really let myself go, and that just won't do at all. I need to get the old, better dressed and happier Eleanor back. I need to make my house into a home with fresh paint and new floors and maybe a mural or two. Above all, I need to find a way to be happy here. As I begin to peel the vegetables a feeling of nervous excitement creeps over me. For the first time since I arrived here I feel hopeful: hopeful about the future, and hopeful that the gloom is beginning to lift and that I might just be on the road to a fresh start.

I chop away at the carrots and allow myself to smile. This is the best I have felt for weeks, and I haven't even had a drop of wine.

5

Harry
January 2018

As soon as I arrive back at the house, I run inside and lock the door behind me. In a vain attempt to calm my frazzled nerves I make myself a cup of tea and fetch myself a biscuit. When I was growing up tea and biscuits was my dad's answer to everything: a bad day, a bruised ego, a broken heart. As a teenager I'd come home from school, my face pale, my eyes swollen with tears extracted by arguments with friends, altercations with bullies or break-ups with boys, and he'd put the kettle on.

"A nice cup of tea," he'd say. "That'll make you feel better."

I smile at the recollection, although the memory is bittersweet. Poor Dad; it can't have been easy for him, raising a daughter all alone. He'd always say that we could talk about anything, and he kept his word, confronting any topic with me no matter how awkward, embarrassing or painful. I remember hankering after stories about Mum, especially as I got older and my own memories of her became faded by time. I'd ask him question after question, badgering him for details until eventually his eyes grew watery and shame got the better of me. As the years passed his answers became well-rehearsed scripts, filled with familiar lines about how wonderful she was, how clever and talented she was, and how much he missed her. This was especially true once he became ill and his battle against cancer blighted our lives. Towards the end he was in so much pain that I suppose he just didn't have the capacity to feel the hurts of the past anymore.

"She was a writer, you know," he said as he lay dying. I nodded, gripped with interest even though I had heard this line a thousand times before. "Before she had you. She was a wonderful writer. I wish I had some of her stories to show you, I wish I could…" His voice trailed off, his thoughts interrupted as they so often were during the long hours it took for him to slip away.

"What happened to them, Dad?" I asked, clutching his hand. "What happened to Mum's stories?"

The question, like so many, remained unanswered. And then, of course, there were the questions which received vague, half-answers, like 'where do you think Mum went?' and 'has she any family she might have gone to?' – questions which came as I got older and for a time, at least, felt a desperation to piece things together.

"I honestly don't know where she might have gone," came the shrugged reply, his eyes always cast down with resignation. "For a time I wondered about Scotland. That's where she grew up and where her family lived, at one time anyway. I think they're all dead now. I never met them, at any rate. The police made enquiries, of course, but…nothing. Always nothing."

Of course, as it turns out, they weren't all dead. My stomach churns bitterly as I reflect once again on how I had a grandmother living up here all that time. Why did he tell me she was dead – was it because that's what Mum had told him, and if so, why? Or did he know of her existence all along? Did he lie to me? Mum, of course, is legally dead; there has been no trace of her for twenty-seven years. Presumably my grandmother knew this, as she made no attempt to leave her estate to her daughter. I narrow my eyes, wondering now what else my grandmother might have known. Frustrated at feeling once again in the dark I shake off the memories, gulping my tea down thirstily and turning my mind to my plans for the rest of the day. The time is getting on; the darkness is drawing in now as the late afternoon gives way to the night. The realisation makes me shudder; during the daylight hours this place's antiquity fascinates me, but at night I'd be lying if I said it didn't give me the creeps a bit.

Deciding that there's still time to accomplish something meaningful I head upstairs, nervously flicking on all the lights as I go. As I walk along the landing I notice again how bare this place is; there's hardly a picture on the wall apart from a few indifferently placed prints of flowers, farm animals and other generic scenes. I furrow my brow. Back in Manchester my flat was full of cherished items: family photos, treasured gifts from Dad, keepsakes which reminded me of Mum. In contrast, there is nothing remotely personal about what my grandmother chose to display. Why? I tell myself that I'm reading too much into it, that in all likelihood she wasn't a sentimental person. Still, I can't help but think that it's strange to hide these things away. Increasingly my hesitation to delve into my family history is overcome by curiosity, and more than ever I want to find the things I feel sure must be here, to study them, to try to uncover their secrets. To try to understand my lost family, even just a little bit.

Gripped by a renewed zeal, I spend the next hour exploring the other bedrooms in the house, raking through the cupboards and drawers to get a sense of what lies within. In two of the rooms I find little more than pouches of decades-old potpourri in the empty drawers, carefully placed to combat that musty scent which occurs in unused furniture. The cupboards in there are similarly devoid of anything interesting, cleared of all possessions as though the space has been left for guests. I swallow hard at this thought, and wonder if one of these rooms was where my grandmother had envisaged me sleeping, instead of that lemon-coloured room I chose last night.

"What do you think, Eleanor, should I have stayed in here? I whisper to myself as I close the door on the final, empty bedroom.

"Or did you think I'd never come here at all? Or did you know I'd come and that's why you've hidden everything away?"

I shake my head at myself, even as the words fall from my lips. I must stop talking to ghosts, especially ones in my head. Especially ones I never knew.

I return to the yellow bedroom, the one where I slept so soundly last night. When I collapsed in here yesterday evening I had been so tired that I had hardly taken a moment to look around, and when I got up this morning my thoughts were so fixed on making a start in the master bedroom that I barely gave it a second glance. Now I take the time to study the space, the furniture, the décor. The painted paper on the wall looks to be decades old, faded by time and peeling away at the edges. Rips in the paper, remnants of blu-tack and empty hooks suggest the presence of posters and pictures long-removed. To one side of the room is the divan bed in which I slept, framed by a teak wood headboard with a matching table to its side. The only other pieces of furniture in the room are a chest of drawers and a dressing table, again fashioned in that same teak wood. I run a careful hand over their surfaces, noting the little dents and scuffs marking their otherwise tidy appearance. Their drawers don't contain much of interest, but they at least contain something: more potpourri, a few empty old notebooks, an address book and an unused diary from 1990. Unlike the other two rooms, the yellow room gives some indication that it was lived in once. My hand stops moving as I realise what this means. This was probably my mother's room. Of all the rooms in the house, I chose to sleep in here, in her bed, where she once slept. I bite my lip, unsure whether to feel comforted or unnerved.

Spurred on by my little findings in the drawers I turn my attention to the cupboard. Unlike my grandmother's room with its grand wardrobe, this room's cupboard is built into the wall, almost a small room with a rail and shelves built in at one side. I delve inside, momentarily excited by what I might find. Sure enough, there are objects within: a very old sewing machine, an embroidery box full to the brim with needles, threads and buttons, and a large box filled with wool. I take these items out, one by one, and sit them on the bed. I wonder who these belonged to. They're in what I feel certain was my mother's room; does that mean they were hers? Did she like to sew or to knit? My dad always told me how creative she was, so it's not hard to imagine her turning her hand to these sorts of pursuits. I let out a heavy sigh. On the other hand, these things could just as easily have belonged to my grandmother. She could have decided to make use of this big cupboard for storing her things once her daughter left home, once she left her life for good, just like she left mine. Filled suddenly with an overpowering sense of despair, I put those things back in their place and close the cupboard door.

I head back downstairs, deciding that I've had enough of sorting and exploring for one day. Disappointment over the day's exploits gnaws at me as I head into the kitchen and try to decide what to make for dinner. I tell myself that I have to be reasonable, that I've only been here for a day, and in that day I've accomplished a lot, exploring every cupboard on the first floor and even making a first trip to the charity shop. I've found out that someone who lived here liked to sew, and that my grandmother had a pretty hip sense of style. That's something, isn't it? That's more than I knew yesterday when I arrived.

I rummage around in the kitchen, examining my pitiful choices for dinner. I realise that I'd meant to pick up some more provisions after going to the charity shop, but I'd been so distracted that it had gone completely out of my mind. I let out a heavy sigh, chastising myself for my earlier behaviour, and for letting my thoughts run wild once again. I'd been bordering on rude to the woman in the shop, and I'd definitely been rude to that man by the roadside. Mind you, I think with a wry smile, he was so cheeky that he probably deserved it. If I'm honest with myself, of course, I know that I wasn't really concentrating on the road, that it was at least partly my fault. As I reach into the back of the cupboard, resigning myself to beans on toast for supper, I resolve to get my thoughts and feelings under control. There's no point ruminating on the past, whether it's mine or my family's. What's done is done, and the rest will probably remain a mystery. I'll just have to learn to live with it.

"Who're you kidding, Harry James? You've never been very good at living with anything. That's why you're here."

The words slip out before I can stop them, and the tears come tumbling after. More memories come flooding to the fore; different ones this time, not those childhood recollections, treasured and tinged with sadness, but an altogether more agonising set of images. These memories are recent, they are raw, and their effect on me is undimmed by the passage of time. His face held close to mine, passionate words teetering on the edge of his lips only to be suspended in favour of lust-filled kisses. Her face as she stands in the doorway, the pain of betrayal heavy in her disbelieving eyes as she sees us and finally understands. The grimy, broken asphalt of the city's unforgiving streets cutting my feet as I run down the road, tear-stained and barely-clothed. That first text message she sent me after it happened, and my struggle to process her venom after a night without sleep. All the text messages she's sent me since; all the times I've read her angry words and not had the strength to reply. God, what a coward I am.

"Maybe this is your punishment, Harry." I cry out. "Maybe that's why you came all the way here to find nothing more than a few old clothes and a sewing box belonging to a woman who didn't care enough to want to know you."

A sob catches in my throat as my sorrow once again gives way to anger and frustration. I lash out at the kitchen cupboard, hitting it with my foot and battering my hand against the worktop until it makes my skin sting. Then I reach over and grab a bottle of red wine; apparently the only sensible provision I brought with me. I unscrew it with self-destructive intent and pour myself a generous glass. I'm miserable and alone: I might as well get steaming drunk.

"I know a woman who does that."

The intrusion of an unfamiliar voice stops me in my tracks. My heart races and my ears prick up, seeking out sounds, trying to determine if the words were real or merely in my imagination. My eyes dart to the closed door which leads into the hallway. I locked the front door, I know I did. Has someone broken in? Is there an intruder out there? There can't be. Intruders don't announce themselves, and they certainly don't start conversations. I look suspiciously at the glass I'm holding. I've had barely a sip of it, nowhere near enough to render me insensible yet. I sniff the contents, trying to discern if it might have gone off. Does unopened wine go off? It's never lasted long enough in my house for me to find out.

"Get a grip, Harry," I whisper. "You're hearing things now."

I move towards the hob and find a pan, emptying the tin of beans into it in an effort to distract myself, to get out of my own head. Besides, I need some sustenance, something to line my stomach if I'm going to pour a ton of wine into it. Nervously I hum, trying to fill the silence of this place which suddenly feels so oppressive. I make a mental note to dig out my speakers tomorrow and set them up in the kitchen.

"Some music while I'm cooking – that's what I need," I mutter, popping two slices of bread in the toaster.

"There's a record player in the living room."

Shit. This time I'm not mistaken. This time I know what I heard, and this time the voice sounds closer, like someone has crept into the room to join me. I don't turn around – I don't dare. Instead I keep my head bowed towards the hob, my eyes focussed on the beans, my hand intent on stirring them to stop them from sticking to the bottom of the pot.

"Who's – who's there?" I stammer, my voice a terrified croak. I can't believe I'm even asking the question. I can't believe I'm even entertaining the idea that there's someone else in this house with me. "Who are you?"

"I might ask you the same question. Where's Eleanor?"

Eleanor. My shock begins to subside, releasing my senses from their suspension, and my mind immediately goes into overdrive. It's a man's voice I can hear; I know that much. His tone is gruff but not unfriendly, and whoever he is, he knew my grandmother. He also knows that there's a record player in the living room, which means he knows this house. I rack my brain, my eyes flitting back and forth between the hob and the toaster as I try to recall everything I've ever been told, every piece of information about my family that I've ever gleaned. I know that this was the Murray family home, that my mother spent at least some of her childhood here. I also know that my grandmother stayed here until her death, when she left the house to me. I turn off the hob and pick up the pan of warm beans as the penny finally drops. In all the parts of this house's story I've been told, one person has been conspicuously absent. I know about my mother, about my grandmother, but no one has ever told me anything about my...

"Grandfather?" The name falls from my lips as a question, and before I can think about what I'm doing, I turn around.

There's no one there. I stare at the closed door, mouth open, pan in hand. I can't believe there's no one there. At that moment I don't know whether to be disappointed or seriously concerned for my mental state.

Before I can think any more, my toast springs up in the toaster and makes me jump out of my skin. Then there is a knock at the door.

6

Eleanor
August 1972

In the final couple of weeks before the school term begins, Anna and I are kept busy with decorating her room. To my surprise we both embrace the task wholeheartedly, and I suspect that in our own ways we are happy to have the distraction. Despite her protestations to the contrary I know that Anna is nervous about starting at her new school, while I am keen to keep looking forward, to stop idling around this house while I obsess about what has passed. Together we keep ourselves occupied, stripping away the old floral wallpaper in readiness for fresh lining paper and some coats of the bright yellow paint which Anna has selected. Very quickly we find that the task of removing the old décor requires considerable physical exertion since it does not come away easily, and I find myself thinking that this house is stubborn, almost immoveable in the face of change.

"It's no good hanging on," I find myself saying, sweat pouring down my face from the sheer effort. "We all must move with the times."

The sight of me talking to a wall provokes one of those teenage disapproving looks from Anna, followed swiftly by us both laughing at my absurdity. I climb down from my ladder then, putting my arm around my daughter and pulling her close to me. I half expect her to shrug me off, to tell me that she's too old now for cuddles, and I am pleasantly surprised when instead she rests her head on my shoulder, just like she used to when she was little.

"I'm glad we're doing this together, Mum," she says to me. "And I'm glad that you seem more like your old self again. You seemed so sad when we first moved here."

"Yes well, moving up here, leaving Manchester – it's taken a lot of getting used to, but I think I'm finally settling in," I reply, giving her a reassuring squeeze. "And it's been fun working on your room with you. Maybe you shouldn't go back to school; I could do with your help getting the rest of this place sorted out." I'm half joking, of course, but as those last words slip passed my lips I realise how much I mean them.

Anna must also detect the sincerity in my words because she frowns at me, concern etched across her young face. "Will you be alright here, when I go back to school?" she asks me. "Dad's out all day at the garage, and you'll be here all by yourself."

The truth in her words pricks at me and I try not to flinch. "I'll be fine, sweetheart," I assure her. "I was only joking. I've plenty to keep me busy." I look around her room, exhaling deeply as I examine the work we've done so far. "This is just the beginning. You'll see; I've got grand plans for this place."

I'm relieved to see my daughter's furrowed brow melt into a huge smile. "That's good! And when I'm around I'll give you a hand, of course I will." She pauses and I watch as she hesitates, choosing her words carefully. "I do hope that you start to meet people though, Mum. We've got some really nice people living near us. It would be nice if you could make a few friends here, like you had back in Manchester."

I give her a tight smile and finally release her from my grasp. "You're a good girl. And I'm sure I'll make friends eventually." It isn't possible for me to explain to my wide-eyed child that I no longer have any friends in Manchester, that those friendships were lost in the fallout of her father's infidelity. That they were never really my friends but his friends, and that I found the prospect of socialising with happy couples far less appealing once the lie which is our marriage was exposed. Nor is it possible for me to make her understand what I realised all too late; that it is important to have friendships and bonds just for yourself, that not everything must always be shared. For that reason, it isn't possible for me to tell her that I have met one of our neighbours, that we enjoyed a strange and inexplicable encounter over a cup of tea, and that I haven't been able to shake off that woman's words or the look in her eyes ever since. Anna doesn't know about it and Bert certainly can't know about it. That knowledge must remain mine, and mine alone.

We complete Anna's room in record time and in a burst of energetic enthusiasm, together we address the dilapidated kitchen walls, bringing them up to scratch with lining paper and a brilliant shade of white. The remaining days of the holidays pass quickly in a blur of fresh paint and aching limbs, of happiness, hard work and exhausted contentment, and rather foolishly I convince myself that the worst times are behind me.

Of course, as always, the dark mood returns with a vengeance, marking Anna's first day at her new school with a regression to my woeful behaviour of recent weeks. It is a rainy Monday morning, the summer heat well and truly broken as the slow march to autumn begins. Anna heads out the door wearing her new uniform and a stoic smile, and I can only stand at the window and watch as she meets her friends on the lane. Knowing I'm there, she turns and gives me a subtle wave before her little group begins its slow, anxious saunter to catch the bus which will take them to their first day, to new teachers, new classmates and new experiences. I wish for a moment that I could go with her, that I could hold her hand and kiss her goodbye on the cheek just as I used to when she was small. Then I remind myself that she's not little anymore, that she is another part of my life which has changed. I am forced to remember that those happy times, too, are gone.

I watch until Anna is completely out of sight, my view of her obscured by distance and high hedgerows, then I watch for a while longer than that. I watch even though there is nothing to watch, the tears welling up in my eyes, the surrounding silence suffocating me. The house is empty; Bert left for work at the break of dawn as usual, and now Anna has gone too. As the hours alone loom menacingly in front of me, a familiar feeling creeps over: I need a stiff drink.

"You have to stop this, Eleanor. You have to pull yourself together." My words dissolve into the bitterest laugh as I head into the kitchen and pour myself a glass of wine. The only thing more tragic than a thirty-nine-year-old woman moping around the house and getting drunk at eight in the morning, is one who loudly tells herself to stop doing it.

One glass of wine predictably becomes three or four, and by eleven o' clock I am snoring loudly on the sofa, one of my best crystal glasses strewn across my chest. Complete inebriation brings on the strangest dream. We are in Anna's room, my daughter and I, sitting on her bed in the corner and admiring our handiwork, just as we did mere days ago. But where the bright yellow paint we applied should be, there is instead a meadow, a wilderness of flowers, a mural of nature in bloom adorning the walls. I watch as the image swims in front of my eyes, the wild grasses blowing on a breeze. Anna looks at me and we smile, both enjoying the sight, both sharing it and understanding its magic. As I take hold of my daughter's hand and squeeze it tight, the door opens and Meg comes in. But Meg doesn't join us; instead she becomes part of the mural, her long black hair and printed skirts billowing in tandem with the natural world, just as they seemed to when I met her. She sees us and she waves but still she does not join us. She is happy where she is, as are we. Not one of us wishes to do anything to disrupt this utter bliss.

Suspended in a state between waking and sleeping, I feel myself smile. I want to paint that mural, and I want to see Meg in it. I want to see Meg, too. It has been just over a fortnight since we met, and I haven't seen her since. I must visit her like she told me to. I must go and see her, when I am sober. Sober. I need to be sober.

I wake slowly, the morning's wine consumption leaving my head feeling groggy and my mouth dry. I wipe away an unattractive slither of drool from the corner of my mouth and force myself to sit up, grimacing at the pain in my head. You'd think that after all the wine I'd drunk in recent weeks, I'd be more immune to hangovers.

I get up and wander through to the kitchen, running myself a large glass of water from the tap and gulping it down thirstily, along with a couple of paracetamol. Despite my delicate state, I find that my mind is surprising alert, abuzz with ideas and an almost excitable anticipation. Normally after drinking myself into stupor I feel dreadful, brought low by the shame, guilt and despair of knowing that once again I have turned to the bottle to ease away my troubles. Instead today my head feels alive and my fingers itch with the urge to create. I want to paint that mural. I want to make real what I saw in my imagination. I want flowers and grasses, blue skies and wild breezes. I want long skirts and flowing hair; I want dark eyes which follow me around the room, trying to steal glimpses at my soul. I want to be reminded of who I am, even when I don't want to remember.

I finish drinking the water and put the glass down on the counter with more than my usual force. My eyes shift over to the bare white wall of the kitchen, the blank canvas which Anna and I prepared, even though I didn't know it at the time. That's it, I think to myself. That's where I must paint this mural.

I go upstairs and fetch my set of acrylics, delicately wiping away the thin layer of dust which betrays their recent inactivity. I get my brushes and palette and other painting paraphernalia, before slipping on one of my overalls. I wonder for a moment if I have the correct equipment, suitable paint and so on. I'm used to painting on canvas or paper, not walls, and I've no idea if what I have for the task will do. Then I decide that it doesn't matter. I have to paint this, and I have to do it today. I have to follow my instincts and make the image that is in my head before it disappears and I am left with only the emptiness and despair once again.

The rest of the afternoon passes in a frenzy of painting. I paint with an energy I didn't know I possessed, putting great eager strokes of colour boldly and spontaneously across the wall as I recreate the meadow which has taken hold of my mind. I depart completely from my usual methodical approach: there is no planning, no sketching, just me and my palette, creating with an urgency and desperation I have rarely felt before. As the hours wear on, my timid, controlled style melts into a sea of careless colour which swirls and blends and makes something otherworldly on my kitchen wall, and after a while I realise that I hardly recognise this work as mine. But it is mine: it is inspired, it is passionate, it is meant. The only time I slow my pace is when I come to paint her, drawing my energies inward as I focus on recreating that hair and those eyes, breathing the shallowest of breaths as though anything more forceful might blow the entire image of her away.

When Anna arrives home a little after four o' clock she finds me recreating the dandelion seeds blown about by the wind; the final few finishing touches of my masterpiece. She stands back, schoolbag in hand, surveying the scene she has returned to and trying to decide what to say. For my part I don't say anything; I carry on with my work and let the uncertain quiet hang. I know that I could make it easy for her, that I could turn around, plaster on a faux smile and trivialise my own work, just as I always do. Today, however, I can't bring myself to do that, to joke about what I've created or worse, to dismiss it altogether. I have no comment, no explanation. All I have is what is before me; the meadow, the flowers, the woman with the raven eyes and those delicate dandelion seeds, all drifting, all making their bid for freedom.

"Wow, Mum." Anna breaks the silence gently, her voice little more than a stunned whisper. Shame niggles at me as I realise that her silence wasn't induced by embarrassment but awe. "Mum, that's amazing. Is that what you've been working on all day?"

"Yes. I told you I'd keep myself busy." I put my paintbrush down for a final time and sit down at the kitchen table, trying to ignore the discomfort in my legs after so many hours spent on my feet.

Anna stays standing, barely able to take her eyes off my work. A smile twitches in the corners of my mouth. It has been a long time since anything I painted left anyone speechless.

"It's so, well, it's brilliant. And so different."

"Is it?"

"Well, yeah." She gives me a considered look before returning her eyes to my wall painting. "I mean, you like to paint nature so it's not different in that way, but the way you've done it is…"Anna frowns, clearly at a loss for words.

"You mean, it isn't my usual style?" I ask. I should really stop teasing her; I know full well that it is a million miles away from how I usually paint.

"Yeah, that's what I was trying to say. I mean it nicely though, Mum. Your paintings have always been really good but this one is something else!"

I give her a broad smile. "Thanks sweetheart. Anyway, how was your day? How was school?"

"Good, yeah, good. I've got loads of homework already though." I watch as her eyes wander over my painting once again. They come to rest on Meg and I await the inevitable question. "Who is the woman you've painted, Mum?"

I give a nonchalant shrug. "I don't know. Just someone I dreamt about once, I think."

"Maybe she's your guardian angel."

"Perhaps," I reply, wondering how much truth there might be in such a fanciful idea. After all, I can't help but think that it was that brief encounter with my enigmatic new neighbour that somehow triggered this wave of creativity currently flooding through me.

To my surprise, Anna comes over and gives me a hug, brief but full of affection. "I suppose I'd better make a start on my homework. I'm glad you had a good day, Mum. I can't wait to hear what Dad has to say when he sees your painting tonight!"

"Ah, yes," I say, the realisation suddenly hitting me that Bert will return at some point, that he will see what I have done. A wry smile passes over my lips as I remember his words to me on that scorching summer's day. He called this house my project – I scoffed at him then, but I'm not laughing now. It is my project; it is my work of art. It is all mine, a gift from my unfaithful husband to renovate, to make beautiful, to perfect. To fix up in all the ways which my life and our marriage can never be repaired.

Anna heads to her room, leaving me alone once again. I get up and pour myself a glass of water, drinking it down thirstily, swallowing whole the ardent words which linger on my lips: for once in my life, my work is passionate, it is spontaneous, and it is unapologetic. I couldn't care less what Bert thinks about it, or about me.

In fact, I realise with a final gulp, I believe I no longer care about Bert at all.

7

Harry
January 2018

I drop the hot pan of beans on the kitchen counter and hurry towards the front door. My mind is still reeling from the last few unsettling minutes. Despite my desire to get away from Manchester and to leave everything behind, I always knew that being this isolated would be difficult for me, that I would struggle with the long silences after the bustle and noise of city life. Nonetheless, I am stunned by how quickly it has got to me; I've only been here for twenty-four hours and already I am talking to myself and hearing voices which are not really there.

The person at the door knocks again, louder this time, and I force all thoughts of imaginary voices to the back of my mind. I need to get a grip, especially if I've got company. I frown then, wondering who is standing outside, my heart beating a little faster as two unwanted names creep into my head. It can't be either of them, can it? They know I've gone; that was obvious from her last message, but they don't know where. No one knows where. No, it can't be them; it must be someone else, someone mundane like the postman or a door-to-door salesman. It might even be no one; I might be hearing imaginary knocks as well as voices. Who knows how deep my new madness runs? I shudder at the thought.

"Come on Harry, pull yourself together." I take a deep breath to compose myself, then I pull the door open, just a little, and peer around.

My first thought is that I'm relieved it's not no one, but my second thought is that I'm annoyed to see who is there. Before I can stop myself I screw up my face. "Oh, it's you," I snap. If I directed such bad manners towards anyone else I would be embarrassed but frankly, I'll make an exception for this man. After the way he spoke to me on the lane as he hovered in front of his broken down truck, he can hardly be surprised.

And indeed, he doesn't seem surprised at all. Instead he gives me an enormous grin, apparently enjoying my irritation. "It's great to see you again, too."

"Well you're the one standing at my front door."

He laughs, and my hackles rise even further. "I think we've got off on the wrong foot earlier today." To my surprise, he extends a friendly hand. "Let's start again. It's nice to meet you. My name's Daniel McCabe."

Reluctantly I take his hand and give it a half-hearted shake. His skin feels coarse, like skin does when it is hard-worked and weather-worn, but his touch is surprisingly warm. His eyes meet mine and I retract my hand quickly. "Harry James," I reply, my tone brusque. "Short for Harriet but no one ever calls me that." I bite my lip. At least, there's no one to call me that anymore.

"Welcome to Kirtlebeck, Harry. It's good to put a name to a new face. We don't get very many new faces around here. That's not a local accent, is it? Where're you from?"

"Manchester," I reply, "and I'm afraid I won't be here very long." The evening air is bitingly cold and I shiver, wrapping my arms around myself.

"I'm sorry to hear that," he replies, and oddly he sounds genuine. "This house has been empty for a while. Mum and I were quite looking forward to having a new neighbour."

"Oh. You live nearby? With your mum?"

He laughs again, but this time it doesn't annoy me. In fact, I find myself warming to his sense of humour. No doubt that's another sign of just how much I'm craving some company right now. "Yes, but I promise I'm not as pathetic as I sound. Mum doesn't keep well, so she moved in with me a few years ago. I have the house further down the lane, the white one with the big windows."

"Hmm," I answer him, trying to recall the cottage he means. I've driven that way a few times now, each time apparently failing to take in any of the surroundings. I shiver again, my teeth chattering as a biting gust of wind encircles me.

"Anyway, I'll let you get on with your evening," he says, seeming to notice my discomfort. "It's too cold to keep you talking on the doorstep."

"It's – it's okay," I stammer, suddenly filled with a desire to prevent him from leaving. "Why don't you come in?"

"I don't know. Should you really be welcoming strangers into your home?" He narrows his eyes at me, but his lips twitch with a smile.

This time it's my turn to laugh; the first time I've done so properly since arriving here. "You'd be right, except you're not a stranger now, you're a neighbour." I open the door wider, beckoning him inside.

He grins at me and steps into the porch. "Well in that case, it'd be rude of me to refuse. I'll not keep you long, though. I'm sure you've got things to be getting on with."

I nod in agreement, but my smile weakens and I turn away so that he cannot see the desperation in my eyes. Desperation for company, to not be alone with my plate of cold beans on toast and bottle of red wine. Desperation to fill the silence with real voices, and not those I have imagined. Desperation, above all, to enjoy some interesting conversation and get away from my overwhelming thoughts about this house, my family, and everything I've left behind.

I lead Daniel through to the kitchen, where the smell of my

abandoned dinner still lingers. Hurriedly I push the opened bottle of wine to one side and hide the filled glass behind the toaster. Although it isn't a crime to drink alone, for some reason I don't want him to know that's how I was planning to spend my evening. Before I can say anything he sits down at the kitchen table and makes himself at home. In fact, I realise, he looks very at home here.

"Can I offer you something?" I ask. "Tea? Coffee?"

He shakes his head. "Too late in the day for that stuff," he replies. "But I'll join you in a glass of that wine you've just shoved out the way."

My face grows warm but I manage to force a smile. "Busted," I say, suspecting that the best way to handle this man is probably with humour. I pour him a glass and reach for mine, glancing at my crusty beans and rather forlorn-looking toast. My stomach rumbles but I decide to resist the temptation to eat my sad little dinner in front of my new neighbour. After all, he said he won't be here long. I suppose I could always reheat it once he's gone.

"I thought most Scots preferred whisky," I say, handing him the glass of wine.

"Most Scots like almost anything to drink," he replies. "Or at least, I do. I suppose I shouldn't pretend to talk for my fellow countrymen and women."

I sit down opposite him and take a small sip from my glass. Suddenly I feel nervous, like I don't know what to say now that we've moved beyond introductions and into my living space. An awkward silence lingers for a moment and I begin to wonder if I've been too hasty in inviting him in, if I'd have been better resigning myself to my solitude and letting him go when he wanted to.

"So, how long have you lived in Kirtlebeck?" I ask, resolving to make an effort. I take another drink from my glass, a longer one this time, and steal a few moments to study his face. Those bright blue eyes immediately draw my attention, just as they did earlier on the lane, but this time I also notice his other features: a strong, unshaven jaw, a thin, straight nose, greying red-blonde hair kept short and neat. The gentle creases around his eyes suggest that he's older than me, perhaps by a decade or more. It occurs to me for the first time that he's actually quite nice to look at, but immediately I push the thought from my mind. After everything that's happened over the last few months, the last thing I need is to become fixated on another man.

"Almost eighteen years," Daniel replies, nursing his glass in his hands. "I moved here to start my own business back in 2000. New century, new chapter and all of that."

"So what do you do?" I ask, intrigued and more than happy to talk about him rather than myself.

"I'm a mechanic. I run the garage in the village. It's a little place but it turns a steady income and the life here suits me." He looks at me pointedly. "I'm not one for city living. I like to take life at a slower pace. You might find that you do too, if you stick around long enough."

"Have you ever lived in a city?" I pursue my line of questioning, ignoring his latter remark.

He nods. "Stayed in Glasgow in the early nineties so yes, I've made an informed choice." He takes a gulp of his wine then grimaces. "Unlike you when you bought this wine. Is this what passes for a drink in Manchester?"

"I'll have you know that I bought that from a shop on my way here!" I reply, trying to keep my voice light. I've spent enough time in this man's company now to understand that he gets a kick out of winding me up.

"Yes, well," he says, taking another, more cautious sip from his glass. "I'll need to bring you a decent bottle round some time and show you what a good wine tastes like."

"That would be nice, thank you," I reply, making an effort to be gracious. "So, eighteen years in Kirtlebeck, eh? Did you know the people who lived here before me?" I ask as casually as I can manage.

Daniel lets out an amused chuckle. "Don't you mean, did I know your grandmother?"

I feel my mouth fall open, but I haven't the presence of mind to erase the shock from my face. Did everyone in this place know about me? "She – she talked about me?" I stammer, my voice small and pitiful.

Perhaps realising that he's stepped into sensitive territory, Daniel's smile fades and he lowers his gaze. "A little," he replies. "I used to help her out from time to time, you know, fixing stuff around this place or fetching her shopping when she wasn't well. She didn't talk much about her family, but she did once mention that when she died this place would pass to her granddaughter. After our, err, encounter on the lane today and then seeing your car parked up here – well, it wasn't hard to figure out who you were." He raises his eyes and looks at me, his expression sympathetic, almost apologetic.

"Is that all she said?" I ask, my voice tinged with disappointment. "Nothing about never meeting me, nothing about wanting to meet me?"

He shakes his head. "Sorry. She didn't talk much about her life, her past, and when she did she said very little – just that she was on her own and had been for a very long time. She seemed like a private person, the sort who kept herself to herself. I assumed she had her reasons for that so I never pried."

I drain the last of my wine from my glass and rub my forehead, weariness and exasperation suddenly getting the better of me. I know that it's not Daniel's fault; I know I shouldn't be cross with him simply for the accident of knowing my grandmother when I didn't. Yet, no matter how hard I try, the feeling of being locked out of my own family, of being a stranger in this place, in this house, eats away at me. Wordlessly I reach for the wine and pour myself another large glass.

Daniel looks down at the wine then back at me. "I'm sorry I can't tell you more," he says. "And I'm sorry you never met her. I didn't know that you were estranged, although I might have guessed that was the case. Your grandmother never seemed to have any family come to visit her. She was quite the enigma, really. She was clearly so alone and yet she never complained she was lonely, never seemed to bother about being here all by herself."

His observation causes a shiver to run through me as I consider how uneasy being alone here makes me. "Don't you think it's odd to live here all of these years, to go to the trouble of making a will which leaves everything to your grandchild and yet never make an effort to reach out to them?" I sip my wine again, regretting the bitterness which has suddenly crept into my voice.

Daniel shrugs. "Perhaps it is. I've asked myself a similar question over the years. Growing up it was just Mum and I. Dad – he, well, he wasn't interested or whatever. The joys of being born in the early seventies to free loving hippies, I suppose. Anyway we haven't seen him for years. In fact, I've no idea where he is, or if he's even still alive. At least you have this house to pick over, to explore and to see what you can find out about your grandmother."

"That's what the solicitor said. But that's what's so frustrating as well," I begin. "There's nothing here. It's as though…" The wine has got me firmly in its grip now and I struggle to find the words, managing little more than a helpless shrug.

Daniel frowns. "What? What is it?"

I let out a heavy sigh. "If you looked around this house, you would see what I mean. It's like anything precious, anything sentimental, anything which could tell a story has been removed. Literally all I've found in the last twenty-four hours is a wardrobe full of very nice clothes, a sewing machine and a knitting basket. It's bizarre, and if I'm honest, I think it's getting to me."

To my surprise, Daniel's concerned face breaks into a smile. "Now, in that respect I might be able to help," he says.

"How?"

"A couple of years ago your grandmother asked me to move a ton of stuff up to the attic. It was all already boxed so I don't know what it was exactly, but something tells me that might be the treasure trove you're looking for."

For the first time since I got here, my eyes widen with delight. "Oh thank you! Thank you!" I gush, trying to resist the urge to jump up and hug him. "I'm so glad you came over to drink my terrible wine."

Daniel laughs. "Oh yes, and about that…" He lifts his glass and drinks the rest of his wine in one huge gulp, grimacing comically at the taste. "Waste not, want not, as they say."

I grin at his silliness, appreciating again his intrusion upon my evening, how he has lightened the mood in this empty house. "Really though, thank you. And I'm sorry about what you told me, about your dad. I grew up without my mum too."

That heavy look of empathy flashes across his face again, but he doesn't press me for any further information. "To be honest, the whole thing just makes me appreciate Mum even more. She had to be everything to me, and she was damn good at it too. And now it's my turn to take care of her."

I nod. "I know what you mean. Dad and I took care of each other. He's…he's gone now. Cancer. Almost eleven years ago."

"I'm sorry to hear that, Harry." The way he says my name sounds oddly endearing and I try to ignore the fluttering it causes in the pit of my stomach.

"Thank you," I reply, before breaking into a small smile. "And I'm sorry to hear you were born in the early seventies – how old does that make you, then?"

Daniel groans, clutching at his heart as though wounded. "Ouch, neighbour," he replies. "I'll be forty-five later this year, thank you for reminding me."

My breath catches in my throat. Forty-five. That's how old he was, too. The man who ruined everything. The man I ruined everything with.

Daniel seems to sense my change in mood. "What? Don't tell me you're even older than me? I wouldn't have put you at a day over thirty-five."

His teasing lifts me from the dark place my mind had wandered to, and I laugh loudly. "I'm thirty, and for that you owe me two bottles of good wine."

The look of genuine surprise lingering in Daniel's eyes tells me that he really did think I was in my mid-thirties. "God, you're an eighties baby," he observes, recovering quickly. "I'm the one who should feel sorry for you. I remember the eighties. It wasn't pretty. I had the haircut to prove it."

I laugh again, and I'm astonished to hear how light-hearted and giggly I sound. Anyone watching us would think we were flirting. Are we flirting? Is he flirting with me?

Before I can think any more deeply on the turn our conversation has taken, Daniel gets up from the table and grabs his coat from the back of the chair. "It's getting late," he says. "I'd better go. I need to check on Mum and besides, I've taken up enough of your time."

I stand up slowly, feeling a little woozy from the wine. I remember that I still haven't eaten anything. "Honestly it's fine," I reply. "I'm actually really glad you called round. We did get off to a rotten start earlier today and it was nice to properly meet you and to make that right."

Daniel's face breaks into the loveliest smile. "I agree," he says. He reaches into his pocket and hands me a business card. "Listen, I'm sure you've got everything under control, but if you ever need a hand with anything while you're here, that's my number on there."

"Thank you," I reply. "That's very kind of you."

He looks straight at me and I see that expression again, the sympathy shining through in those bright blue eyes. "It can't be easy, coming here alone and having to deal with all of this. I'm here to help if you need it."

I repeat my appreciation of his offer and quietly show him to the door. After he leaves I lean hard against the front door for a few moments, my senses dulled by wine but my mind nonetheless keen to rake over the evening's events. It's only my second night here and it's been a strange one; a disrupted dinner, an empty bottle of wine, an imagination running wild with voices and an unexpected guest. My thoughts linger for a few moments on my visitor; funny how he seemed so hateful earlier today and yet now all I can think is how he made me laugh, how he warmed this old house with his presence, how he lightened my mood. Then again, I tell myself, I'm so alone here that perhaps someone with half his charm would have had exactly the same effect. I also remind myself how susceptible I am to the appeal of the older man, and how I must never allow myself to get caught up like that again.

I scrape my uneaten meal into the bin and leave my dishes to soak until morning. All that wine on an empty stomach has left me feeling exhausted, and I crash into bed easily, fully-clothed and without a second thought. I drift off peacefully in the lemon-coloured room, all thoughts of Manchester, my grandmother, this house, even Daniel suspended. I need to sleep now, there's nothing else for it. Everything else must wait until tomorrow. The dishes. The attic. The voices…

"Sleep well," someone whispers.

But I have already gone; I am fast asleep and I don't hear them. And at that very moment, alone as I am in the dark, that is probably for the best.

8

Eleanor
August 1972

I wake around three in the morning, although in truth I am unsure if I have properly slept. My head is pounding and my mind reels over the night's earlier events, or at least, the parts that I can remember. It began, as it always does, with a glass of wine, a drop of celebration and vitriol enjoyed while cooking the evening meal. I was, I recall, recklessly happy about the mural I had created, about what I had achieved, about the glory I had managed to carve out from a day which had begun so hopelessly. I decided that in these circumstances a glass of wine was permissible; I wasn't drinking out of misery but out of joy. I was drinking in the same way that every other person I know drinks. I was only having one. I wasn't getting carried away.

Then Bert came home and things got out of control.

I stagger out of bed, careful not to disturb the snoring lump strewn next to me. The last thing I want is for him to wake, for there to be more words between us. It was only in the heat of argument that I realised how little I had spoken to him over the preceding weeks, how truly we had become strangers in this house, and how comfortable I was with that fact. I hated talking to him; I despised his expectation that I would explain myself, that I would justify my actions to him. So I raised my voice, louder and louder, stifling his demands with a shrill holler, letting out all the anger and all the resentment I had been holding on to for so long. My screams were brief but cathartic, and in those moments I realised that I owe this man absolutely nothing.

I tiptoe along the landing, a shawl draped over my shoulders to warm me against the cool night air. My mouth is desert dry and my throat is as rough as sandpaper; drinking and yelling certainly take their toll on the body. I walk past Anna's room, grimacing as I am reminded of the other ill-effects of my behaviour. Poor Anna, having to listen to all of that. All my efforts to keep the truth from her have come to nought. She can be in no doubt now about how her father has wronged me, about how I truly feel.

It began with the mural, of course. To say that he wasn't delighted with my artwork would be an understatement. My art for Bert belongs on paper, in neat little sketchpads which can be locked away and forgotten about, or delicate framed images which can be put aside and dismissed with ease. As far as he's concerned, my art is not meant to be bold or confrontational, it is not meant to dominate, to force you to look at it, to make you pay it some attention. Bert likes art the same way he likes women: meek and mild, demure and undemanding. Easy. Bert likes easy things best of all.

I saw his mouth fall open as soon as he walked into the kitchen and laid his eyes upon it.

"What do you think then, Albert?" The half-empty glass of merlot in my hand had emboldened me and I was ready to goad him.

"Christ, Eleanor," he replied with a slow shake of his head. "What have you done to the kitchen wall?"

"It's called a mural," I answered him as though talking to a child. "Well, you did say this place was mine to make nice."

"Yes – to decorate, to put some nice paper on the walls. I never suggested that you turn our house into the flamin' Sistine Chapel.

What on earth were you thinking?"

"Oh! What a good idea!" I replied, pouring myself another glass of wine and ignoring his question. "I could create some religious frescoes on our bedroom ceiling…"

He came closer then, his eyes dark and serious. "Don't mock me, Eleanor."

"Why not? You're completely ridiculous. Pathetic, even. Yes, you're pathetic." I cannot describe how good it felt to finally say it.

He drew himself upwards, looming over me, and I waited to feel the sting of his hand across my cheek. I don't know why I thought he'd hit me; as a husband he has many failings but being quick to use his fists isn't one of them. But tonight, as he stood in front of me, his venom-filled eyes boring into me, I believed I might have pushed him too far. A deeply horrid part of me almost wanted him to strike, to give me the smallest satisfaction of provoking some feeling from my husband other than his usual disapproving disregard. Alas, no, he couldn't even give me that, and in the end he just shook his head, his lips possessed by an ugly snarl.

"You're completely insane," he replied. "Just take a look at yourself – a barking mad drunk with shabby clothes and a terrible haircut spending her days drawing on the walls and necking bottles of wine. I'm glad you never leave the house – you're an embarrassment."

Tears pricked in the corners of my eyes but I refused to let them fall. "Is that why you fucked that tart?" I asked through gritted teeth. "Is that why you betrayed me and my daughter?"

"Oh, so that's what this is all about!" he scoffed. "I should have known. Do me a favour, Eleanor, and leave our daughter out of this. This has nothing to do with Anna and you know it. This is about me and you. This is about me and you and whatever the hell you decided to do to our kitchen wall."

"There is no me and you!" I began to scream then. "This isn't a marriage, it's a living hell! I hate you, you selfish bastard! I hate you for what you've done to me, for what you've brought me to. If I am so awful, so ugly, so disgusting, then it is you who has made me this way. It is you who has taken everything from me…" my words gave way to my trembling lip and the tears began to fall in earnest. I hated myself for crying; I hated myself for crumbling in front of him, but I couldn't help it. The mural, the wine, the events of the past few months – all of it, I realised, had left me raw and vulnerable. I was wounded. I was battle-weary. I was drunk.

Bert had no empathy, of course. He never does. "I don't have time for this, Eleanor. I'm going back to the garage. I've a lot of paperwork to catch up on. Someone in this house has to pay the bills."

He walked away without another word, leaving me to sob over the cooker as I finished preparing our meal. Dinner was a lonesome affair; Anna made herself scarce in her room on the pretext of still having a lot of homework to do, while I choked and snivelled my way through a bland plate of macaroni and cheese along with a bottle of wine which was sufficient to send me on my way to oblivion. By the time Bert came home I had passed out in bed; I vaguely recall stirring as he climbed in beside me, groaning drunkenly in protest at his presence. Even now the thought of him lying there next to me lights a fire of indignation deep within my belly. How dare he think he can share our marital bed after what he said to me, after he showed me how little he cares.

Far from sleep and unwilling to return to my bed I wander in the dark, finding my way to the living room window which looks out on to the lane. This point has been the furthest I have ventured for weeks, the nearest I have got to the outside world. If I go outdoors it is only into the secluded back garden; I never venture out the front or along our gravel driveway, and I certainly don't go into the village, let alone along to the next town. For reasons I still barely understand, I have felt the need to lock myself away, to confine myself to this big old house which hardly feels like home. Yet now, as I gaze out into the night, I feel the urge to leave this place rush through me. Suddenly I want to take a walk down the lane, to breathe the fresh, cool night air. Impulsively I grab my jacket and throw on my shoes and walk stealthily towards the door. I hesitate as my hand grips the handle; what sort of person goes out for a walk in the middle of the night? What will I say if anyone sees me? And in any case, where on earth do I want to go at half past three in the morning?

As I ask myself that final question, the image of her grows in my mind. I smile. Of course. I know exactly where I want to go.

I open the door and step out into the silent black. The breeze is slight but chilling and I pull the collar of my coat up higher around my neck. I creep down the lane, taking care to keep my footsteps light. The last thing I want is for Bert to wake and find me outside in my nightgown; he already thinks that I've lost my mind. I walk down the lane, which is very dark, far darker than I had appreciated when indoors. Sunrise is several hours' away yet and tonight's moon is periodically obscured by moving cloud. I squint under the insufficient glow of the streetlights dotted sparsely over me, and I begin to wish I had brought a torch.

After a few moments I reach the first dwelling beyond mine. It is a humble cottage, sitting low beside the lane, partially obscured by a set of mature, unkempt conifer trees. Overcome with curiosity I draw closer, standing to one side of an old rusted iron gate upon which is placed a carved wooden name plate: *Thistle Cottage.*

"This is it," I breathe. "This is her home."

I startle as signs of life stir within and a light flickers on, almost as though Thistle Cottage is responding to my whispered words. My heart begins to race as I step back into the shadows of the trees. It's the middle of the night; Meg, like everyone else, is surely fast asleep. I can't have woken her, can I? She can't possibly have heard me out here, can she? What will I do if she finds me out here? What will I say? How will I explain myself?

A hand touches me lightly on the shoulder. Adrenaline surges through me and it takes every fibre of my being to prevent myself from yelling out. Slowly I turn around, my eyes wide with the strain of seeing in the dark, and if I'm honest with myself, with an unhealthy dose of fear. In the re-emerging moonlight I am relieved to see Meg's dark gaze fixed upon me, her expression somewhere between inquisitive and startled. The sight of her face calms me and I feel my heart resume its regular soft beat within my chest.

"Eleanor? It is you. I heard a noise out here. I thought someone was trying to break in. You gave me a real fright."

Her words bite at me and I feel the heat of shame rise in my cheeks. "I'm so sorry, Meg. I didn't mean to scare you, I was just, just…"

"…wandering around in the dark in the middle of the night?" She finishes my sentence for me and I'm relieved to see a wry smile emerge on her lips.

"Yes, something like that," I reply. "I couldn't sleep, and I needed some air. I'm truly sorry to have woken you."

"Oh, don't worry about that," she replies, the light, easy tone returning to her voice. "I hardly sleep anyway. I tell you what, seeing as we're both awake, why don't you come in for a while? I'll make us some tea, fetch a couple of blankets and we can get cosy and talk about why neither of us can sleep. How does that sound?"

"That sounds lovely," I reply. "If you're sure?"

"Of course I'm sure," she breathes. Before I can give a final murmur of assent, she has taken me by the hand and led me inside.

The interior of Thistle Cottage is small and dimly-lit, the air laced with the musty scent of old mahogany furniture. Meg leads me to a tiny living room and bids me to sit down on an antique chair nearest to the fireplace. Wordlessly she places a blanket around my shoulders and leaves the room, presumably to boil the kettle. I sit quietly, enjoying the petite homeliness of her cottage which sits in stark contrast to the large rooms and high ceilings of my house. I take a moment to admire the original features which Meg has clearly lovingly maintained, from the open fireplace to the exposed beams on the ceiling, to the ancient wooden floor dressed only by a deep red Persian rug. On the walls a collection of small stitched landscapes catches my eye and I can't help but wonder if she made them. I am about to take a closer look when Meg returns, carrying a tray of tea and biscuits.

"It'll soon be time to start lighting that again," she says, nodding briefly towards the fireplace as she puts the tray down on a small table and begins to pour the tea. It strikes me momentarily how bizarre this scene seems, taking place in the middle of the night.

"I bet it's so cosy in here with a roaring fire in the grate," I say wistfully. "You have a lovely home, Meg."

She flashes me a beaming grin as she sits on the seat opposite. "Thank you. As do you, of course. How are things coming along at Kirtlebeck End?"

"Quite well," I reply, tentatively lifting my cup. "Anna and I decorated her room. It looks lovely. Then we gave the kitchen a lick of paint, and…" I hesitate for a moment, though I'm not sure why.

Meg looks at me, her interest piquing in those deep brown eyes. "And?"

"And I took your advice. I started a mural. In the kitchen. I've finished it, in fact," I pause, sipping my tea and wondering why my attempt at an explanation is so chronic. "What I mean is, I created a mural in my kitchen."

Meg gasps, clasping her hands together excitedly. "Oh, Eleanor, that's wonderful news! What is it like? When can I see it? I bet it's amazing. Oh, I do wonder what you will do next!"

I draw a deep breath. "It's a meadow scene of sorts and yes, of course you can come over and see it. It was you who gave me the idea, after all. In fact, I've featured you in it. Well, a lady who looks like you." I expect to be embarrassed by telling her this but strangely I'm not. In fact, I feel proud; prouder than I've ever felt about anything I've created.

"Oh, Eleanor!" she squeals. "Now I really can't wait to see it!"

I give her a grim smile. "Yes, well, you'll have to be quick, I'm afraid. I suspect I'm going to have to paint over it."

A frown creases her brow. "Paint over it? But why?"

"Because Bert hates it," I explain without hesitation. "We had a huge row about it this evening. I think that's part of the reason I couldn't sleep."

Meg bites her lip and I can see that she is considering what to say to me. "But you like it, don't you? Why must it go just because your husband doesn't like it?"

"I think you just answered your own question," I reply, rather more flippantly than I mean to. "He's my husband – what he says, goes. That's been the truth of it for all of my married life. We left Manchester because he said so, we moved here because he said so." I pause, stopping short of telling my new confidante exactly why we moved. "And now, if he says my mural must go, then so it shall be." I grit my teeth, fighting back the tears which I can feel brimming under my eyes. Even as I say it, I know that I won't be able to bear it. I can't get rid of my mural, and I can't stop painting them, either. For the first time in years I feel alive, literally and creatively. I know that I must carry on.

Meg smoothes her skirt over her lap. Her eyes are cast down but I sense that they are filled with sympathy. "This is exactly why I like to live alone," she says quietly.

"Yes," I reply. "And for that, I envy you."

She looks up at me then. "But you wouldn't be without your daughter, surely?"

"No, of course not," I say. "But I could live quite happily without Bert for the rest of my days."

"Because he hates your mural or because he made you leave Manchester to come and live in Kirtlebeck?"

"All of that and more besides." I gulp down the last of my tea and glance at the clock on the mantelpiece. "But that's a story for another time. I'd better go; I've kept you up long enough and Bert and Anna will both be up in an hour or so. If I'm not there to make them some breakfast, I don't know what they'll do."

I intend those words to be spoken in jest but they come out sounding sad. Meg gives me another understanding look. "You can change things you know, Eleanor," she says to me.

A shadow of regret passes over my face before I can prevent it. "I think it's too late for that, and in any case, I'm not sure I'd know where to begin," I reply, getting up from my seat.

"We must all start somewhere." Her words follow me to the front door. "I think you could do anything you put your mind to."

I give her a final, grateful smile. "Then you have more faith in me than I do, Meg. But thank you, and thank you for the tea."

I return home a little before sunrise, creeping inside and finding my way on to the sofa. I intend just to lie down for a few moments, to wait until I hear the familiar sounds of the house stirring, but instead I fall into a peaceful, irresistible slumber. I sleep so soundly that I don't wake when Anna gets up; I don't wake when she comes downstairs, and after finding me sleeping, gets on with making herself and her father some toast. I don't wake when Bert comes into the living room, his eyes bleary with tiredness, his sigh heavy as he assumes that I have been up in the night, drinking myself back into a stupor. I don't wake when he swears under his breath, calling me a useless drunk once again. I hear it all, but I don't wake. I choose not to wake. Unlike so much of my sleep over the previous weeks, this sleep is dreamless and restorative, and I decide to indulge myself in it. After all, if I'm going to spend the day creating something meaningful, I must be well rested.

In my sleep I sense Bert leave the room. I allow myself a little smile. I will begin another mural today and what's more, I will paint it in our room. I don't care what he thinks and I don't care what he will say. After all, Meg was right: I can do anything I put my mind to.

9

Harry
January 2018

The following day I wake early, my head pounding and my empty stomach growling at me in protest. After a few moans and groans I force myself out of bed, grabbing a packet of painkillers and a glass of water from the bathroom as the kitchen just seems too far away. Feeling slightly disgusted with myself for sleeping in my clothes I jump into the shower, yelping as tepid water hits my skin. I really must get to grips with how the boiler works in this place. But on the bright side, the cool water refreshes me and I emerge moments later, more awake and ready to get on with my day.

I head back into the bedroom to dress, throwing on an old pair of jeans and hoodie. If I'm going to spend my day crawling around an attic, I need to make sure I'm comfortable. I sit down at the dressing table and give my hair a cursory brush while I try not to examine my appearance too closely. My skin is pale and blotchy and my eyes are heavy; sure signs that I drank too much and ate too little last night. Unimpressed by what I see in the mirror I allow my eyes to wander, examining the reflected image of this room. I wonder how many times my mum sat right here on this stool, brushing her own hair, applying her make-up, or simply gazing as I am now? I wonder about the things this mirror saw over the years, the conversations it bore witness to, the reflections of my family's life it contained. I wish then that I could glimpse at it and see more than just myself; I wish I could see what it knows, what it remembers.

"Don't be stupid, Harry," I mutter. "What do you think this is, some sort of fairy tale? It's just a mirror."

I avert my gaze from the mirror's reflection and look down at the table itself. After only a couple of days here I have already littered it with my things; face cream, hair brush, perfume, and my phone. My phone. I swallow hard as my eyes come to rest upon it. I haven't switched it back on since the day I arrived, when I received that text message from her. I wonder how many more messages she's sent me since. I wonder what she's said. I wonder how I would feel if I switched it on and read her words to me. I pick up the phone, my finger hovering tentatively over the button which, if pressed, will bring it back to life and along with it, all those memories of what I've left behind. My hands shake and my heart pounds; do I really want to do this to myself right now?

No, I decide, I don't. What I want to do right now is make myself a cup of tea and some breakfast, and after that I want to go into the attic and find those boxes Daniel told me about. I want to see what's inside them, and I want to know what they can tell me about my family. Anything else is just a distraction.

After demolishing a bowl of cereal at lightning speed, I waste no time in trying to figure out how to get into the attic. The access door is in the ceiling at the end of the landing, and I climb up on a chair to open it. It swings open relatively easily, greeting me with a ton of dust and thankfully, a ladder which pulls downwards. I know from what Daniel told me that he was up there just a couple of years ago, and since he placed boxes up there I assume that the attic space is at least partly floored and that it has lighting. Nonetheless before climbing up I grab my torch and tie a scarf around my face to protect my mouth and nose. I feel pretty stupid but I remind myself that I've no idea what condition the space is in or what else might be up there. I can't be too careful, especially when I'm here all alone. If I was to collapse up there after inhaling something nasty, no one might find me for days, weeks even. With a small shudder I push the unpleasant thought away, and satisfied with the precautions I have taken, I climb inside.

The air in the loft is cold, and rather predictably, thick with dust. I shine my torch into the darkness, groping around for a light switch. Eventually I find it dangling by a string and I pull it with some urgency, hoping that it works. I breathe a sigh of relief as the light flickers on, illuminating the room with a dingy yellow glow. If I'm honest with myself, I've always found attics a bit creepy, and this one is no different. As I look around I find myself shivering, my eyes gazing uneasily at the old wooden beams covered with cobwebs. I wonder how big the spiders are up here. I really don't like big spiders; in fact, I really don't like any size of spider at all. My mind races, and I can't help but wonder what else might live up here...

"Cut it out," I hiss to myself. "You'll be hearing voices again next."

I reign in my fevered imagination and focus instead on the task at hand. The boxes are easily found; indeed, there is little else sitting up in the attic at all. I smile when I observe how neatly they have been placed. Daniel took great care in putting them up here; he must have suspected that they contain important things, or at least, things of value to my grandmother. Then again, I think to myself, Daniel strikes me as the sort of person who would always be attentive, no matter what was asked of him. My stomach gives a funny flutter at the thought; I don't like it, and I push both the thought and the feeling to one side.

I open the first box I come to, carefully removing the brown tape holding the top shut. I am keenly aware of the way my heart is hammering in my chest; I know I'm like a child opening presents at Christmas, but I just can't help it. The anticipation of what I might find inside is almost too much to bear. Fortunately, this first box doesn't disappoint, and I almost squeal with delight when I pull away the last cardboard flap to reveal a set of sketchbooks. I lift the first one out and run my hand carefully over it. Its edges are yellowed with age but otherwise it is in immaculate condition. My heart skips a beat when I read the name written on the front of it: Eleanor Murray. Eleanor – my grandmother. This sketchbook belonged to her.

I turn the front cover over tentatively, conscious that the pages contained within it are old and possibly fragile. Fortunately, an examination of the first page quickly reassures me that the paper is still robust, and I set about thumbing through the rest of the book. Every page has been filled with drawings, and the pictures which greet me delight my eyes. The entire book contains a set of city scenes: bustling streets, buses, town parks, rows of terraced houses lining cobbled streets. The images are from another time; my knowledge of past decades is scant but I'd guess from the vehicles and the fashions that these pictures were drawn sometime in the sixties. It's only when I turn over another page and spot a familiar landmark that I get a sense of place, and I gasp with surprise.

"That's Manchester Central," I whisper. "When did you go to Manchester, Eleanor?"

I run my fingers delicately over her drawing of the railway station as it looked to her all those years ago. During my childhood the station was left derelict and unused, until its conversion into a conference centre over ten years ago. Looking at this drawing now, it's funny to think that I never saw it serve its original purpose; I never saw the platforms, I never saw the trains come and go. I never saw it as she saw it.

"You're full of surprises, Eleanor," I say. "Let's have a look at what else you've hidden up here."

The next sketchbook sits in marked contrast to the first. For one thing, it is incomplete, with only about half of the pages drawn upon, and many of the pictures themselves are unfinished. Secondly, this sketchbook doesn't contain any of the urban images that my grandmother so excelled at in the first. Instead, every image is of the natural world; birds, trees, flowers, babbling brooks, grassy meadows. The style is different, too, the pencil strokes running wild and free, more passionate, less controlled but also, I think, less certain. On one page my eyes come to rest on a little chaffinch, perched on his branch. I smile, studying his cheery demeanour as he readies himself to fly off in an unknown scene, to an undrawn abyss. Like many of the images in this sketchpad, the chaffinch too remains incomplete.

"I wonder why she never finished you," I say, tapping his little beak.

"She's good, isn't she?"

That deep, male voice startles me and I just about jump out of my own skin. I bite my lip hard to stop myself from yelling out, and then force myself to take a few deep breaths. This is ridiculous. I have to stop imagining things. I have to stop hearing voices which are not, which cannot be there.

"I'm not talking to you," I say with all the determination I can muster. "I'm not answering you. You're just my imagination. You're not really there."

"Of course I'm here. And you did just speak to me."

"I'm not…" I stop myself, realising that I'm about to tell the voice in my head that I wasn't talking to him, but myself. God, how absurd. I take another deep breath and rub a hand over my brow. I really am losing my mind.

I put down the sketchbook in my hand and continue raking through the box, making a conscious decision to ignore the voice. Perhaps if I don't acknowledge it, it will stop. Perhaps if I force myself repeatedly to observe reality, to understand that there cannot be anyone talking to me right now, eventually my broken mind will get the message.

And yet, despite my determination, the voice keeps talking.

"I was just saying that she's a good artist," he continues. "I don't think I tell her so often enough, but she is. It was Eleanor who drew those pictures, I presume you realise that. Who are you, anyway? And where is Eleanor? I've been home for ages now and I still haven't seen her, or Anna. Where's Anna? They're my…she's my…"

"Oh for fuck's sake!" I cry out, putting my hands over my ears.

"How dare you speak to me like that under my own roof."

I groan, realising that this voice isn't going to stop, no matter what I do. "This isn't your roof," I say with a resigned sigh. "It's mine. Now go away and leave me alone."

"But…go where? And what do you mean this is your house?"

I spin around, throwing my arms up in despair. "I mean that I own this place! Just stop it! There's no one here. I can't see anyone here. I'm losing my mind." My irritation dissolves into tears and I clasp my head in my hands.

"But I can see you. I'm standing right near the ladder which leads back down into the hall. Can you really not see me?"

"No," I say with a sniffle, "I can't."

"How strange."

"That's one word for it," I mutter. I glance back at the boxes. Every fibre of my being is telling me to ignore this, to carry on sorting through my family's possessions and stop indulging in my wild fantasies. And yet, something deep within my gut is drawn to this voice, wanting me to engage with it, with him, to see what stories he can share. Call it desperation or curiosity, but at that moment I feel compelled to ask him a question: "What's your name?"

"Robert Murray," he replies. "But everyone calls me Bert."

"It's nice to meet you, Bert," I say, my mind racing as I try to figure out what to say next. What should you say to someone who isn't really there? "You mentioned Eleanor before. Was she — is she your wife?" I ask, choosing my words carefully.

"That's right. And Anna's my daughter. Have you seen them?"

I shake my head. "No, I'm sorry, Bert," I reply. "I haven't seen them. I haven't seen them because they're dead."

The moment that final word rolls off my tongue, the lights go out. I feel my breath quicken, my heart beating faster. I reach for my torch, thankfully still tucked away in my pocket, and turn it on, shining it frantically around the room as I walk back towards the light switch. I pull the cord. Nothing happens.

I stare in disbelief at the light, all manner of thoughts sprinting through my mind. It's one thing to hear a voice, to hold a conversation with your own imagination. Admittedly it's crazy, but it's also possible to understand it, to appreciate the power of the mind and what it can do when someone has been under considerable stress then finds themselves all alone in an old house. But the light going out at that very moment, then refusing to come back on? Of course, it could just be a power cut, or the electricity tripping out due to bad wiring. But on the other hand, it could be…

I pull the cord again. Still nothing happens.

"Bert?" I say gently. "Did you turn the lights off?"

"Yes," comes the reply.

"Don't you think that's a little childish?"

"You said my family are dead." This time he sounds upset.

"I know. I'm sorry. But I'm afraid it's true, and…and Bert, I think you might be dead too. I think that's why I can't see you." Even as I speak the words, I struggle to believe them. How is any of this rational? How can it possibly make any sense?

"I think you might be right." His voice is really small and I find myself feeling really sorry for him. "But you still haven't told me who you are and what you're doing here."

I take a deep breath. "Well…" I begin, unsure exactly how to frame my response. The last thing I want to do is make him even more upset; he might lock me in here and leave me to perish. "Actually, I inherited this place from Eleanor, when she…she passed away. Bert, my name's Harriet. I think I'm your granddaughter."

The light flickers back on, and I breathe an enormous sigh of relief.

"Anna's grown up? She has a daughter of her own?"

"Yes, Anna did grow up and she did have me." It feels strange to call my mum by her name. "But Bert, I haven't seen my mum since I was three. She disappeared and I never heard from her again. After all these years, well, I assume she's dead."

"After all these years? What year is it?"

"It's January 2018," I reply.

"Oh, Christ."

"I know. I'm afraid all this is rather a lot to take in, for both of us." I frown, trying to gather my thoughts, trying to understand how on earth I'm holding a conversation with someone I can't see, someone who isn't really there, in the physical sense at least. "What's the last thing you remember?" I ask him, deciding to suspend disbelief. Can he even have memories?

"I – I don't know," Bert replies.

"Well, when you first spoke to me last night in the kitchen, you asked where Eleanor was. Were you expecting to find her here? With Anna?" I prompt him.

"I suppose I was."

"Alright. So what does Eleanor look like to you, how old is she, when was the last time you saw her? And Anna too, what is she like?"

"Eleanor's…well, Eleanor's just Eleanor. Very pretty, although she says she's getting on a bit now. She's always covered in paint, always creating something – but you know that, you've looked through her books. Anna's a lovely girl. A bit quiet, spends a bit too much time in her room, but she's at a difficult age, I suppose. Or at least, she was. I can't believe they're dead. I can't believe I'm dead. I just walked back into this house last night, I had something to say to Eleanor. I forget what it was now…"

My ears prick up. That unsettling cold I felt rush by me on the afternoon I spent sorting out Eleanor's clothes comes immediately to mind. "Last night? So you weren't here before that?"

"No. At least, I don't think so."

"I see." I push the memory away. It must have really been a draught, then. "It's a bit strange that you only came back last night. I always thought that, err…if spirits stick around after death, they tend to stay in the same place. Not that I really believe in any of that paranormal stuff." I can't believe how ridiculous I sound. I don't believe in ghosts, yet apparently I'm talking to one.

"I'm not paranormal! And don't call me a spirit."

"Sorry." I let an awkward silence hang for a moment. "I take it you don't remember when you died, either?"

"Christ, you're blunt." The irritation in his voice makes me wince and I resolve to tone down my line of questioning. "No, I don't. I think if I remembered that then all this would be a lot easier to work out, wouldn't it?"

I look over at the boxes, still stacked behind me. "Well, maybe there are some clues packed away in there. I'm going to start bringing them downstairs, so if you could manage to leave the lights on for ten minutes, that'd be great."

It's a weak attempt at sarcasm and Bert, quite rightly, doesn't answer me. As I begin the back-breaking task of carrying the boxes down the ladder, I wonder about the bizarre conversation I've just had, or I imagined I had. After all, it isn't beyond the realms of possibility that my overactive mind has invented this character to give me someone to talk to, to comfort me during this lonely time, or to satisfy my deep need to find out more about my family. And yet, a part of me hopes that he is really here, that he has come back to this house, and that the reason for his return is to meet me, the granddaughter he never knew. The prospect of this excites me, although my happiness is tinged with a disappointment that he is the only one who has come back. My grandmother, my mother – both of them remain silent. Both of them are a mystery which always feels as though it is just beyond my reach.

As I bring down the final box and place it with the others on the landing, I am filled with a renewed sense of desperation. I don't know what I'm looking for, I don't know what I want, but I do know that these boxes had better contain what I need. If they don't, I'm afraid that Bert and I will be stuck in the dark forever.

10

Eleanor
August 1972

The mural in my bedroom is much larger and one week after starting it, I find that I am not even half way to finishing. Unlike the instinctive, broad brush strokes of my kitchen meadow, my approach to this piece is painstaking, almost bordering upon obsessive. Until the kitchen mural I had always been a slow painter, careful in my technique and sure enough, when it comes to turning my attention to my bedroom, my previous spontaneity gives way to patience and preparation. I take the time to strip and repaint the whole room, taking care to prime my chosen wall in readiness for the image which swims around in my head: birds in full song, trees in full leaf, rivers rumbling over rocks, cutting across a landscape in bloom. I want my bedroom to be filled with life, to be comforting and inspiring in its connection to the natural world which I love so much. Since I am still reluctant to venture far outside, I decide that it makes sense to bring nature home to me.

The idea for my mural came to me after my night-time visit to Thistle Cottage, and I reflect that it was perhaps partly inspired by those little landscapes on Meg's walls, and partly motivated by my interest in painting wildlife. The concept is also, I think, in keeping with my kitchen meadow theme, and it appeals to me to have some consistent imagery around my home. This time, however, there is no compulsive painting with reckless abandon. There is no drinking on the job, either; the early stages of my project mark my longest period of sobriety for months. Instead, with a clear head, I commit the image in my head to paper, drawing it in my sketch pad and meticulously marking out its placement before even daring to place the first drop of paint on the wall.

This is how a proper artist does it, I tell myself. This is what I should have done with the kitchen mural. Just think how polished I could have made it look, if only I had taken more time.

The problem is, I prepare so much that when the time comes to begin to paint I am filled with anxiety, making my early efforts slow and timid. Even as my work progresses I find that these thoughts do not ease, my mind growing increasingly hyper-critical of each and every stroke, and after a while I begin to doubt that I have any creative ability at all. At one point, I feel so dreadful about my work that I consider stopping altogether, simply abandoning it half-finished like I did with the chaffinch and so many other projects before. Bert does nothing to encourage me, of course, continuing instead to make his snide remarks about painting on walls at every opportunity and even choosing to cease sleeping in our room altogether on the grounds that the smell of paint is bad for his health.

"It gives me a headache," he complains, but to my surprise he refrains from criticising the work itself. Perhaps even that most insensitive of oafs senses the fragile state of my self-esteem and has decided that it isn't worth rocking the boat. Or perhaps he's just too busy nursing his sore head to care. Either way, I can't help but pray that his move out of our marital bed is a permanent one. The fact that he removes not only himself but all of his belongings to one of the spare rooms gives me more than ample reason to hope.

The morning that my crisis of confidence reaches its crescendo is also, mercifully, the next time that Meg comes to visit. Opening the door and seeing her friendly face comes as such a blessed relief that I almost haul the poor woman inside.

"Goodness, Eleanor!" she exclaims. "Are you alright?"

Wordlessly and without warning I fling my arms around her. "Not really." Today she smells like fresh linen and shampoo and I can't help but breathe her in.

Fortunately, Meg doesn't seem to mind my overly-tactile gesture and returns my embrace with a tight, comforting squeeze. "I just came over to see how you were, and to see the mural, of course." She releases herself from my grip and looks me squarely in the eye. "Unless you've painted over it already?"

I give her a watery smile. "No, I haven't. Bert hasn't asked me to, although I'm not sure why, given how much he obviously hates it."

"Well, that's good then. So what's the matter?"

"I've started another mural," I sniff, brimming with self-pity.

"Eleanor that's fantastic!" Her enthusiasm dissolves almost immediately into a concerned frown. "Isn't it?"

"Well it would be, if it was any good," I reply. "I'm beginning to think that my success in the kitchen was a fluke. This mural is turning out just like so many of my past projects – it's an abject failure. I can hardly bear to look at it."

Meg tilts her head to one side, her expression at once considered and empathetic. For a few moments she says nothing, she just studies me, those deep, dark eyes penetrating my soul, asking their unspoken questions and receiving, I suspect, my unsaid answers. It is an easy silence, the sort which normally passes between old friends not new acquaintances. It is this realisation rather than the silence itself which begins to make me feel uneasy.

"You're the only person who ever looks at me like that," I say, almost without thinking.

"Like what?" she asks.

"Like you know me. Like you really know me."

She smiles. "Would it help if I took a look at your mural? The unfinished one, I mean, although of course I want to see the one in the kitchen too. I'm not much of an artist, but I might be able to help."

"Not much of an artist," I scoff. "That's not true – I've seen those little embroidered pictures in your home. They're exquisite."

For the first time since meeting her, I see storm clouds gather over her face. "I didn't make those. They were a gift from someone I once knew."

My interest piques at the mystery contained within her words, but her expression tells me not to ask anything further. Not for the first time it occurs to me how little I know about my new neighbour and I begin to wonder if her enigmatic persona is innate or well-rehearsed.

Those eyes read my expression once again and seem not to like what they see. "Oh, it's nothing dreadful," she adds with a dismissive flick of her wrist. "Just an old friend – sadly we lost touch. That sometimes happens, doesn't it? I'm sure you understand, what with you moving away from your life in Manchester." The factual way she says those words bites at me and I have to do my best not to flinch. "Shall we go and take a look at this mural, then?"

I nod, dumbly leading her in the direction of my bedroom. We are half way up the stairs before I realise that I hadn't actually said that I wanted to show her my work. My heart sinks. I can only imagine that she saw the desperate, pathetic assent written all over my face, too.

A strange feeling washes over me as Meg wanders into my personal space. No one ever comes into this room other than me, and until recently, Bert, and it feels weird to watch this woman I barely know sit herself down at the foot of my bed and lean back on her hands as she surveys the half-finished work before her.

"Hmm," she muses, "I do see what you mean."

"What? That it's a complete disaster?"

"No – it's not that bad. In fact, it's quite beautiful, but I do see why you're struggling with it. It is missing something."

"I know," I agree, plonking myself down beside her. "I just don't know what that 'something' is."

She wraps her arm around my shoulder and leans her head in towards mine. Her closeness is a comfort, and I allow myself to be enveloped once again in her linen scent as we sit quietly, both contemplating the work before us.

"I think it's the light that is the problem," she says after a while.

"What, the daylight in here?" I ask, confused.

"No. The light in the painting. There is too much of it. You need some darkness as well. The darkness is where you will find the depth."

"Is it?"

"Come on now," she replies, giving me a playful squeeze. "I think you know that better than anyone."

"What do you mean by darkness?" I ask her, ignoring her cryptic remark. "I want something nice on my wall, something which cheers me and makes me think about all the things I love. I don't want to be frightened each time I go to bed at night."

"Dark doesn't have to be scary though, does it? You can use darker colours to create all sorts of beautiful things – a night sky, filled with stars, for example."

"Hmm, I do love space," I muse. "I haven't been able to stop listening to David Bowie lately. Maybe I should go the whole hog and paint the cosmos. That would certainly be different from a daytime sky." Even as I say the words I'm excited by the image assembling in my mind, the idea of the universe in all its spectacular, mysterious glory keeping watch over my earthly scene of birds and flowers.

"Eleanor, I think that's a truly wonderful idea!" Meg exclaims. She releases me from her grasp and rises from the bed, taking a few enthused steps towards my painting. "Yes…yes, I could absolutely see how that would work. You are so clever, my friend."

I beam at her. "Thank you, but I think you have to take some of the credit for giving me the idea in the first place."

"Oh, nonsense," she replies. "I have none of your great talent. I can't wait to see how this is going to turn out."

"Mmm," I reply, getting up off the bed. "It does seem a shame to paint over the bright blue sky I've started, though. Perhaps I should just carry on and leave the design as it is, I could always..."

She walks over to me then, silencing me with a soft finger placed delicately on my lips. Those deep brown eyes gaze intently at me and I sense that some wisdom is forthcoming. "Eleanor," she says to me, although the use of my name is redundant; she has my full attention. "Sometimes in order to rebuild, you have to be prepared to destroy first." She lowers her finger and those eyes lighten, but I would be a fool to believe that I was no longer beholden to the power of either. "Come now, I've still got to see this kitchen mural!"

We leave my bedroom for the kitchen, Meg leading the way as though this house, like me, is hers to own and command. When we get to the kitchen I put the kettle on, leaving Meg to make her quiet study of my first, hurried attempt. Out of the corner of my eye I watch her face, trying to decipher what she thinks of it. Her expression remains serious, her brows slightly furrowed and my heart sinks as I realise that she doesn't like it.

"I did paint it rather quickly," I say as I hand her a cup of tea. I take a seat opposite her. "I'm afraid my haste has made it look rather sloppy."

She gives me a brief nod. "Yes, your technique definitely doesn't seem as controlled. It's pretty, but I think what you're working on upstairs has the potential to be much better."

"Do you think I should just paint over it?" I ask with a sigh, sitting down beside her.

"Not at all," she retorts, her face finally breaking into a smile. "Your husband hates it. That's more than a good enough justification for keeping it, I'd say."

"I'll drink to that," I joke, toasting her with my tea cup and taking an enormous gulp.

But Meg doesn't join in with my foolish revelry. Instead I watch as her eyes slide around the room, settling their gaze upon the multitude of empty wine bottles sitting on the counter. "You drink quite a lot, don't you, Eleanor?" she asks.

I give a nonchalant shrug. "It's a bad habit I've developed of late, but I've got it under control. It's nothing to worry about." My heart thuds hard in my chest, beating in time with the lie as it slips from my lips.

"Were you drinking when you painted the kitchen mural?"

I feel my cheeks grow warm. "Yes."

"But you haven't been drinking while painting the mural upstairs?"

"No." Despite my best efforts I find myself growing defensive. "Why? What does it matter? Don't you like an occasional drink, Meg?"

Her stare grows ice cold at my indignation. "This isn't about me. You do better work when you're sober. If I was you, I really would stop drinking altogether."

"Advice noted." I knead my fingers together, my knuckles turning white with agitation. My head knows she's right, of course, but my heart gives me only one response: giving up will be easier said than done.

An awkward silence descends over us in the wake of our heated exchange. In our brief friendship – yes, I realise I am already beginning to regard her as a friend – this is the most disagreeable we've been with each other, a fact which makes me feel tense. I glance at her, noting her impassive eyes and clenched jaw, and sense that she feels the same way.

"I've run out of wine in the house anyway," I say with a forced chuckle. "So it should be easy enough to avoid temptation. Mind you, I'm running out of paint too, which presents a separate issue."

"Can't you just buy some more?"

I almost ask whether she means more wine or more paint, but my intuition tells me that this isn't a moment for jokes. No, this is a moment for complete and frank honesty with Meg, and with myself. "If only it was so straightforward. I have no money of my own and I doubt Bert will be willing to finance more childish experiments, as he calls them. And besides…" I hesitate, struggling to find words which won't make me feel foolish. "Besides, I don't actually venture far these days."

"Yes, I know," she says, and to my surprise she reaches over and pats me sympathetically on the hand. "I live down the lane, remember. I never see you out and about."

I give her a weak smile. "The furthest I've been since we've lived here is your cottage."

"Yes, I know."

"I don't know why I find it so hard to leave this place." I shake my head at myself. "It's not like I love it or feel especially attached to it. In fact, I don't feel anything towards it. I don't feel anything towards a lot of things – this house, my marriage, myself."

"I don't think that's true," Meg replies, her concerned expression dissolving into the saddest smile. "On those subjects, I think you feel a lot of things – anger, resentment, hate? Am I right?"

I nod.

"So if you feel so badly about those things, there must be others which make you feel good, right?"

I nod again.

"Name them."

"My daughter," I say, the words spilling forth before I can even consider them. "I am fiercely proud and protective of my daughter. My art, especially my murals. They have lit a fire inside of me. They make me feel alive again, like I have a purpose inside these four walls, like I have a mission to bring the world in here, to me, to have all the things I love out there right in front of me every day because then one day I might be able to feel happy again." Before I can stop it my lip trembles and a tear falls.

"And what things do you love out there?" she asks.

Instinctively I close my eyes, growing wistful as more tears seep out from under my eyelids. "Meadows filled with flowers, rivers full of fish, forests thick with trees where birds can be found chattering on their branches. A beautiful rolling landscape perfected by the orange glow of a setting sun. I love everything from the lush green of summer to the brown decay of winter; I love the challenge of trying to capture in art what nature has already made so sublime. I love it all and I hate myself for hiding from it, especially now that I am far from the city and so completely surrounded by it."

I open my eyes and look at Meg, who meets my gaze with an intensity I've never seen before. For a moment we just sit there, looking at each other. Then, before I can say anything else, before I can apologise and ridicule myself for pouring out my feelings, she gives me an enormous smile. "I assume Bert keeps some money in the house?" she asks me.

"Yes."

"And I assume you know where he keeps it?"

"Yes," I say again. "Why?"

"Go and fetch some money," she instructs me, struggling to suppress a giggle so infectious that I almost find myself laughing too. "I know an artist who needs paint far more than Bert needs his secret stash."

"Meg!" I scold teasingly. "You're wicked!"

"I know," she replies. "Now go and get the money and get yourself ready."

"Ready for what?"

She gives me a delicious grin. "Ready for the big wide world, Eleanor. You and I – we are going out."

11

Harry
January 2018

I haul all the boxes down the stairs and into the living room and close the attic up, hopefully for good. I decide that if I'm going to spend the rest of the day examining these items which, for whatever reason, my grandmother decided to stow away, I might as well make myself comfortable. After bringing down the final box I sit down with a well-earned cup of tea and take a few moments to catch my breath. I realise that this is the first opportunity that I've had to spend any real time in the living room. The décor is long overdue a refresh but the old-fashioned furniture suits the room and the sofa, although worn, is soft and comfortable. At the centre of the room is a beautifully carved fire surround framing a large, open fireplace. I imagine how cosy a lit fire must make this room when it is cold outside, much like today, and make a mental note to find out where I can buy firewood next time I'm out at the shops.

"Aren't you going to put a record on?"

Bert's voice startles me and I almost spill tea on my lap. "Oh, I had forgotten about that."

"Well, you did say in the kitchen last night that you like to listen to music."

"You're right, I did. Although I think more than anything it was the silence which was getting to me. Something tells me that's not going to be such an issue from now on." I'm half-joking, but also half-disturbed by what I'm saying. I suppose it's true, though; those who hear voices are never alone. "Anyway, I've nothing to play on it. All my music is on my phone."

"Your music is in your telephone? Don't be daft!"

I gulp down the last of my tea. "Yes, well let's just say that technology has moved on somewhat since you last roamed the earth. Whenever that was."

"Eleanor always had a good record collection." He sounds wistful, and my heart lurches a little in pity as I realise that's the first time he's talked about her in the past tense. "Look in the cabinet under the record player. My records were always in there, too."

I rummage through the cupboard as instructed and pull out a pile of records. I thumb through them, examining each one in turn. Many of the bands and singers I've never heard of, and I'd guess quite a lot of it wouldn't be to my taste, but some famous names stand out. "So, which one of you liked David Bowie?" I ask when I reach the third of his records.

"That was Eleanor. His music was a bit weird for my liking, but she was really keen on it, especially around the time of the moon landing. All that space stuff seemed to capture her imagination."

"I see," I reply, raising my eyebrows a little as I study Bowie's expression on his Hunky Dory album sleeve; eyes gazing upwards, lips parted, hand placed dramatically on his head like a golden era movie starlet. Like many of the others, the record is in immaculate condition and I guiltily speculate as to how much it might be worth now. "The moon landing – that was 1969, wasn't it?"

"Yes, why?"

I smile. "That means you were still alive then. It's our first clue and we haven't even gone through all the boxes yet." I don't mention that I could, of course, go upstairs and fetch my phone, that I could do a search for Robert Murray and see what the world wide web can tell me about when he might have died. For one thing, I'm not sure after his earlier phone remark that I want to try to explain the internet to someone who's probably been dead for years. And secondly, searching for information in these boxes feels like far more fun than turning on my phone and confronting everything else that is likely lurking on there.

Bert groans as I take the Bowie record from its sleeve and place it on the turntable, a little clumsily as I'm not really certain of what I'm doing. I'm relieved when it starts to play, the sound surprisingly rich and seamless. I half expected the record player not to work after sitting idle for so long. Goodness knows when it was last used. A shiver runs through me as I realise the last person to touch it would have been my grandmother.

"Sorry, Bert," I say, "but the music was your idea."

"I'll survive," he mutters. "Are you going to look through those boxes then, or what?"

"Alright!" I throw my arms up in mock exasperation. I wander back over to the boxes which I have abandoned haphazardly in the middle of the room. "Where will I start then?"

"The smallest one," he replies. "Like a kid at Christmas – start small and work your way up."

I grin at the pleasant image his words provoke, and pick up the smallest box as suggested. I carry it over to the sofa and place it on the floor beside me, ripping apart the brittle box tape with little effort. I gasp with delight as I unveil the contents. Photographs – loads and loads of photographs. Some are sorted into albums, stacked carefully at the bottom of the box, but most are simply bundled up and bound with elastic bands.

"Some of these might jog your memory, Bert," I say, holding up a handful for him to see, even though I don't even know where in the room he is. He doesn't answer me, and I don't prompt him for a response. I've spent enough time talking to him already to understand that when he wants to talk, he will.

For the next hour or so I pour over the photographs, stopping only to remove the record when Bowie stops playing. Through these images finally I feel as though I'm getting to know my family, through a lens at least. Rather predictably, the albums contain the most precious memories: Bert and Eleanor's wedding day, Anna's baby photos, her christening, her first Christmas, and so on. All the photographs in the albums are black and white which only adds to the feeling that they're special, that they're from a lost time. I examine their faces, committing them to memory: Bert's dark eyes, his thick moustache; Eleanor's slim, severe face, her hair growing ever shorter through the years; and Anna, my mum, her features constantly changing as she grows. Tears of sadness and joy well up in my eyes as I study my mother's childhood; abundant, confusing tears which threaten to overwhelm me and turn me into a sobbing wreck. I force myself to suppress my bubbling emotions, to maintain a clear, objective head. Crying won't help me piece together my family's story. Only a keen eye will help me to do that.

The bundles of photographs don't seem to be in any order at all, and I find it difficult to make any sense of them. Thankfully a few have had dates scrawled on the back which gives some guidance, but beyond that I have to assess their age from whether or not they're in colour and the approximate ages of my family in them. The images they contain are very ordinary; family outings, summer's days spent outdoors, the occasional birthday, but for me this only increases their importance. About halfway through my exploration I find one of Eleanor and my mum standing outside this house, posing in front of a rather smart looking car. On the back is scrawled a description, and a date: new home at Kirtlebeck End, 1972.

"I took that one," Bert says.

"I wondered where you'd gone," I reply. "So you only moved to Kirtlebeck in 1972? Where did you live before that?"

"Manchester."

"Manchester! How strange — that's where I grew up." A thousand thoughts run through my head then, about Mum, about Dad, about how they met, about how they ended up back in my mum's childhood city. About all the things I don't know. About all the things I might never know. "Well, that explains Eleanor's Manchester sketches, then."

"I had to cajole Eleanor into having that photo taken," Bert says. "She wasn't very happy with me that day."

"Oh?" I ask. "Why not?"

"She was upset about moving away from the city."

I study the photograph more closely. "Actually, I can see that she's not very pleased. Anna – my mum – she's grinning, but Eleanor looks quite stony-faced. I suppose it would have been a big change, moving from a busy city to all this silence. It's taking me some getting used to."

"Yes, well, Eleanor blamed me for it. We didn't always have a very happy marriage."

Bert doesn't elaborate any further and I don't feel inclined to ask. Dead or not, it seems wrong of me to pry into the dynamics of their relationship. "Mum is around twelve or thirteen in this photo, isn't she?" I ask, changing the subject slightly. "I know that she and my dad were born in the same year – 1959."

"Yes, that's right. 15th September 1959. A day I'll never forget."

I stare long and hard again at the photo, Mum's happy teenage face gazing back at me as she leans into her mum and smiles for the camera. She looks content, settled, like she has the whole world at her feet. I wonder then what changed, what happened to her that meant she felt she had to leave me and never come back. "I wish I could have known her. I wish she'd been there when I was growing up." My voice shakes with emotion and I hold my breath to stop myself from crying.

"I'm sorry, Harriet," Bert says. His voice is strained, awkward even, and I wonder if it's because for the first time since we met, he's conscious of his lack of physical presence. After all, this is certainly a moment which calls for a hug, or at the very least a comforting pat on the shoulder. Bert can offer neither, and I suspect that jars with him as well as me. God knows, I need a hug right now. "You had your dad though, didn't you? Where's he now?"

"Dead," I reply. "Cancer. Just over a decade ago."

"Oh, I am sorry. So you really are all on your own?"

"I am as you find me," I reply, holding my arms out wide. "But there's no use in weeping about it. Such is life. All any of us can do is play the hand we're dealt." I bend down, picking up another pile of photos and thumbing through them absent-mindedly. "I do find it odd that you can remember so many details about your life, but you can't remember when or how you died. Do you think that's a self-defence thing? I suppose if we all remembered the moment of death then we would arrive in the afterlife feeling pretty scarred, and…" I stop talking as a small cluster of photos catches my eye.

"And what?" Bert asks.

"Nothing." I shake my head. My train of thought switches entirely to the images in my hand. Unlike all the other family shots, these pictures are just of Eleanor. I study her face, noting how different her expression seems from all the other photos I've seen. Here there isn't that deadpan Eleanor, her face stern or her smile suspiciously forced. Here she looks happy, proud, standing tall and gleeful in front of some beautifully decorated walls. My eyes scan the backgrounds behind her and I see glimpses of trees, meadows, birds and skies. It takes me a few moments to realise that the images aren't wallpaper; they're paintings.

"Did Eleanor do some wall paintings?" I ask Bert.

I sense him hesitate for a moment. "Yes. Yes, come to think of it, she did."

"Where?" I ask. "Here?"

"Yes, not long after we moved here, I think. She painted one in the kitchen and one in our bedroom. She called them her murals. It was her way of making the place ours, I suppose."

"Hmm," I muse, studying the photos again. "They look incredible. I wonder why she papered over them."

"I don't know," Bert replies. "I don't recall her redecorating those rooms, anyway."

"…which probably means that you were gone by then," I interject. This whole situation with Bert is still surreal to the point of insane, but in my own way I am beginning to make sense of it.

Feeling suddenly restless, I get up off the sofa and pace around. "I'd like to see these murals. Would you mind if I stripped away the paper so I can have a look?"

"It's your house now," Bert answers me, his voice gruff. "Do as you wish."

"I know, but it feels only right that I should ask you first." I continue to walk up and down, my mind trying to formulate a plan. I don't have the right equipment for stripping walls, and although that is easily resolved with a trip into town to buy supplies, I'm also nervous about doing this job alone. This will be a delicate task; if I'm not careful, by removing what covers them I could damage the murals underneath. The easiest way forward would be to pay someone to come and do this, someone with some expertise, but I'm acutely aware that such extravagances would leave my already finite pot of funds even more depleted.

"What are you thinking about, Harriet?" Bert asks.

"I'm thinking I'm really not qualified to do this on my own," I admit. "The last thing I want to do is ruin Eleanor's murals whilst trying to uncover them."

"What about that Daniel fella? He said he'd help if you needed it. Maybe you could ask him."

I frown deeply. "You were there when Daniel visited too? You listened to us talk?" I ask. I feel an indignant heat rise in my cheeks at the thought of my private conversation being overheard, my wine consumption being witnessed, and my suspiciously-close-to-flirting behaviour being observed.

Bert, however, doesn't seem to notice. "Of course I was there. I told you, that was the night I came back here."

"Okay. We're going to have to set some ground rules if you're going to be here. I need my privacy, Bert."

"Don't worry, I haven't been wandering in while you're in the shower or anything like that…"

"I should hope not! I'm your granddaughter, for heaven's sake!"

He falls silent for a moment, and I can tell that he's thinking. "I keep forgetting that's who you are. It sounds so strange to hear you say it."

"Yes," I reply. "Well, this entire situation is weird. Daniel is a good suggestion, though. I'll give him a call in a little while."

"Why not now?"

"Because right now I'm busy with these boxes," I snap. I'm also still busy avoiding my phone, but of course I don't tell him that. "Why the hurry?"

"Because when you're dead you realise that it's best not to put things off." His tone is huffy and I can tell he's annoyed with me.

"When you're dead I'd have thought you'd realise that in fact you've got all the time in the world," I bite back. I'm not in the mood to be bossed around from beyond the grave.

"Yes – all the time in the world to find out that everyone you loved has gone and there's nothing you can do about it."

"I'm sorry Bert, but that's not my fault, is it?" I spread my arms wide, gesturing around me. "I didn't ask for any of this – this house, Eleanor, my mum, you…"

"You're right; you didn't. I'm sorry."

I let out a heavy sigh, dragging my hands down my face in exasperation. "What are you doing back here, Bert? Why haven't you moved on to…to wherever it is you're meant to go?"

"I don't know," he replies in a voice so forlorn that my heart breaks a little.

"Then I'm sorry for that," I say, softening my voice as I begin to regret my harsh words. "Come on, let's finish going through these boxes."

"Actually, I think I'll leave you alone for a little while. As you said, you need your privacy."

"Oh Bert, I didn't mean…" I let the words fall away, realising that there's no point in arguing with him. "Suit yourself," I say with a shrug.

I spend the rest of the afternoon rummaging through the remaining boxes. True to his promise, Bert is quiet. I don't know if that means he's left the room or if he's merely giving me the silent treatment; I don't sense his presence, so except when he talks to me, I never know whether or not he's there at all. I brush the cross words we exchanged earlier to one side and decide to enjoy the peace, focusing all my energies on examining my family's treasures. In two of the boxes I find the rest of Eleanor's life's work, from books filled with pencil sketches to larger painted pieces on paper and canvas, packed away in bubble wrap and brown paper. It's clear to me from the careful way in which these items were stored that they were considered precious, and it baffles me a little that they were stowed away in the attic at all. Although I don't have much of an eye for art, even I can see that much of what my grandmother created was good - surely someone with that much talent and passion would want their work to be displayed, not hidden away.

"As ever, you're a mystery to me, Eleanor," I mutter, before putting her paintings back as I had found them.

The final box I open is the largest one, and I gasp when I see that it contains my mother's personal effects. Everything has been crammed inside, from teddies, ornaments and trinkets to school reports, notebooks and diaries. At the bottom of the box I find a number of folders filled with papers. Intrigued, I pull them out and leaf through them, trying to get a sense of what they are. All the papers have yellowed, but the words on them are clear enough to read, written in bold ink and with a neat, controlled style. My heart flutters as I run my fingers over the first page; I've never seen my mother's writing before. My eyes absorb the title at the top, and before I can stop myself I begin to read aloud.

"Margaret Escapes, by Anna Murray. Margaret hated boarding school. It was the dullest, most self-obsessed place she'd ever had the misfortune to live. It was worse even than being at home with Mother and Father, and that was saying something…"

My eyes flit across the first few paragraphs, taking in the text at a pace. It's clearly a story, written by my mother during her youth, perhaps for a school project or perhaps just for fun. I flick again through the remaining pages and realise that they all contain stories. A slow smile of delight spreads across my face. I recall Dad's stories about Mum's writing, and my frustration at never being able to see any of it for myself. Her adult works are lost to me, just as she is, which makes today's find all the more precious. How lucky I am to have found these, to be able to read the work of her formative years. Carefully I tuck the pages back in their folder. These will be my bedtime reading while I live here. These will be the way in which I get to know my mum, even just a little bit.

By the time I finish it is late afternoon, the daylight fading fast as the long winter's night begins to fall. Hurriedly I close the curtains and put on some lights, trying to make the house feel cosy and less unsettling. I still don't like night-time here; the solitude and the silence seem that much harder to bear during the dark hours, and for the first time since he stopped talking to me, I start to wish I had Bert's voice for company. I think about calling his name, then quickly decide against it. He's the one who went off in a sulk. He can talk to me when he's ready.

I head upstairs, resolved instead to give Daniel a call. I'm still reluctant to switch on my phone, to have to confront the bile which is no doubt lying in wait for me. However, I know that I don't have any choice; I want to see Eleanor's murals, and I'm not daring enough to strip those walls on my own. I turn my phone on, screwing up my face with a painful reluctance. Maybe if I just ignore my messages, if I just dial Daniel's number without so much as glancing at my inbox. Maybe that would be the best course of action.

I key in Daniel's number, putting the phone to my ear swiftly so that my eyes can't linger on the screen. After two rings he answers, his tone uncertain as my number will have come up as unrecognised.

"Daniel? It's me. It's Harry."

He relaxes, and we have a light-hearted chat about how we are and how we've spent our respective days. I thank him again for his tip about the boxes in the attic and tell him about some of the exciting things I've found. I laugh a little at myself when I get to the part about wanting to strip two walls on the strength of some intriguing photographs. Then I bite the bullet and ask my favour.

"Of course I'll help you," he says without hesitation. "How about Saturday afternoon?"

"Saturday's perfect," I reply. "Thank you so much."

"My pleasure," he says. "I'll bring the wine."

"Wine?" I ask. "For wallpaper stripping?"

"Good wine," he corrects me. "For drinking, once we've finished."

We end our call after a few more wine-related jokes. Slowly I draw my phone away from my face, the amused grin provoked by our conversation fading as my eyes are drawn to the little envelope icon at the bottom of the screen.

Eleven messages.

I let out a gasp. I wonder how many are from her.

I wonder if any are from him.

Against my better judgement I open my mailbox. My eyes widen as I scan the messages, and a clenched fist instinctively finds its way to my mouth, my teeth chewing on my knuckles to prevent me from crying out. So much anger, so much hatred. So many demands that I tell her where I am, that I understand that I can't get away, that I know that I can never be forgiven. So much venom that I will never be able to erase from my mind. I hold my breath as I delete each message in turn. Perhaps it would be best if I changed my number. I know what we did was wrong, but surely I don't have to put up with this harassment forever.

Then the alert sounds, and another new message is received. My fingers are poised to delete it too, but then I realise that it isn't from her; it's from him. My heart races as I read his words; the warm memories, the lust, the passion flooding uninvited to the fore. It's the first time I've heard from him since I left, and his message to me is short, simple, and suddenly puts her rage in perfect, painful context.

I've left her. I want you. Tell me where you are.

12

Eleanor
August 1972

The day which greets us is fine and bright, with only a brisk westerly breeze hinting at the possibility of rain. Deciding not to trust the weather I bring my raincoat and umbrella, then feel decidedly overdressed when I see that Meg has merely cast a patterned shawl around her shoulders. I follow her brisk, purposeful footsteps down the lane, trailing slightly behind her, partly due to my lack of fitness, and partly because I am still reluctant to venture far. For those first few yards I hold my nerve, but when we pass Thistle Cottage and round the corner I realise that my house is no longer in sight and I feel myself begin to panic. My pace slows to almost a standstill, my heart races and my whole body feels as though it has broken out in a cold, clammy sweat.

I can't go out, I tell myself. I can't leave my house; why would I? I'm safe there, but I'm not out here. Out here, I can see the whole world, and the world can see me. Out here, anything could happen. My stomach lurches at the dreadful possibilities and I struggle to catch my breath.

"Meg!" I call out between gasps. "I think I'm going to be sick!"

I stagger to the edge of the lane, gripping the old stone wall with both hands as I empty the contents of my stomach all over the grass verge. Meg comes over to me, rubbing my back gently, watching me retch and splutter as the vile acid burns the back of my throat.

"It's worse than I thought," she says quietly. "I had no idea you were this bad."

"Neither did I," I reply, wiping my mouth with the back of my hand.

"You made it down to my cottage," she reminds me, pushing my hair back from my face as I straighten myself up.

"Yes – in the middle of the night when no one was around. And your place is only a stone's throw from mine. I suppose I could just about cope with that," I explain. "And besides, I really wanted to see where you live. I really wanted to see you." I feel my cheeks begin to redden at the honesty of my explanation.

"I'm glad you did," she replies, giving my shoulder a brief squeeze. "And if you can make it to Thistle Cottage, you can make it into Annan to buy art supplies."

"You have more confidence than I do." My grim reply rolls off my tongue before I can stop myself.

Unperturbed by my negativity, Meg takes hold of my arm, giving it the gentlest of tugs, bidding me to come with her. "I have every confidence in you," she insists. "Annan isn't very far at all, and I will be with you every step of the way."

At a break in the wall we leave the lane and head down a rough woodland track which leads, after some time, to a perfect riverside path. It's a shortcut, she tells me, as she slips her hand into mine. Her fingers are soft, warm and reassuring, and I find that the gesture calms me. We walk like that for some time, hand in hand, no words passing between us as we simply absorb the serene beauty of our surroundings and enjoy the shelter which the thick trees provide from the wind and from prying eyes. Not a single living soul passes our way for what seems like miles; it is just her and I, together. It occurs to me then how peaceful I feel, and how I wish I could always feel this way. How I wish it could always be

Meg and I, together. How I wish I could always feel the comforting touch of her skin against mine. The thoughts confuse me but I do not push them to one side. Instead I relish them, exploring them in quiet contemplation, wondering if I could paint them, wondering if I could ever do them justice.

We arrive in Annan just over an hour later. Meg takes me directly to a quaint little craft shop, fully stocked with everything I could ever need and more. Together we pick out some supplies, keeping a careful eye on price as my budget is limited. I only took a small amount of the money Bert keeps hidden away; his stash of cash, as Meg called it, is vast enough that I thought a modest sum going missing might go unnoticed. Bert has always kept a lot of money in the house; it was a habit he formed early in our marriage back in Manchester and one which he has continued with ever since. I don't know why but then, I suppose I've never asked, and now I don't care – I'm just glad his money was there for the taking. As it turns out, what I took is just enough to cover my costs but sadly not for any extras, which is a shame as I spot some lovely good quality canvasses stacked in the corner.

"They'd be good for a future project," I whisper to Meg. "If only I had enough money."

"There's always another day," she tells me. "And you've got the mural to finish first."

Our whispers earn us a very wary look from the shopkeeper, who serves me without much idle conversation. His aloof manner unsettles me and when the time comes to pay, I find myself fumbling around awkwardly with my money.

"I still haven't got the hang of these new coins," I joke, which is not entirely untrue; despite decimalisation happening over a year ago, I still remain hopelessly attached to the old pounds, shillings and pence. As I look up at his grey, suspicious eyes, however, I sense he knows it is his manner, rather than the lack of a sixpenny bit, that is bothering me.

I leave the shop in a hurry. It is just after noon now, the late summer sun high in the sky, and I feel hungry, tired and desperate to get home. All the fresh air, the exertion, the interaction with other people has exhausted me, and I long for the safety and solitude of Kirtlebeck End.

Meg seems to sense the shift in my mood. "Come on," she says, taking me firmly by the arm. "I think that's enough for one day."

I give her a grateful smile. "Thank you," I reply. "You've come all this way with me, though. Surely you've got somewhere you need to go, errands you have to run while we're here?"

"Not at all. I'm here to support you, and if you've had enough then so have I."

"That shopkeeper was really strange with us," I ponder as we walk. "Don't you think he was very offhand?"

"I didn't really notice," she replies with a shrug. "Perhaps he just didn't recognise your face. Some people can be like that with those they don't know. And I suppose you are a stranger in this town," she adds, clearly trying to tease.

"Yes I am, but surely you're not, Meg? Wouldn't he have recognised you? You told me you like to paint; surely that shop is somewhere you go from time to time?" I screw up my eyes, realising I don't even know how long Meg has lived around here.

The smallest hint of a sad smile lingers on her lips. "Yes, I've been there a number of times before. At one time a lot of people around here would have known me, but nowadays, I tend to keep to myself. I doubt that silly man even recognised me." She giggles lightly but the sorrow in her eyes remains. We keep on walking out of town, arm in arm, the bag containing all my paints weighing heavily on my other hand. The earlier silence returns to linger between us as I struggle to find any topic of conversation which doesn't involve asking Meg why she chooses now to remain so alone. It is only when we reach the edge of our woodland route that it occurs to me that Meg might be avoiding asking me the same question, that she might be wondering what brought me to Kirtlebeck in the first place, and what caused me to shut myself away.

We walk briskly, reaching the lane which leads back to Kirtlebeck End in record time. Breathless from the exertion, Meg sits down on a fallen log and bids me to join her.

"Just for a few moments," she assures me. "Then I'll take you home."

I answer her with an obliging nod. Sweat trickles down my spine beneath the raincoat I never needed and I realise that I could also do with a well-earned rest. Now that we are far from the town my eagerness to return home has dissipated somewhat, my earlier agitation being replaced by the soothing reassurance which my countryside surroundings provide. My home, I am coming to realise, is not the only sanctuary available to me in this quiet, unassuming part of the world.

"I meant to give you this." Meg hands me a piece of paper. "I grabbed it off the noticeboard in old grumpy's shop. I thought it might be of interest to you."

I study the little flyer, my brows furrowed with intrigue. "Art captures art," I say, reading aloud. "Photographer seeking collaborative projects with fellow creatives for exhibition of local talent."

"I thought you could call the number and find out what it's all about," Meg explains. "Maybe once your mural is finished they'd like to take a look and incorporate it into their photographic display? See, there's a name on there – Emma McCabe. She must be the photographer."

"Hmm," I muse, folding the flyer carefully and tucking it into my pocket. "I'll see how the mural goes first. But thank you, Meg. That was very thoughtful of you."

She waves her hand dismissively at me. "It's just a flyer."

"I know, but…" I hesitate, unsure how to best explain myself. "For someone who doesn't know me that well, you seem to have such confidence in my work – more confidence than I could ever muster. If it wasn't for you, I wouldn't have gone out and bought paint today. Heck, I'd probably have let my paints run out then given up in despair. If it wasn't for you, I wouldn't be painting murals at all." I give her my best smile. "It seems that you're a good influence on me, Meg -," I stop speaking abruptly, realising that I don't actually know her surname.

"Meg Roberts," she interjects as though reading my mind. "Roberts is my maiden name. I've never been married." Her voice remains light but something about the way her jaw hardens tells me that I'd be best not to pry.

"Well, Meg Roberts," I reply, smiling, "that is probably the most I have discovered about you in our short but enjoyable friendship."

"I'm not the easiest person to get to know, I suppose," she replies, her tone thoughtful and her face remaining straight. "I'm very good at keeping people out, and not so good at letting them in."

I stop laughing, sensing that there is a story to come, that Meg is about to make some revelation to which I should listen. I don't ask, however; I just sit beside her and wait. After all, in the short time we have known each other she has always afforded me the courtesy of not asking too much, of offering friendship and support without scratching hard at the source of what pains me. She has accepted me as I am in a way which is unlike any other I have ever known. The very least I can do is to be the same way with her.

"A long time ago, there was a man…" she begins, faltering after those first few words. The way she bites her lip is beautiful and I can't help but reach out and clutch her hand. "He was very talented, very creative, and I loved him very much."

"Was it him who made you those little landscapes I saw in your home?" I ask, but in truth I already know the answer.

She nods. "Yes. He made those little keepsakes when he was in love with me. I keep them so that I might always remember those happy times."

"So what happened?" I ask tentatively, aware of the tears which are welling up in her deep brown eyes.

"What always happens with men when they fall out of love with you," she snaps bitterly between gritted teeth. "He abandoned me – intellectually, emotionally and finally literally. He became someone else, someone so different that by the end there was nothing left of him. By the end he was a vacuum; his heart was so dark and I couldn't take it anymore."

"So he left you?" My mind reels over her cryptic, almost nonsensical words. "When did this happen? You said it was a long time ago but you look so young, how can it be…?"

"Isn't that your husband's car?"

My neck snaps up, the beginnings of a heartfelt discussion well and truly interrupted by the rumble of Bert's Ford Cortina as it rolls along the lane. It's a nice new car, instantly recognisable, its bold red colour contrasting sharply with the green of the surrounding foliage. Bert has always said that in his line of work it is important to drive a good looking car, that it gives the right impression.

"It's a lovely car," Meg remarks, her thoughts once again in tune with my own. "What does he do for a living?"

"He's a mechanic. He runs his own business – the new place in the village, just past the Post Office," I explain, repeating verbatim what Bert has told me since I have never actually been there.

"He must be doing well, to drive a car like that, and of course to own a house like yours."

"Hmm," I muse, keen to end the discussion, partly because I'm old-fashioned enough not to brazenly reveal our financial affairs, and partly because frankly I'm embarrassed that I know so little about our fortunes, good or otherwise.

Bert's car grinds to a halt. Instinctively I grab Meg's hand, pulling her with me towards some bushes which hide us from view. The last thing I want is for Bert to see me, for me to have to explain where I've been and what I've been doing. Above all, the last thing I want is for Bert to meet Meg, for him to cast his approving gaze over my beautiful new friend. The very thought of it makes bile rise up into my throat and I have to resist the urge to gag.

Meg, perhaps sensing my unease, doesn't ask me why we're hiding. Instead she crouches beside me, still holding my hand as we watch Bert climb out of his car. A frown creases my brow as he walks round to the passenger door, opening it carefully, an enormous smile plastered on his face.

"Who is he with?" Meg hisses. "And why is he stopped here? He's not even five minutes' walk from your house."

Her questions hang heavy in the air as I hold my breath, unable to bring myself to answer them. I know why he's stopped here, and I know who he's with. I know who it is that he doesn't want me to see.

And then, of course, I see her. She's just as lovely as she always was, with her long blonde hair, her bright blue eyes, her tall and slender frame. She looks like a supermodel and I wonder once again what on earth that pretty young thing sees in my husband. Whilst he's not unattractive, the years are certainly catching up with Bert, and the lines on his face and his expanding girth are beginning to betray his age. She must think him good in bed, I think sourly, my mind wandering back to that day I caught them together, naked under the sheets in our bed, a young woman and a man past his prime. I remember the looks on their faces, matching expressions of what at the time I presumed to be guilt. Now, seeing them together all these months later, I realise that it wasn't guilt I saw, but regret. Regret at being caught. Regret at being found out. Regret that their pleasure had been interrupted by the dowdy middle-aged wife, the figure of fun at whose expense they no doubt enjoyed endless callous laughter. The wife who foolishly agreed to move hundreds of miles away in a vain attempt to move on, to fix the unfixable. The wife they are continuing to mock, even now.

Tears well in my eyes so fiercely that I struggle to blink them away.

"You'd better walk from here," I hear him say. "It's a small village and people talk. You've got the key for the cottage, haven't you?"

The tart nods and I can't suppress my grimace as she kisses him on the cheek.

"Are you sure about this?" she asks him. "What if your wife sees me here?"

"No chance of that," Bert scoffs. "She never leaves the house, which is probably just as well, given the circumstances."

"Really?" she asks. "Why?"

Bert shakes his head and my heart thuds indignantly at the familiar sight of his disapproval. "You know what Eleanor's like – a law unto herself. Spends her days painting on the bloody walls and drinking herself senseless."

The tart touches his arm so tenderly that I struggle not to vomit in my mouth. "Aren't you worried about her?" she asks.

The trees rustle in the breeze, rendering Bert's answer inaudible. Of course, I know him well enough to know what it is. He isn't worried. In fact, he hasn't given me a second thought for months.

"Eleanor?" Meg repeats, her hushed voice laden with concern. "What's going on? Who is that?"

Angrily I brush my tears away. I can barely bring myself to look at Meg; I know one glimpse of her worried face will be all it takes for me to break down completely. All I can manage is a weak shake of my head, a signal that I'm not yet ready to talk, to commit to words the hatred, the rage and the despair I have kept within me for so long. I am not yet ready to tell her my story, to describe my utter disbelief and humiliation as its latest chapter unfolds before my eyes. To my relief, Meg doesn't press me. Instead, she squeezes my hand; it is such a reassuring and comforting gesture that in that moment I almost swear she's the only person in the whole world who understands me at all.

We watch in silence as the tart makes her way down the lane, Bert taking a moment to gaze after her before getting back in his car and driving away. Even after they have gone we sit for some time, staring quietly ahead, each of us contemplating what we have witnessed with a potent mix of bewilderment and fury. Meg continues to hold my hand tightly in hers and I realise that she will have guessed most of my sorry tale. Her gesture is one of solidarity and of sympathy. She barely started to tell me her story and I haven't yet spoken mine, but nonetheless we understand enough to know that we are kindred spirits. We are both the woman who is no longer the object of desire. We are both the woman scorned.

"What happens when men fall out of love with you," I say, my voice shrill with suppressed emotion as it repeats Meg's earlier words in a way which is neither a statement nor a question.

Meg turns to me slowly and I can tell she is considering how best to help. "What will you do now?" she asks.

I ruminate on her question as I look around me, allowing my senses to be momentarily distracted by my surroundings; the creak of the tree branches as they are teased by the breeze, the scattered logs of storm casualties past, the wild flowers encroaching obstinately on to the rough footpath. I am surrounded by all this beauty, I think, and yet I make so little of it. I dreamt of places like this when I lived in the city; I craved them, I coveted them. Yet now, when I can indulge in it all I lock myself away; I pity myself and I give those around me cause to pity me or worse, to mock me, to betray me again and again right under my nose. Why can I not find it in myself to do better, to have courage? Why must I always hold myself back? Why can I not be more like Meg? Why can I not be beautiful, enigmatic, independent? Why can I not escape from Bert, from Kirtlebeck, from our life together?

The answer to that last question pains me like shards of glass piercing my skin – because, of course, I have nowhere else to go. The rest, however, I might be able to do a little more about.

Twigs crunch underfoot as I stand up rather more abruptly than intended. My hand feels numb from Meg's unrelenting grasp but I relinquish her hand with as much grace as I can muster.

"Eleanor, where are you going?" she asks, following me back towards the lane.

I wipe my eyes and keep on walking, my mind racing as the events of the last few minutes overload my senses. I don't know what's going on; I don't know why the tart is here or what sort of game Bert is playing by bringing her back. I don't know why he insisted we move here only to humiliate me all over again. And above all, I don't know why any of this should bother me. I don't love him anymore, and I know that he no longer loves me. We are just two people, living in the same house, tied together by a child, by cowardice and by convention. And yet it does bother me; seething fury bubbles under my skin and although I ball my fists to contain it, I know that it must be let free. It must have an outlet, one made of paint, of sweat, of vitriol. Of vengeance. Of darkness. The darkness where the depth is found.

I turn back to Meg, standing tall, my sudden determination writ upon my face. "I'm going back to Kirtlebeck End. I need to finish my mural."

13

Harry
January 2018

By the time Saturday arrives I am restless with the need for some distraction. Bert continues to keep up his vow of silence, leading me to wonder if I really did imagine our conversations after all. Unable to convince myself that I have truly plumbed the depths of insanity, I spend my time searching for proof of Robert Murray's existence, for details which verify the tales he told me about who he was, and about his life with Eleanor and Anna. When the house, true to form, throws up nothing helpful beyond the photographs I've already seen, I resort to typing words into an internet search bar – 'Robert Murray, Kirtlebeck, death'. Nothing of any use appears and I am left frustrated, staring at the image of a man in a wedding photograph and wondering who he really was and why he's no longer here.

I also spend some time reading some of my mum's collection of stories. I discover that my mum wrote prolifically, and that many of the stories concern the character called Margaret. The more I read, the less it feels like this was a school project; instead I begin to believe that this was the beginning of my mum's passion for writing which my dad always spoke so wistfully about. After I finish reading 'Margaret Escapes', in which Margaret runs away from boarding school in the wake of the chaos caused by a fire which she started, I read 'Margaret Joins a Commune' and 'Margaret Falls in Love'. I enjoy reading about the adventures of this tearaway teenager my mum imagined; how she goes from spirited schoolgirl to peace-loving hippy who falls hard for a young artist with big, blue eyes. I find myself imagining my mum as she sat at her desk, ruminating on her ideas, scribbling them down, throwing screwed-up pages over her shoulder before finally settling on what worked. I wonder where she drew her inspiration from; friends, books, stories she heard? Or was this her way of enacting her own teenage rebellion from the safety of her bedroom?

I suspect I'll never know, that I'll only ever be able to read between the lines of what she wrote. Nonetheless, I am determined to read all of her stories while I'm here. It will never make up for not knowing her, but at least it might allow me to understand the young Anna, the creative girl with a fevered imagination. The woman she grew into, the one whose heart was hard enough to let her leave, will always remain a mystery. It's a realisation which pains me just as much as it always has, but at the same time I'm beginning to wonder if perhaps that's for the best. Perhaps I'm learning about the best version of her. Perhaps I will have to content myself with that.

When Daniel finally arrives around lunchtime I am sitting in the living room, putting Eleanor's record player to good use once again while I flick through the family photos for what feels like the hundredth time. I jump out of my seat almost as soon as I hear him knock at the door, then immediately chastise myself for being so desperate for company. Hadn't I wanted this? Hadn't I wanted to get away from everything, to start again? Hadn't some part of me wanted to experience life in a rural idyll? It's not as though I've been as alone as I'd envisaged; the conversations I've had with my dead grandfather have seen to that.

"Which reminds me," I mutter as I hurry towards the porch, "you'd better be quiet this afternoon, Bert. And no eavesdropping on us, either!"

My comment receives no reply, and I wonder once again where he's gone.

I open the door to Daniel who stands there, wine in one hand and a large shopping bag in the other. "Chateauneuf du Pape," he says, handing me the bottle, "and dinner for tonight, once we've had the great unveiling."

"Thank you," I say, "although I was rather hoping you'd bring ladders and some wallpaper remover."

He hands me the shopping bag and gestures over his shoulder. "Don't worry, I've got everything we need," he assures me. "Although we're going to have to be careful how we do this so that we don't damage what's underneath."

"Yes we are," I agree. "So, no wine until we've finished."

Daniel flashes me a grin. "Wouldn't dream of it," he replies. "I'll bring in what we need, and then let's get started, shall we?"

Daniel brings in the tools while I take the bag through to the kitchen and inspect the goodies he's brought us. I have to say I'm quite taken aback; I was expecting maybe a couple of pizzas and a tub of pre-made salad, but instead I find a roast for two, complete with potatoes, trimmings and dessert. My heart lurches into my mouth; this is the sort of food he used to cook for me, on the nights we stole together whenever she was away. This is date night food. Part of me hopes that I haven't given Daniel the wrong idea by asking for his help, whilst another part of me wonders what I will do if I have.

"All that needs to go in the fridge," Daniel says, poking his head around the kitchen doorway.

I startle slightly, lifting myself from the depth of my thoughts and giving him a small smile. "You really didn't need to go to all this trouble."

"It's no trouble. I hope it's not too presumptuous – I kind of feel as though I'm inviting myself for dinner. But at the same time, I figured we'd be hungry by the time we finish all of this. And besides, I've seen what you've been living off over here, or rather, the lack of what you've been living off." Spotting my quizzical expression, he elaborates: "Saw your plate of beans and toast the other night."

"Oh!" I laugh. "Yeah, I never even ate that in the end."

"That's exactly what I'm getting at." His face is stern and I feel like I'm being told off. I push the notion to one side rather than dwelling upon it and allowing it to irritate me. I got annoyed with Bert and it drove him away, for now at least. The last thing I want to do is the same thing with my kind and helpful neighbour.

We get to work, starting in the master bedroom as the wall is bigger, and I suspect, the task will be more arduous. We use the photographs of Eleanor to identify the correct wall, which is the one directly opposite the bed. I wonder about the choice of wall. Bert said that she wanted to make the place her own, that painting the murals was her way of doing so. I suppose there's no better way to do that than to paint something in your room, your private space. I suppose that Eleanor picked that wall on purpose, that she wished not only to stake her claim on this space, but to see her work every morning when she woke, and last thing before she went to sleep at night.

"Today will be the most time I've spent in this room since I've been here," I remark to Daniel. We've started with the softly, softly approach first, and we're working carefully with sponges, dampening the paper before we try to remove it.

"Oh? I take it you've not been staying in here, then?"

I shake my head. "Feels too personal in here. Too much like it's still her space...like it's still Eleanor's space. I'm staying in the yellow room just down the hall. I think that might have been my mum's room."

"Is that why you're staying in there?"

"Actually...no. I just picked a room when I got here. The notion that it was hers came to me later. Funny how things work out like that. I'd like to think that wherever she is, she's watching over me and is glad I'm staying in her old room. But I think that's probably just me trying to be sentimental about someone I never even knew."

Daniel glances at me and I see the clouds gather in his eyes. "Sometimes those are the people we're most sentimental about."

"Wisely put." We're both quiet for a few moments and I suspect that Daniel, like me, is contemplating the deep waters we've already strayed into. Keen to keep the conversation going and avoid long silences – God knows I've endured enough of those – I swiftly change the subject: "I hope I haven't caused you any inconvenience today. I mean, Saturday is probably a busy day at the garage, and you've got your mum to look after too."

He chuckles at me. "It was me who suggested Saturday. I only normally work Saturday mornings, then I take the rest of the weekend off. I've got a couple of lads who pick up the slack on Saturday afternoons and have done for a while. I'm getting too old to work six days a week. And Mum's fine for a few hours so don't worry – if it had been a problem, I wouldn't have offered."

"Well, thank you, again," I say. "Not everyone would give up their time for someone they barely know."

"No, that's true," he concedes, his voice low and controlled as he carefully peels at a corner of the paper. "But if you'll excuse me for saying it, you seem like you need a friend."

I nod, conscious of the grim expression which has grown upon my face. Of course, he's right; I've no one in the world who cares about me right now. The memory of those messages on my phone springs uninvited into my mind, haunting me, plaguing me once again. Everyone who has ever been in my life is either dead or hates me with good reason, and the only person who wants me at all, really shouldn't. I brush off the thought, forcing my mind back on to the task at hand. For all that my new neighbour appears to be very intuitive, he can't possibly know the half of it. He can't possibly realise just how true his suspicions are.

The bedroom wall takes several hours to strip, and the task is every bit as painstaking as we had imagined. It's also completely worth it, and I can't help but gasp as Eleanor's work is revealed, little by little. Uncovering her mural is like building a jigsaw; with the removal of each bit of paper a new piece falls into place, and I think I've understood its meaning until the next part is revealed and I'm lost once again. By the time that the last sheet of wallpaper is removed, my hand is clapped over my mouth in disbelief. I knew from her sketchbooks that Eleanor was talented, but this work is something else altogether. It is rich with colour yet dominated by darkness. It is beautiful, but it is also unnerving. Nature, the earth, the universe – all represented on her wall, all drawn towards a deep blackness. I'm no art critic, but it seems to me that her painting is as much about death as it is about life. I stare at it, my eyes wide. I wonder why she painted it. I wonder why she wanted this image in here.

"The damage is minimal," Daniel remarks, pointing to a couple of areas where the paint has come away. "It's quite something, eh? It's funny – to look at her you'd never have thought she had it in her."

"I'd love to know what inspired it," I say, still unable to take my eyes off it. "She looks so happy in the photos, standing next to it with a huge smile on her face. I wonder why she covered it up, when she was clearly so proud of it."

Daniel shrugs. "Ah, the questions we'd ask the dead, if only they could speak."

"Yes, if only…" I reply, thinking immediately of Bert, although in his case, it seems the dead has decided to stop speaking.

"Maybe she just needed a change," he suggests. "Maybe after a while she had enough of seeing it. It is quite, well, intense for a bedroom wall. Bedroom décor is supposed to be peaceful and relaxing, isn't it?"

"A mechanic, a chef, a wallpaper stripper and now an interior designer – is there no end to your talents?" I tease, giving him a playful nudge.

He grins at me. "I can assure you that my bedroom is a haven of tranquillity."

I feel the heat rise in my cheeks and I look away, inwardly

chastising myself for my flagrant joviality. I should know that jokes seem to lead to flirting between us; I should know where the line is and how not to cross it. I'm thirty years old, for goodness sake; I'm not a silly young girl, naïve and vulnerable to the charms of an older man. I never was; if I'm honest with myself I have always known what I was doing, what I was getting myself into. I've been here before; I know where it leads and I know the cost. A broken marriage. A broken heart. A broken Harriet.

A cold, deeply unwelcome breeze runs behind me, making the hairs on the back of my neck stand on end. I wonder for a moment if it's Bert, then remember that I never usually feel his presence in that way. I also remember that I've felt the cold rush by me in this room before, that I attributed it to a draught. I try to rationalise it once again, yet the unsettled feeling growing in my gut tells me it's something more, that someone is here, someone I haven't met yet. I shiver, wrapping my arms around myself and glancing at Daniel, looking for clues that he felt it too. If he did, he shows no signs of discomfort. My heart sinks. I'm probably imagining it. I'm probably making myself feel chilled, allowing myself to be preoccupied with all the icy, brittle thoughts running through my mind.

After a moment's awkward silence, Daniel clears his throat. "Right, let's get working on that kitchen wall, shall we?"

I nod. "Yes, let's."

I hurry away from the wall, sponge and bucket in hand, keen to see what Eleanor's kitchen mural has in store for me, keen to try to discern more about my grandmother from the images she created. Keen to provoke more questions than I can ever find answers to. Keen, more than anything, to leave strange breezes, borderline flirtation and painful memories in the bedroom, where I can only hope that the darkness on Eleanor's wall might be able to consume them.

14

Eleanor
September 1972

For the next fortnight I paint almost continuously, casting wild strokes upon my wall like a woman possessed. Gone is the notion to plan, to design, to exercise caution and control over my work. Instead, instinct takes over; a feral, primitive urge so intense that it drives me to paint as though my life depends upon it. And in some ways, I realise, my life does depend upon it. I spend my days alone, my child at school and my husband forever absent, my only visitor a single friend who is as reclusive as I am. My life is empty and bordering on meaningless, effortlessly contained within the faded walls of the house at Kirtlebeck End. Only my murals give me any sense of purpose. Only my creations can offer me any escape from this life at all.

The only time I leave my bedroom is when I need to wash and I need to eat. I seldom see Bert, who keeps the hours of a dedicated workaholic with a mistress on the side. Even when he is at home we give each other a wide berth; he has no interest in seeing my work, and I have no interest in knowing his opinion on it. I'd say that I've no interest in him altogether but I know that's a lie - the festering fury I feel every time thoughts of that day on the lane creep into my mind is a testament to that. However, it is a blessed relief that I don't have to see him. My emotions are raw, open sores splattered all over the wall. I can't account for what I'd do if I was forced to confront him with them.

Anna, perhaps sensing my singularity of purpose, becomes ever more self-sufficient, and though I am hopelessly obsessed with my work I feel guilty for leaving my daughter to fend so completely for herself. As the laundry and housework begins to mount up she takes these on too, even turning her hand to ironing her father's clothes in addition to her own school uniform. She is quiet, stoic and accepting, and I can't decide if I should be proud or deeply worried about her. Knee-deep in paint and creative fervour I might be, but even I can see that our living situation isn't healthy for a girl of her age. I invite her to join me as much as I can, using every excuse under the sun from needing a cup of tea to just wanting her company. I realise that this is mostly to reassure myself, to ease my own rotten conscience, but Anna plays along, sitting and watching me paint the evenings away with a pencil in her hand and a homework textbook set upon her lap. She seems content enough but her quietness unsettles me, and after a while I can't help but hanker after some knowledge of what is going through her mind.

"I think what you're doing is amazing, Mum," she tells me one evening, offering up a rare insight into her thoughts.

"Thanks, sweetheart," I reply, turning around and trying my best to give her my full attention although the ceaseless urge to paint has me wrapped in its tentacles.

She pauses, watching me for a few minutes as I return to my work. The silence between us hangs heavily, and gradually my attention is drawn back towards her.

"Is everything okay?" I ask, glancing down at her textbook. "At school, I mean? You study very hard. I worry you'll overdo it."

She frowns at me. "You're seriously worried that I'm doing too much schoolwork?"

"No, of course not," I reply. "I'm proud of how bright and studious you are. But it isn't good for you to study all of the time –

you have to take a break once in a while."

She slams her book closed in mock outrage. "Like you do from painting?"

"Point taken," I say, inwardly impressed by her quick retort. "And stop frowning at me. You look like your father when you frown."

The way I spit out my reference to Bert makes Anna wince and I feel an immediate pang of guilt at hitting an obvious raw nerve.

"Sorry," I say. "I shouldn't have said it quite like that. Of course you look like your dad at times. You are his daughter too."

Anna looks away, a nonchalant shrug rolling off her shoulders. "It's alright, Mum, honestly."

"No, it's not," I insist, finally putting into words the thoughts which have been plaguing my mind. "Your father and I are going through a difficult time, I think you know that, but that's no excuse for me making unkind quips about him in front of you."

She chews the end of her pencil, her gaze fixed upon me. "What about the unkind things you say to each other when you argue?"

I feel my cheeks begin to colour. "What about them?"

"I heard Dad call you a barking mad drunk."

"Yes."

"And you called him a selfish bastard."

"Yes. I'm sorry you heard that. I really am. It can't have been nice to hear your parents speak to each other like that." Despite my best efforts I feel my lip begin to tremble, hot tears spilling down my cheeks. A dozen images flash through my mind before I can stop them. The insults. The indifference. The lies. The betrayal. The two of them on the lane, her pretty face full of concern as he spilled out his woes, his eyes fiery with lust as she walked away. All the things I've been trying to erase, all the memories I have worked so hard to paint away, to cast out into the cosmos, to suffocate and suppress under layer upon layer of thick acrylics.

Anna gets up and throws her arms around me. "Oh Mum, I didn't mean to make you cry."

I give her a watery smile and pull her back from me, looking at her beautiful, innocent little face. "You didn't. None of this is your fault. Never, ever think that any of this is your fault."

A solitary tear rolls down Anna's cheek and it is enough to almost break my heart in two. "I'm just sad that moving here hasn't fixed things like you hoped," she says. "And I'm sorry that Dad hates your murals so much."

I choke out a laugh. "I think his displeasure at me painting on the walls is probably the least of our problems, but I do wish that he could appreciate them too, even just a little bit."

My efforts to lift the mood fall flat and the uneasy silence returns. Instinctively I pull Anna in close to me, hugging her for dear life, hoping beyond hope that my affection reassures her in ways which my words alone cannot. "You're a good girl," I whisper. "And I'm always here for you, even if sometimes I seem like I'm not."

"I know," she replies. "I hate Dad for cheating on you."

My heart sinks as my suspicions are confirmed. Anna did indeed hear every word of that dreadful row. "Please try not to hate him," I say. "He is still your father, when all is said and done." Those words don't come easily but I know that I have to say them, for her sake if not for my own.

"But I feel so angry, Mum. I don't know what to do! How can I just make those feelings go away?"

I release her from my embrace and pick up my paintbrush. "Channel your anger into something productive," I suggest. "Although I suspect you're already doing that, with all the studying you've been doing."

"What else can I do then?" she asks.

I give her a wry smile. "Well, for a start you could stop doing his ironing!"

Anna laughs, and I breathe an inward sigh of relief. The moment lightens and our peaceful routine resumes, but I suspect we both appreciate how the understanding between us has deepened, how in many ways our hurt is a shared wound. Quietly

Anna continues to study and I get back to my painting, my hands busy, my mind preoccupied with one thought: if only I could take Anna's pain away. If only I could put it with my own. If only I could paint it like I paint my own sorrows.

As Meg suggested, I focus my efforts on creating the mural's darkness. I fashion a great, elaborate cosmos, allowing it to grow from the top corner in glorious juxtaposition to the earthly scene with emerges from the bottom of the wall. In the centre of the wall the two images meet, trees and birds reaching up towards the stars, seeking their embrace, taking their place within the universe in a triumphant swirl of colour, flight and ambition. Completing this final part gives me the most intense feeling of joy. It is then that I experience, perhaps for the first time in my life, the greatest sense of satisfaction with my own work. I am proud of what I have accomplished, even if I can hardly believe myself capable of it. I have created something beautiful, something magical, something otherworldly. Something which is mine. Something which I can wake up to each morning, something which will remind me that I have choices, that I can steer my own path, and that I have left my mark, however small, upon this world.

Meg comes by just as I complete the final touches, her sense of timing remarkable. My mouth falls open with surprise as I open the door to her pretty face, her eyes glinting with obvious anticipation.

"I've just finished," I say, wiping my hands on a paint-sodden cloth.

"I know." She grins at me. "Can I see it?"

"Of course," I reply, beckoning her inside. "But how did you know?"

She shrugs. "I just did. Call it intuition or you know, ESP or whatever."

"Ha! A lucky guess, then," I reply.

"What, you mean you don't believe in magic?" Meg shoots me a playful look.

I shake my head. "Do you want to see the mural or not?"

Another broad smile is her only response as she almost runs towards my bedroom.

"You remember where you're going, then," I call after her.

"As if I could forget!" she replies.

When I finally catch up to her, she is standing in the centre of my room, hands clapped over her mouth, gazing at the wall before her. I hang back in the doorway, watching her reaction with an unexpected sense of pleasure. She doesn't need to say a word; I know she loves it. She loves it as much as I love it.

"Well, Eleanor Murray," she begins, her deliberate annunciation of my full name giving me shivers, "you certainly figured out what was missing."

"You like it?" I ask, drawing closer to her.

She turns to face me, rewarding me with those deep, dark eyes. "It is without doubt the most incredible piece I have ever seen. The way you've worked the two scenes together, the way you've varied your style..." she wanders closer, pointing up in all different directions as she demonstrates what she means. "See here, it's so controlled, so intricate, but then here, it's all explosions of colour, all reckless abandon, before dissolving into that wonderful darkness up there. That's the deepest part – at first glance it seems blank, but if you look closer you can see it harbours so much feeling."

"Thank you," I whisper. "That's so kind of you. Thank you."

"I don't say it to be kind," she replies. "I say it because it's true. I knew you could do it. I knew you had it in you. You just had to focus, to channel your energy, and dare I say it, lay off the wine for a while! I take it you managed to kick the booze into touch?"

"Yes," I say, laughing as I sit down on the edge of the bed. "Yes, I haven't had a drink for weeks. In fact, until you mentioned it I'd barely given it a thought. I suppose I've been so wrapped up in my painting that I've thought of little else. I'm just lucky that Anna has kept me going with tea and sandwiches, otherwise I'd have faded to nothing."

Meg sits down beside me. "She seems like a real treasure," she remarks, smoothing out her long, patterned skirt.

"She is. She knows about her father – what he did, with that woman," I blurt out, my words falling clumsily from my tongue.

"She knows that the woman is here?"

"No, thank God. She just knows that he had an affair. She doesn't know anything more than that. She says that she hates him and I feel terrible because deep down that makes me glad, even though I know it's not right."

To my surprise, Meg shrugs. "You can't expect her to adore him in spite of knowing what he's done. She is human, after all. Let her hate him, and let her let him know that she hates him. It seems to me that so far your husband has got off scot-free, and he must know it, given that he's bold enough to bring his bit on the side up here and dangle her under your noses. Maybe Anna's hatred is his punishment for what he's done."

"Hmm," I reply, unconvinced. "It just all feels so bitter, I suppose. We were supposed to move up here for a fresh start, to put the past behind us. And yet here I am, all these months later, still dwelling on it all, still allowing my anger to fester. I don't want it to be like that for Anna."

"You can't leave the past behind if your husband insists on bringing it with him," Meg answers me, and I find myself taken aback by her bluntness.

"True," I concede, "but still, I can't bear the thought of Anna suffering because of all this. It's her birthday soon. I think I will do something nice for her, something unexpected, maybe surprise her with something. Hopefully that might make her feel better."

"That's a good idea. And what about you? What will you do to make yourself feel better?"

A bemused smile suppresses the frown which hovers above my eyes. "Well, I've painted this mural, haven't I? Surely that's about as cathartic as it gets!"

Meg's eyes rest intently on me and I know that some insight is coming. "Yes, but there's something else on your mind, isn't there?"

"How do you know that?"

"I told you – intuition."

I bite my lip, hesitating for a moment, almost disliking the way in which my friend seems to be able to read my thoughts. "I've been thinking about going out again. I haven't left this place since our walk into Annan, and now that the mural is finished…" words fail me and my voice trails off under the scrutiny of Meg's unnerving gaze.

"Are you thinking of going anywhere in particular?" Meg asks me. I know that she already knows the answer.

"Perhaps a walk around the village," I answer her, almost ashamed of how coy I am being.

"It's not wise to go looking for her, Eleanor. It won't do any good."

I clasp my hands together hard, trying to control the heat of the anger which rises up from my gut. "Won't it? I can just imagine the look on her face. She thinks she's safe, sitting pretty somewhere, happy in the knowledge that she won't encounter me since Bert assured her that I'm some kind of weird loner. I'd show her. I'd show both of them."

"Yes you'd prove them wrong about you, but what then? Where would that leave you? How would it do you any good at all? How would it help Anna, who would surely get to hear about it?"

I feel my face crumple and before I can stop them, warm tears trickle down my cheeks. "You're right. Of course you're right. I just – all this time I've spent working on the mural, keeping myself busy, but at the back of my mind there's always been her and him. The knowledge that she's so near, that he's brought her here and placed her under my nose, it festers under my skin like a disease, poisoning me, eating away at me bit by bit. I thought if I threw myself into my art, if I gave voice to my emotions through my mural, then all my rage and resentment would go away. Now I realise that there's so much of it, I don't think I can ever be rid of it."

Meg casts a tender arm around my shoulder and draws me in

close. "You can keep painting though. Keep painting and painting and painting until Bert, the woman, the horrible things he's done are all far, far away."

I give her a grim smile. "How can that ever be the case while he is here, under the same roof?"

Meg returns my smile, but she doesn't answer me. Instead she gets up, walking about towards my mural as though to give it one last thorough examination. "Can I make a suggestion?" she asks.

"By all means," I reply.

"There's only one person you should be tracking down right now," she says, "and that's Emma McCabe."

I frown at her. "Emma who?"

"The photographer, of course!" Meg throws her arms up in mock despair. "Don't tell me you've lost her details?"

"No – I'm sure I have them somewhere," I say, hesitating. "They're probably still in my coat pocket."

"Well, fetch them then! There's no time like the present! You can give her a call right now."

Slowly I get up from the bed. "Are you sure she'll be interested? Maybe this isn't the sort of thing she's looking for."

Meg walks over to me, placing her hands on my shoulders and looking me wearily in the eye. For a moment I feel like a child, bracing herself for a lecture from an all-knowing parent. "She wants to capture art, Eleanor. This is art! You could be right – she may not like it. On the other hand, she may adore it. You won't know unless you call her."

"Okay," I concede with a resigned sigh. "Message received and understood. I'll go and fetch the flyer."

I head downstairs to find my jacket. Meg follows closely behind me and I feel momentarily irritated at the way she seems to be monitoring my every move, as though she doesn't believe that I'll actually have the gumption to make the call. I locate the flyer with ease and spurred on by my irritation, I go to the telephone in the hallway to phone the photographer. I dial the number swiftly and without hesitation, giving Meg a pointed look as I put the receiver to my ear. It is only when I hear the phone begin to ring that my heart starts to pound a little harder.

"Hello?" someone answers in soft, feminine tones.

"Hello," I say in my best telephone voice. "Is that Emma McCabe? My name is Eleanor Murray. I'm phoning with regards to your advertisement."

Meg grins at me, nodding her head as we speak. My earlier irritation dissipates as I realise that she was right; this is a call I needed to make. This is something I need to try to do, not to ease my guilt about Anna or soothe my pain over Bert but simply for me and for my art. I need to focus and I need to believe. I need to trust Meg's mysterious wisdom and see where all of this leads.

On the other end of the line, the voice's interest piques. "Yes this is Emma. You mean the flyer for 'Art captures Art'? Excellent! Do you have something to show me?"

I take a deep breath. "Yes," I reply. "Yes I do. I have a mural on my bedroom wall. I would be delighted if you would come to see it."

"Wonderful," Emma replies. "I take it you're a local artist?"

"Yes," I say. "I live in Kirtlebeck. And I am an artist."

The significance of those words don't strike me until after they have slipped from my lips. I shake my head in disbelief at my own willing, confident description. I am an artist. I live in Kirtlebeck. Kirtlebeck is my home. I am an artist. I'm not a drunk; I'm not a hermit. I'm an artist who just picked up the phone to tell a stranger about her work without so much as a second thought.

Next to me Meg looks ready to burst with delight as my conversation with Emma progresses well. "I knew you could do it," she breathes.

I nod. So did I. For the first time in all my life, so did I.

15

Harry
January 2018

"I wonder who she is."

We finish stripping the last sheet of paper off the kitchen wall, revealing an earthly, beautiful scene. The colours have faded a little, probably thanks to sunlight from the window which would, at one time at least, have illuminated this part of the room. Nonetheless, the image is still striking. Again, Eleanor's focus is on the natural world, but there is no cosmos here; just long grasses, flowers, and bright skies. At the centre of it all is a woman with flowing black hair and dark eyes, her hands grazing over the meadow as she runs. Her happy face tells me she's meant to be in harmony with the scene around her, but for me there is something about her darkness which disrupts it. I stare at her, mesmerised, and futilely repeat my question:

"Who is she? Why did Eleanor paint her on the kitchen wall?"

Daniel chuckles at the indignant tone in my voice. "Yes, she's quite the mystery, isn't she?"

I shake my head. "I've never seen her before. Not in any of the photos I've found, at any rate. Mind you, everything I've found so far has been of the family – of my family. Just the three of them;

no one else." I ponder this for a moment, wondering at its significance about the kind of life they might have led.

"Well, whoever she is, you have to admit it's another lovely painting. You should be proud, Harry. Your grandmother was clearly very talented."

"Hmm," I muse. I might feel pride if she'd been someone I'd actually known, but that's not something I wish to confess to Daniel. "I'm not sure. I mean, the meadow is stunning, but I'm not keen on the woman. There's something about her which unnerves me."

"Oh, I don't know about that," Daniel replies, hands on hips as he examines her one more time. "I'd say she's quite stunning."

I can't help but roll my eyes. "Well, you're a man," I quip. "You would say that."

Our wall-stripping endeavours complete, we clean up and make a start on dinner. My stomach growls hungrily as I put the roast into the oven, reminding me that once again I skipped lunch. I hope to goodness that Daniel doesn't hear the noise. He probably had a point when he remarked that I didn't seem to be living on much, but in my defence no one in my position would be managing to feed themselves particularly well. I'm jobless, friendless and not far away from penniless; until I sell this place the pot of money I have to live on is small and finite. So, with the exception of kind neighbours bringing culinary gifts, beans on toast will have to do.

"Will I make us a brew?" I offer, gesturing towards the kettle which has had considerable use during the course of the afternoon.

Daniel makes a face. "No, that's quite enough coffee for me. I've never known anyone who drinks tea in the quantities that you do."

I grin at him. "Maybe it's a northern thing."

"Scotland is north," he scoffs.

"You know that I mean – northern English. Drinking lots of tea, chip butties, gravy – all northern things."

He smirks. "If you say so."

"I do say so!"

"You're speaking to a man who originates from the country of haggis and the deep-fried Mars bar. I'd say we have the monopoly on delicacies."

I throw my arms up in mock despair. "So what would you like to drink, then?"

"Wine, of course." He reaches for the bottle I left sitting on the counter. "I'll pop the cork; you find us some glasses."

I oblige, reaching up into one of the cupboards and locating the two glasses we used the first night we met. They're reassuringly robust-looking things, with thick stems and a pretty cut glass design. "I've never tried haggis," I confess, placing the glasses down on the counter in front of him.

Daniel pours the wine, periodically glancing up to meet my gaze. "Well, the thing you have to understand about haggis is that it has so many versatile uses. I mean, traditionally it's eaten with neeps and tatties – turnip and potatoes, to the unacquainted. But equally, it can be enjoyed battered, deep fried and served with your beloved chips, put in pies or even in more exotic foods. For example, I make some superb haggis nachos."

"Oh?" I say, intrigued. "Scotland meets Mexico, eh? Sounds like you're quite the cook as well as a wine connoisseur."

He nods, throwing me a meaningful glance. "It's what life's all about, isn't it? The little rewards; the small, everyday things that are there for savouring, if only we take the time to notice and enjoy them. Otherwise we're no better than miserable peasants, living on pottage."

"Or beans on toast," I add with a smile.

He laughs. "Yes! Or beans on toast."

We sit down at the kitchen table, each with one eye on the roast which is cooking away nicely in the oven and filling the room with delicious smells. We relax into the evening, both happy to put our proverbial feet up after a hard day's graft. I sit quietly for a few moments, running my finger over the top of my glass and allowing my mind to wander a little. I'm tired, bone weary in fact, but today has probably been the nicest day I've had since I've been here. I feel a sense of satisfaction in achieving something, in revealing something of Eleanor's which was hidden and perhaps getting a little closer to knowing her. But more importantly than that, I realise, I haven't been alone. In fact, I've enjoyed some good company; kind, friendly company which has lifted my spirits and brought a smile to my face.

That smile must creep on to my lips then as Daniel flashes me an intrigued look. "A penny for your thoughts," he says.

I laugh. "A penny! It'll cost you more than that, I'm afraid."

"Oh – they must be some good thoughts, then."

"No, not really," I retort, sipping my wine. "I need to charge a lot because I'm skint."

Daniel gestures around him. "Surely not?"

"I suppose you could say I'm house rich and money poor," I say with a shrug. "But anyway, all I was thinking was how much fun I've had today." For some reason, the admission makes the heat rise in my cheeks.

Before I can look away, Daniel captures my gaze. "Me too," he replies. He holds my eyes with his for just a second longer, then raises his glass in a toast. "Here's to great Saturdays spent unveiling lost treasures."

I chuckle, raising my glass and clinking it against his. "Cheers," I say, before taking another sip. The wine is strong and warming, and I remind myself to drink slowly. Wine on an empty stomach is a sure way to end up tipsy before dinner is even served.

"So, Harry James, what's your story?"

I nearly splutter on my drink. "Goodness – it's a bit early for a question like that, isn't it? I'm only on my first glass of wine and already you want to know all my secrets."

Daniel shakes his head, his face serious but his eyes dancing with amusement. "Not secrets. Just some background – you know, what life was like before you came up here." He must note my aghast expression because then he adds: "Come on, you know loads about me."

"No I don't," I protest.

"You know more about me than I do about you."

I have to concede that's probably true. "There really isn't very much to tell," I reply. "I am as you find me – my parents are dead, my grandmother is dead, and now I have this house to sort out and sell."

A look of sadness passes over Daniel's face at that final word. "Have you thought about not selling? I mean, this is your ancestral home of sorts."

"No, I wouldn't want to live here long term. It's so large that I would be lost in a place like this. And although, as you say, it's part of my family's history, I don't think I could ever feel truly at home here. There's – there's too many ghosts."

Daniel looks up, his blue eyes wide. "Ghosts?"

"Not literal ghosts," I reply quickly, although my mind wanders immediately to Bert and I almost have to cross my fingers behind my back. "You know what I mean – there's probably too much history here. And it's very eerie at night."

Daniel laughs. "Now that I can believe, especially when you're on your own." He pauses to sip his wine. "Have you – have you always been on your own?"

Despite my best efforts I feel my face grow serious. "If you're asking me if there's ever been anyone significant in my life then, yes, but not anymore. What about you?" I ask quickly, keen to deflect from my own woes but also suddenly intrigued to know more about him.

"Divorced," he replies with a grim nod. "For almost twenty years now."

"Oh, I'm sorry to hear that," I say.

"Yes, well, I can't say it was the most pleasant experience of my life, catching my wife in bed with a close friend. I mean, that's the sort of thing that would give anyone serious trust issues." He drinks again, a gulp this time. "I've dated a bit since but nothing's ever worked out."

"I'm sorry," I say again, swallowing hard. I'm aware that I've been sorry twice but I realise I don't know what to say. What can I say? What possible comfort can I give – me, the one who has been the other woman?

"It's alright," he replies, even though we both know it isn't. "As sad as it sounds, I'm just glad I've got Mum living with me. I like company, and it can get very lonely on your own, can't it?"

I nod, feeling the heat of shame rising in my cheeks again. I know better than most what loneliness can do. It was loneliness, in part, which drove me into his arms.

"So the person in your life, the significant one, it didn't end well, I presume?"

I frown. "What makes you think that?"

"Your face when I forced you to mention it. Did he, or she, did they break your heart?"

I take a deep breath. "He – we...let's just say hearts were broken and leave it at that. I'm really not great at talking about this stuff." I know my tone is abrupt but I can't help it. After what Daniel's just confided in me, I'm hardly about to confess to being a willing participant in destroying a marriage.

He holds his hands up in mock surrender. "Alright. So tell me about life in Manchester? There must be a job, a home, some friends you're hurrying back to, once all this is done?"

I take a deep breath, trying not to crumple as Daniel's question prompts me to think about everything I left behind. "I had a job, yes, in a hotel. Just admin and reception work, you know, but it paid the bills. I had a little flat, and of course I had a few friends too."

He raises his eyebrows. "Had?"

I nod. "Yes, I gave up the lease on my flat and resigned from my job when I came up here." I try to keep my voice even, my words factual. I can't tell him that it was his hotel, his life I was drawn into, his world I existed in. I can't tell him that my closest, dearest friend was his wife. I look away, glancing at Eleanor's mural on the wall, my thoughts roaming to the grand cosmos upstairs. I swallow hard. I can't tell him that I was merely a small planet orbiting his sun and that once the supernova happened, I was left for dust.

"But why?"

I give a small shrug. "I needed to sort this place out, and I didn't know how long that would take me."

The expression on Daniel's face tells me that he senses my half-truths. "So do you plan to go back to Manchester, once this place is sold?"

"I don't know." At least that part is true. I genuinely don't know what I will do after all this is over; indeed, I don't know what I will do with the rest of my life. I only know that if there's any justice in the world, I will spend it alone, without love, in penance for all the pain I've caused.

The oven beeps, signalling that our food is ready and mercifully interrupting Daniel's line of questioning. A shiver comes over me as I stand up, and I notice that despite the heat of the oven, the temperature in the room seems to have dropped a couple of degrees. At first I assume that I'm imagining it, that it's the cold turn of my thoughts which are having this effect on me, but then Daniel gets up and rubs his arms.

"It's odd how chilly it's got in here," he remarks.

"This place could do with re-insulating, amongst many other things," I say, busying myself with serving our dinner. I wonder for a moment if Bert is making his presence felt. Usually I only know he's around if he speaks to me, but I suppose there's a first time for everything. On the other hand, given the nature of the conversation Daniel and I have just had, I'd much rather that Bert had listened to me and made himself scarce.

"I can light a fire in the living room after dinner, if you like," Daniel suggests.

"That would be lovely, but I've no firewood."

He grins at me. "Ah – but you do. It's in the hut outside. Put it there myself last winter. There should be plenty left."

I let out a small laugh as I hand him his plate, grateful for the lighter turn of our conversation. "I'm beginning to think that you know this place better than I do," I reply.

We eat and wash up quickly, neither of us relishing the kitchen's chill despite the warming, delicious food we enjoy. We take dessert with us to the living room, where as promised Daniel lights a fire. I pour each of us a final glass of wine, emptying the bottle, and we get comfortable on Eleanor's worn old sofa. Outside night has fallen; the sky is tar black and judging by the light white dusting on Daniel's head when he returns from the hut, it has started to snow. In here, however, is warm and cosy, the world out there removed from view by the thick curtains drawn over the windows. I finish eating the very delicious fudge cake which Daniel provided, then snuggle down against the faded cushions, glass in hand, eyelids heavy, a look of weary contentment etched on my face. For once it's nice to enjoy this place at night, to feel relaxed rather than on edge. For once it's nice to have some company, other than the dead, during the long dark hours.

"You're tired," Daniel observes. "I'll go soon and let you get to bed."

I shake my head in weak protest. "Please don't. Not yet, anyway." I almost reach over and grab his hand but stop myself just in time.

"You're a mystery to me, Harry James. You choose this solitary existence and yet you obviously don't like to be alone." Those bright blue eyes gaze at me and I'm forced to look away.

"Neither do you."

"That's right, but I didn't choose it. If it was down to me I'd still be happily married, maybe with some kids by now."

"What makes you think I chose to be alone?" I ask. "I didn't choose for everyone in my life to disappear, to leave me, to die…" Tears burn in my eyes, threatening to fall and I find I have to stop talking.

"Do you still love him?"

"Who?"

"The man - the reason you left everything."

I suppress a gasp, not wanting to let Daniel see how close to the truth he's come. "No," I reply. "I see him for what he is now. Do you still love her, your ex-wife?"

The laugh which emerges from him is bitter and strained, and for a moment I glimpse a different Daniel, a man from a time before he found peace and refuge in a little village in southern Scotland. "No. For a long time I did, and I hated myself for it, too. But not anymore." He takes a long sip from his wine glass, long enough for me to think about all those vile messages she's sent me and whether they're a sign that she's filled with love and hatred too.

"His name was Mark," I blurt out. It feels strange to say his name now, like I'm talking about something lost, something remote, something that was once bigger than those few letters can attest to but is now nothing more than a memory. I'm not even sure why I said it at all. I hold my breath, forcing myself to say nothing more.

Daniel smiles. Kindness lingers in his eyes and I allow myself to breathe again. "Her name was Joanna," he says simply enough, but in a tone which tells me she's never gone completely from his thoughts, even after all these years.

Before I can say anything else, he gets up and walks over to the record player. "I always wanted to play something on this but I never dared to ask Eleanor." He picks out an album and places it on the turntable. I don't recognise the music which plays; it's slow, soft and sounds like jazz, and I realise it's probably one of the albums I passed by when flicking through the record collection the other day.

Daniel turns to me and holds out his hand. "Dance?"

I look up at him, and there's something about his expression which prevents me from hesitating. I take hold of his hand and let him pull me towards him. We stand close, but he's careful to maintain a polite distance even though part of me, the part which has drunk wine and craves the comfort of being touched, wishes he wouldn't. I sway with him in time to the music, one hand still in his, the other hand placed gently on his shoulder, the proximity of his body to mine filling me with a conflict of contentment, heat, and desire. I am shocked to realise this, and yet I do not pull away. As much as I want to, as much as I know I should do, I cannot deny myself the warmth of being in someone else's arms.

"I'd like to see you again, while you're here." His quiet words caress my ear, and a shiver runs down my spine.

"Me too," I reply, as a shameful, blissful smile finds its way on to my lips.

16

Eleanor
September 1972

In the middle of the month Anna's birthday rolls around and just like that, my daughter becomes a teenager. Her special day arrives on an especially wet and miserable Friday and it takes every scrap of willpower I have to get myself out of bed early to make her a birthday breakfast, just as I have done every year since she was a little girl. After indulging in a feast of crusty bread and jam Bert joins us and together we watch her open her gifts. At first I feel myself grow tense at his presence, and I must remind myself that she is his daughter too, that we must suspend our marital hostilities for today and remember that we are parents, that among all the discord and estrangement we also have some shared joy.

Of course, even the arrival of our only child's birthday cannot work miracles and we sit far apart, avoiding eye contact, focussed only on Anna and her smiles of delight as she opens up all the things she asked for. When the last gift is unwrapped she thanks us both, but she comes over only to me for a cuddle. After our recent conversation about her father I am unsurprised, but a quick glance at Bert's face confirms that he is taken aback and hurt by the sudden loss of his daughter's affection. I try my best to feel sorry for him but I can't. Perhaps Meg was right; perhaps this is his punishment for all that he has done.

Anna heads off to school in an excitable mood, and I linger in the doorway listening to her chatter and giggle with her friends as she meets them on the lane. After school we plan to have a party at home for her, with a few of her friends coming over for dinner and…well, whatever teenagers do to celebrate someone's birthday. I try my best to remember what I would have wanted to do at that age but swiftly draw a blank. Times were different back then; when I turned thirteen the war was barely over, and everyone I knew was thinking about how to rebuild their lives rather than what entertainment might be most appropriate for a thirteen-year-old's birthday party.

"Are you too old for party games now, do you think?" I asked Anna a few days ago when this quandary first crossed my mind.

"What, like pass the parcel or pin the tail on the donkey?" The amusement in Anna's voice told me the answer.

"What will you do, then?" I replied, feeling a little exasperated. "I need to know in case there's anything I need to prepare."

Anna gave me a nonchalant shrug. "I don't know. We'll just sit around and talk, I suppose. Maybe listen to some music. Could we use your record player in the living room? Maybe borrow your David Bowie record? My friends love Bowie."

"Sure," I said, "help yourselves – you know where all the records are. I'm sure Dad won't mind if you borrow his, either."

Anna made such a disgusted face that I had to hold my breath to stop myself from laughing out loud. "No thanks," she said. "Jazz is for old people."

"Fair enough," I answered her with as straight a face as I could muster. "Oh, one more thing, is it just girls coming to this party?"

"Mum!" she bit back. "Of course it's just girls. The last thing any of us want is boys spoiling our evening."

"I see," I replied, unable to hold back my smile this time. "Well, sounds like an easy night for me to get ready for. Just some food, no boys and plenty of Bowie."

"Exactly," she said.

That was the end of the conversation, but not the end of my thoughts on the matter. I secretly celebrated my daughter's continued disinterest in the opposite sex, even though I knew it couldn't last. One day, she would meet someone and the feelings we ascribe to love would capture her in their stealthy claws. As I stand on the doorstep, listening to my beautiful child bound down the lane with her gaggle of girlfriends, my thoughts return to that dark place where all my resentment for Bert festers, and where all my fears for Anna's future are found. Part of me hopes that a boy never sweeps her off her feet, that she never meets a man she wishes to marry. That way at least I can be sure that she will never have to suffer as I have done, that she will never have to pick up the pieces of a life shattered by pain and betrayal.

An early autumn breeze as cold as my thoughts rushes past me and I shiver, pulling my cardigan tighter around my waist. Behind me I hear Bert rushing around, readying himself no doubt for a day at the garage, or perhaps a day in bed with his mistress. Either way, I am pleased that he will be out of the house and far away from me. Today I have much to do, and not all concerning Anna's birthday. Today I also have a photographer coming to visit, to see my work, and hopefully to capture what is the product of one of the most inspired and most tortured periods in my life. Before the chilly breeze can attack me again I go back inside, shaking off the weariness produced by my early start, digging deep for as much determination as I can muster.

"Do you need anything from the shop?" Bert calls to me as I walk into the kitchen.

"Like what?" I reply, my words resuming their clipped character now that Anna is out of earshot.

Bert sticks his head around the door. "You know, food, things for Anna's party?"

"No," I say, turning on the kettle. "I think I have everything I need. Besides, I can always nip out into the village later if there's anything I'm missing."

Bert frowns so deeply that I have to turn away so that he can't see me smirk. "Can you?" he asks, hovering in the doorway. His sudden discomfort delights me and I wish that I could keep my face straight enough to turn around. "That's news to me. I thought you never left these four walls. I thought you didn't have any money, either."

"There's a lot you don't know about me, Bert."

The rumble of the kettle as it boils fills the silence that descends between us as Bert thinks about what to say. I lean hard against the worktop, taking a few deep, steady breaths in an effort to master my emotions, to control myself enough to be able to turn and face him. If I'm going to look him in the eye for the first time in weeks, I can't afford to give anything away.

The kettle clicks and Bert springs back to life. "Well I wish I'd known that you were prepared to do some shopping. You've no idea how much running around I've had to do to get all of Anna's birthday presents in time."

"I'm sure it's been hectic for you," I reply, stirring my tea. "After all, you've got so much on your plate – a new garage business to run, a new home which desperately needs some attention…" I add milk to my tea, finishing my sentence in my head. And a mistress to fuck. Oh, how I wish I could bring myself to say it.

I turn around just in time to see him standing before me, the confusion written all over his face. "Well yeah, Eleanor, actually it has."

I smile sweetly as I take a sip of my tea. "Anything I can do to help, just say the word."

He kisses the top of my head so tenderly that for a moment I am almost transported back to the old times, the times before he did things and we said things and it all went sour. Then I remember where we are now and the ghost of his lips on my scalp almost makes me shudder.

"Thank you," he says. "I'd better get to work."

I press my tea cup to my lips and watch as he walks out the

front door, closing it firmly behind him without so much as a backward glance. Before I can stop it a giggle escapes from me, a high-pitched mischievous noise causing my tea to splutter over the top of my cup. Losing all self-control, the giggle grows into a cackle, a wicked, twisted, bitter sound rising deep from within my belly. *I can nip into the village…there's a lot you don't know about me, Bert…anything I can do to help…* My mind replays my words over and over. I don't know where that conversation came from; certainly, it wasn't one I planned to have. I didn't plan to be so damn passive-aggressive, to toy with his emotions or to mess with his head, but the fact that I have done gives me a strange and unfamiliar feeling. I feel victorious. I feel empowered. I feel alive. I feel ready to get organised for Anna's party. I feel ready to show this photographer my mural.

"Well, that'll make you think twice about letting your tart out around the village, won't it, Bert?" I ask the closed door as my laughter subsides. "You stupid, ridiculous man." My vitriol feels like velvet as it slides off my tongue. It doesn't matter that no one can hear me, that only this house bears witness to my vehemence. What matters is that after all these weeks of drinking, of misery, of self-pity, I am finally seeing clearly. I am finally rebuilding my defences. I am finally taking some control of my life. I am, at long last, filled with a sense of purpose that even my selfish, deceitful husband will struggle to erode.

I head upstairs, my footsteps falling hard, pounding to the beat of victory and defiance. There's a lot my husband doesn't know about me. If that conversation this morning has surprised him, then he hasn't seen anything yet.

My visitor arrives in the early afternoon, just as I am putting the finishing touches to my chosen attire. It takes me far longer than it should to get ready, and I surprise myself with just how desperate I am to make a good impression. I am also surprised by the abject poverty of options coming from my wardrobe. For the first time in months I am taking a good look at what I have to wear and I don't like what I find, my cupboards and drawers filled with little more than faded jeans, old shirts and baggy sweaters. Little wonder, I think bitterly, that Bert was so rude about my clothes. He was right; they are shabby, but then they are a reflection of me, and I have been shabby for a very long time.

Reluctantly I settle upon my least distressed-looking pair of flared trousers and a shirt fashioned with a bold floral design. The latter item is probably the single nicest thing in my wardrobe and I realise, to my shame, that I have hardly worn it. Until today it seemed too bright and too colourful for someone who for so long sought nothing other than to fade into the background, to disappear. Until today this shirt never seemed like the right thing to wear. Now it feels like the only thing I can wear – quite literally, in fact, since a rigorous examination of my cupboards has revealed that I have no other choices. I fasten the buttons and smooth down the collar just as the photographer knocks at the door. I glance at myself in the mirror and let out a slow, uneven breath, casting a final, critical eye over my appearance. I hope it is enough. I hope that I am enough. My mind preoccupied with doubts, I run downstairs and answer the door.

Thankfully, my worries about the photographer's visit prove to be unfounded. Emma's warm manner and gentle enthusiasm fills my home within minutes, reassuring me and putting me at my ease. As soon as she comes inside she throws her arms around me just like we are old friends, telling me that she is so pleased to meet me and so excited to see my work. She is lovely, I'd guess around ten years younger than me, with long wavy blonde hair and gorgeous bright blue eyes. After spending so long critiquing my wardrobe I find myself carefully studying her clothes; an impeccable pair of bell bottomed jeans paired with a beautiful embroidered blouse, and a matching bandana tied around her head. The bandana reminds me of Meg; it gives Emma the same hippy appearance, although that is where the similarities end. Emma might have only been in my home for a few moments, but she radiates an openness and light which I have never seen in Meg. My enigmatic friend might dress like a free spirit, but her dark, sorrowful eyes and cryptic words about lost love suggest that she is anything but. Shaking off thoughts of Meg, I decide that I like Emma's style and I make a mental note to try to find a blouse like hers. If I can ever pluck up enough courage to take some more money from Bert's stash and venture back into town, of course.

I lead Emma up to the mural, watching with stunned pride as she gushes admiration almost as soon as she enters the room. First Anna, then Meg and now Emma; the only three people to have really looked at this mural, and all of them have had such a strong and positive response. It really is hard to believe. It really is quite overwhelming.

"So tell me," Emma says, turning her gaze back on me, "what's the story with this piece? What's it about? What made you want to paint it?"

I feel my cheeks begin to burn in response to the sudden onslaught of questions. "I, er…I…" My mouth feels dry and my words falter.

Emma gives me a sympathetic smile. "Sorry, I didn't mean to interrogate you. It's just that usually I like to get a bit of background first, about the artist I'm working with and about their work. It helps me to work out how best to do the shoot, what sort of pictures to take, and of course, how best to include the artist."

My eyes widen with surprise. "You want to take photos of me as well?"

"Yes, of course," she replies. "I apologise; I probably wasn't very clear about that on the phone, was I? I'm really keen that this project is about artists as well as the art they create. I want to reflect each artist's life, from the exciting to the mundane, to bring out a sense of what inspires them, what drives the artist to create. I also want to try and make it fun, to reflect each individual personality." She looks at me, her face straight with concern. "Is that alright? Oh, I do hope so! Your work is wonderful, Eleanor. I'm really keen to capture it, and you."

I hesitate for a moment, watching as the pleading look grows in

Emma's eyes. "I'm sorry. I've just never thought of myself as the subject of anything." I gesture helplessly at my clothes. "I'm not exactly dressed for the occasion either, am I?"

Emma glances briefly at my clothing. "Is that what you would normally wear, you know, just on an average day at home?"

I give a little laugh. "No. To be truthful, I'd probably be wearing some faded old jeans and a paint-splattered t-shirt. I only put these on because you were coming over." I bite my lip, realising how pathetic that sounds.

Emma puts her arm around my shoulder in a gesture which once again reminds me of Meg. Instead of feeling reassured I feel even more ridiculous. "Listen," I begin, "I'm really sorry to have wasted your time, but perhaps it's best if we don't do this."

"Eleanor," she says to me, so close that I can feel her breath on my neck, "your work is brilliant. You are brilliant. It would be a real shame not to at least give this a try. How about you change into something which makes you feel more comfortable, then we can try some shots and have a little chat about your work? Once I've developed the photos I'll come back and we can have a look at them. If at that point you don't like what I've done, then they never have to see the light of day, I promise."

I take a deep, considered breath. "Alright," I reply. "If you promise…"

She releases me from her grasp and gives me a cheeky grin. "I do solemnly swear it," she says. "So you've absolutely nothing to lose. And besides, I know already that we are going to do something amazing here today. I know that you are going to love these shots."

I return her smile with hesitation, still wondering what on earth I am getting myself into. "I hope you're right," is all I can manage in reply.

17

Harry
January 2018

That night I sleep fitfully, my rest disturbed by the wind outside as it howls and whistles through the gaps in the aged windowpanes. When I dream what I see is as vivid as it is disturbing; horrid images of that woman, the one Eleanor decided to paint on the wall, the one with the black hair and haunting eyes. Except, in my dreams she is not confined to the wall but living, breathing, moving; a hellish mannequin made flesh, following me, trying to talk to me although I cannot hear what she has to say. In the end she grows angry with me; I see the rage burn red in her gaze and she starts to scream. It is then that I can hear her; in fact, her cries are all I can hear, the pained, anguished sound echoing through my slumber and continually bringing me back to the surface of wakefulness. When I wake for the final time and see that there is daylight outside, I am relieved to finally make my escape. For all that I enjoyed myself yesterday, for all that I felt delight in seeing Eleanor's work, I wish that I'd never uncovered her.

I wish that Eleanor had never painted her.

I drag myself out of bed, wrapping myself in my warm dressing gown to keep out the biting chill which greets me. I shiver and touch the radiator, expecting that the ancient boiler has given up completely, but to my surprise it feels warm. How is that possible, when the room is so cold?

"Bloody heating system in this place is useless," I mutter. At least now I know there's firewood outside. It's Sunday; it's freezing, and I have no plans after yesterday's hard graft. Perhaps a day spent in my pyjamas and keeping warm in front of the fire is just what I need.

I make myself some tea and toast, taking care all the while not to look at that woman on the wall. I toy with the idea of covering her up again, but then decide it would be a shame not to see the rest of the mural, which is really very pretty. Still unnerved I don't linger in the kitchen, instead taking my breakfast to the living room and lighting a fire with the leftover wood from last night.

Last night. My thoughts linger there as I eat, a nervous flutter occurring deep in my stomach every time I think about how our night ended. The dancing; the wine; the fire; the whispered words. I wanted more, I know I did, and yet I know I shouldn't. I hardly know Daniel, and even if I did, I should not allow this to go any further. I'm not here to fall for anyone; I'm here to sort out this place and get on with my life. Daniel's questions yesterday made me realise that I'm free, that once this house is sold I can go anywhere, I can do anything. But I have to keep the promise I made to myself, the day she found out about us, the day I left him for good. I have to be alone. I deserve to be alone after what I did.

Anxious for distraction, I pick up one of Mum's stories, tucking my feet up on the sofa as I begin to read. Sadly, today's instalment of the 'Margaret' series provides little comfort. Until now I have relished reading Mum's uplifting, adventurous tales, but in this one the story takes an altogether murkier turn. The title, Margaret is Betrayed, should have been enough of a warning for me. Margaret's starry-eyed love for the artist, who Mum never names, is shattered when she discovers his infidelity with several of the beautiful models who pose for his work. When she confronts him, the artist admits his liaisons freely but denies any wrongdoing, telling Margaret that this is the life she has chosen with him. Broken and with nowhere to turn, Margaret attempts suicide but is saved by another woman in the commune who urges her to find the remedy for her fractured heart in revenge. Despite the heavy, emotive subject matter, Mum's prose is so cool and factual that it feels unnervingly detached, which only adds to the sense of foreboding. I finish reading, shaking my head in disbelief. Where did she get such an idea, and at such a young age? Surely this sort of subject matter was far beyond her years at the time, and yet she handles it with such objective maturity. I don't know whether to be impressed or if I should wonder about Mum's state of mind. I take another bite of my breakfast and put the story away. That's enough reading for one day.

"Sore head after all that wine last night?" Bert's disapproving tone booms at me and I almost drop my toast in alarm.

"You're going to give me a heart attack doing that!" I reply. "So you're speaking to me again, are you?"

"You're the one who said you needed some space. And you told me to keep quiet while you were entertaining that fella."

"You know his name is Daniel," I bite back, "and I wasn't entertaining him, he was helping me as you suggested he might, remember?"

"Looked like you two were getting up to more than a bit of DIY."

"Oh, so you were spying on me then!" I feel my hackles rising. Why is it that conversations with Bert always end up infuriating me?

"I stayed quiet. I was just keeping an eye on you. You are my granddaughter, after all."

The concern in his voice touches my heart and I relent a little. "Alright," I say, "although I am a grown woman. I'm perfectly capable of looking after myself."

"From where I was standing, it looked as though you were going to end up in bed with him."

My cheeks burn and I can't decide if it's due to indignant rage or embarrassment that there may be a modicum of truth in Bert's words. "He's my neighbour! He's just trying to be a friend to me." I cross my arms over my chest, taking a defensive stance against the invisible, unknown quantity hovering somewhere in my living room. "I don't have to justify myself to you."

Bert laughs. "No, you're right, you don't. But take it from me as a hot-blooded male: that man is smitten with you. He's got that whole 'love at first sight' thing going on in his eyes. If you keep encouraging him, there can only be one outcome."

"A former hot-blooded male," I correct him. "In case you've forgotten, you're dead."

"Trust me, that's not something I'm likely to forget." His words are more muted, and for a moment I feel bad for subduing him with a reminder of the hard truth.

We are both silent then, the atmosphere hanging heavily between us as we both consider the argumentative turn our conversation has taken once again. I think about apologising for my unkind comment, but something stops me. Perhaps it's stubbornness, or perhaps it's an acknowledgement that Bert's own rude remarks probably make us even, but either way I keep my words to myself.

"Harriet, if you like the man there's no shame in it." Bert's tone is more conciliatory this time. "I mean, he's a bit older than you but there's nothing wrong with that. You're single, after all, aren't you? Well, that's what I heard you tell him."

I throw my arms up in despair. "Is there any part of last night that you didn't listen to, Bert?"

"I told you, I was keeping an eye on you. You told him that someone broke your heart. Is that why you came up here?"

"I'm not discussing this with you."

"Well, I think you need to discuss it with someone. It might as well be me. It's not like I can tell anyone, is it?"

I hesitate, but I know he's right. Thoughts about Mark, the message he sent me, the messages she sent me, the confusion it all causes me to feel about Daniel swirl around my mind. It would be good to get it off my chest. "I didn't say that my heart was broken," I tell him. "I said hearts were broken. And yes, if I'm honest with you, I came up here to escape."

"Escape from what?"

I take a deep breath, composing myself, trying to bring myself to talk about it, to say words aloud which have spun around in my head for weeks. "Mark was married," I tell him. "To my friend, Deborah. My very good and loyal friend, Deborah. My relationship with Mark, it…it was an affair."

"Oh. I see."

I screw up my face, feeling almost physical pain as I force myself to confront this. "No, I don't think you do. You don't know the agony my actions have caused. Deborah and I go back years. When Dad died, she became all I had; she helped me pick up the pieces of my life. Then she met and married Mark – he's older than her, older than both of us. Everything was fine until I found myself out of work just over a year ago. Once again Deborah was there, and she asked Mark to give me a job in his hotel. We…we got close, working long hours and late nights together. One thing led to another, and…well, you can imagine the rest. The worst of it was, it wasn't a one-off. This went on for months – lying, sneaking around, betraying Deborah time and time again. And all the while I knew how wrong it was, but it was like I just couldn't stop myself. It ended when she caught us together at Christmastime. It was then that I decided to come here, to escape – as if I could ever really escape my shame and my guilt," I add bitterly.

Bert is quiet for several long, agonising minutes, and I begin to wonder if he's fled the scene after everything I've just told him. I wouldn't blame him if he had, if he decides never to talk to me again. Who would want a granddaughter like me – someone so deceitful, so callous, so treacherous? My heart sinks. I can only imagine what Daniel would think if he knew.

"I had an affair." He speaks so quietly that at first I think I've misheard him. I want to believe I've misheard him. "Your grandmother found out about it, too. That's why we left

Manchester and moved to Kirtlebeck."

For a moment I just sit and stare, dumbstruck by his admission as surprise, sadness and pity run through me. Poor Eleanor. No wonder she looked so miserable in so many of those photos. She must have been in such pain, such anguish. She must have been humiliated. My thoughts creep back to the messages on my phone. She must have been all the things which Deborah is right now.

"Aren't you going to say anything?" Bert tries to prompt me. "I suppose we're not so different, you and I. Turns out we both loved the wrong people."

I'm about to argue, to refute his words, to attempt to frame my wrongdoing as somehow less than his. But then I realise that he's right; he betrayed his wife, I betrayed my friend, and neither act can be the lesser of the two evils. We both sacrificed our loyalties for a misplaced love, and then we both ran away to this place to hide, to seek sanctuary while our worlds fell apart. The depth of our similarities strikes me then, and it is almost too much to bear.

"Eleanor had a breakdown when we came here." My silence sparks a monologue from Bert and the story begins to pour from him. "The paintings – the ones you've uncovered on the walls – she did those in 1972, not long after we moved in. She was in a dark place at that time."

"A place you drove her to." My condemning tone speaks as much to my own guilt as it does to his.

"Yes. Yes, perhaps. I couldn't stand to be around those paintings. I could hardly bring myself to look at them. They say more about what I did to her than Eleanor could ever have put into words."

"Bert, who's the woman on the kitchen wall?"

"I don't know."

"You don't know? How can you not know?"

"Well, she's no one I ever knew. And I told you, I couldn't bear to even glance at those paintings, never mind ask Eleanor questions about them. Maybe she isn't anyone. Maybe Eleanor invented her to, you know, represent something."

I shudder, my mind wandering again to the darkness in the woman's gaze, the horror of the dreams I suffered last night. "She seems too vivid, too real to be made up," I say. "Maybe Eleanor had a friend, someone you didn't know about. Maybe Eleanor kept secrets from you, too."

Bert attempts a laugh but it is hollowed by sadness. "Secrets. Everyone has secrets."

Upstairs several doors slam shut, and I just about jump out of my skin. I clasp my hands over my chest, readying myself to get up and investigate. Outside it's still a windy day. I must have left a window open. This place is draughty at the best of times.

"I'll be back in a moment," I say to Bert. "I'd better go and sort this out before…"

A great, dull thud halts my words and stops me in my tracks. I look up at the ceiling, my heart racing, banging hard in time to the sound of footsteps in Eleanor's room above. The air around me grows ice cold, and I watch in mesmerised horror as the fire dims in the grate, its bright embers smothered and then extinguished by some unseen, oppressive force.

"Bert," I begin. "Bert, are you still there. Is this – is this you?"

No answer.

"Bert," I repeat, trying to reassure myself with a forced, incredulous chuckle. "Bert! Cut out the ghost crap now, you're frightening me."

Still no answer.

Above me the footsteps grow louder, banging down hard on the ceiling. Across the hallway another door slams. Then another. Then another.

Oh God, I have to get out of this place.

I run to the living room door, which I had closed to keep the heat in the room. I try to turn the old brass doorknob but it is jammed in place. Desperately I pull at it, harder and harder until my fingers are sore from the effort, but still it doesn't turn. Tears of frustration and terror race down my cheeks as I begin instead to bang on the door, hitting it hard with my fists. The banging above me continues, finding a rhythm with my own thuds, at once frightening and mocking me.

Who is this? What do they want?

Why are they in Eleanor's room? Does this have something to do with the mural?

The banging stops and for a moment there is silence. I press my ear against the door, listening, my eyes wide, my breath ragged. The footsteps move along the corridor and down the stairs – thud, thud, thud. They draw closer.

They're outside the living room door.

Knock. Knock. Knock.

I try to scream but no sound emerges. Futilely I flee, seeking sanctuary next to the large living room windows. I slump down on the floor, drawing my knees under my chest and tucking my head into my folded arms. I squeeze my eyes shut. If I can't see it, it's not there. If I can't see it, I can't be scared.

"Bert," I whisper. "If you're there please help me. I knew there was someone else in this house. I'm right, aren't I? There's someone else here."

Still no answer.

The living room door opens and the footsteps approach. The air around me turns colder still, so cold that my whole body shakes and my teeth begin to chatter.

The footsteps stop. I feel eyes upon me.

"Whoever you are, I mean you no harm. Please don't hurt me." My voice is muffled by my arms but still I don't dare look up.

Icy fingers trace my hairline, stroke my head, caress my shoulder. Frozen breath besieges my ear with whispered words: "I'm disappointed in you. You're as bad as him."

Before I can digest the meaning of these words, before I can utter a response, a hand taps on the window and a familiar voice calls loud enough that I can hear it through the old single glazing. A voice I couldn't be more glad to hear. "Harry, it's me."

Around me the room grows warmer; I hear the fire roar back to life in the grate and I sense the icy presence withdraw. Reassured by the returning heat I finally dare to open my eyes, immediately turning around to see Daniel's face pressed against the window.

"Oh thank God," I say, dragging myself off the floor and running for the front door. Giddy relief rushes through me, my eyes are tear-strewn, my limbs are clumsy and my body is still shaking from my ordeal. But I don't care. I don't care about anything right now. I only care that I am safe and that Daniel is here.

I only care about seeking refuge from whatever it is that means me harm.

18

Eleanor
September 1972

Despite my initial misgivings I find that I enjoy my photoshoot, and as the afternoon wears on I grow more relaxed, placing myself entirely in Emma's hands and allowing her to direct me as she sees fit. Emma is so easy to work with; she is clearly passionate about her work and she is also highly professional, setting up scenes and enacting her ideas with confidence whilst being respectful of me and my art. As suggested I change into my daily attire, donning some old jeans and a paint-encrusted t-shirt, removing the little mascara I had applied to leave my face clear and devoid of makeup. Emma completes my messy, devil-may-care look by ruffling my overgrown short hair, and for some shots, even smearing paint on my arms and face.

"Just to leave everyone in no doubt that you are an artist," she giggles as she admires her handiwork.

"Very authentic," I agree.

We chat almost constantly throughout, pausing only for me to pose and smile at the required intervals. Emma's subtle efforts to find out more about her subject are not lost on me, but I find that I don't really mind opening up to her questioning to a certain extent.

I tell her about my family, about my daughter, about our relocation from Manchester to Kirtlebeck but I keep the story factual, I give her the bare bones, I leave the emotion out. When she asks about the origins of the mural I stick with the safe story, the tale of the restless artist stuck in an unfamiliar village and a house desperately needing renovation. A mural or two, I explain, seemed like the most obvious way to deploy my skills and brighten the place up a bit. I congratulate myself on my evasiveness, on my ability to wear a suitable mask, if only for an afternoon.

"So what does the mural represent?" she asks me. "What made you want to paint this particular mural on your bedroom wall?"

"Well, it's all about nature and the cosmos, I suppose. They're two of my favourite things so I thought I'd bring them together. It started as a piece about nature but then a friend suggested that it needed something more, some darker elements. Her comments inspired me to think bigger, and there's nothing larger or darker than space. Before I knew it, I had settled upon bringing the universe into my bedroom, so to speak. I'm a bit of a David Bowie fan so making my room into a space oddity wasn't an enormous leap of imagination." I laugh nervously at my weak attempt at humour.

"Wow," Emma remarks. "Sounds like you've got a good friend there. The cosmos part is certainly what draws the eye – it's dark and sombre in parts, but then there are the swirls of colour which totally capture the imagination. It really is stunning, Eleanor. Your husband and daughter must be very proud."

My face betrays me and for a moment the mask slips. Like the best interrogator, Emma notices straight away. "What?" she asks. "Don't tell me they don't like it?"

"My daughter loves it," I reply. "My husband, well, not so much."

"Really?" Emma asks, placing her camera down and coming to sit beside me. "Oh, do tell!"

I struggle to stifle a small snigger at her mischievous enthusiasm to hear my sorry tale. "It's ridiculous really. Bert was the one who suggested that I make this place my own, that I deploy my talents on its improvement. I suppose he just doesn't like what I've done very much."

"That's such a shame. So, what happens now? To the mural, I mean."

I shrug. "Nothing. It stays where it is."

"He hasn't asked you to paint over it? Not that I'm suggesting that you should, of course. In fact, you absolutely shouldn't."

I draw a deep breath. "No, he hasn't. Actually, he hasn't made any comment on this particular mural at all. Now, the first one I did, the one in the kitchen, that caused a fair bit of trouble and for a while I thought I might have to paint over it. But I haven't; instead, I've done another one and I'll probably do another now that this one is finished. I'd like to think that even if he doesn't like my work, he understands that this is something I need to do and is prepared to tolerate it," I add, my words sounding far more reasonable than I feel.

"But if he hasn't said anything about this mural, how do you know he doesn't like it?" Emma asks, her brow furrowed as she tries to make sense of what I am telling her.

"I think him moving out of our room tells me everything I need to know," I scoff.

Emma claps her hand over her mouth, her eyes wide with surprise. "Oh dear, Eleanor!" she exclaims through her fingers. "What a story! I am sorry that this is the price you're having to pay."

"I'm not sorry," I reply. "But I'd appreciate it if you'd keep what I just told you to yourself. We've just moved here as you know, and I like to keep these matters private."

"Of course," she promises. She gets back on her feet and stands, hands on hips, surveying my great work of art another time. "You know, what you've just told me makes me see this work so differently."

"It does?"

"Yes – I can see the anger in this piece now. I see the rebellion, the sense of lashing out and breaking free, just like those swirls of colour."

"I'm not sure that's what I was thinking when I painted it."

"It might not have been, but it's in there. I think that the way you feel always finds its way through in your work somehow. And the context in which you painted it; a new home, an unfamiliar place, a disapproving spouse, makes the act of painting this an act of defiance, don't you think?"

"I don't know. I've never thought of myself as much of a rebel."

Emma picks up her camera and smiles. "Well, you are. And we're going to capture that rebellious streak. Would you mind showing me the kitchen mural you mentioned? I'd like to photograph you with that one as well."

Her request takes me by surprise, and before I can stop them, the fragments of memories run unabated through my mind. The wine, the misery, the self-loathing. The epiphany of a dream, the frenzy of spontaneous brush-strokes, the loss of control and the triumph of creative passion. The colours splashed boldly all over my kitchen wall; the image which speaks of beauty, of mystery, of destruction, of pain.

Emma clearly notices the look of hesitation on my face. "If you'd rather just stick with this mural then that's fine. After all, this is the one you invited me to photograph."

"No it's okay," I reply, giving her a weak smile. "As you said, I've got nothing to lose. But I warn you, it's quite different to the bedroom mural."

"Now I am intrigued," she says, following me out of the room.

I lead her downstairs, my heart pounding hard as we go. If Emma wants to capture the personality of an artist, then there's certainly a different Eleanor to be found in this piece of art. The question I must ask myself is, is that Eleanor someone I want this friendly stranger, and indeed the rest of the world, to see?

Emma leaves just after three, giving me precious little time to get organised before Anna and her friends come in the door and start her birthday celebrations in earnest. As I dash around the kitchen filling jugs with juice and arranging a buffet of vol-au-vents, sandwiches and sausage rolls on to plates, my eyes creep back towards my first mural and my heart flutters. Before leaving, Emma assured me that she would be back in touch once she had developed the photos, to show me the results of our shoot and to get my assistance in choosing the best shots for the exhibition. At the mention of that word I had swallowed hard; as stupid as it sounds, I had forgotten that these photos would actually be placed on display, that I and my work would be part of something which people could come and see and admire or, indeed, critique.

Proving her astuteness once again, Emma picked up immediately on my hesitation. "It'll be alright," she promised me. "I won't include anything in the exhibition that you're not comfortable with."

"Where is this exhibition going to be?" I asked her.

"I'm still firming up the details," she replied, "but there's a community gallery in Lockerbie who are very interested in my project. I'm hoping the exhibit can be placed there in just a couple of weeks' time."

"Goodness," I replied my mouth growing increasingly dry, "that's no time at all."

"You're telling me!" she retorted with an amused smile. "It's been such a lot of work trying to pull all of this together, but it'll be worth it. Doing this project has brought me into contact with so many artists and craftspeople across the area; I can't wait to bring it all together in the exhibit and shine a light on their talent. And you never know, you might get a commission or two out of it," she added, winking at me.

"Oh, I'm not sure I should be let loose to paint on anyone's walls apart from my own," I answered as lightly as I could manage.

"Don't be so quick to put yourself down, Eleanor," Emma said. "You're a great artist with something interesting to say. Hopefully when you see these photos you'll start to recognise that about yourself."

I turn my back on my kitchen mural, brushing off her words. Part of me hopes that Emma is right, of course, that I will view the photos and myself in a positive light. But for now at least that part of me is silent, and the part which worries, which frets over what these pictures might look like and what they might reveal, takes over. It's that part of me which weighs heavily, which feels like a stone sunk deep into my stomach. I contemplate this feeling for a moment, frozen in the middle of the room, a plate of food in one hand and a jug of orange squash in the other. Then the front door clicks open and Anna and her friends burst in like a gust of wind, the silence of the house interrupted by their excitable voices. Immediately I respond, straightening my posture and fixing a relaxed expression on my face. Time to wear my mask again, I think. The mask of mother, of host, of happy housewife. The mask of contentment. The mask of joy. The mask which conveys to the world all the things I want them to see and conceals all the things I want to hide away.

"Hello girls, good day?" I call as I walk into the hall.

Cheerful young faces greet me and unthinkingly I mirror their smiles. Yes, I remind myself; pretending is easy. After all, I've been doing it for a long time.

Anna's party goes on until around eight o'clock, when parents come to collect their offspring in dribs and drabs. All are polite and gracious but reservedly so, prompting me to remember once again the consequences of locking myself away instead of getting to know the people here. The reminder is unwelcome and causes me to hanker after seeing the one friend I have made since arriving in Kirtlebeck, who I haven't seen since the day I completed my mural. As I start clearing away leftovers and washing the dishes I make a mental note to call by Thistle Cottage and check on the woman who, I suspect, is in need of a close confidante just as much as I am.

Bert arrives home just as I finish tidying up. He saunters in, characteristically weary, still wearing his oil-soaked overalls as though to prove to me that he has definitely been at work rather than committing yet more infidelity.

"The garage was busy today," he says, answering my quizzical stare as we meet in the hallway. "I barely stopped for a cuppa, never mind something to eat. Got halfway home and realised I still had this thing on."

"Yes, well, you'd better go and change," I say, my raised, disapproving eyebrow making it clear that this is an instruction rather than a suggestion. "The last thing we need is oil all over the walls."

"I don't know – you could always paint a picture with it, I suppose," he retorts with a chuckle.

I don't share his laughter but continue to stare, eyebrow still elevated, arms folded.

Bert clears his throat, apparently deciding to change tack. "Tell you what, I'll just take this off right now, then there's no risk to the walls, right?" he suggests, removing his overall and folding it over his arm. "Now, what's for dinner? I'm starving."

"Leftovers." I shrug the reply as I head back towards the kitchen. "Help yourself."

"Oh, of course," he says, following me. "How did Anna's party go?"

"Well, I think. She seems happy anyway."

"That's good. I thought she was in a really odd mood this morning."

"Was she?" I put the kettle on; not because I really want a cup of tea but because it's something to do.

"Yes," he says sullenly between bites of a sausage roll. "You probably didn't notice, but she didn't even give me a hug this morning after she opened her gifts. She always gives me a hug. I suppose now that she's a teenager she's too 'cool'." The way he emphasises the word 'cool' by creating quotation marks with his fingers almost makes me laugh out loud. Then I remember that I know the real reason why Anna has ceased to indulge in father-daughter cuddles and my sense of humour is immediately dampened.

"I hadn't noticed, no," I lie. "As you say, probably just all part of growing up."

Bert squirms against the kitchen counter, refusing to be pacified. "Do you think she knows anything about, well, you know…?"

I stare at him blankly. "About what?" I ask, trying to torture him, trying to force him to say it.

"About what I did," he sighs. "About my unfaithfulness."

"Oh yes, she knows," I answer, holding him in my cool gaze.

"What? You told her?"

"Of course not. She overheard us arguing about it a few weeks ago."

Bert frowns, clearly trying to recollect. "Oh! You mean when you were drunk and yelling at me about it? Well yes, thinking about it now I'm surprised that the whole damn village doesn't know."

"Don't try to turn this around on me," I fire back at him through gritted teeth. "I'm not the one who fucked someone else in our marital bed. I didn't lie, or betray, or humiliate you. You're not the victim here, Bert."

"Oh, and you are?" Bert throws his arms up in exasperation. "You're not exactly without your flaws, are you, Eleanor?"

"I've never betrayed you." I stare at him hard, unblinking. I will not be subdued. I will not cry this time.

"No, you've just made my life a bloody misery, every step of the way. If I looked elsewhere for love, for comfort, for support, it's because I learned long ago that my wife is incapable of giving those things."

My heart clatters painfully in my chest, his words wounding me. "If I'm so dreadful, how do you cope now?" I ask him, wearing the sarcastic tinge to my voice like a suit of armour.

His dark eyes bore into me as he wipes crumbs from his moustache. I know him well enough to realise that he's weighing up my question. He's trying to decide what I might know. He's trying to figure out how best to lie to me. "What sort of a ridiculous question is that?"

"Well, you've left her behind, haven't you?" I continue, pursuing him with a sick sort of glee that I really ought to be ashamed of. "You're stuck up here with your awful, dead-hearted wife now. How on earth do you manage? Maybe you should get yourself another bit on the side, another pretty young thing to help ease your suffering…"

Bert bangs his fist down hard on the counter and despite myself, I jump. A heavy silence follows, Bert gazing at his hand as though he is unsure what to do with it next. After a moment he rubs it, soothing his skin and retreating from his anger. "I'm not going to continue this discussion with you, Eleanor. It does neither of us any good, and it's certainly not the sort of thing I want our daughter to be hearing. I think our overheard rows have done enough damage, don't you?"

He walks away, leaving me standing, suspended, at a loss as to what to say or do. I forget all about the boiled kettle, leaving it to go cold as I ponder our hopeless impasse. How do you handle a man who closes down a conversation? How do you confront a husband who so adeptly sidesteps your anger? How do you challenge someone whose eyes fill with cold indifference even as he accuses you of harbouring the very same darkness in your soul?

"You know, I thought this morning we were starting to get somewhere." He calls to me from the hallway, but he doesn't turn around. "But, as always, you're just not prepared to try to be happy. You just can't let things go."

It's only when I hear his footsteps landing heavily on the staircase that I close the kitchen door and allow my tears to fall. I sit down, laying my head on the kitchen table, sniffling silently. Why do I do it? Why do I begin these discussions, why do I try to goad him? It always ends in the same way, and it never does me any good. Why, instead of talking to him in riddles, making twisted jests about taking up with another woman, can I not bring myself just to ask him the straight question: why is she here? What on earth possessed you to move us all this way, tearing us from our lives, only to install your mistress in a cottage in the village? What is it that you're not telling me? What is it that I don't understand?

I look up from the table and dry my eyes, steeling my resolve. Bert was right about one thing: I can't let go, and I'm never going to be able to let go until I get to the bottom of all of this. It's time to close this part of my life down for good. It's time to have answers. It's time to get closure.

It's time to find her.

19

Harry
January 2018

Under any other circumstances I would have felt mortified at throwing myself into a man's arms like some sort of damsel in distress, especially when it is a man I've known for mere days. Yet when I open the door to Daniel and embrace him like my life depends on it I feel nothing but comfort, warmth and familiarity. I feel nothing but good. I feel like I've known him all my life, and that finding myself in his embrace is the most right and natural thing in the world.

He gathers me in without hesitation, holding me with strength and acceptance. Only his words to me betray his surprise: "Harry? What on earth is going on?"

I can't help it then; the fear, the terror, the shame all comes pouring out of me, a sweeping tide of emotion I cannot hope to stem. "Did you not see it?" I sob, my voice muffled as I press my face against his chest. "Did you not see that...that thing in my living room just now?"

"What thing?" he asks. "All I could see was you, sitting under the window. What were you doing down there, anyway? I knocked at the door and there was no answer. I was...well, I was worried about you."

His concern only makes me cry harder, and for a few minutes I am rendered speechless, soaking the front of his jacket with my tears as he gently strokes my hair. If I wasn't so upset the intimacy of the moment would have surely made me retreat. But right now I need his care, his affection. I need him, more than anything else in the world.

"Shall we go inside?" he whispers.

I nod reluctantly, still fearful that something untoward is lurking in the house. Perhaps sensing my hesitation Daniel takes the lead, grasping my hand tightly as we go into the living room. My legs feel weak as I sit down on the sofa and I look around me, swallowing hard. The room is so warm and cosy, and it all looks so normal; the fire burns again in the grate, and not a thing is out of place. Perhaps I imagined it; perhaps I fell asleep and had a bad dream. Perhaps there was nothing in here, after all.

Daniel sits beside me, his hand still gripping mine. "What happened Harry? You look like you've seen a ghost."

I shake my head, exhaling a shuddery breath. "I don't know, I…something was in here with me. Something which made a lot of noise and made the room turn cold. Something which touched me, which spoke to me. I can't explain it but…" I hesitate, suddenly realising how crazy I sound.

"But?" Daniel prompts me.

I close my eyes, almost unwilling to acknowledge these words as my own. "I think there's something in this house, and I think it wants to frighten me."

Daniel sits back a little. I keep my eyes closed but I can sense him studying me, searching for what to say. I prepare myself for an onslaught of denial, of rationality, of lectures about the dangers of spending too much time alone. God knows, these are all thoughts which are racing through my head right now, competing with the ones which tell me that I know what I saw, I know what I heard. I know there is something terrible in this house.

"I was joking about ghosts before, but do you think that's what it was?"

I open my eyes then, immediately meeting his bright blue gaze. "Do you think I'm losing the plot?"

"No, of course not. I mean you could have dreamt it. It is warm in here – maybe you nodded off in front of the fire…"

I shake my head. "No, I don't think so. I was talking to Bert when it happened." The words slip out before I realise what I'm saying. Shit, shit, shit.

Daniel frowns. "Who's Bert?"

I take a deep breath. There's no way around this; I'm going to have to come clean. "Bert is my grandfather. My very rude, very dead grandfather."

"You've seen your grandfather's ghost?" His brows are raised and I can't decide if it's surprise or disbelief written on his face.

"Not seen, no, but he talks to me. I hear his voice. I know that sounds insane – it probably is insane."

Daniel looks over his shoulder, as though seeking someone who isn't there. "Is he talking to you now?"

"No. He stopped talking when it happened and I haven't heard from him since."

"Maybe it was Bert who was trying to frighten you."

"I don't think so. I mean, he's good at making a nuisance of himself but I don't think he means me any harm. Although when I next speak to him I'm going to give him a piece of my mind for disappearing and leaving me to the mercy of whatever it was." I shudder again at the thought of it. Daniel moves his hand up to my shoulder as though he's trying to hold me steady. "The noise it made, the coldness it cast into this room, the way it whispered in my ear – it was horrid." I look around, suddenly fearful that even recounting the tale could provoke it to come back.

"What did it say?"

"It told me that it was disappointed in me, that I'm as bad as him."

"What do you think that means?"

I shrug. "I don't know," I reply, although even as I say it, the guilt which niggles at me tells me that I do know, I do understand its meaning. I know what it must have heard me tell Bert. I know which confession of mine spurred it into such malevolent action. "I wonder if it was Eleanor," I add, thinking aloud.

"I doubt it. Why would your grandmother want to frighten you like that?"

"Maybe she's pissed off that I'm talking to Bert. They didn't exactly have a happy marriage, you know. He told me so himself." I don't elaborate any further. The last thing I want to tell him is what Bert did to her. The last thing I want him to know is how alike Bert and I really are.

Daniel looks at me thoughtfully, tilting his head to one side as he tucks a stray lock of hair behind my ear. His touch makes my stomach flip, even though the look in his eyes tells me that he thinks I've lost my mind. "I can't see Eleanor ever disliking you, Harry. I'm sure that if she was here, she would feel blessed to know you."

"Thank you," I reply, giving him a grateful smile. "Thank you for listening to me. I know you must think that I'm crazy."

Those fingers trace my cheek before dropping back down by his side. "I don't think anything of the sort. I think you're lovely, Harry, and I…" he allows his words to trail off, his sentence finished instead by the look in his eyes. For the briefest second I see his longing, his sadness, and then it is gone.

"You what?" I say with shallow breath, willing him to continue. Willing him to touch my hair and my cheek again. Willing him to kiss me.

He grins, breaking the spell with forced cheer. "I almost forgot why I came over. I thought you might like to go for a walk with me." He points to a rucksack which I hadn't even noticed him place on the floor. "I even brought sandwiches. What do you say? From the sounds of what has happened to you this morning, it would be good for you to get out of here for a while."

I nod in agreement. Daniel's right; some fresh air and a change of scenery would do me the world of good. I've spent so long inside this house, wrapped up in its contents and its mysteries that I've barely taken a moment to look outwards, to appreciate what lies beyond in this quiet, picturesque corner of Scotland. I don't plan to stay here long; indeed, after today's events I wish to leave even sooner. It would be a shame not to explore the area while I can. It would be a shame to confine myself here with only fear and ghosts for company.

"Sounds like a great idea," I reply, seizing my opportunity to escape for a while.

Daniel takes me down the lane, his hands stuffed into the pockets of his jacket in defence against the biting cold. I'm glad of my thick coat and woollen gloves, and can't help but think that he looks a little under-dressed for the time of year. He talks all the while, pointing out all the cottages which populate the lane and telling me anecdotes about the people who live in them, all the people in this small community whom I have never met and frankly, probably never will meet. More interesting to me are his stories about the cottages themselves. There are no house numbers around here, he tells me. All the cottages have names, mostly taken from flowers and plants: rose, flora, lavender, heather. The only property which doesn't, which bucks the trend, is the big house at the end of the lane. My house – the house at Kirtlebeck End. Apparently it needs no grander name than that.

When we reach his home, the white one with the tall windows, I half-expect him to stop, to perhaps suggest that we call in and see his mum, and I'm disappointed when he doesn't. I don't know why, but I find myself suddenly taken with the idea of stepping into his world, of meeting his family, of discovering more about him. I remind myself to mind my own business. After all, my determination to solve mysteries hasn't exactly yielded positive results so far.

"Your house is nice," I remark as we hurry past.

"I had it built myself," he replies. "There was a derelict cottage on the land; it had been empty for years and was a bit of an eyesore. Folk used to complain about it, so when I moved here I decided to buy it for demolition and have my own place built from scratch."

"I'm impressed," I tell him, wishing to see inside now even more. "So if all the cottages here are named after flowers and plants, what name did you choose?"

"Thistle Cottage," he replies, "after the cottage that stood there before."

"Thistle Cottage," I repeat. "How lovely."

With a final glance at Daniel's unexplored haven I walk on, bitten by cold air, curiosity and the strangest desire to have seen the shell which stood before Daniel brought beauty to bear.

Daniel takes me off the lane and on to a woodland path which, he explains, leads all the way to Annan if followed to its conclusion. Partway along the path begins to chart the course of the river in an area so beautiful I could gasp. Even at this time of the year, when the landscape is all browns and whites it is stunning, and I can only imagine how magnificent it looks in full bloom, illuminated by the summer sun. For a moment I feel a stab of regret that I won't be here to see it, that by then the house will be sold, that I will have left this place and gone far away for good. Then I remind myself that as much as I might feel drawn to this place, that I might have found refuge here, there are a growing number of reasons to get away.

As though sensing that my thoughts are taking flight, Daniel slips an arm around my shoulders and tethers me to this moment. I don't pull away, even though I know I should. I keep allowing him to touch me, and he keeps wanting to; there is only one place this leads and it's not somewhere I should allow us to go. But I know, as he knows, that the urge for comfort, to not be alone, is stronger. Escape, refuge, solace – those are the things I truly came here for. I was a fool to think I could find them simply by remaining on my own. I'm a fool now if I think I can ever find them in that big, old house, devoid of life and filled with ghosts.

"You're beautiful, Harry."

His compliment breaks my train of thought and I stare at him, surprised. "Did you bring me out here just to seduce me?" City girl bolshiness takes over for a moment, and I disappoint myself as I hear such attitude slip from my lips.

He recoils, rebuilding his defences. "No. No! I brought you here because this is where you needed to be, and I'm sorry, I just got caught up in the moment." He tries to recover himself with a laugh but I see the sadness appear again in his eyes.

"I'm sorry; that was unkind of me. I'm just…I don't know, I…"

The touch of his lips stems the flow of my words. His mouth against mine is cool, cooler than I expected, and I suspect that we're both chilled by the freezing air around us. His touch is gentle and delicate, soft and lingering; it is not intrusive, it doesn't ask for more. The two of us remain there, pressed together, suspended in the moment, neither of us daring to move lest we break what we're clinging to beyond the point of all repair.

When we finally part our breath clouds us and the kiss evaporates into the ether.

He strokes my cheek with a tenderness beyond reason, given we've known each other barely any time at all. I watch the mist as it gathers in that blue gaze and wonder what he wants to say to me. This is the Daniel I've glimpsed only once before; sorrowful, vulnerable, filled with longing. Now he is here, his soul as bare as the trees around us, and I can hardly breathe for the intensity of him.

"If only we had met in another time," he says to me.

Those are not the words I was expecting. "What do you mean?"

"God, if I had met you before, things could have been different."

"Before what? I don't understand."

"I'm sorry for kissing you. It was wrong of me, but I just had to. Since I saw you that day on the lane, I haven't been able to think about anything else. It's why I keep coming back – I tell myself to leave you alone, but it's like I can't help myself. If you'd sent me away it would have been easier, but you invited me in, you asked for my help, you saw me how I wanted to be seen, and I…I'm mesmerised by you."

I stare at him, my mind lost in his riddles. "I don't want you to leave me alone," I mutter, taking him by the hand. "I don't want you to stop kissing me."

"But you're going to leave."

"Someday, yes. But not yet. There's still work to be done."

He nods. "There are still questions to be answered."

"Yes, indeed," I reply, grim-faced. It has long since dawned on me that I may never get the answers I seek. I may never know the truth. I may never know my family at all.

Much later we walk back to Kirtlebeck End in peaceful silence, both unable to resurrect the easy humour between us but equally content to do without it. I absorb my surroundings once more, enjoying the grey, dim light as it fades in its march towards night, darkness growing in its place, the rising moon creating shadows and mystery around us. I look left and right, examining the little cottages on the lane, all lit up inside now, the glow of lights peeking around drawn curtains. Only the house at the top of the lane, my house, remains in darkness. As we draw near I feel my throat grow tight and dry. I don't want to go inside. I don't want to be in this place alone. Not tonight. Not ever again.

I turn to face Daniel, asking him the inevitable question before I can talk myself out of it: "Will you stay?"

His response comes without hesitation. "Yes, of course I'll stay."

The relief I feel is enormous and unspoken, but I know he senses it. I realise that's why he couldn't say no, even when we both know that this only leads us further down a path that neither of us is sure we should tread at all. In gratitude I kiss his hand, lightly and with a timidity which surprises me. I've never been backwards when it comes to men, but there is something about his words earlier which strikes at my core, which speaks to my own sadness, my own regrets.

We go inside, put the lights on and light a fire. We eat, we drink, we talk, and our homely glow joins all the others as we spend our evening reassured by each other's company, banishing cold, banishing darkness, banishing solitude.

Banishing unwelcome spirits for tonight, at least.

20

Eleanor
September 1972

I am forced to sit on my hands, figuratively speaking at least, for the whole long and rainy weekend which follows Anna's birthday celebrations. Mercifully Bert spends most of the daylight hours at work, leaving Anna and I to our own devices in the house. The temperature outside drops by a degree or two, exposing for the first time the difficulties in keeping such an old home warm. Inwardly I curse the place for not having central heating, a luxury which we had installed in our home in Manchester not long before Bert made us up sticks and move. To combat the cold Anna and I decamp to the living room, lighting the fire, cosying up together in front of the television and watching nothing much. We make a sorry pair, Anna suffering from the inevitable flat feeling which follows the euphoria of a party, whilst I am restless, willing it to be Monday morning when the house will be empty and I can get on with my mission.

Perhaps sensing my strange mood, Anna tries to draw me out, but with little success. "Are you thinking about a new project, Mum?" she asks me, guessing that my agitation is rooted in a creative urge.

I give her a gentle smile and reach over to stroke her hair. "Not really, sweetheart," I reply. "To be honest, I think I need to give painting a rest for a little while."

Anna makes a face at me but says nothing, and we both continue staring blankly at the box in the corner of the room. My daughter might be disappointed, but it's true; for now, at least, my head is bereft of inspiration and my thoughts are decidedly focussed elsewhere. Right now, all I want to do is get to the bottom of Bert's sordid affair, to figure out where this sorry business leaves me and to take control of my life, once and for all.

By Monday my impatience soars, and I can't get Anna or Bert out of the house fast enough. Bert makes some snide remark, reckoning that there must be a plain wall somewhere in desperate need of painting, which I ignore, of course. Anna looks hurt as I usher her towards the front door, telling her that she'll be late, even though we both know that's not true.

"My friends won't even be waiting for me yet," she complains as I hand her coat to her.

"Well, don't keep them waiting," I reply. "Be prompt, for a change."

"Don't I even get a kiss?" Her doe eyes are almost too much to bear.

I give her a peck on the cheek. "Of course. Now off you go."

I watch her for a moment as she makes her way slowly towards the lane. The weather, at least, is crisp and bright, with the sun making a welcome reappearance after the weekend's dismal performance. I give her an encouraging wave as she glances over her shoulder at me. I can't feel too bad about making her hang about outside when the day is so perfect.

"At least you get asked for a kiss goodbye," Bert grumbles as he pushes past me. "I feel like I don't exist sometimes."

I don't even deign his remarks with a response. I can't; I don't have anything nice or comforting to say. After all, if Bert feels left out in the cold, then it is a misfortune entirely of his own making.

Once Bert and Anna are out of sight, I waste no time in getting ready to put my plan into action. After hurriedly washing, dressing and making a vague attempt at clearing all the dishes dumped on the kitchen worktop, I decide that I can't wait any longer. I throw on my coat and rush out of the front door, leaving all manner of domestic chaos in my wake. Today I don't care; today I have more important matters to attend to.

I walk at a pace down the lane, enjoying the fresh morning air as its awakening chill fills my lungs. At least the weather has decided to show me some good favour; I can't imagine trying to do this in the pouring rain. After a few moments I arrive at my first stop. I pause, enjoying the sight of Thistle Cottage as the autumnal sunlight sets its white walls aglow. The last time I visited it was the middle of the night and the place was shrouded in trees and gloom. How different it looks in the daytime, I think. How much more inviting. How much less mysterious.

Tentatively I knock at the door and await an answer. I feel nervous, although I'm not sure why. I tell myself it's because Meg isn't expecting me and I feel awkward about turning up unannounced at her home again. I suspect, however, that in fact my anxiety stems from knowing what Meg's response to my plan is likely to be. Deep down I know she won't like it, and I know that it's going to take all of my powers of persuasion to get her involved. My worry heightens when my first knock goes unanswered. I wander round the side to a window, trying to peer in and spot signs of life. Heavy net curtains, however, obscure my view. Where could she be? Like me, Meg isn't someone who has many places to go. She usually can be relied upon to be here, in her cottage, or at my front door, or wherever I need her to be…

"Meg!" I return to the front door and call through the letter box. "Meg, are you in? It's Eleanor." The silence which answers me makes my heart pound even harder in my chest. I need her. I can't do this without her.

"Can I help you?" an elderly man walking his dog calls to me from the lane. It's so unusual to see anyone walking up the village's end that I startle.

"No, it's okay, I…" I stammer, instinctively stepping back from the door. "I'm just looking for Meg, that's all, but she mustn't be in."

The man shakes his head at me, a look of concern flashing across his lined face. "Meg?" he says, repeating her name as a question. "I don't think I know a Meg round here."

Before either of us have a chance to say anything further, the door creaks open and I'm greeted by the sight of my friend peering around it, her eyes heavy and her face pale.

"Come inside," she instructs, her voice a hollow rasp as she grabs me by the hand. I have time only to give the man the briefest of obliging nods before I am pulled into Thistle Cottage.

Meg shuts the door behind us and leans hard against it, closing her eyes and taking several laboured breaths. I wait at her side in silence, unsure what to do or say. The light inside Meg's home is dim, but it is enough to illuminate the fact that my friend does not look like her usual self. Gone is the bright smile, the spring in her step. This Meg looks weary, weak, down-trodden. This Meg looks like I felt when I first met her.

"Meg?" I whisper. "What's the matter? Are you unwell?"

"Bloody nosy neighbours," she says, still not opening her eyes. "Bloody people always sticking their noses in where they don't belong."

"What do you mean?" I ask. "Who's been bothering you? If you mean that man out there, he had no idea who you were, said he'd never heard of you."

Her eyes flicker open and she settles her dark stare upon me. "Did he? Well, good. The more people forget about me, the better."

I shake my head at her, my confusion written all over my face. "I don't understand," I begin. "If someone has upset you, you can tell me…"

"It doesn't matter now," she interrupts, forcing a tight smile on to her lips. "Come on, we'll take some tea and have a chat. It feels like a lifetime since I last saw you."

Meg leads me into the living room which, like the hallway, is utterly deprived of daylight. "Will I open the curtains?" I ask, hoping that the question will be taken as a helpful offer rather than a criticism.

"No, please don't," she calls from the kitchen. "Too much light gives me a terribly sore head. Some days I find it easier to dwell in the dark. Today is one such day."

"Oh, I'm sorry to hear that," I reply. "I was going to ask you if you'd like to come out with me today."

Meg returns from the kitchen and hands me a mug. "And go where?" she asks.

I take a deep breath. I might as well get straight to the point. "I'm going to find Bert's mistress," I say. "You know - the woman we saw getting out of his car on the day we went to Annan. I know you advised me not to go looking for her, but I just can't let this rest now that I know she's here. I hope you can understand that."

Meg gives a brief nod as she sips her tea. "I see. And how do you plan to find her?" she asks. "Surely you're not going to go door-to-door."

"No, of course not. I believe there's a shop in the village so I thought I'd ask there. Newcomers are always noticed in small places, no matter how much they try to keep their heads down. It shouldn't be hard to narrow it down to a couple of addresses."

"Alright. And what do you intend to do once you find her?" Those dark eyes pin me down under their quizzical gaze and I feel the room grow even smaller around me.

"That I do not know," I answer her, deciding that honesty is the best policy. "I'd like to confront her, to ask her what is going on and why she's here, but I don't know if I'll be able to, if I have the stomach for that today. But at least I'll know where she is, at least I'll be able to keep an eye on her and Bert." I pause. Hearing my thoughts aloud for the first time makes me realise how crazy this whole idea sounds.

"Hmm," Meg replies, taking another drink from her tea cup. "I meant to ask you, how did your meeting with the photographer go? Did she come and take some photos?"

"Erm, yes…yes, she did," I reply, caught off-guard by her abrupt change of subject.

Meg's face brightens. "Well, that's good! So what happens now? Have you told Bert? I'm sure the whole thing will have gone down like a lead balloon with him."

My hackles rise at her latter question. "No, I haven't told Bert. He won't be interested and frankly, it's none of his business. I'm just waiting now for Emma to get back in touch. Once she's developed the photos she's going to come over to the house and we will go through them before the exhibition. She seems like a lovely lady – I think you'd really warm to her. Perhaps you'd like to join us and see her work for yourself?"

Meg's posture stiffens at the suggestion. "No, it's fine," she says shortly. "I'm sure I can see them another time. Thank you for the invitation, though."

"You're welcome," I reply, a frown creasing my brow. "You really aren't keen on meeting people, are you? I can't help but wonder why you made an exception for me." My tone is teasing but I think we both know that I mean every word.

Meg looks away and it's immediately obvious that she isn't going to answer my question. "I'm really not feeling great today, Eleanor. I don't think I can come with you to find this woman you're looking for."

My heart thuds hard in my chest and it takes all the strength I can muster not to wear my rising panic on my face. It's not fair, I tell myself. She's not well. It's not fair to rely on her so much. I need to be stronger, to overcome my fears, to learn to rely on myself. "Oh Meg, I am sorry. I should never have just turned up out the blue and asked this of you. I think I'll go. You need to rest, of course you do. I hope you feel better."

"It's alright," she replies meekly. "I'm sorry I can't come. Will you be alright on your own? I know how you get about venturing far."

"I'll be fine," I assure her, plastering on a smile. "It's only a short walk into the village. Going out isn't as hard as it used to be, thanks to you." Despite my brave words my stomach flips. I feel like my heart is about to explode.

As I get up from my seat Meg reaches out and grabs hold of my arm. I startle; her touch is ice cold. "Promise me something, Eleanor," she says.

"What?" I ask. "What is it?"

"Promise me that if you find her, you won't confront her. Not today, at least. Just watch her, get the measure of her, but don't do anything yet. It isn't the right time."

She looks at me squarely and for the first time I see an odd glint in her eyes which I can't quite read. "Alright," I reply. "Although I'm not sure it'll ever be the right time."

"The time will come," she insists, still holding me in her freezing grip. "And when it arrives, you'll know. Then you'll have what's due to you."

I frown at her. This is all so strange; the way she's speaking, the look on her face, none of it is like the Meg I've come to know at all. "I don't understand," I admit. "What do you mean?"

Meg smiles and releases me from her grasp. "Revenge, of course," she says with a small, weary sigh as she sits back in her chair. "When the time comes, you'll have your revenge on both of them."

I leave Meg and walk outside, the bright morning light causing me to squint after being shrouded in the darkness of Thistle Cottage. As I head along the lane and towards the village, I try my best to shake off the uneasy feeling which this morning's encounter has stirred deep within my stomach. Meg was certainly not her usual smiling and enthusiastic self; her shine was dimmed, somehow, just like the light in her humble home. Immediately I dismiss the thought. Of course she didn't look happy, I tell myself; she admitted that she wasn't feeling well. I'm simply reading too much into the situation. Besides, I need to leave Meg behind for today and focus on the task at hand, the one I set myself, the one which has been eating away at me all weekend. Yet, no matter how hard I try, the sight of Meg's pale, drawn face continually creeps into my consciousness, her words about revenge making my blood run cold through my veins. Something about her isn't right. Something doesn't make sense. But then, I reflect, a woman is entitled to her mysteries, to her secrets, to her unanswered questions. After all, how many people in my life must have said the same about me?

I round the corner and I am confronted by a sight which makes me catch my breath. There's no time to agonise about what I'm doing, to panic about being out on my own. There's no need, either, to play the amateur sleuth, to pluck up the courage to ask searching questions at the shop or to interrogate passers-by, for there she is, bold as brass, standing on the doorstep of a little terrace house. And there, standing in front of her and waiting to be invited inside, is Bert. All thoughts of Meg are immediately suspended as I scramble backwards to ensure I am not seen. I peer back around the corner just long enough to see Bert walk inside with her and to hear the door slam shut behind him. I let out a heavy sigh, my breath creating clouds in the chilly air. What now, I ask myself. What do I want to do now that I've found her? What do I want to do now that I know Bert is there with her? Meg's words ring in my ears: don't confront her. Just watch her, but don't do anything yet. The memory makes my stomach flip. How I wish Meg was here with me. How I wish I wasn't doing this alone.

Stealthily I nip down the lane which runs behind the terrace row, counting the gates until I identify the one which I think belongs to her house. I try the latch; to my relief it is unlocked. Without even thinking about what I'm doing, I slip inside. I'm greeted by a small yard, cobble-stoned and bare but for a couple of dustbins placed next to the wall. Feeling suddenly exposed I duck down between them, obscuring myself from view as I shuffle towards the window, peering inside as much as I dare. My heart lurches as I see two figures, a man and a woman, a tall, beautiful goddess with her arms folded and a middle-aged man, gesturing wildly. It's them; it's definitely them, and from what I can hear through the window, which has been left slightly ajar, they're arguing.

"I'm sorry, my love," I hear Bert saying. "It was Anna's birthday on Friday and work was non-stop this weekend. I just couldn't get away."

"But we agreed – we agreed you would call in every day! I've sat here for three days, stuck in the middle of nowhere, wondering if you were ever going to come back." Her voice is raised and she is clearly agitated. I stifle a scoff. What a self-centred cow. What does she want him for every day, anyway? My mind whispers the answer and my heart stings with spite. She wants him. She loves him. But clearly she doesn't trust him.

His voice is lower now and I don't catch all of what he says but it sounds like: "I'll always come back for you." Bile rises in my throat and I think about leaving. I don't need to witness this. I don't need my hatred for him to be compounded any more.

Whatever his exact words were, they appear to have the desired effect. Her defences disintegrate and she wraps her lean arms around him. She says something but her words are muffled and I can tell that she is crying. Well done, Bert, I think. You've managed to bring another woman to tears. Aren't you good at making us so miserable?

She releases him from her embrace and they both walk from view. Instinctively I crawl to the other side of the bins, pressing myself between them and the wall. After a moment the back door clicks open and Bert walks out. Terrified of being seen, I keep my breath shallow and for some inexplicable reason, I squeeze my eyes tight shut.

"I'll take care of you, just as I promised," I hear him say. "I'll protect you from all of this. It's my fault, after all. It's all my fault and I promise you that I will make it right."

"I'm so frightened, Bert," she answers him, her voice hoarse. "What if we didn't run far enough? What if he finds us?"

True to his character, Bert doesn't answer her. Silence follows.

Not daring to look up, my mind paints a picture of him kissing her tenderly on the lips, stroking her cheek, then walking away. It is only when I hear the gate click shut and the back door close that I muster the courage to open my eyes. I wait for a few moments, and then as quickly and quietly as I can manage, I make my escape back on to the lane and then slip out of the village. I walk briskly, rushing away from the cluster of dwellings until eventually the houses become sparser and I enter the quiet idyll of trees and hedgerows which leads to Kirtlebeck End. It is then and only then that I find myself able to take a few deep, calming breaths and to reflect upon all I have just seen and heard. Clearly, Bert and that woman are still lovers. Clearly, he has brought her here because he cares deeply for her and she for him. Nothing is surprising about either of these facts. Nothing about them inspires fresh hurt; they can only ever deepen the existing wound. What I was surprised to learn is that there is obviously more going on here than a mere sordid affair. All that talk about protection, about running away, about being found – whatever is going on, Bert and his mistress are up to their necks in it.

I walk back up the gravel driveway leading to my home and unlock the front door. For all these weeks I have thought of this place as both a sanctuary and a prison, a place where I can hide, where I can lock myself away. What I heard today gives that idea additional significance – this house, this sleepy village, this quiet life could all be keeping us safe. But safe from what? What has Bert got himself into? What have he and that woman done? That woman's words ring in my ears – what if he finds us. He. Who is he? A jilted lover? A husband? Either of those seem likely. But why is she so frightened? Why did they both have to run away?

I step inside and lean heavily against the door. My quest today has only served to provoke more questions, questions which must be answered. I must know what's going on. I must understand what it all means and what the consequences are.

Above all, I realise, I have to know if Anna and I are in danger.

21

Harry
January 2018

I wake with a start, curled up in the corner of the bed in my mum's old room. It's early; the lack of daylight disorientates me and it takes me a good few moments to remember where I am. Flickers of dreams linger in my consciousness, making me feel torn between the waking world and the one I've just left. It was a happy place, quite unlike any I've visited for a while; since I've been here my head has been full of other people's lives, other people's memories. Other people's ghosts. Last night I remembered myself, not the guilt-ridden woman who ran away from Manchester, but the girl I was before that. The young girl who had a father, and for a time, a mother. The girl who had a childhood. I dreamt about those times; I played by the sea with my dad, I ate ice cream on the beach with my mum. I saw her face, her smile, so real I could reach out and trace it with my fingers. I don't know if what I saw was a memory; it might have never happened at all. But whatever it was, it made me feel content for a little while.

My smile evaporates into the gloom and I remember everything that happened yesterday. I remember what I heard, what I felt, and what was said. I remember that I didn't go to bed alone.

I turn over, reaching into the space where last night he lay down beside me. It is cold and empty, and I don't know whether to feel sad or relieved. Last night, nothing happened and everything happened. I asked him to stay with me. I asked him to share my bed. I asked him to hold me, to ward off the spirit which I felt certain would return. He did all this without question; he stroked my hair and lulled me to sleep with the gentle rise and fall of his chest as he held me in his arms. But he did nothing more. He asked for nothing more. Perhaps he was right not to; perhaps he is sensible to exercise the caution which I seem determined to throw to the wind. Yet the thought of what might have been plays on my mind. Why is it that whatever I do or don't do always seems to leave me with regrets?

If only we had met in another time.

I groan at the memory of his words. What is wrong with this time? What is wrong with now?

I think about getting up, but in truth I don't want to set a foot out of bed until daytime arrives. This place frightens me in the dark, even more so after what happened yesterday. I wish then that Daniel had stayed, that he hadn't slipped away while I was sleeping. I wish I wasn't all alone.

"Bert? Are you there?"

I sigh as only silence greets me. I'd have even forgiven him for being in my bedroom, just this once. I'd have even answered the impertinent questions about what happened last night which he'd no doubt have had in store for me. I'd have asked a few of my own, as well; what happened to him yesterday, why didn't he try to help me when I needed it most?

Why has he been silent ever since?

"Talking to someone?" Daniel startles me as he peers around the bedroom door, a cup of tea in his hand. "Bert isn't in here, is he?"

"I thought you'd left already!" I shake my head as I pull myself upright. "No. He seems to have gone for now." I smile gratefully as he hands me the drink. "Thank you for humouring me. I'm still sure you must think I'm crazy."

His face is serious as he sits down beside me. "I already told you, I don't think that. I believe you, Harry. And I wouldn't leave without saying goodbye."

I sip my tea. "I could get used to this – usually I have to make my own brew in the morning."

My joke provokes a smile but once again I see a glimmer of melancholy in his eyes. He reaches over and caresses my cheek. "Unfortunately I'll have to leave you now."

Instinctively I draw my knees up to my chest. "Oh?"

"Monday morning – time for work."

"I see." In the midst of everything else, I had completely forgotten what day of the week it was.

A look of concern passes over his face. "If you're worried about being here alone, why don't you call in on my mum? I know she's been wondering about our new neighbour and would love to meet you."

"I'm not sure. I mean, I'd love to but I don't want to just turn up on her doorstep unannounced."

"Honestly, she won't mind. Tell you what, I need to go home first before I head to the garage. I'll mention that you might drop in."

"Okay. Thank you, Daniel. Thank you for everything. You've been so good to me."

He kisses the top of my head as he gets up to leave. "I wish I could be more for you, Harry."

I want to ask what he means but I know my question will go unanswered. "Will I see you later?"

He doesn't answer that either. He just turns and smiles, a warm smile which tells me he will be back when he can, that he would stay if he could.

Then he leaves me to the darkness and the silence.

I spend the rest of the morning in bed, wrapped up warm under my sheets and absent-mindedly flicking through a magazine. I know I ought to apply myself better, that there are things in this house which need to be done. I know too that if I wish to read I could fetch one of Mum's stories, that I could delve further into her formative creative work just as I promised myself I would do. Something about this prospect makes me hesitate, however; the last story I read was so dark, and I'm not in the mood to wander into any painful places today, even imaginary ones. So, fashion and celebrity gossip it is. Anything light which can distract me from thoughts about frozen breath in my ear and icy fingers tracing my scalp.

At one point I even grab my phone, turning it on before remembering that I was meant to be avoiding it as far as possible. Before I can put it back down I see that I have messages again. My heart sinks; there's only two this time, at least, but I know without reading them who they will be from. I think about ignoring them but decide against it. If I'm ever going to face up to what happened, I need to be prepared to face them, even if only through modern media.

The first is from Deborah, telling me what I already know.

He's left me. Says he loves you. You're not even here and you're still fucking things up for me.

And the second is from Mark.

I'm going crazy without you. I've tried calling but your phone is off. Please, please come back to me. I love you.

The world stops for a second, and it takes me a few moments to remember how to breathe. I try to remember what I felt when he touched me, when he kissed me for the first time. I try to remember what it was like to have him look at me, to have him smile at me. I try to remember if I loved him, or if I just thought I did. But all I can see when I try to think clearly is Daniel; his face obscuring the view, his touch capturing me, his eyes making my heart race. In the end I throw my phone down, frustrated and disgusted with myself. How pathetic I am, succumbing again to the charms of an older man, a man I barely know, a man who has made it clear to me that nothing can happen. I'd be better off spending my time reading more of Mum's depressing tales.

I sigh. I'd be better off figuring out how I'm going to reply to the people I once called friends. I'd be better off selling this place and getting out of here for good.

After a late breakfast and several more cups of tea, I get dressed and decide that I can't stand the solitude any longer. Old houses are noisy houses, and every creak, every groan, every bump I hear sets me on edge. Unable to spend a moment longer torturing myself, I throw on my coat and head out down the lane to Daniel's house. The fresh air will do me good and besides, he did say that his mum would like to meet me. I realise I don't know anything about his mum; I don't know her name, how long she's lived in Kirtlebeck, or how well she knew my grandmother. This last realisation causes hope to spike within me. Perhaps if I'm lucky she will have some interesting stories to tell about Eleanor. She might even remember Bert. She might even remember my mum.

I knock on the front door a little too enthusiastically, desperate for company and eager, I realise, to peer inside Daniel's world. After a moment or two a woman answers, looking warily around the door to see who's there. She's elderly, although she doesn't look as frail as perhaps I expected, given Daniel's remarks about her health. Her face, though heavily lined, is pretty, framed perfectly by long silver-blonde hair which rests on her shoulders.

Her bright blue eyes stare inquisitively at me. "Yes?"

"Hello," I say, feeling suddenly rather awkward. "I'm Harriet. I'm your new neighbour. I've just moved into the house at Kirtlebeck End."

She opens the door wider as her face breaks into a welcoming smile. "How lovely to meet you, Harriet." She extends a hand towards me and shakes mine warmly. "I'm Emma. I had noticed that someone new was living in that house."

My brow furrows momentarily at her vagueness. Has Daniel not told her anything about me? "Yes, well, Daniel suggested that I come down and introduce myself. I hope I've not called at a bad time?"

Her eyes widen. "Daniel? Oh, erm…I see. Yes, he might have mentioned something, come to think of it. My memory's not too good these days, I'm afraid. Please though, do come in." She turns away, but not before I see the confusion clouding her face. I relax a little, beginning to understand. When Daniel told me that his mum doesn't keep well, he must have meant that it's her mind which troubles her.

I follow Emma along a wide, modern hallway, flanked on either side by walls thickly decorated with framed photographs. We go into the living area, which I realise forms part of a large, open space running into a dining area and kitchen. I find the lack of separate rooms in this place appealing; there's nothing hidden, nothing stifling about this house. Everything is laid out, seen, flowing free. I smile; I can imagine this is exactly how Daniel likes to live. Perhaps once I've sold my grandmother's home, this is the sort of place I should buy.

I glance at the walls, painted in a seamless magnolia and once again filled with the most beautiful photographs, mostly portraits of people captured in all manner of interesting places. "Your pictures are beautiful," I remark.

Emma nods, bidding me to sit down. "Thank you, that's very kind. I was a photographer for many years. Can I fetch you some tea?"

I shake my head. "No, thank you. I won't keep you long. I really just wanted to come and say hello."

She smiles at me. "Well, it's very nice to meet you, and it's nice to see that big old house being lived in again, as well. Is there – is there just you, I mean, do you have family with you?"

"No. Just me."

She raises an eyebrow. "That's a big house to be rattling around in, all on your own."

I clasp my hands together in my lap. Talking about the house makes me feel agitated. "Well I don't think I'll be there for very long. I inherited it from my grandmother, so really I'm just here to clear out the contents and arrange its sale.”

“So you’re Eleanor’s granddaughter?”

I nod, trying to hide my surprise at her question. Either Emma’s memory really is terrible, or Daniel hasn’t told her anything about me at all. “Did you know my grandmother well? My family wasn’t close so I never really knew her.” I hope my carefully chosen euphemisms suffice as an explanation. I really don’t want to have to tell the family story yet again.

Emma hesitates. “Not really in recent years, no. I only moved to Kirtlebeck ten years ago to live with Danny.” The affectionate way she shortens his name makes me smile. “He used to go up to the big house to check on her, help her out. She was a bit of a recluse, to be honest.”

“Yes, he told me about that.”

“Oh. He did?”

“Yes, he said he did odd jobs for her, but that she was very reserved.”

“I see. You’ve seen a lot of Danny, then?”

“Quite a bit. He’s been very kind, very helpful since I moved in.” I choose my words carefully. She is his mother, after all. She’ll have seen it all over the years: the girlfriends, the heartbreaks, the divorce. She might be forgetful, but I’ll bet she’s also protective. “So you didn’t know Eleanor at all?” I feel the disappointment growing in the pit of my stomach.

“Oh, I did, when we were younger women. Before Danny was born, in fact.” She gets out of her seat and walks over to one of the walls filled with photos. “Come here and I’ll show you.”

I wander over, my eyes drawn to where Emma is pointing. It takes me a moment to recognise Eleanor, to reconcile her smiling, glorious image with the dour expression I’ve grown used to seeing in family shots. But there she is, brush in hand, paint smudged on the end of her nose, eyes creased to near closure as she laughs without restraint. And there, behind her, is the bedroom mural, the darkness of the cosmos swirling unapologetically in the background. “Oh wow,” I gasp. “I’ve never seen her looking like that before."

"I took that in the autumn of '72," Emma says. "It was part of an exhibition I ran over in Lockerbie, showing off our local talent. Eleanor responded to an ad I placed in the paper and asked me to come and see her murals, and that's how we met."

"1972," I muse. "That was the year they moved here."

Emma nods carefully, as though she's trying to remember. "Yes, I think that's right. They moved here from Manchester. New business opportunity for her husband, or something like that. I think it was a hard time for Eleanor – for your grandmother, I mean. She seemed very lonely."

"I've seen the murals," I tell her. "She'd covered them up but after I found some photos of them I knew I had to see them for myself. They're incredible."

"Yes, they are. I think painting them helped her through it all. I remember her telling me that the move had been all her husband's doing. I don't think she felt as though she was in control of her own life."

I think about what Bert told me, about how upset Eleanor had been about the move, about the affair. I wonder if Emma knows about the affair. "Did you know my grandfather?" I ask as casually as I can manage.

Emma frowns. "Not really, no. I only met Eleanor a handful of times while we worked together for the exhibition. And of course, her husband disappeared not long after that so..."

"He disappeared?"

She looks straight at me, and I can see the surprise on her face. Surprise that I didn't know. Surprise at how little I know. "Yes, I remember seeing the appeal in the paper. Must've been later in '72 that he went missing. It was all very strange. I don't think they ever found any trace of him."

"My goodness, I can't believe it. Poor Bert. Poor Eleanor. Poor Mum." I cover my mouth with my hands, my mind reeling with the shock of this new piece of information. I think about Bert, his restless spirit still present in that house. What became of him?

Clearly he's now dead, but he doesn't remember when he died, he doesn't remember what happened. I think too about the other spirit in the house, the one which petrified me with its cold touch and whispered words, the one I feel sure is Eleanor. Perhaps she, like me, is simply looking for answers. Perhaps she is searching for Bert…

"I'm sorry." Emma interrupts my racing thoughts with the gentle touch of her hand on mine. "I suppose it's old news around these parts, and I just assumed that you knew."

I drop my hand to my side, regaining my composure. "Unfortunately I don't know a great deal about my mother's side of the family. Mum left when I was a little girl, so…" I let my words trail off, but my face tells the rest of the story.

Emma's gaze grows sympathetic, which only serves to make me feel even worse. "I'm sorry – there isn't a great deal more I can tell you, Harriet. I don't think I ever met your mother, though she would have been a girl if I had, and my acquaintance with your grandmother ended after the exhibition finished. Though I do believe I heard that she got some commissions out of it. In fact, that exhibition probably marked the beginning of her career around here. She really was a very fine artist."

"So you never got back in touch with Eleanor, even when you moved to Kirtlebeck?"

"No. As I said, she kept herself to herself. The only person who had anything to do with her was Daniel." Her face is impassive but the rigidity of her posture suggests that there's something she's not telling me. Like so many things here, I suspect I will never discover what that is.

Sensing that I've taken up enough of her time, I get up from my seat. "I'd better get back now, but it's very nice to have met you, Emma." I offer her a hand and a smile, masking my growing frustration. A missing mum, a reclusive grandmother, and now a disappearing grandfather – the more I discover, the more it seems like a family story without a conclusion.

Emma shows me to the door. "So, have you any plans to see

Danny again?" she asks.

I resist the temptation to raise an eyebrow. Her defence of her son is really quite something. "No specific plans," I reply. "He just pops in from time to time. I suppose in some ways it's a habit, from when he used to help my grandmother."

"Yes. Perhaps." Emma's eyes are wide, searching. "Just – be careful, Harriet."

I frown at her. What a strange thing to say. "Careful – why? What do you mean?"

"Just be careful with his feelings, and with yours. You're exactly his type, and when he falls for a woman, he falls hard. Please, trust me. You must take care."

"Okay. Thank you for the advice." My response is feeble but I don't know what else I can say that won't sound irritable or petulant. We're both grown adults, for goodness sake. And besides, he's made it clear that he's drawn a line between us, a line he will not cross. It seems to me that he's perfectly capable of protecting his feelings, and mine, of course, are my own concern.

As I turn away Emma calls after me: "Please do call again! It was lovely to meet you!" Her tone is light and friendly, as though those words of warning had never been uttered at all.

I don't turn around. Instead I trudge up the lane, putting thoughts of Daniel to one side, resigned to return to my home filled with secrets I may never know and spirits whispering words I'd rather not hear.

22

Eleanor
September 1972

It is a little after nine in the morning and I am sitting down, a sketch pad balanced on my knee, a cup of coffee in my hand and a pencil tucked behind my ear. I have been up since before dawn, restless and unable to sleep. Every single chore which my mind could conceive of was completed by the time the sun had risen, and now that Bert and Anna have got up and gone out, I am left here to fester in silence and agitation. To combat this, I am trying to busy myself, to take my mind off things by seeking solace in a reliable favourite pastime. I haven't drawn anything in my sketchpad for weeks, not since I began that sorry little chaffinch in the summer. For so long all my creative energies have been focussed upon the walls of this place; the great canvasses upon which I have painted beauty, magic, anger and despair. I need to find my way back to the small, to the ordinary, to the things I used to do before the madness took over. I need to learn how to take comfort in my art again. And yet, I sit here and stare, the page remaining blank, my mind racing and distracted, my feet tapping wildly on the hard floor. Today, I fear, will not be the day I discover my old self again.

I let out a heavy sigh and put down my empty cup. I suppose I shouldn't be surprised that I can't draw. There is too much to worry about, to fret over. There is too much plaguing my mind. It has been several days since I witnessed Bert and that woman together, and the scene has been replaying in my mind ever since. Her anxiety and fear, his tenderness and sincerity – it all echoes around my head, endlessly torturing me with unanswered questions. I have analysed each word spoken between them again and again, trying to extract some new meaning, some clue as to what is going on. When I couldn't satisfy myself with that, I found the courage to venture out once again, to return to her house and crouch down once again beside those bins in an effort to witness a new scene, to possess another piece of the puzzle. But after all that I was out of luck – Bert never returned while I was there, and all I got to see was that woman doing her housework or watching television.

If I'm honest with myself, I hung around longer than I should have, deriving some measure of twisted pleasure from watching her, undetected. I was, to quote Meg, getting the measure of her, studying this person who has caused me so much pain and heartache. I thought briefly about taking things a step further, about making some noise and trying to frighten her. It wouldn't be difficult; given how on edge she clearly is about this unnamed threat she fears. However, when it came down to it I didn't have the nerve and in the end I came away, disappointed and frustrated, and more perturbed than ever.

Today I don't even have the option to be able to go and spy on her. Yesterday afternoon Emma finally got back in touch and we agreed that she would call round today to review the photographs. As a result, I have no choice but to suspend my investigation, and to put all questions of Bert and that woman and what they may or may not have done out of my mind. Instead, I have something else to worry about, something else which stops me from wanting to draw and makes me restless and sleepless. Those bloody photographs. That bloody exhibit. I can only imagine what I look like, how ridiculous I will seem. Why on earth did I let Meg talk me into making that call? Why did I allow Emma to lead me, to capture me posing like a peacock next to wall paintings which no sane person can possibly have any interest in? Why couldn't I just tell them no and insist that they leave me alone?

The clock on the mantelpiece chimes and I am startled briefly from my whirring thoughts. Irritated, I brush my sketchpad off my lap and wander over to the window. I am expecting Emma to arrive any minute and the wait is, quite frankly, killing me. I don't know what these photos are going to be like, I don't know if I'll adore or detest them but either way, I just want to get this over with. I linger for a few moments, carelessly tracing my fingers over the condensation which has gathered in the corners of the window panes. Autumn is in full swing now; as the end of the month draws near the temperature grows ever cooler and the leaves begin to yellow and curl on the trees. Soon those leaves will fall, leaving the branches bare in their wake. It occurs to me for the first time how thick the foliage is, how well it surrounds and shields this house. I let out a heavy sigh, lamenting the impending loss of it. How much emptier, how much more exposed it will feel to be here during those bleak winter months.

A plume of smoke trickles upwards before my eyes, its source the chimney on the lowly cottage further down the lane. I watch the soft grey swirls caress the morning sky, my mind turning to the friend who is not herself. After the unsettling nature of my last visit to Thistle Cottage, I had resolved not to call on Meg again at the moment, to leave her in peace and to wait for her to make contact with me once she was feeling better. Now I wonder if that's the right thing to do, if instead of keeping my distance I should try to help. After all, Meg has so often been there for me, supporting me with my art, getting me out of the house, giving me advice, and yet here I am, agonising over whether to visit her or not. I shake my head at myself, despairing at my shortcomings. I never know how to be with people. I never know what to do for the best.

Footsteps crunch across the gravel, drawing nearer until Emma comes into view. Spotting me at the window, she gives me a broad smile and a friendly wave. I wave back, drawing a deep breath as I head to the front door to greet her. Yet another thing in my life that I have got myself into and I don't really know how to handle. But at least she's here and I can find out what this cheery, enthusiastic young photographer has in store for me. At least I can get this over with, one way or another.

"I'm so sorry it's taken me this long to come and see you!" Emma says the moment I open the door. She is radiant today, her cheeks pink with the cold and an enormous smile set irrepressibly on her lips. "You have no idea the amount of rushing around I have been doing, trying to get this thing organised."

"I can only imagine," I reply, taking her coat and beckoning her through to my living room. "Can I fetch you something to drink? Tea, coffee?"

Emma shakes her head as she sits down. "That's very kind but no thank you. I'm afraid I can't stay too long – I've a meeting with the gallery in Lockerbie straight after this and I'll really have to keep an eye on the time. The buses through Kirtlebeck aren't exactly frequent, are they?"

"No," I reply, letting out a light chuckle which I hope will disguise the fact that I've no idea if the buses here are any good because I've only left this village once, and that was on foot. "It is a bit of a backwater here, I suppose."

"Yes but it's a beautiful wee place," Emma counters. "I would happily live in a small village like this. I can only imagine how idyllic it must be, how wonderful to have so much peace and space in which to be creative. You must find that, surely? I imagine you must notice a huge difference after living in Manchester."

"Hmm," I nod, sitting down opposite her. "My life here is certainly different. I suppose it would be fair to say that it can be an inspiring place, at times." My eyes shift nervously towards the leather folder placed neatly next to her. "Are those the photos from our shoot?"

"Oh, yes! Goodness, I'd better not keep you in suspense, had

I?" Before I can say anything else, Emma opens the folder and starts to spread the photos over the coffee table. "Please, have a good look at them all and tell me what you think. As you can see, I took a lot of different shots but I'm really only looking for two or three for the exhibit. I'd love to get your opinion on which ones I should use." She gives me a cautious look before adding: "If you like any of them, of course. There's still no obligation for you to be a part of this, if you don't want to be."

I give her a meek smile and as she asks, I take the time to study each one in turn. I have to admit, I'm impressed. My worries about looking like a deranged middle-aged woman with a paintbrush are immediately allayed. In these photos I look many different things: sometimes serious, professional and demure, at other times wild, carefree, and liberated, but never crazy. I look like someone who should be taken seriously. I look like an artist who cares deeply about her work, who believes in it, who believes in herself.

"Emma," I breathe. "These are incredible. Thank you for making me look so, well, wonderful."

Emma grins at me. "The camera doesn't lie, Eleanor. You look that way because you are wonderful, and your work is wonderful. I just capture what is already there. So, can I take it from your reaction that you're willing to be included in the show?"

I put the photos down and clasp my hands together, my nerves returning. "I really don't know. The more I've thought about being part of this show, the more terrified I've felt. You have to understand, I'm not someone who normally puts herself out there, who likes to be the centre of attention…"

"And yet you called me," Emma counters. "You asked me to come and look at your work."

"Yes," I concede. "Yes, I did do that. Call it a rare courageous moment helped by the support of a good friend."

Emma raises her eyebrows at me. "The same friend who encouraged you to paint the mural?"

I nod. "The very same."

Emma draws a sharp breath and shoots me a considered look.

"Eleanor," she says. "I'd like to show you some more photos that I took, if that's alright?"

I feel a frown grow across my forehead. "Photos of me? I thought you had shown me all of the ones you took."

"There are a few others which I held back. The quality isn't as good as the light is a bit all over the place. Here," she says, handing them to me, "you can see what I mean for yourself."

I flick quickly through the photographs. Emma is right; there is a definite issue with the lighting. In some of them I am illuminated, surrounded by a bright light, the source of which is unclear. In others the light randomly decorates the images with white, glowing spots. I look up at her, furrowing my brow. "Perhaps there was something up with your camera? Or something went wrong when you developed them?"

"That's what I thought at first, although it's weird how some of the photos have turned out this way and others haven't. But now I'm starting to wonder."

"Wonder what?"

She smiles at me. "Well, don't you think there's something ethereal about the light in those pictures? Maybe you've got a guardian angel."

I let out an amused laugh, remembering what Anna said to me weeks ago, when I painted the first mural. "Goodness! You sound like my daughter. I very much doubt I have one of those."

"I'm serious, Eleanor. I've heard of other photographers capturing things like this, but this is a first for me. It's quite exciting, actually. And it makes sense when you think about it. Your friend encouraged you to paint that wonderful mural, then encouraged you to get in touch with me so I could capture it. It was obviously meant to be."

"You think my friend is my guardian angel?"

Emma laughs. "No, but your guardian angel could have brought her into your life to be a good, supportive influence on you. I would take comfort in it, Eleanor; someone is looking out for you. And I know I'm biased because I'm excited by these shots and really want to include you in the show, but if I was you I would also follow this and see where it leads. After seeing these pictures, I firmly believe that this is the path you're meant to be on."

I pause, considering her words. I can't deny that Meg has been a good influence on me, encouraging me to paint, to stop drinking, to participate in this exhibit and generally to concentrate on my art rather than on my marital problems. In many ways, she has been the driving force behind my efforts in recent weeks; if it wasn't for meeting her, I probably wouldn't be where I am now, sitting with these beautiful photographs of me and my work.

"Perhaps you have a point," I say, putting the photos back down on the coffee table.

"So...?" Emma looks at me, eyebrows raised, her face filled with hope.

"Alright," I exhale. "Alright, I'll do it. I'll be part of the show."

Emma clasps her hands together in excitement. "Brilliant! I can't tell you how pleased I am. Do you have any preference about which photos I use in the exhibit? Or any photos that you really don't like?"

I shake my head. "Not really, they're all great. Well, except the ones with the weird lighting. Now that I'm thinking about it, I actually find them a little bit creepy."

Emma picks one of them up and studies it again. "Really? I think they're magical."

I shrug. "Well, beauty is in the eye of the beholder, as they say."

"Indeed," Emma replies. "Indeed it is."

The sudden sound of the front door bursting open causes me to jump out of my skin. "I'm sorry," I say to Emma by way of answering her quizzical expression, although I'm not sure what I'm sorry for. "Excuse me for just one moment."

I wander out into the hallway to find the source of the intrusion. It's too early for Anna to be home, and the door was locked, I'm sure it was. Therefore, the only other person it could be is my husband. I frown at the realisation, my heart thudding hard in my chest. Bert never comes home in the middle of the day. What is going on?

I am confronted with an empty hallway, which serves only to deepen my anxiety. Above me I hear footsteps. "Bert? Is that you?" I call up the stairs. I glance at the living room door, mindful that my guest is listening. "You're home early. Is everything alright?"

After a few painful, quiet moments, Bert peers down over the banister. "What?" he asks me. "What is it?"

"I was just checking it was you," I reply, growing indignant at his abrupt manner.

"Of course it's me. I do live here. I'm just looking for something and then I'll be out of your way." His tone continues to be offhand which in itself is not unusual; Bert and I have hardly been renowned for our conciliatory interactions of late. Nonetheless, there's something about him which is amiss. He is not his normal cool, careful self. He seems unsettled, almost panicked by something. My mind wanders back to the conversation I overheard between him and that woman. Perhaps something has happened. Perhaps they've been discovered. Perhaps he hasn't been able to protect her like he promised. I bite my lip, unsure if the prospect of this delights or terrifies me.

I glance again at the living room door. Any further questions will have to wait until later. The last thing I want is for Emma to hear us arguing. "That's fine," I say smoothly. "It's just that I have a visitor in the living room with me."

"A visitor?" I watch as his face reddens like an awful beacon hanging over the railing of the stairs. "What kind of visitor? What do they want?"

I pause, letting the silence linger for just a moment longer than is comfortable. He thinks that whatever trouble he has got himself into, it has found its way into our house. And what's more, he thinks I'm completely ignorant, that I'm perfectly unaware of any of what is going on. I know it's terrible, but I relish the opportunity to torture him for a few sweet moments. "Oh, it's just an art thing," I reply in the end. "You won't be interested."

Bert forces a grim smile to his lips. "No, no," he protests, coming down the stairs. "Tell me. I'd like to meet this visitor."

His sudden approach flusters me. "Well, she's a local photographer. She's very interested in my murals, she…"

Bert doesn't give me the chance to finish my sentence. Instead he breezes past me and flings open the living room door. Meekly I have no choice but to follow behind him. My moment of power is over. It is my husband who is once again back in control.

I walk in just as Emma has got to her feet. "Hello," she says, extending a friendly hand to shake his. "I'm Emma. You must be Eleanor's husband. You have a very talented wife. Her murals are just wonderful."

"Hmm," says Bert. He takes her hand slowly, warily, as though this pretty young photographer wasn't at all what he expected to find, as though he was expecting someone else altogether. "And what interest do you have in Eleanor's work, exactly?"

"I'm organising an exhibition of local talent. It's called Art Captures Art – essentially I have been photographing local artists with their work. It's been a really fun project and a great way to shine a light on all the talent tucked away in our quiet corner of the world."

Bert frowns at her. "And where will this exhibition take place?"

"At the community gallery in Lockerbie. I'm meeting with them again later this afternoon but it looks almost certain that it will open in just over a week's time."

"You see," I interject, "it's just a local art thing, like I told you."

"Oh, but I'm hoping it'll become so much more than that," Emma adds. "I've already spoken to the local press and they're very interested in covering it. I think the publicity for the artists involved will be considerable."

"And the benefit for you; that will presumably be quite considerable as well?" Bert snaps, his face reddening once again. I shudder at his tone.

"Well, yes," Emma replies. Her face retains its amenable expression but the curling of her fingers into her palms suggests she is feeling anything but. "Like any project, there is a mutual benefit for all involved. My work is on display too, as they're my photographs…"

Bert puts up his hand, silencing her. "I'm sorry," he says, "but my wife can have no part in this. I won't allow it."

Emma looks at Bert, then at me. Her expression is impassive but her eyes are ablaze, challenging me to say something, to do something. She's right, of course; I can't just accept this, I can't let all my work and all of her work go to waste simply because my philandering husband wills it so. I feel my anger swell and churn deep within my stomach and I take a deep breath, trying hard to suppress it. Not now, I say to myself. You can't lose your temper now. Not in front of Emma. Instead I meet her gaze, giving her the briefest of nods, telling her that I will handle this, that I will fight for it.

"Albert," I begin, as gently as I can manage, futilely trying to sweeten him with his nickname. "I have already made up my mind and given Emma my answer. I am going to be part of the exhibition."

But Bert doesn't look at me. He doesn't acknowledge me. He acts as though I haven't spoken at all. "You have to understand," he says to Emma. "My wife is unwell. She isn't fit to participate in this. It will only make her condition worse."

"Condition?" Emma repeats. She looks at me, aghast. "Eleanor, what condition? Is this true? Are you sick?"

"No," I begin. "No, I…" I step towards her, reaching out, trying to find the words to refute what he's saying, to explain. There's nothing wrong with me, I want to say. I don't understand why he's saying this. Tears sting in my eyes and begin to fall unabated down my cheeks. Tears of frustration, of confusion, of humiliation. Tears of rage.

Before I can utter another word, Bert grabs hold of me and pulls me back. "You can see how upset this is making her," he says. "I think it would be best if you leave now."

"Alright…yes, yes of course," Emma stammers, gathering up her belongings. "I'm sorry, I won't take up any more of your time."

She rushes towards the front door, grabbing her coat on the way. Bert follows closely behind, ushering her out, ensuring that he is rid of her. "Please accept my apology," he says. "Eleanor should have told you. I'm sorry she has wasted your time."

Emma turns back, smiling sadly at me. "She hasn't," she says. The soft, sympathetic look in her eyes tells me that those words are intended for me. "It has been lovely getting to know you, Eleanor. It has been an honour to see your work. I hope you are feeling better soon."

I try to smile back at her but my trembling lips fail me. "Goodbye Emma," I reply.

It is only once Bert has closed the door behind her that I allow my rage to soar. I fly at him, beating my fists against his back, his chest, any part of him upon which I can lay my hands. "You bastard!" I scream. "You bastard, I hate you!" I don't care if I hurt him. Every last thing which was mine, which gave me purpose, which gave me hope, has been taken from me by this man. All these weeks I have spent convincing myself that I can tolerate him, that I can be indifferent, that I can bear to live by his side if I carve out a path of my own, if I find a space and a purpose for myself. Now I realise what a fool I have been. He will never let me have peace. He will never let me breathe. He will never let me have anything which is truly mine and mine alone.

Bert grabs hold of my wrists, his strength overpowering mine. "Stop it, Eleanor," he instructs, his voice eerily quiet and calm. "This will do no good."

"Why?" I yell as hot tears of fury continue to pour down my face. "Why did you do that? Why did you stop me from doing the exhibit? And why did you tell her I was ill? Why did you lie and humiliate me like that?"

He lets go of my arms and sighs wearily, almost pitiably at me. "Come into the living room," he says to me, refusing as usual to answer my questions.

"Why should I do anything you say?"

Bert gives me that hard stare, the one that tells me not to

challenge him, the one that tells me I'd better obey.

"Because for once in your life, you need to listen," he replies, in a voice so cold it makes me shudder. "This insanity has gone on for long enough. We need to talk."

23

Harry
January 2018

I creep back into the house, desperate not to disturb the spirit which I feel certain still lies in wait. Eleanor's spirit. I shudder even as my mind names her, frightened that the mere thought of her name will be enough to summon her. Part of me wants her to reappear, wants her to talk to me. It's the part of me which is curious, which agonises over the missing details, the unanswered questions. I want to know why she, like Bert, is still here, why she isn't at peace. I want to know about her life, about her marriage, about her paintings. I want to know if she knows what happened to my mother.

And then there is that other part of me, the frightened part, the part which is riddled with guilt. The part which knows exactly what she meant when she told me that she's disappointed in me, that I'm just like my grandfather.

My grandfather. Bert. Where is Bert?

The door clicks closed behind me, and once again I am submerged in this house and its secrets.

"Bert?" My voice hisses out a whisper. "Bert? Are you here?"

No answer comes. The wooden staircase creaks and my heart

beats a little faster.

"Bert?" I repeat, steeling my resolve. "I need to talk to you. I've found something out. Something which might help us figure out what happened to you."

"Harriet?" His voice is faint, muffled, far away. "Harriet, is that you?"

"Yes, it's me." Elation at hearing his voice runs like a river through my veins. He's rude and impertinent, he invades my privacy and by his own admission he betrayed my grandmother, but he means me no harm and right now he's all I've got.

"Can you let me in? I can't get in."

My smile fades as I hear the desperation in his voice. "How can I – how do I do that?" I ask. "What do you mean you can't get in? You're dead. Surely you can go anywhere you choose?"

"I don't know. It's not like it was before. The way isn't clear. Everything is so dark and…I don't know, but please, help me."

"What can I do?"

"Try opening the door."

I frown, feeling foolish as I turn the handle and stand there, the door wide open, beckoning thin air to come inside. After a moment a rush of cold sweeps past me. I am taken by surprise; if that was Bert, then that is the first time I have actually felt his presence. I shiver, folding my arms across my chest. I hope it was Bert. I hope I haven't invited any other ethereal visitors in.

"Did it work? Are you inside?"

"Yes. Yes, I'm here." His voice is nearer, clearer this time.

I close the door, letting it slam shut. If anything else is lurking out there, I want it to know it's not welcome. Of course, deep down I know that she is probably already inside, but I don't want to think about that. I can't bear to think about that.

"Where've you been?" I cross my arms, partly because I'm cold and partly because I suddenly feel defensive. "You've been gone for two days. You left me to the mercy of…that thing, that spirit, whatever it was."

"What do you mean? What spirit?"

"The day before yesterday, don't you remember? We were talking in the living room when all that banging started above us. Then there were footsteps and the room, it went so cold, and I couldn't get out and you were silent and…" My voice breaks and before I can stop them, the tears come.

"I'm sorry Harriet, I don't remember any of that."

"How is that possible?" I whisper, my question aimless, hopeless, without answer.

"We were talking about our infidelities, about our secrets. I remember that."

"And then?"

"And then – nothing. Suddenly I couldn't hear you. Suddenly everything was black and I felt so very far away."

"She forced you out," I say quietly, barely able to consider the implications of my words even as they fall from my lips. "She didn't want you here."

"Who?"

"Eleanor." My eyes dart around the hallway as I speak her name, as though she might appear at any minute. "I think she's here, Bert. I think she's still in this house."

"No. You're talking nonsense," he says. His voice lowers an octave; grows gruffer, almost threatening. "It's not possible. I would know. She'd have made sure I knew."

I throw my arms up at him in despair. "What other explanation is there?"

My question hangs on a difficult silence. I know Bert won't answer. I know he doesn't have an answer. No one has any answers in this place.

I walk to the kitchen and switch on the kettle. I need some tea, some refreshment. I need to get my head straight, my thoughts in order. There are so many stories here, so many things I don't understand about my grandmother, about my mum, about Bert. So many riddles, so many loose threads. Maybe it's time that I stopped picking at them. Maybe it's time for me to just let all this go and move on with my life. Maybe that's what coming here was really about, after all; to accept that there are no answers. To accept that I will never know.

"What did you mean before, when you said you'd found something out about me?"

"Oh, so you are interested in something I've got to say, then?" I pour hot water over my tea bag, add milk, and stir vigorously.

"Don't be so bloody sensitive. Christ, you remind me more of Eleanor each day."

Something about the way he says that makes my blood run cold.

"I spoke to Emma today. My neighbour. Daniel's mum. I doubt you'll remember her as she said she didn't really know you. She knew Eleanor, though. Apparently they collaborated on a project in autumn 1972 and she took photographs of Eleanor's murals for a local exhibition. Ring any bells?" I pause, sipping my tea, waiting to see what he has to say.

"Perhaps. I do remember Eleanor wanting to work with a photographer on something. I don't remember it going ahead, though. That was often the way with Eleanor – lots of ideas, many of which never came to anything."

"Well, it did go ahead," I tell him. "But that's not the most interesting part."

"It isn't?"

"No, it isn't. Not long after the exhibition, you went missing. You were never found, either."

"Oh."

"Oh? Is that all you've got to say? This is really significant, Bert."

"Is it? Why? I don't remember anything about going missing."

I sip my tea. "I figured as much. I think that's when you died, Bert. Think about it: every memory you've related to me has taken place before that point. You remember moving here. You remember my mum as a child. But you don't remember anything after that. If you'd run away, if you'd gone on and started a new life somewhere, surely you'd have other memories? The only plausible explanation is that you were dead." I tap my hand on the kitchen counter, satisfied with the strength of my own logic.

"Christ, don't sound so pleased about it."

"I'm not! I'm just glad to get an answer to a question for once. Even if that answer only creates new questions."

"Such as?"

"Such as what happened to you, why did you disappear? How did you die? Honestly Bert, are you not interested at all?"

He answers me with silence, and I feel my hackles rise.

"You know what I think?" I ask him, even though I'm not sure if he's still there. "I think you remember more than you're letting on. I think you know things about what happened back then and you don't want to tell me. I think you're hiding something. Am I right?"

A further prolonged silence confirms my suspicion that once again Bert has walked out on our conversation.

"Dammit!" I bang my hand on the kitchen counter in frustration. I'm furious; furious at Bert for his evasiveness, for his convenient memory loss, for disappearing all those years ago and leaving no clue as to why. I'm furious at him for not being around, for not knowing my mother as she grew up, for not knowing me. I'm furious that my mum left me. I'm furious that Eleanor lived here all these years and never tried to reach out to me. I'm furious that no one seems willing or able to give me the answers I seek.

More than anything, I realise, I'm furious at myself for caring when clearly none of my family ever cared about me.

I don't bother with dinner; I'm not hungry and besides, there is nothing to eat in this house anyway. I chastise myself for neglecting to take care of the basics; I have been so caught up in trying to solve mysteries that I haven't bothered to shop, or clean, or do my laundry. Nor have I really knuckled down to clearing this house of its contents and getting it ready for sale. Tomorrow I will do better, I tell myself. Tomorrow will be a fresh start. Tomorrow I will finally focus on what is important, on what I came here to do.

I grab the pile of my mum's stories and take them upstairs, tucking myself under my duvet as though my bedsheets can ever give me the comfort I seek. It's too early to go to bed but the house is cold, its ancient boiler once again failing to heat the radiators beyond lukewarm. For a moment I wish that Daniel was here, cuddled up close beside me just as he was last night. I brush the thought aside. My attachment to him is as ridiculous as it is confusing. He's right to push me away, to make it plain where we stand. It's clear that both of us in our own way have broken hearts to mend. It would be wrong of us to lean on each other, especially when we both know that I'll be leaving soon.

With a heavy sigh I pick up where I left off. I know I'm just torturing myself by reading Mum's words, by trying to get to know her through mere prose on a page. Yet part of me still believes that although they're fiction, these stories form part of her truth, her life, her childhood. I give a shudder as I read the title of the next instalment: Margaret Gets Revenge. Clearly the bleak turn that these stories had already taken is about to get much worse. I shake my head in amazement. Such darkness so vividly imagined must have come from somewhere, must have been inspired by something. What made my mum write all this?

Margaret's story continues after her narrow escape from death by her own hand. Still nursing a broken heart, she tries to soothe her pain by formulating a plan for revenge on the man who betrayed her. His artwork has gained some renown, and he leaves the commune to live independently, setting up a small studio in a cottage in a nearby village. Margaret, jealous of his success and infected with a bitter fury, tracks him down and goes to the cottage. She confronts him, declaring her anger but also her love for him. For a moment, her wish to have her revenge dissolves and she weeps, pleading with him for a chance at a life together. The artist, however, is indifferent, telling her that their time together meant little to him. She was just one of many starry-eyed young women who had inspired him, he says, but now her moment with him has passed and she is no longer of any use to him as a muse.

Margaret flies into a rage; she realises that there is no future for them together, but she also understands that she cannot bear anyone else to have him. Consumed by a thirst for vengeance she murders him, beating him with one of his own sculptures which is so heavy she barely understands how she is able to lift it. Even when he is dead she keeps hitting him, delivering blow after blow to his body, to his head, to the face she loved so deeply.

"In the end there was nothing left of him; only blood and darkness in his place."

I whisper those words, over and over again. I try to imagine my mum, sitting where I am now, writing the scene of sheer violence which I am clutching in my hand. I wonder about what was going on around her, about her life with a reclusive mother consumed by the urge to create, and with a father who was suddenly, inexplicably absent from her life. Did she write these stories after he went missing? Was this tale of betrayal and vengeance her way of pouring out her feelings of grief?

"Margaret lit a fire then, cleansing the cottage with heat and flame. When her dress caught she made no effort to curb the fire's appetite. Instead she lay down next to the artist and closed her eyes, her hand resting on his still chest as the flames consumed them both. The fire raged, their flesh blackened and their hearts charred but at least now they would always be together."

I exhale loudly in disbelief as I rest the pages on my lap. Such mature, insightful, terrible words; words which were surely far beyond her young years. After reading this I can't decide whether my mother was a genius, or profoundly disturbed.

I fall asleep shortly after I finish reading, sinking into that horrid restless state between sleeping and waking where the lines between what is real and imagined are blurred. In my mind's eye I see myself standing in that cottage in the midst of the fire, surveying the scene of death and destruction as the flames lap like waves at my feet. In the middle of the room lies Margaret, embracing her lover just as Mum described. I can't see him clearly, perhaps because my mind doesn't wish to conjure the horrors she has inflicted upon him. I can see Margaret, however; my mind recreates her to look just like my mother did in all the photographs I've been pouring over – pretty, pale, but dead. I stand for a moment, just staring at her. How can someone so beautiful, so apparently angelic, commit such a dreadful crime as this?

I'm about to turn away, to leave this dream and rouse myself, but then she opens her eyes.

"Wait!" she cries out. "I know you're there. Don't go!" Her voice is soft but commanding, and I find myself frozen to the spot.

"Why?" I ask her. "You're dead and I shouldn't even be here."

"Yes, you should. You're exactly where you're meant to be."

I frown. Around us the fire dissipates, begins to smoulder. "What do you mean?"

She clambers to her feet, slowly, ghoulishly, her flowing dress still aflame.

"You need to know the truth, Harriet. You won't be able to rest until you know the truth."

She walks towards me, an amused chuckle escaping from her lips. The mask she wears is still my mother's, but she corrupts it somehow, twisting that formerly pretty smile into something altogether crueller, her eyes shining at me with hate-filled contempt.

"Leave me alone!" I cry out, staggering backwards. "What do you want from me?

Her laugh grows louder and louder, her amusement at torturing me evident. "I want you," she says. "I want you."

"Why now?" I yell at her. "Why now, when you never wanted me before? Why did you leave me, Mum?"

But she doesn't answer, and I know for certain then that this woman is not my mother, not really. Instead she reaches for me, her hands almost grasping at my shoulders, almost taking me and keeping me here, trapped within this nightmare. Almost making me hers. Almost.

Because then, thank God, I wake up.

24

Eleanor
September 1972

Swiftly I make my way down the lane, sheltered by the darkness of the moonless sky. Above me the tall trees swish and strain against the power of the wind which has brought cold air and heavy rain to Kirtlebeck. It is an unsettled, autumnal night, far from conducive to venturing out before dawn. I have been awake for many hours now; I can feel tiredness prickle at the corners of my eyes, but I had to stay up. I had to wait for Bert to go to bed. I had to wait to make my escape. In truth, I am still surprised that I had any means of escape. After the way our conversation ended earlier today, I thought Bert might have locked me in the attic or chained me to the stairs. After all, he made it quite clear that he thinks I'm mad, or dangerous, or both.

"You must see how unwell you've become over these past few months," he said to me once he'd finally got me to sit down in the living room.

I shook my head fiercely at him. I could see well enough where this was going and I was determined to refute his ludicrous assertions. "Unwell?" I asked. "What do you mean by unwell? There's nothing wrong with me. I'm perfectly fine. You're the one who is sick – cheating on me, making attempt after attempt to destroy my happiness. What happened today is just the latest example of that."

"What happened today was that I was forced to protect you for your own good. You cannot go through with that exhibition – the attention, the exposure, the criticism, it will destroy you." He put his head in his hands, playing up his exasperation, but I wasn't fooled.

"Destroy me? And who are you, to be the judge of what will destroy me?" I got to my feet, pointing an accusing finger at him. "I think it is you who has done me the greatest harm; you and your other woman."

"Oh for God's sake Eleanor, let it go! What's done is done – you said so yourself, the day we moved up here. You promised then that you'd put all of this in the past where it belongs, that we'd move on together as a family. Instead you've turned it into a weapon, throwing it at me at every opportunity."

"How can I put it behind me when you…you…" my words faltered and I fell silent. I was about to tell him that I knew she was here, that I knew he'd brought her with him, but I stopped myself just in time. Bert talked of weapons; that knowledge, I realised, is the only weapon I have against him.

"I what, Eleanor? I have done everything I can possibly do to make amends. I moved us away, I started again with you and Anna in this lovely house, in this peaceful little village. God knows, I've had to build my business again from scratch. Do you know how hard that is?"

"Don't pretend you did it for us," I replied through gritted teeth. "You did it so that you could run away." I used those words intentionally, of course. I didn't want to admit what I know, but I did want to torture him with some of it.

His eyes widened at me. "What do you mean by that?"

I shrugged, giving him a sweet smile. "Oh you know, Albert. You know exactly what I mean. You needed to absolve yourself, to break ties with your filthy little affair. What happened – was it no longer so appealing once it ceased to be a secret? Maybe it wasn't just me who discovered the truth, maybe she had a husband who found out too…"

"No," he interrupted me. His voice was cool but his face was red enough to tell me that I'd hit upon a grain of the truth. "I chose my family. I chose you, and look what it got me. A crazed alcoholic wife who locks herself away and paints on the walls. And then, if that wasn't bad enough, she plans to participate in an exhibition and bring the evidence of her mania to the attention of the local press! Can you imagine the repercussions of that, Eleanor? Can you imagine what people would think? Can you imagine how the kids at school would behave towards Anna after the news of your insanity became public?"

"I am not insane!" I screamed at him. "It isn't insane to resent your cheating spouse. It isn't insane to express your creativity on the walls of your home. It isn't insane to want to meet likeminded artists, to collaborate with them, to try to make a name for yourself in a place where no one knows who you are! God I wish I had left you! I wish I'd had the strength to take your daughter far away from you!"

Bert sat back in his chair and scratched his jaw, and my hackles instantly rose at that familiar, irritating gesture. There he was, trying to handle me once again. "But you didn't leave," he replied, his tone sickeningly nonchalant. "You stayed. You made your bed and you're lying in it. And now I'm warning you: mend your ways, Eleanor. Stop dwelling on the past, stop scribbling on walls, and stop wandering off and advertising your lunacy to the world. Because if you don't, I will have you locked up. I've had enough. I will not put up with anymore."

I will not put up with anymore.

The wind blows hard against me, but in truth I am unsure if it is that or the memory of Bert's warning which makes me feel chilled. I'd be fooling myself if I thought that Bert's ultimatum hadn't frightened me, that it hadn't left me feeling hopelessly caught in his web of lies and deceit. That is why I've stayed up for all these hours, why I've waited until his watchful eyes are closed before leaving the house. I don't know what to do; I don't know how to overcome him, and I badly need some help and advice. I desperately need to find a way to use the only things he doesn't know about to my advantage: my knowledge of that woman's whereabouts, and my friendship with Meg. Right at this moment, under the cover of darkness, I need to talk to Meg.

I arrive at Thistle Cottage, slipping quickly through the gate and up the footpath. Inside I can see that the lights are on, and my heart warms momentarily at the realisation that, once again, my friend is there for me when I need her. My brisk knock at her door is answered almost immediately, and the sight of her face almost causes me to cry out with relief until I notice her ghastly pallor and heavy eyes.

"I've been wondering when you'd call again," her voice a weak whisper as she lets me inside.

"God, Meg, you look worse than ever! Don't you think you should see a doctor?" Momentarily I forget my own troubles, overcome instead with guilt. I should have checked on her. I should have visited sooner. What sort of a friend am I?

"Doctors can't do anything about what's ailing me," she replies curtly, "and neither can you. This sort of sickness never goes away."

We both pause for a moment, lingering silently in the narrow hallway. Meg doesn't invite me into the sitting room, and I realise that my visit tonight will be short. I want to ask her about this dreadful, apparently incurable illness, but something stops me. Something tells me that my questions would be futile, that she isn't going to reveal any more.

"I'm really sorry to bother you again," I say quietly. "I've not been a very good friend to you, have I? I always seem to need so much from you, but I never return the favour."

Meg reaches out and touches me gently on the arm. "You've been a great friend. I'm just not very good at confiding in people, as I think you've probably realised by now."

"I wish you would tell me what's wrong…" I begin, but Meg cuts me off, placing her fingers softly against my lips.

"Please Eleanor, don't worry about me." She gives me a measured look, those dark eyes reading me once again. "I think it's you we should be worried about. You're a deathly colour. What's happened?"

I take a deep breath. Aware of the late hour, I try to relate the whole sorry mess to her as succinctly as I can manage. When I get to the part about Bert telling Emma I was mad and asking her to leave, I see Meg's hackles rise for the first time, her pale face flushing with indignation. By the time I conclude the tale with the details of his horrible ultimatum, she is almost shaking with rage. I have never seen her look this way before, and I realise that it both excites and unnerves me.

"How dare he," she mutters through gritted teeth. "How dare he do this to you."

"But that's just it, isn't it?" I say with a weary sigh. "He's my husband. He's a man who has cheated on me, who has uprooted me from my life, who has isolated me, who has belittled who I am at every turn. He has done all this and yet I have stayed with him – call it cowardice or misplaced loyalty, but for whatever reason, I haven't left. He knows that he can pretty well do whatever he pleases, safe in the knowledge that I'm not going to do anything about it."

Meg narrows her eyes at me. "But something's changed this time. This time you are going to do something." I can't decide whether her words are a question or an instruction.

"I have to," I reply with a resolve which surprises me. "I can't live like this anymore. It's bad enough knowing that he's moved his mistress into the village, that he's carrying on with her again under my nose, but I could have put up with that, I could have ignored it if…"

"If he'd allowed you to have your art." Meg finishes my sentence for me and wraps me in her delicious, floral embrace.

"Oh Eleanor, this is all so terrible for you."

"Yes. You know better than anyone how cathartic those murals have been for me," I say, my voice shaking with emotion as a tear tumbles down my cheek. Her arms are warm and comforting, to the point of allowing me to unravel completely. I bite my lip hard, trying to keep myself in check.

"But he can't allow it," Meg continues. "He can't help himself; he has to suffocate you. He has to take everything from you until there's nothing left."

I nod, my weeping eyes wetting her shoulder. Once again, Meg is right. Once again, she expresses the truth about my life better than I ever could.

"So, you can't allow him to carry on like this," she continues. In contrast with her loving embrace, her voice is coldly factual. "You have to act now. This is your last chance, Eleanor. You have to have courage, otherwise you're at risk of losing yourself altogether. I saw it almost happen before, when I first met you. I saw the darkness growing behind your eyes. I watched as you almost drowned yourself in wine and misery. You pulled yourself back from the abyss, you found meaning and purpose in your work but if you allow Bert to take that away from you…" her voice trails off, but I understand her meaning well enough. "Trust me, I know what it's like to be left with nothing."

"By the man you told me about? The one you once loved?" I ask, recalling that strange conversation several weeks ago.

"Yes," she replies, her tone brittle. She releases me from her tight grip. "Like you, I had a choice to make."

"I don't even know what my choices are," I tell her. "This is just like being back in Manchester and finding out about his affair all over again. I couldn't leave – I had nowhere to go and no one to turn to. And I had Anna to think about – I couldn't bear to leave her with him, but I knew I didn't have the means to take her with me. I felt trapped then and I feel trapped now."

"But this isn't like last time," she insists. "This time you are prepared. This time you know what's going on, and can use that knowledge to your advantage, surely."

"I know some of what's going on," I correct her.

Meg frowns. "What do you mean by that?

"I don't know." I recall the day I spied on Bert and his tart together, eavesdropping from behind the bins while they talked about their fear, about how they had run away. "I just have a niggling feeling that there's more to all of this than meets the eye."

"Even if that's the case, you still know that his other woman is here, somewhere. Did you find out where he's hiding her?"

"Oh, yes I did." In the midst of today's developments, I had forgotten that I hadn't told Meg about that. "In fact, it was surprisingly easy to find her. I actually saw the two of them together on her doorstep, not an ounce of shame between the pair of them."

"But they didn't see you?"

"No."

"Good." Meg allows herself a small smile. "Then you still have the element of surprise." Briskly she turns on her heel and grabs her shawl from the hook on the wall and starts wrapping it around her shoulders.

"What do you mean?" I ask. "What are you doing?"

"I'm coming with you, of course," she replies, that smile growing ever broader. I note the pink returning to her cheeks and the excitable glint lingering in her eyes. Strangely, despite the late hour, she looks restored, like the Meg I first met.

"But where are we going?" I pursue my line of questioning but in truth I already know the answer.

"To see that woman," she replies, "and to deal with this situation once and for all. I told you the last time I saw you that you would have your revenge when the time was right. Well, now is the time."

"But what am I going to do? Confront her? What good will that do?"

Meg takes hold of my hand. "Just follow my lead," she says, her voice suddenly quiet and calm. "I will be with you, every step of the way. Just do as I tell you and everything will be fine. You're going to have everything that is due to you, Eleanor. You're going to bring Bert's sordid little world crashing down. It's time for him to know what it's like to lose everything."

Before my stunned, addled mind can muster a reply, Meg flings the front door open and leads me out into the cold, blustery night. I follow her dumbly, unsure what I'm letting myself in for, but putting my complete trust in her nonetheless. After all, she's done me nothing but good since we met, and it's not like I have any better ideas. In fact, I'd say that without Meg's help, tonight and over the past few weeks, I would still be floundering in an ignorant, drunken, self-pitying stupor. Perhaps Emma was right; perhaps I do have a guardian angel leading me down the path I'm meant to be on.

Nonetheless, as Meg and I reach the lane, staring into its unending dark, I find myself swallowing hard. I tell myself that it is the unsettled night which is unnerving me, sending shivers down my spine. I tell myself again that Meg is just looking out for me, that the excitement in her eyes and secrecy on her lips are perfectly normal. I tell myself that blind faith is good. I tell myself that it'll all be worth it in the end.

And yet, as she clasps my hand ever tighter, pulling me insistently towards the dim village lights, I can't shake off the feeling that wherever Meg is leading me tonight, there will be no turning back.

25

Harry
February 2018

Over the next few days, I make a concerted effort to re-establish some normality in my life. Long, frozen January finally ends, and I decide to use the coming of a new month as a fresh start. I knuckle down to the tasks I have set myself, clearing and cleaning the rooms in this house and arranging for a local charity to collect some of the furniture which, although old fashioned, is too good to simply throw away. As the days pass the house looks increasingly bare, but I find that I am encouraged rather than depressed by that fact. Empty rooms mean progress. Empty rooms mean I can soon leave this place behind.

The hours, although busy, are spent alone, and after a while I do begin to hanker after some company. I try talking to Bert, but when he doesn't answer, I start talking to the house instead. I tell it that it will make a lovely family home for someone new, that what I'm doing is the best thing, that it can never be a home for me. I tell it that I'm sad that I will never know the story it contains, but that I'm starting to come to terms with it. I tell it that I'm grateful for what I do know, for what it has shown me about my family. I thank the house for this; I know more now than I did when I arrived here, and I'll have to be content with that. I tell it that the terrifying dream I had about that woman was a wake-up call, making me realise that I was delving too deeply, that I was allowing my mind to run wild.

"A fevered imagination is what happens when questions go unanswered," I say to the house, and it's true. Between unexplained disappearances, unnerving murals and frightening adolescent fiction, there's enough crazy stuff in my family's story without me adding to it. I had a dream and nothing more; I allowed my mind to retell my mum's story, to bring her protagonist to life, to give her Mum's face and put words in her mouth. I heard her tell me that she wants me, that I need to know the truth, but really that was my subconscious speaking. Well, I don't need to know the truth. I don't need to know anymore.

In the midst of getting this house in order and laying my family history to rest, I also try to get some closure on my own past, plucking up the courage to finally respond to the messages from Deborah and Mark. My replies are brief and lack detail; I don't tell them where I am now or what I'm doing, but I do try to give both of them what they are due from me. In many ways my words to Deborah come easier; she was wronged by me, I know that, and while I would never expect forgiveness I want her to know how sorry I am.

I'm truly sorry for the hurt I've caused you, I say to her. *I know that my apology will never be enough but please know that I love you and hope you can be happy again one day.*

Replying to Mark is harder, mainly because I'm still not sure what I feel, or what I ever felt, for him. Was it love? Can it ever be love when what you had together was built upon betrayal and deceit? In the end, I settle for letting him know where he stands. If I want to move on with my life, then it's only fair to give him the chance to move on with his.

What we did was wrong, I tell him. *We were both to blame. I need to move on, and I think you do too. I hope you can find happiness again.*

When I check my phone a day later, neither of them have

replied. I decide that's probably for the best.

In the quietest moments, the ones which exist in the lulls between all this activity, I find myself thinking about Daniel. I haven't seen or heard from him in over a week, not since the morning when he left me in bed to ponder his subdued, bewildering declaration: I wish I could be more for you. I think about the time we've spent together, the moments we've shared, the way our easy friendship quickly transformed into something altogether more intense. I think about the things I told him, and the things I didn't. What if he knew the whole story about my affair with Mark? Would he still speak to me? Have my crazy stories about ghoulish grandfathers and paranormal phenomena already served to frighten him away? I glance out the window from time to time, contemplating whether I should wander down the lane and call at Thistle Cottage, casually enquiring after him. After all, it's not like him to remain out of touch for so long; since we met barely a day has passed where we haven't seen each other. But then…but then…

But then he kissed me, and immediately barriers were erected. Perhaps by keeping his distance he's simply seeking to protect his heart, and mine.

Besides, I think as I walk away from the window for the umpteenth time, I can only imagine the level of interrogation I would get from his mother if I asked to see him. That woman's defensiveness of her son really is something else.

On an unusually mild Tuesday morning, I finally bite the bullet and pack away Eleanor's record player and vinyl collection. I know I've been putting this off; the empty living room they now inhabit, stacked rather sadly in a corner, is a testament to that. There's something deeply personal about those items; Bert said enough about them for me to realise how much they must have meant to Eleanor. If I'm honest, I know that I've half-convinced myself that their removal will somehow result in some vengeful act from a ghostly Eleanor who, already furious with me for giving her cheating spouse the time of day, will decide that disposing of her David Bowie records is absolutely the last straw.

Hurriedly I sneak the items out of the house and into the car, stowing them away in the boot where they can't be seen by prying ethereal eyes. I know I'm probably being ridiculous, but after that horrid experience I had, the ice I felt, the noises and the condemnatory words I heard, I decide that I can't be too careful. If it is Eleanor who haunts this house, and I still believe that it is, then I don't want to do anything else which risks provoking her wrath.

I place a couple more boxes on the back seat, filled with lamps, vases, a candelabra and other miscellany which seemed too good just to throw away. I plan to drive to Annan and drop everything off at one or two of the charity shops; while I'm there I also intend to pick up some provisions since my fridge is empty and I've spent the last couple of days living on cans of tomato soup and toast. My mouth waters at the thought of a good, wholesome meal, and I realise I haven't eaten well since the night Daniel cooked for me. Quickly I push the thought from my mind, before all those other memories can take hold, the ones which contain warm fires, heartfelt conversations, and the feeling of his arms around me as we danced. Obsessing over the details of our time together will do me no good. I take a deep breath, inwardly disciplining myself. It's time to dispense with it all: my past, this house, my family's story, and Daniel. It's time to move on. Again.

I turn the key in the ignition. My little car judders and chugs, stirring briefly to life, but then the engine cuts out. I groan. I don't need this today; I've got things to do.

"Come on, come on…" I urge it, trying again, turning the key harder as though sheer force and willpower can make the engine start. Again the car considers my command, its motor whirring and straining for several seconds before cutting out completely.

"Shit. Shit!" I bang my hand against the steering wheel. I can't believe this has happened now, just when I was getting somewhere, just when I was making progress. My mind wanders to the contents of the car's boot and my eyes shift suspiciously back towards the house, seeking any sign of life from beyond the grave. Is it possible that this is Eleanor's doing, just so she can stop me from taking her record player away? I shudder, remembering how she put out a roaring fire and turned my living room ice cold. If she could do that, then breaking a car engine is probably nothing to her.

"Bert?" I whisper. "If you're there, I could really do with your help right now."

"I'm here." His voice is characteristically gruff. "Sounds like you've got car trouble."

"Yeah. I think Eleanor did it. I have her record player in the boot. I was going to take it to the charity shop."

"I've told you, it's not Eleanor in that house. I would know if it was."

I narrow my eyes. "Who else could it be? Wait, are you admitting that there is someone else in there?"

"Could be the spark plugs. Or the carburettor. Have you tried adjusting the choke?"

I throw my arms up in despair at Bert, once again dodging a direct question. "It doesn't have a choke, it's fuel injection. God, who made you an expert?"

"Well I was a mechanic," he retorts. "No choke then, eh? Times have changed."

"You were a mechanic," I repeat. It's funny; all the questions I've asked Bert about my family and yet what he did for a living was never one of them.

"Isn't that Daniel fella a mechanic as well?"

I nod, which seems silly as I've no idea if Bert is even in the car, or if it's just my voice he's picking up on. It's the first time we've spoken outside of the house, and if I wasn't so preoccupied with my current car trouble I'd give more thought as to how all this talking to the dead stuff works. But right now, I don't have time for the questions lingering at the back of my mind, about how he moves around, why he can't always access the house, and where he goes when he isn't in my home. And even if I did, he probably wouldn't answer them anyway.

"Why don't you give him a call? Ask him for his help?"

I sigh, thinking again about how many days it has been since we last saw each other, since we last spoke. "I really don't want to bother him. Besides, I left my phone in the house."

"Well, go and get it."

I glance warily at the front door. "I don't think that's a good idea. If Eleanor's pissed off enough to break my car, then God knows what she'd do to me if I set foot back in there."

"It's not Eleanor in the house, Harriet."

"Then who is it?" I raise my voice far more than I intend to and immediately regret it. Every time I get cross Bert stops speaking to me, and the last thing I need right now is another one of his silent treatments. "I'm sorry. I just – I just don't need this right now. I just want to get on, to get away. I just want to see this through and move on with my life."

"Didn't Daniel say he runs a garage in the village? Why don't you wander down there and see if someone can come up and have a look under the bonnet? That way you don't have to get your phone, and you don't have to bother Daniel specifically. Although I suspect if he's there he'll be the one who wants to help you," Bert adds mischievously.

"I wouldn't be so sure about that."

"Why? Don't tell me you pair have fallen out?"

"It's a long story."

"You can tell me later then. Now go on, go and find Daniel's garage and get this car fixed. Oh, and Harriet?"

"Yes?"

"If his garage is the one next to the Post Office, then it's the same one that I used to run. I loved that place. I built it up from scratch, you know." His voice sounds wistful for a moment.

"Hmm," I reply, getting out of the car and cutting him short. I don't mean to be rude but after weeks of Bert evading my questions I'm not now prepared to listen to tales of his business success. "As you say, I'd better go."

"Yes, yes, of course," he replies. "Take care, Harriet."

"I'm only walking into the village," I scoff.

"I know, but…" he hesitates for a moment. "Sometimes little places like this are the worst for things not being as they seem."

I throw my bag over my shoulder. "Don't I know it," I mutter as I begin my walk towards the lane.

I find the garage easily enough, at the heart of the village and surrounded by a cluster of attractive little dwellings. The Post Office appears to be long gone, but the attractively renovated home bearing the name The Old Post Office which sits next door confirms that Daniel's garage is indeed the same one Bert had all those years ago. Despite my determination to focus on the task at hand I can't help but marvel at the coincidence. Times change, people come and go, but the places they lived in and the buildings they inhabited remain, connecting the generations in so many often unseen ways. It makes me think for a moment about the house at Kirtlebeck End. In recent days I have allowed myself to become detached from it, to see myself as someone who is just passing through. Now, I realise, I am as much a part of its story as Eleanor, Bert, Anna, and the many other people who lived there before, and in turn the house is a part of mine. Not knowing my family's story doesn't alter that at all. The house knows. The house has witnessed it all.

I wander over to the forecourt, a touch of nerves creeping into my steps. It is certainly a busy little place; inside the building I can see a couple of cars up on the ramps, and outside several others sit waiting. I can hear the vague hum of a radio providing a soundtrack to relaxed chatter and the clatter of tools. Finally, I walk inside, the smell of engine oil filling my lungs as I look for a friendly face. Despite my earlier insistence on not bothering Daniel, now I find myself hoping that he's here. Bert was right, after all; he would want to help me. He is my friend. He is my only friend.

"Can I help you?"

A man approaches, his blue overalls covered in oil, his lightly lined face red and sweating. He wipes his hands on an old rag and flashes me an inquisitive look. "Break down, is it?"

I frown. "Yes. How did you know?"

He chuckles lightly. "You look flustered. Is the car in the village?"

"Yes, well, sort of. Up the lane, at the house at Kirtlebeck End."

He nods. "I'd heard a young woman was living up at the big house."

I flinch, wondering if it was Daniel who had told him. Wondering what else he might have told him. "Are you able to come up and take a look? I'd be ever so grateful."

The man hesitates, glances over his shoulder. "We're pretty stacked out with work this afternoon, hen. Tomorrow would be the earliest we could manage, I think."

"I see," I reply, the heat of desperation rising in my cheeks. Tomorrow means losing another day. It means another night of tomato soup and toast. It means facing the wrath of Eleanor's ghost when she knows that she's successfully grounded me, that I have no means of getting away. "The thing is, Daniel gave me his card. He said if I ever need help just to get in touch."

The man's face darkens. "Daniel?" he repeats. "How do you know Daniel?"

"We met a while ago," I explain, exaggerating a little. It can't hurt to make this man think that we're old friends. I look around me. "Is he…is he here?"

The man's expression is grave, his eyes suddenly heavy and glistening with tears. I know then what he is about to say. I read his words before he even utters them, and my breath catches in my throat as it all falls into place. Daniel's words. Daniel's demeanour. His sharp wit and humour under which lies such loneliness, intensity, and sadness. The way he turns up just when I need him. The way he disappears for days without explanation. The way he looks at me like I'm someone he already lost. Suddenly, it all makes sense.

"I'm really sorry to tell you, hen," he says, almost choking out the words. "But Daniel is dead."

235

26

Eleanor
September 1972

By the time we reach the village, I am chilled to the bone. Meg, seemingly unaffected by the freezing wind despite being utterly underdressed in her simple shawl, silently indicates that I should walk in front and take us to the woman's house. The prospect of me leading the way causes me to falter for a moment and immediately I chastise myself for being such a coward.

Meg notices too. "You have to," she reminds me. "I don't know the way. This is your life, Eleanor. Take control of it."

"I know," I hiss, my snappy tone thankfully diluted somewhat by the strong gusts howling around us. "I still don't know what the hell I'm actually doing here. I still don't know what you expect from me…"

"I expect nothing more than you should expect from yourself," she hits back. "Now, take us to her house. Is there a back way in? That way there's less chance of us being seen."

I nod, and with a potent mix of resignation and fear, I take us along the street and up the alley which leads to her back yard. Her house, like those surrounding it, is in complete darkness. Not a soul stirs. As quietly as I can, I open the gate and tiptoe inside, Meg following closely behind me. For the first time tonight I feel grateful for the wind; the whistles and groans it produces do a great job of masking any careless noise we make. Of course, I think, it could equally betray us, carrying our small sounds along with it and taking them to the unwanted attention of a night owl neighbour or insomniac passer-by. Immediately I dismiss the thought, telling myself to stop being negative. Not everything must end badly. Not everything lets me down. Meg's presence here with me tonight is surely proof of that.

I duck down behind the bins, instinctively finding my way to that familiar spot. Meg does the same, taking a moment to adjust her shawl and tame her dark hair. We sit for a moment in the shadows, both catching our breath and taking stock of the situation. Only the barest amount of light filters in from the nearby street lamps; even so, I can see well enough to note that enduring strange look in my friend's eyes – wild, excited, and, I think, faintly amused.

"Well?" I ask her. "We're here. What do we do now? We can't sit here all night."

"We need to get into that house, of course," she replies.

"What are you suggesting? That we break in?" I feel my heart begin to race at the very idea. I've still no idea what I expected to happen tonight, but an act of criminality certainly wasn't what I had in mind.

"Goodness, no! Although I quite like the idea of frightening the life out of her." She gives an unsettling giggle. "You'll just have to knock on the door."

"What, me? Now? In the middle of the night? I don't know, Meg, shouldn't we just come back in the morning?"

"No," she says flatly. "There's no time like the present. Honestly Eleanor, how can you expect to be rid of this woman if you're not even willing to confront her?"

Her words bite at me but I have to concede that she has a point. "But what should I say to her? How should I handle this?"

Meg flashes me a smile and touches me lightly on the shoulder.

"Just follow your instincts. You'll know what to do."

I gaze back at her for a moment, trying to find the reassurance I need in that pretty, friendly face. But tonight her beauty is obscured by that odd expression, the one I can't read, the one which fills her eyes with restlessness and makes her smile seem strained, almost forced.

"Alright," I say in the end, sighing with resignation. "Alright. It's not like things can get any worse, I suppose."

Tentatively I emerge from my hiding place and creep over to the house. I raise my hand and give three timid taps on the wooden door. The deep sound seems to reverberate through the silent night air, causing me to step back into Meg, who stands behind me. I am shaking like a leaf, partly because I am so cold and partly because I am terrified. We wait for what feels like an eternity but no sound comes from within, no light flickers on and no footsteps approach to answer us.

"I don't think she heard us," I whisper, stating the obvious.

"Try again," Meg hisses back. "Knock on the glass this time. Knock harder."

"But what if someone hears us?"

Meg looks over her shoulder. "There's no one around. And besides, there's no law against knocking on someone's door."

"There might be at two in the morning," I mutter to myself.

Before I can knock again, the light inside flickers on. I hear the soft beat of footsteps as they come towards us. I hold my breath, preparing myself for her coming to the door, for what she might say, for what she might do. I had been so caught up in what I was going to do that it took until now for me to even consider her response to my visit. Will she be surprised, upset, angry? Do I even care?

I wait and wait, growing increasingly agitated. She doesn't open the door; instead, those footsteps divert into the kitchen, where the light goes on and the sound of running water can be heard. It dawns on me then that we are not the ones who woke her, that she is not aware of our presence outside, and that something else is keeping her up in these night-time hours.

"She doesn't know we're here, Meg," I say, my words so quiet that they are barely audible.

Meg doesn't answer me. Before I can comprehend what is happening, she reaches forward, scraping her long fingernails down the wood of the door. She repeats the action over and over again, scratching and scraping like an animal. Except that, unlike a dog or cat frantically trying to get the attention of its owner, her movements are even, rhythmic, filled with intent. They are the actions of someone in complete control, who understands what needs to happen, who knows what she wants and how to get it. They are the sorts of actions which I can only aspire to.

Inside, I sense her hear us. The kitchen light goes off and silence falls. We listen and she listens, stood still like pieces on a chess board, each trying to decide our next move.

"Hello?" Her voice comes at us, muffled by the thick wood of the door. "Who's there? Bert, is that you? Has something happened?"

Meg nudges me hard in the ribs, causing me to yelp. "It's – it's me. It's Eleanor," I mumble, realising as I speak that she might not even remember who I am. To her I am just Bert's crazy wife, a figure of fun, a mere inconvenience. "It's Bert's wife," I add, feeling the heat of humiliation rising in my cheeks. Sensing my agony Meg takes hold of my hand, squeezing it tightly.

A difficult silence descends, disrupted only by the blowing breeze. She's thinking, I realise. A thousand and one thoughts are racing through her mind. Bert's wife? What is she doing here? How did she find me? What does she want? All the thoughts that I know I would have, if I was ever in her position.

Except I'm not. She's the lover. I'm the woman scorned.

"Eleanor?" Her voice is surprisingly gentle, although she still doesn't open the door. "What are you doing here?"

I look helplessly at Meg. She stares back at me, her eyes burning with impatience, gesturing that we need to go inside.

"I – I need to talk to you," I stammer.

"At this time of night? Does Bert know you're here?"

"No." I try to ignore my hackles rising at her insinuation that I am somehow accountable to my treacherous, uncaring husband. "Can I come in?"

The jangling of keys gives me my answer. She takes her time in opening the door, allowing it to shuffle slowly over the thick pile carpet. She peers around at me, dark circles under her eyes illustrating her wary gaze. She looks tired and on edge, and once again it occurs to me that something must be keeping her up at night. Something other than her lover's wife coming to call.

She opens the door wider, bidding us to come inside. Wordlessly she leads us away from the back door and into a small living room. Despite the late hour and my growing anxiety at the difficult conversation which must surely follow, I can't help but take a look around. Her home is cosy and recently modernised, its fresh décor and new furniture sitting in sharp contrast with its antique stone exterior. A bitter taste creeps into my mouth as I compare it with the draughty dilapidation of my home. Trust Bert to keep his mistress in a palace while his family have to make do.

"Is this rented?" I ask, gesturing around me as I take a seat in an immaculate armchair.

She nods. "Bert made all the arrangements…" She stops talking, perhaps sensing that I don't need to hear what she has to say.

"He's good at that, isn't he? Arranging things." As soon as I utter those words, I regret them. Resolving to be more conciliatory, I swallow down my spiteful tone. I flinch as it burns like bile in my stomach.

Thankfully the woman doesn't try to answer me. "What do you want, Eleanor? And how did you find me? Did Bert tell you I was here?"

"No!" I scoff. "Even Bert isn't cruel enough to rub my nose in his sordid little affair. Actually, he is cruel enough, but perhaps he's not brave enough. After all, he does believe I am insane. Perhaps he's worried what I would do."

The woman raises an eyebrow at my rant and I see a concerned look flash across her face. "I think you're harsh to call him cruel. I'm not sure you understand him at all."

I give her a hard stare. "That's easy to say when you're the bit on the side," I snap.

She holds her hands up in surrender. "Yes, of course. I'm not a part of your marriage. That's between you and Bert."

"No, you're not a part of it. You're an appendage, a blight, a fucking pustule." I look to Meg for support and see from her face that she likes my words.

The woman begins to rise from her seat. "Look, if you've come here just to trade insults, I think it would be best if you leave." She begins to walk towards the back door. Feeling panicked, I follow her.

"No. Listen, sorry, you're right. I've not come here to yell at you." I let out a heavy sigh and rub my brow, my head suddenly aching with fatigue.

"Then what are you here for, Eleanor?"

"I don't know." I look helplessly at Meg, who has joined us in the hallway. "To just talk, I suppose. To find out what's going on. To ask you to please leave."

"Leave?" She latches on to that final word as she walks into the kitchen, pouring herself a glass of water and gulping it down thirstily.

I stand in the doorway, watching her. I have to admit, even in her dressing gown and slippers, with her face devoid of makeup and her hair dishevelled, she is a beauty. I still have absolutely no idea what she sees in my husband.

"You want me to leave?" she repeats again, wiping her mouth with the back of her hand. "Do you have any idea what you're asking of me?"

"Do you have any idea what you being here is doing to me?" I retort. "My daughter already knows what her father did back in Manchester. She knows why we came here. She hates him for what he has done. Can you imagine what it will do to her when she finds out that you're here?"

"You weren't supposed to know that I'm here," she says quietly.

"Obviously. What man would want his wife to know he's fucking someone else? Getting found out was the cause of all his problems last time." I scoff.

"No, you don't understand. If Bert keeps things from you both, it's to keep you safe. You don't know the half of what has gone on…"

"Well please, enlighten me."

She stares at me and for a moment, she looks like she's about to tell me something, as though some long-withheld truths are teetering on the edge of her pink lips. Then she presses them tightly together, and I can see that she has stepped back from the brink. "I can't."

I narrow my eyes at her. "You can't? Or you don't want to?"

"Both." Her gaze softens, and she looks at me with such pity that I feel the depths of my stomach begin to burn with fury. "It isn't for me to tell you, Eleanor. This is a conversation you need to have with your husband."

"Bert will never tell me anything, you know that."

"Perhaps that's true. I believe he thinks he's protecting you."

"From what?" I feel my voice lift an octave as my anger begins to break free. "The only thing I need to be protected from is my philandering husband. That man has ruined my life, sucking the joy from me bit by bit, denying my creativity, destroying the person I used to be…" My lip trembles and to my utter shame and humiliation, the tears begin to fall.

"Stop crying, Eleanor. Don't show her any weakness," Meg mutters from behind me. Her words cause me to startle; for a moment I had forgotten my friend was there.

"Oh Eleanor." The woman steps forward, touching me tenderly on the arm. "I don't think you can hold Bert responsible for all of that, can you? He talks about you a lot, you know. He worries about you, about your moods, about your drinking, he -"

"You don't know what you're talking about," I growl, my voice so deep and feral that I barely recognise it as my own. "You need to leave, you need to go right now and get far away from this place. You need to leave us alone."

"She's not going to leave, Eleanor," Meg hisses.

"No. I'm sorry but I told you already, I can't leave." She gives me a hard stare, a determined look etched upon her pretty face. I know then that she means what she says, that she isn't going anywhere. I know then that my situation is completely hopeless.

"Oh God!" I cry out, covering my face with my hands. "What am I going to do?"

"You need to go home and talk to Bert. And get some help. I really think you need to get some help," she replies.

"You need to end this once and for all," Meg whispers in my ear, stroking me gently on the arm.

"End it? How?" I mutter back.

"The only way these things can ever end." Before I know what she's doing, Meg guides my hand up towards the nearby knife stand, wrapping my fingers around the handle of the largest, sharpest blade.

I draw out the knife slowly, and watch as the woman's eyes widen. She backs away from me, pressing herself up against the kitchen counter. "No," she begins. "Don't do this Eleanor, we can talk about this, we can work something out."

I move towards her, taking several deep breaths as I try to block out her pleas and steady my trembling hand. I feel terrified, horrified and sickened, but also strangely empowered. For the first time in a long time, I am holding all the cards. For the first time in a long time, I am in complete control.

"Just remember what they've done to you," Meg calls out from behind me. "Just remember how Bert threatened you, how he wants to have you locked up. You know why he wants to do that, don't you? You know it's so that he can be with her instead."

I draw close to her, watching with delight as her face dissolves into tears. "You don't have to do this," she repeats. "It doesn't have to end this way."

I grit my teeth, staring hard into her weeping eyes. "Yes it does."

"I've been waiting for someone to come and end things like this, but I never imagined it would be you."

"You really are on the run from someone, aren't you?"

A flicker of confusion passes across her tear-stained face. "So you do know?"

"Not everything," I confess. "But enough to know you're both in trouble."

"Listen, Eleanor, I'll tell you everything if you put the knife down," she offers, her voice shaking with the recognition that she's just played her last bargaining chip.

"You know, I don't think I really want to know the gory details anymore," I reply, a twisted chuckle escaping from me before I can stop it. "I do want to know one thing, though."

"What?"

"Your name. I've never known your name."

"Barbara. Barbara Bevan."

"It's nice to meet you, Barbara."

"You're a crazy fucking bitch, Eleanor."

Her coarse language throws me for a moment, just long enough for her to push her hands against me and make her desperate bid for freedom. Her attempt is futile, of course; I am faster and stronger than she is, fuelled by my rage and a newfound taste for power and revenge. And besides, Meg still stands near the doorway, blocking the exit while she enjoys the show. I pull Barbara back by the hair and glance at my friend, my eyes pleading for a final piece of reassurance.

"Do it," she instructs.

I nod and smile. There can be no clearer guidance than that.

I've never thought that I would ever kill anyone, and it is over far quicker than I would have expected. I wield the blade like an expert, drawing a line across her throat with the precision of an artist intent on her craft. Blood spatters like paint, decorating that pristine kitchen in minutes, disrupting its clean surfaces, creating chaos on its perfect floor. I am reminded of my murals, the depth, the fury and the darkness they harbour, the way they interrupt the faded walls of my home with their boldness and grandeur. This scene, I realise, is the ultimate work of art. It is the final act of releasing all those feelings which, I know now, my murals could never hope to contain forever.

I let go of Barbara's hair, her lifeless body hitting the floor with a dull thud. "What now?" I ask Meg.

She gives me a big smile, one which tells me that she's pleased, that she's happy. That she's proud of me. "Our work here is done. Time to go home," she replies.

I nod, stepping over the body and walking towards her. I reach out for her hand and she offers it gladly, her cool fingers providing the strength and sustenance I find I suddenly need.

"You did well tonight," she says, giving my hand a quick squeeze. "There is one more thing, however."

"What is it?" I ask, my voice sounding muffled and dazed.

Her grin grows broader. "Don't forget to bring the knife with you."

Realising that it's still in my hand, I tighten my fingers around the handle, noticing for the first time how my sweat has dampened the cold metal of my murder weapon. My heart pounds hard with fear and fascination at what I've just done. I've just killed my husband's lover. I've just slit the throat of a woman whose name I hadn't known until moments before. I've just taken a life.

Feeling suddenly overwhelmed, I grip Meg's hand tighter. "You won't leave me, will you?" I ask her with the desperation of a child.

"Of course not," she replies. "I'll come over to your house tomorrow. You have a phone call to make."

"Do I?"

"Yes, of course you do. You need to phone Emma McCabe and tell her that you will be part of the exhibition."

I nod meekly. Meg's hushed tone is forceful enough to make me understand that I shouldn't argue. She's right, of course. Why else did I come here, if it wasn't to rid myself of that woman, to make a stand against my husband and have my revenge for all that he has done? If I stop now, if I give up and surrender myself to Bert's wishes, then everything I did tonight will be for nothing. I have to follow this path I'm on; I have to see where it leads.

Above all, I realise, I have to find my freedom, even if it costs me everything. Even if I have to keep on killing for it.

27

Harry
February 2018

I hammer hard on the front door of Thistle Cottage, my loud bangs reverberating down the lane in tandem with my sobs. My heart pounds hard in my chest and fresh tears streak my face. I don't care if I make a scene. I don't care if concerned neighbours and friends come to see what's going on. I'm a mess; everything is a mess. I've spent all these weeks trying to unearth my family's secrets, disturbing ghosts probably best left to rest, and all the while the one person I knew in this godforsaken place who I counted among the living was actually dead too. I'd laugh at the irony of it if I wasn't so distressed. I really liked him; really, really, liked him. I was deeply, hopelessly attracted to him. I think one day I could have loved him, if I didn't already. The past tense I apply to these thoughts only serves me to cry harder, and my whole body shakes as I drive my fist at the door one more time.

Finally, Emma answers. She looks at me, her eyebrows raised, her bright eyes knowing.

"So, you know the truth, then." Her words come out as a statement of fact rather than a question.

I nod, biting my lip hard in a futile effort to quell the tears which keep clouding my vision.

"I think you'd best come in."

She leads me to that bright, airy sitting area where we sat and made small talk merely a week ago. I look around, noting once again those cleanly decorated magnolia walls I had so admired on my first visit. I'd been drawn to the neat clarity of this place then, but now I find it bare, almost barren, as though something has been stripped away and is notable by its absence.

His absence.

I take a deep, uneven breath as I sit down on the sofa. Emma says something about fetching us some tea and I nod blandly, unable to focus my mind on mundane niceties like warm drinks and biscuits. Given what we're about to discuss, I almost wish she'd offered me something a little stronger. Like wine. A good, red wine, just like that nice bottle Daniel brought for me.

But how could a ghost bring me wine? Or did I imagine it? Did I imagine him?

Emma hands me a warm mug and sits down opposite me, flashing me a small smile, half-grim, half-apologetic.

"Did he ever live here?" I ask, unsure why I've decided to begin with that question.

"Yes. Yes, this was very much his home. He designed it, had it built, and lived here until his death."

Her use of that last word feels like a punch in the gut. "And how did he…when did he…?"

"Six months ago." She closes her eyes for a moment and I sense that she's guarding her own emotions. "He was fixing his truck by the roadside. Damn thing had broken down again. Someone came speeding along the lane, they never saw him, and…" She doesn't give words to the rest of it. She doesn't need to.

"That's how I first met him," I say quietly. "I was driving back into Kirtlebeck from Annan and I saw him under the bonnet of his truck. He said he'd broken down. He also accused me of whizzing down the lane."

She gives a wry smile. "That sounds like Danny."

"But how could I have met him like that? How is any of this possible?" I'm not sure if my question is directed at Emma or simply at myself.

"I've seen him too," she replies. "The first time was the day of his funeral. I nearly fainted when he walked back into this house as though nothing had happened, as though we were burying someone else that day. I saw him a lot in those early days, but recently his visits have been less frequent. I wondered if he was starting to, you know, move on, but then you turned up at the house and it all made sense. I realised then where he had been going instead." Despite the heavy subject matter, I sense amusement rather than hurt in her voice. "He did always like a pretty face," she adds with a grin.

"That day I came round here, why didn't you just tell me the truth?"

"Well, for one thing it came as a bit of a shock to have a young woman turn up on my doorstep and start telling me that she'd been talking to my dead son. Even worse to then realise that this young woman believed he was very much alive. How was I meant to break it to you? Besides, it wasn't my secret to tell. Danny is – was a good man. I believed he'd tell you himself when he found the right time."

"But he didn't," I bite back, my sorrow dissipating into anger. "I only found out when I went down to the garage to get help with my car. The poor old guy I met was almost in tears when he told me."

Emma sighs. "Sounds like you spoke to Joe. He's taken the place on now. Danny and him were close. He's taken his death very badly." Her voice breaks and she closes her eyes again. "Losing him has been hard for all of us."

"I'm sorry," I say quietly, feeling suddenly guilty for turning up unannounced with my tears and my questions. Whatever sadness I feel about Daniel's death can only be a fraction of the pain Emma is going through. "I can't even imagine what this has been like for you."

Her eyes grow serious and she reaches over to pat my hand. "Oh, I think you and I have more in common than you might think. We're both alone, and we're both surrounded by ghosts."

Adrenalin bursts unpleasantly through me as she says those words. I think about Daniel, about Bert, about Eleanor. I think about how haunted I feel, how powerless I am in that house, left alone to face their ethereal whims. "What do you mean by that?" I croak, my mouth suddenly dry.

"I haven't been very truthful with you, Harriet," she admits. "I haven't told you everything I know about that house, about your family."

"Don't worry," I quip. "You're not the only one."

Emma narrows her eyes at my sharp remark but doesn't question me further. Instead she gets up from her seat and walks over to the sideboard, opening a drawer and rummaging to find something. When she returns I see that she's holding a set of photographs.

"Aside from talking to my son, has anything strange happened to you since you arrived at that house?"

I nod, thinking immediately of Bert. "You could say that. Why?"

She hands me the photos and returns to her seat opposite. Hurriedly I flick through them, a frown growing between my eyes. Much like the photos Emma showed me when we first met, they all feature my grandmother striking various poses in front of her murals. However, unlike those shots these are mostly unclear, out of focus, or decorated with sharp spots of bright light. In some of the photos the brightness surrounds Eleanor, seeming almost to consume her while she smiles, apparently oblivious to it. I glance once more at the living image of her, shuddering as my mind is drawn back to that day when she placed her cold, dead fingers on my scalp. I turn the photos over and place them on my lap.

"For years I've wondered about those images," Emma muses. "The camera doesn't lie. It can't lie. It picked up something that day, something Eleanor and I couldn't see but which was there anyway. Something which was very attracted to her."

My skin crawls as my mind wanders over the unexplained, the inexplicable. The creaks, the groans, the draughts, the whispers, the ice. For a brief second I entertain the idea that none of this was Eleanor's doing, that it was something or someone else altogether. The thought is so terrifying that my blood runs cold. However unnerving I find the idea that Eleanor is trying to frighten me, the notion that some unnamed force is at work is far worse. Better the dead you know than the dead you don't.

"Maybe it was just a trick of the light," I suggest. "Or perhaps a problem arose when you developed them."

Emma gives a light chuckle. "I seem to remember that's exactly what your grandmother said when I showed them to her." She takes the photos back from me and gives them a swift study. "I told her that I thought she might have a guardian angel. Of course, if she did then they didn't do a very good job of looking out for her. Her life here must have been pretty intolerable."

"You mean because my grandfather went missing?"

She eyes me carefully. "Not just that, although of course that would have been awful. There were a lot of rumours about him, a lot of unpleasantness surrounding his disappearance. Not long after he went missing a woman was found murdered in one of the cottages in the village. That sort of thing doesn't happen in little places like this, and the press were all over it like a rash. I remember reading that she'd lain undiscovered for weeks, that a neighbour had grown concerned about the smell coming from the place and had gone in to find her lying in the kitchen with her throat cut." Emma screws up her nose. "It was all very gruesome, and to make matters worse the police investigation leaked like a sieve. Very soon connections were made, connections which involved Manchester and extra-marital affairs, all of which seemed to lead back to your grandfather. Poor Eleanor was the talk of not just the village but the whole area. Almost overnight it seemed like no one knew her and yet everyone knew all about her. It must have been hellish."

"So the police thought that my grandfather committed some sort of crime of passion and then, what? Ran away for good to escape punishment?" I can hardly believe the words I'm uttering. I can hardly comprehend that Bert, my grandfather, might have done something so unspeakably dreadful. By his own admission he was an adulterer, but a murderer? How was that possible? What could have happened to make him do such a thing?

Emma nods. "I believe that was the theory, although I don't think they could ever prove it."

"Do you think there could be any truth in it?" I don't know why I'm asking, other than to torture myself with the possibility.

"Well, from what I saw all those years ago, your grandparents were far from happily married, and in my experience volatile situations tend to bring out the worst in people. But, murder? I suppose we'll never know now." Something about her carefully chosen words makes me flinch.

"Poor Eleanor," I muse. "Imagine having to spend all those years wondering if it was true or not and never having any answers. And my mum, what must she have made of it all?"

"I think she took it very badly."

"I thought you didn't know her?"

"I didn't, but I heard things from time to time. Back then I knew a lot of people, heard a lot of gossip. She was really quite troubled, I think. She had a reputation for being a bit of a tearaway. Got herself into some trouble with the police, I believe. She left the area in the end, probably as soon as she could. Presumably that's when she went to Manchester and had you."

I nod, thinking not for the first time about my mum's state of mind. The trauma of Bert's disappearance, the dark, violent stories she wrote, the way that years later she was able to just abandon me – it all adds up to someone who was profoundly disturbed. I've felt many things about her disappearance over the years; anger, confusion, regret. Now, for perhaps the first time, I just feel sorry. Sorry for what happened to her. Sorry that she didn't get the help she needed. Sorry that having her own child and making a life with my dad wasn't enough to help her heal.

My face must have fallen in tune with my thoughts, as Emma moves to sit by my side.

"Perhaps I shouldn't have told you all this," she says, giving my shoulders a gentle squeeze.

"No," I reply. "I'm glad you did. Even if it's all bad news, I'd rather know than not know. I've spent my life not knowing."

"How old were you when your mum left?"

"Three."

"So when was that?" Her eyes brighten, alive to possibilities, and I realise she's making connections.

"I don't – I don't know which month exactly, but it was some time in 1990. Why?"

"I think your mum came back here." She pats my hand with a touch of triumph. "I was still living in Lockerbie then. I remember that year clearly because it was Danny's last year at home with me before he took an apprenticeship in Glasgow. I was out shopping in town one afternoon when I spotted them; I hadn't seen Eleanor for years but I knew her straight away. She looked older, of course, and was more smartly dressed than I remembered her ever being, but it was definitely her. It was only afterwards that I realised the young lady she was with must have been Anna. I remember thinking how ill she looked, so pale and thin. Poor thing must still have been suffering, even after all those years."

"She came back here," I mutter quietly, shaking my head, trying to force those words to sink in. "Did you speak to them? Did they say anything to you?"

"No. I'm not sure if Eleanor even saw me, much less recognised me, or if she would have come over to speak to me if she had. She looked uncomfortable, on edge, as though she didn't want to be there. I just didn't have the heart to bother her, if I'm honest. Sometimes I wish I had. I think she probably needed a friend."

"Instead she became a recluse," I muse.

Emma nods her agreement. "She'd never struck me as the most sociable person but yes, if her later years are anything to go by, she certainly decided to shut herself away in that big old house. Mind you, I suppose having the whole world talking about you would be enough to make most of us go into hiding."

"I wish I knew what my mum was doing here. I wish I knew why she left me. I wish I knew where she was now." The lump I've been suppressing in my throat begins to grow and I feel tears prick in the corners of my eyes.

Emma takes hold of my hand, that glassy look returning to her eyes as she gives me a sympathetic stare. "I know," is all she manages to say. "I know."

I leave Thistle Cottage as afternoon becomes evening and the light begins to fade. Street lamps spring to life as I walk up the lane, a thousand thoughts creating chaos in my already addled brain. Today has been exhausting and devastating in equal measure; if it hasn't turned my already pretty screwed up world upside down, then it's come astonishingly close. I ruminate on it all, almost numb with shock about the information which Emma provided. My rude, adulterous, frustratingly evasive grandfather might also be a murderer. My mum, too traumatised to raise her own daughter, might have sought refuge in her childhood home. And that home, which is now my home, might contain more things which go bump in the night than I had previously accounted for. So many possibilities. So many maybes. So many answers which only provoke more questions.

Who was the murdered woman? Was she Bert's lover? Why would Bert kill her? And if he didn't, who did?

What happened to my mum to throw her life so horridly off course? Was she unable to come to terms with her father's disappearance, or is there something else in her story which I'm just not seeing?

What are those strange auras on Emma's photographs? Yet more ghosts, or simply a trick of the light? Is there such a thing as a guardian angel?

"Poor Emma's probably just seeing things which aren't really there," I mutter dismissively, before pausing as my own words bite at me. After all, if anyone has been seeing things which aren't really there, it's me.

Tears prick behind my eyes as my thoughts return to the reason I called on Emma in the first place. My friend, my only friend, is dead. Daniel is dead; he was dead before he even met me. That is the only thing I know for certain right now, and it's the most painful truth of them all.

"You managed to fall for a ghost, Harry," I say. "That's even more pathetic than getting involved with your best friend's husband."

I shake my head, realising that I've started talking to myself again. I suppose it's better than talking to the dead.

I draw near to my front door, a sense of trepidation filling my already thrumming heart. Next to the house sits my car, still broken, still packed up with all the things Eleanor loved. I wonder then if she's waiting inside, armed with more chilling anger, ready to let me know exactly what she thinks about my attempts to clear away her life. As I reach into my pocket for my key I notice a piece of paper hanging out of the letter box, flapping a little against the growing breeze. I pick it up, unfolding it as I wonder who it's from. Who in all the world is there to come round here and leave me a note?

When I open it, I see immediately who it must be from.

I love you. Please forgive me.

The handwriting is bold and red, and smudges as my tears fall upon it. I clutch the note to my chest as I hurry inside, my fear of this house overcome now by sheer sorrow, by complete and utter grief. By the sense of isolation brought by the realisation that I'm all alone in the world and that everyone I've ever cared about is dead and gone.

He is dead and gone.

I sink down in that great wide hallway and weep — for my mum and my dad, for Eleanor and Bert, for Daniel. For the fact that I was always too late. For the fact that I was never enough. For the fact that my life is as empty as this place.

I am empty. I am forgotten. I have only ghosts for company. I am just like the house at Kirtlebeck End.

28

Eleanor
October 1972

I check my appearance over one last time and give my reflection a reassuring smile. I am pleased with how I look, my makeup immaculately applied, my hair tamed into place. Even my clothes, which are usually a let-down, aren't too bad. I have opted for that same bright, floral shirt which I had abandoned just before my photo shoot, and have matched it with a neon hairband and some large, colourful earrings which I borrowed from Anna after letting her in on my plans for today. This is the most effort I've put into my appearance in a long time and I'm pleasantly surprised by how good it makes me feel. I've spent so long not caring, so long neglecting myself; I realise now that things have to change. I have to change. I have to reinvent myself, starting with my dowdy wardrobe.

My daughter stands in the doorway, a copy of Jackie magazine in one hand and a hairbrush in the other. "You look good, Mum."

I turn around, smoothing my hands over my shirt. "Do you think so? Maybe the earrings are too much?"

"No." She laughs at me. "Trust me, they suit you. They really make you look the part."

"So you think I'll fit right in with all those arty types?" I ask, wiggling my hips.

"Well, that depends," she replies.

"On what?"

"On whether arty types tend to dance like Pan's People." She hides her face behind her magazine in faux-shame at her cheekiness, but I can see from the way it shakes that she is laughing. I laugh too. She's such a good girl; I think I can permit a little teasing once in a while.

"It's a shame you can't come with me," I say, meaning every word. I would have loved her company this afternoon.

"I know. But I promised Alison I would go over to her house to study. I told you about that test we have next week. I know Alison is really worried about it and I'd feel terrible if I let her down."

I give Anna a reassuring smile. "I know. I'm being selfish but it would have been nice to have you there."

Her expression is apologetic. "It would have been nice to have been there to support you, Mum. I do feel bad about you going on your own. I wish Dad could be a bit more understanding, then he could go with you rather than forcing you to sneak around behind his back."

"It doesn't matter," I shrug. "And besides, I won't be on my own. I have a friend coming with me." This is the closest I've come to telling Anna about Meg and as soon as the words slip out, I hesitate.

Anna's interest piques. "A friend? Someone you've met through doing this exhibition stuff?"

"Sort of."

"Oh, that's nice. I hope I get to meet her one day."

I smile and walk towards the door, giving my daughter's hair a gentle stroke. "I hope so too, sweetheart." I glance at my watch. "Now then, I'd better hurry up and catch that bus to Lockerbie. You know what Sunday services out here will be like."

Anna nods. "What time do you think you'll be home?"

"I've no idea. It starts at four o'clock, but I honestly don't know how long it will take. I presume you'll be home at dinner time? There's food in the fridge, if I'm not back and you want to make yourself something."

"Okay," she replies, "and what should I tell Dad, if he's home from the garage before you get back?"

Her question forces me to stifle a snigger. "Tell him you don't know where I am, that you got back and I'd gone. I don't want him to think you're involved in this and besides, a little bit of mystery will do him no harm."

Anna's expression is obliging but something in her eyes tells me she's hesitant. "Alright Mum, if you're sure."

I give her shoulders a small squeeze. "Of course I'm sure," I reply, and it's true; I've never been more sure. I check myself in the mirror one more time. I am a confident, brilliant woman with a gift to share with others, and today that is exactly what I am going to do. I don't care what Bert does or doesn't know, whether he finds out where I've gone later today or whether he never discovers the truth at all. I know what I want and I've set myself on a course to get it. It's already too late for Bert to stop me.

Briskly I walk down the lane, illuminated by the sunshine on a bright autumn day. It is the first day in October, and while the heat of the summer has long since been extinguished, today it is unseasonably warm. I run my hands down my smartest jacket, feeling glad that the favourable weather meant I could dispense with my very unflattering raincoat. I take a deep, satisfying breath. Everything is falling into place: I feel great, I look great, the weather is great. Today, I feel sure, will be the icing on the cake, the epitome of everything I've worked for. People will see my work and hopefully, they will admire it. The press will write a story about it. I may even get some commissions, just as Emma suggested.

I smile. Emma. She had been very surprised when I phoned her with the news that I could take part in the exhibition after all.

"This is great news," she said. "But what about your husband, what does he…"

"He's had a change of heart," I lied. "He understands now what this means to me."

"Of course," she replied. "Well, it's not like you should need his permission anyway, is it?"

"No. But I have it, all the same." My voice was unnaturally clipped as I struggled to swallow my own deceit. I looked at Meg, who stood by my side, nodding vociferously, her dark eyes wide and understanding.

"That is good news, Eleanor," she answered me in a tone which sounded less than convinced by my story. "Everything is ready for the opening on 1st October. It shouldn't be too difficult to squeeze your images back in. I was half-hoping that you'd be back in touch. Your work is so special; it would have been an enormous shame if people didn't get to see it."

We exchanged a few more pleasantries before ending the call. As I hung up the phone, a pang of guilt and anxiety reverberated through me about what I had done, and what I had committed myself to. It must have shown on my face because Meg picked up on it straight away.

"Don't worry," she reassured me. "You've done the right thing."

"Have I? What if Bert finds out? What if he turns up at the gallery and ruins poor Emma's show?"

"I doubt it," she replied with a snigger. "I bet he won't even notice that you've gone. Something tells me he will have other things on his mind just now."

"Meg, don't."

"Don't what? Oh come Eleanor, don't tell me you're having regrets about last night."

"You say it like it was nothing, like I went out and had too much to drink, maybe woke up next to some handsome stranger and committed a little infidelity of my own."

Her face darkened at the mere suggestion. "Don't say that – not even in jest."

"I'm not joking, Meg. I was so angry, so resentful of them both – I still am. But what I did, what I found the strength to do, I can't believe that I…I took a life last night." I whispered the words, letting them hang between us for an awkward moment. Feeling the tension, the adrenalin, the sheer terror of the last twenty-four hours suddenly hit me I clutched my forehead. "I've got a headache. I think I need to lie down."

Once again, Meg took charge of the situation. "You need to get a hold of yourself, Eleanor. No looking back now, only forward. Last night you did what had to be done, and today you took the first step towards your future. You know who you are, and you know what you want, so now you just have to go and get it."

"You make it sound so simple."

"It is simple. Well, as long as you get away with it. I take it you covered your tracks and dealt with the knife?"

I nodded, recalling its hiding place in my bedroom cupboard, wrapped in cloth and well concealed in a shoe box. "Yes, I don't think anyone will find it."

"Good. Remember, there are only two types of people in our lives: those who help and those who hinder. Rely on the first type and get rid of the latter. If you do that, you won't go far wrong, trust me. You do trust me, don't you, Eleanor?"

"Of course. Always," I replied, reaching for her hand. "I wouldn't be anywhere without you."

Thankfully, that is the only real difficult moment I've had. As I draw closer to Thistle Cottage, I congratulate myself on how well I've coped. It's been a little over a week now since it happened, and apart from a few bad dreams and nasty flashbacks, I've excelled as the gatekeeper of my thoughts, hardly allowing myself a moment to think about it, let alone to feel any remorse or regret. I've no idea if Bert knows, if he's visited her house and stumbled upon his nasty surprise. Given the frequency with which she expected him to visit, I would be surprised if he hadn't, but in any case he is hardly ever around and when he is, he plays his cards close to his chest, just as he always has. After a few days of wondering, I realised it didn't matter anyway. Bert will never suspect me; no one will. As far as he's concerned I'm just mad Eleanor; a drunk, a recluse and a laughing stock. In fact, I think now with a bitter curl of my lip, that has to be the best alibi of them all.

As I reach the thick trees surrounding Thistle Cottage, Meg comes stumbling out of her gate. I notice that she looks tired, her face pale and drawn. I've seen that weary look before, the day that I turned up unannounced at her house and tried unsuccessfully to persuade her to come looking for that woman with me. However, today there is something different about her, something I can't quite put my finger on, something restless about the way she hovers at the wall, waiting for me.

"Everything alright?" I ask her. "Are you unwell?"

"Not unwell exactly," she replies, "but I don't feel much like myself today. Perhaps I shouldn't come to the exhibition."

I feel my face fall. "Oh but Meg, I need you. I can't do this on my own."

"No, you don't. Listen, I'm just not sure I should be there. All those people…I think my presence will be a problem. Don't you think it'll be a problem?"

"Why on earth would it be?" I ask, incredulous. "It may be busy. In fact, I hope it will be busy! But one more body in the room won't make any difference."

She stares at me for a moment, drenching me in that dark gaze. I know her well enough now to recognise that she's trying to figure out what to say, that a thousand words are racing through her mind and she's deciding which ones will best fit the situation. I flinch as I realise that she reminds me of Bert and how he tries to handle me. Why is it that everyone in my life feels they must manage me, carefully navigating or even manipulating my feelings for their own gain?

"Fine, don't come then," I say, folding my arms tight in front of me as I breeze past her and continue my walk. "I haven't got time to argue about this. I've a bus to catch."

Behind me I hear her sigh. "Alright. I'll come for a little while, if you really want me there."

I stop, turning around a little too triumphantly as I allow her to catch me up. "Thank you, I appreciate it."

"You're welcome." She gives me an apologetic smile, tucking her long dark hair coyly behind her ear. "If I'm coming though, I do have one request to make."

"Oh?"

"Just – just don't make a big deal out of me being there, will you? You know I don't like to be around lots of people. I'd rather just fade into the background. It's your day, so please, just pretend like I'm not even there."

"Of course." A concerned frown creases my brow and I glance at my friend. "I'm sorry, I'm being very selfish. I should have appreciated how hard this is for you. I know you well enough to understand that you prefer your own company."

She looks at me sideways, giving me a tender smile. "And your company. You know I like your company, Eleanor. I've never had a friend like you."

Now it's my turn to look coy. "Me neither."

"Promise we'll always be there for each other."

"I promise."

Meg takes my hand and holds it tight, all the way to the bus stop. The lane is quiet but even if it wasn't, I don't care. I don't care who sees us, or what they think. All that matters is that we're together. All that matters is us.

We sit at the back of an empty bus, our conversation stilted whispers as we bump along the winding country lanes to Lockerbie. Meg sticks initially to easy topics, asking about how Anna is doing at school, whether she is settled, whether she seems happier with things as they are. I express my amazement at how well my daughter has adapted to all the changes, how expertly she has dealt with our recent ups and downs, and how grateful I am for the support she's shown towards my creative work.

"She's such a good girl," I say, beaming with pride. "She's

studying with friends today, otherwise she would have come with us."

"And how's Bert?" Meg asks, apparently deciding to steer the conversation into murkier waters.

"Oh you know, Bert is Bert," I reply, my hushed tone decidedly nonchalant. "He's never around, and when he is he has little enough to say for himself."

"Do you think he knows yet?"

"About…her? I don't know. Perhaps. Shouldn't he, by now?"

"But there's been no sign of her being discovered, has there? No wailing sirens, no police going door to door…"

"Meg! Shh!" Instinctively I look over my shoulder, which is silly as there's no one around apart from the driver, who can't possibly hear us. Nonetheless, her choice of words sets me on edge.

"Don't you think it's odd? If Bert has found her and not alerted the police?"

"I've no idea what to think," I snap. "I don't wish to think about it at all, to be honest – what I did, how easily I did it…" I shudder as my mind momentarily wanders back to that forbidden place. "If you're right though, and he has found her and not reported it, I can only think that would have something to do with whatever trouble they were both in. That night I went to find her, I told you that I saw them both together. What I didn't tell you was that they were talking about being in some sort of danger, like they'd had to run away from someone or something. Whatever it was, she was really frightened."

Meg's eyes widen and I can see that she is digesting every delicious detail. "So you've no idea what they were running from?"

"No," I sigh, "and I doubt I ever will. But if it's bad enough to flee hundreds of miles north, then it's not beyond the realms of possibility that it's bad enough to conceal a murder, especially if…" I pause, the penny finally dropping.

"If?" Meg prompts me.

"If Bert thinks her death is linked somehow to the trouble they were in."

Meg draws a sharp breath. "Well, that would certainly explain it. It makes you think though, doesn't it?"

I frown at her. "Think what?"

"About the sort of man you're married to. About what he might be capable of."

I give her a grim smile. "True. But when it comes down to it, all of us are capable of doing things we'd never dreamed of. Surely I'm living, breathing proof of that."

Despite the bus's meandering course we arrive at the gallery in good time, just a few moments before four o' clock. The place is already really busy, which both surprises me and induces that familiar nervous, sinking feeling in the pit of my stomach. All my earlier confidence and bravado dissipates and I shrink back for a moment, intimidated by a room full of jostling, chattering bodies as they move around, casting their critical eyes over the work on display. A smiling waitress greets me, offering me a glass of orange juice from the tray balanced carefully on her arm. I take it gladly, gulping it down in an effort to soothe my throat which, like my mouth, has grown suddenly dry.

"Calm down," Meg whispers in my ear. "You can do this. You've come such a long way. Remember what you were like when I first met you. Remember that day we went to Annan and it took all your strength just to leave the house. You're not that woman anymore. You're free of her now."

"I still don't like crowds," I hiss back.

"Neither do I, but I'm here for you. Now go on, go and do this, go and show how great you are. This is just the beginning for you."

"You're right." I take a deep breath and force myself into the room, perusing the displays in an effort to mingle in, to look friendly and sociable. Even in my anxious state I can't fail to notice the immaculate presentation of the work on display, and the impressive quality of both Emma's photographs and the artwork captured within them. I spot my photos and feel pride rush through me; we look impressive together, my murals and I, and I'm certainly in good, creative company with the many painters, sculptors, weavers, knitters and designers featured here. I look around the room again and realise how silly I am. These people are all here too; like me they have put their work out there for admiration, for criticism, for plain indifference. Like me they have been brave, and no doubt like me they are also now a little bit nervous. Strangely this realisation helps me to relax. I'm not alone. In fact, I'm part of a community, all brought together by a touch of Emma's magic.

"I'm so glad you're here." Emma's velvety voice greets me. Before I can respond she pulls me in close, giving me an enormous, warm hug.

"I'm so glad to be here. Well done Emma, this exhibition is wonderful. You're an inspiration."

She releases me from her embrace. "Thank you Eleanor, that means the world to me. I'm so proud of what we've all done, how this has all come together."

"Well I would say it's a success. Just look at the turnout today!"

"Yes, well, most of the folks here are the subjects of the photos, like yourself, and their families. But there are a few journalists hovering around, so you might find you get asked some questions. There are photographers too, some from the local press and a few friends of mine who I've asked to capture today's event. So I hope you don't mind but they'll be snapping away." She gives me a mischievous wink.

"That's alright."

"Good. Thanks again for coming, Eleanor. I was worried you wouldn't manage to get away."

A small frown creases my brow. "Worried? Why?"

She steps a little closer to me and lowers her voice. "You don't have to put up with it, you know. I'm sorry, I know it's not really my place to interfere; you hardly know me so tell me to mind my own business if I'm overstepping the mark. But there are ways out of your situation, there are people who can help." She labours those final words, giving me a meaningful look.

"It's not like that," I reply, my voice suddenly sounding really small. "He doesn't hit me."

"There are many ways that a man can be cruel to his wife," she replies. "I'm just saying that this is 1972, not the dark ages. You don't have to stay. You have choices."

I nod and give her a weak smile, recalling the choices I have already made and the things I have already done. My heart beats hard in my chest, and that great wave of horror I've spent the past week suppressing washes over me. "Thanks Emma, I appreciate it."

She smiles warmly. "You're welcome. Now, go and mingle! You look like you're all on your own over here."

"Oh – I didn't come alone. I brought a friend with me." I point towards the corner of the room where Meg is hovering, far away from the assembled crowds. "You see the lady over there, with the long dark hair? That's my neighbour, Meg. She's the friend I told you about, the one who has been so supportive."

Emma follows my finger, screwing her face up in confusion. "Over in the corner? I can't see anyone, Eleanor."

"She's there – she's right there. She's standing on her own, she's wearing that long skirt and shawl – she's wearing what she always wears."

Emma lets out a nervous laugh. "Really, I don't know who you're talking about. There's no one there. Maybe she nipped out, maybe she…Eleanor, are you feeling alright? You look awfully pale."

I stare in front of me, watching Meg as she stands there, plain for all the world to see. Or at least, so I thought. "She's wearing what she always wears," I repeat, my voice a panicked whisper, my mind racing to make sense of the lie I now know my eyes must be telling.

Meg looks over at me, her brown eyes playful, that familiar smile teasing her lips. Then she reads my awful expression, and her face darkens. She knows that I know. Whoever she is or whatever she is; she knows that the world has intervened and forced me to see the truth. A sickening desperation rises from my gut. I want to reach out, to call her over to me, to take her by the hand and never let her go. Yet I know there's no point. I know now that she isn't really there, that she was never really there at all.

Meg knows it too. She gives me a sad little wave, and then she disappears.

29

Harry
February 2018

That night I expect to dream about Daniel, about his mischievous smile, his intense gaze, the feeling of his arms wrapped protectively around me as my mind recreates him, makes him flesh. Makes him mine. But I don't; instead, I dream about Mum, about Eleanor and Bert, about what might have happened. Vivid, awful images plague me as I slip into a restless sleep, taking hold of my mind as I fall deeper and deeper into the nightmare. I see Bert arrive home, his hands and face covered in blood, a look of shock and horror carved out on his pale face. I hear Anna's blood-curdling scream as she sees her father, still wielding the blade that killed his lover. I hear Eleanor's raw, heartbroken sobs as she is confronted with the truth, as she is forced to listen to what he has done. I see Bert leave and never come back. I see a silent home, a mother and daughter shrouded in grief and surrounded by auras, by ethereal presences intent on their purpose. Protection? Harm? Which it is, I cannot tell.

I wake with a start just before dawn. Partly awake, partly still gripped by my dream I find myself searching for those auras, for those little lights hovering around me. But there is nothing here, only the gloom and the darkness of a world not yet wakened. I let out a sigh as I turn over. Silent, dark, empty. I'm not sure why I ever expected anything else in my life.

"Bert." Despite myself I whisper his name, my desperation for company, any company, overcoming my dread of confronting him. Of asking questions. Of what he might say in response.

"Bert? Are you there?"

No answer comes.

"You knew about Daniel, didn't you? You knew he was dead all along?" I lay the bait and lie still, holding my breath as I wait for him to bite.

Still no answer comes.

"What happened to that woman, Bert? Back in 1972, did you kill her then run away? What happened to you then? Did you kill yourself?" I go for the jugular this time. I'm sick of dancing around memories, of selective amnesia. I'm sick of evaded questions. I want to know the truth.

But still he doesn't respond. With another heavy sigh I close my eyes and pull the covers over my head. I don't know why I expected anything else. Bert has only ever told me the story he wanted to tell. He chooses to forget the rest, to build a wall of silence around it, to bury it, and I think that tells me everything I need to know. I think it tells me that it's true, all of it. I think it tells me that he was a killer. I think it tells me that he was a coward. I think it tells me that he was the ruin of his family, and the architect of his own demise.

When I wake again it is daylight, the brightness of a clear late winter's day peeking through the gap in the curtains. I startle, a burst of adrenalin brushing off any remnants of sleep as I realise I can hear tapping coming from downstairs. Ever since that day when Eleanor made her presence felt with the noise and the cold I have been on edge, unable to relax in this house. I get out of bed, wrapping my dressing gown around me, telling myself to be rational. The sound I can hear is someone knocking at the door, that's all. It's probably the mechanic from Daniel's garage, coming up to look at my car, just as he'd promised.

"There are a few living people here, Harry," I remind myself. "It's not just the dead who come calling in this bloody place."

I run downstairs, too flustered even to concern myself with the fact that I'm answering the door while still in my pyjamas. At one time I would have cared; I would have thrown on a pair of jeans and a jumper and made it look like I'd been up for hours. Now I'm not bothered what people think. I'm not concerned if I give the impression that I've slept all morning, and I couldn't care less if people speculate as to why that might be. I'm not worried if people want to gossip about the woman living on her own in the big house; I don't care if they want to trade salacious stories, just like they did about Eleanor. It might have been enough to drive Eleanor into hiding, but it can't do that for me - someone as alone as I am can hardly become a recluse. Instead, I'll be leaving soon. I'll be selling this house and giving them someone else to talk about. There's nothing left here for me now.

"Thank goodness, my car really needs…"

I stop mid-sentence when I see that it isn't the mechanic standing in front of me. He looks at me, and I at him, those blue eyes of his seeming to communicate a thousand feelings, a hundred apologies, a handful of regrets. He's wearing that same jacket, the one which never looks warm enough – why did I never notice it was always the same jacket before now? His posture is shrunken and his face is drawn and pale; he is not his usual, buoyant self but then, how could he be? How could he be anything other than dead?

"Daniel," I whisper, unsure what words I can muster other than the utterance of his name. "Daniel, I…"

"Can I come in?" He looks over his shoulder, and I realise in an instant he's checking to see if anyone is watching us. Or rather, if anyone is watching me, standing on the doorstep in my dressing gown, talking to myself.

I nod, standing aside to let him in, wondering all the while if he could just walk through me. Wondering what that would feel like. Slowly I raise my eyes to meet his, taking in the image of him one more time. I look for signs, for the things I might have missed before I knew the truth – evidence that he is an apparition, that he isn't really there. And yet I find nothing; he looks so present, so corporeal. He looks so alive.

"You held me," I begin, shaking my head. "You danced with me. You kissed me. How is any of this possible?"

"I wish I knew the answer to that." His voice is serious, clipped, holding back emotion.

"No," I begin, unwilling to accept any more unanswered questions. "You brought me wine, and tools. You brought me dinner, for goodness sake! What are you, a conjurer as well as a ghost?"

"Perception versus reality," he says with a shrug. "I think that we both saw what we wanted to see and indulged ourselves in it. Except the tools – they came from Eleanor's shed," he adds with the faintest flicker of a smile which he must know isn't appropriate.

I put my head in my hands, unable to face up to the extent of my self-deception. Unwilling to consider what else in this place might not be real, what else I might have imagined.

"I'm so sorry, Harry."

"Your mum sees you too." I brush off his apology, instead seeking comfort in knowing that it's not just me who talks to the dead.

"But not like you see me." He takes my hand and brings it towards his face. I gasp a little as I feel the coolness of his skin, the roughness of the stubble on his cheek. "With you I'm not a memory of what was; I'm not someone to mourn, to cry over. With you I feel alive again."

"I wouldn't be so sure about the crying part," I reply, feeling the heat of tears rising once again in my eyes.

He lets go of my hand. "I know, and I'm sorry. I never wanted you to find out that way. I wanted to tell you myself but the moment never seemed right. The way you looked at me – the way you always looked at me, I didn't want to lose that. I knew that once I told you, you would never look at me in the same way again."

I lean into him, hoping, trusting that I will be able to feel his chest against my cheek, his heart beating against my ear, the warmth of his arms as he wraps them around me. And he does; immediately, instinctively, wordlessly, we hold on to each other as though that alone is enough to make sense of this, to make things right.

"You're colder now," I whisper as the tears begin to fall.

He places a kiss on top of my head. It feels wet, as though he too is crying. "I know," he says. "That's what I was afraid of."

I close my eyes, trying to stem the flow of tears, trying to ground myself in this moment. I don't know how things will be now that I know what he is. I don't know if he will be like Bert, appearing and disappearing, sometimes there but often out of reach. I don't know if one day his last links with this world will sever, if he will fade away, if he will move on. I don't know whether this moment is our last moment, or if I'll ever see him again.

"I wish we had met sooner, Harry. I wish we'd had more time."

"I know. Me too."

"That day I saw you on the road. I was just so drawn to you. I had to see you again, I had to get to know you. I had to fall in love with you, even though I knew I was only torturing myself. Even though I knew it could never go anywhere. It's not fair. We could have been so good together."

I shake my head, pulling away from him. "I'm not as great as you think I am, trust me. Back in Manchester I did some really horrible things; I hurt people I cared about and I didn't even have the courage to stay and face up to them." I look him squarely in the eye as he stands there, his face impassive, awaiting my confession. "In your note you asked me to forgive you, but actually it's me who should be saying sorry. I've not been honest with you, Daniel."

A flicker of confusion passes over his face. "What note?"

"The one you left on the door yesterday, telling me that you love me and asking me to forgive you."

He gives me a sad smile. "Well, I do love you and I am sorry, but I didn't leave you a note."

"If you didn't, then who did? Bert, maybe? I mean, declarations of affection don't seem to be his style, but he certainly has plenty to beg forgiveness for, from the sounds of what your mum told me yesterday, and…"

My words catch in my throat as Daniel seals them in with a kiss. His lips, like his arms, are cold yet soothing as they linger gently against mine. For a minute I suspend all thoughts about notes, about Bert, about apologies, about what is or isn't or what might have been. Instead I stay in the moment, kissing him, as though we're two people on the cusp of happiness. As though we're two living, breathing lovers with our whole lives together to look forward to. The dream is so irresistible that for a split second I almost believe it.

"I love you, Harry," he says again, cupping my face in his hands as he holds my gaze with his. "It doesn't matter to me what you did before you came here. All that matters is that you did come here, that we got the chance to meet."

"I had an affair with my friend's husband," I blurt out, the heat of shame rising in my cheeks as more tears spring forth. "I broke her heart, then I left and broke his, too."

"Harry, it's okay, you don't have to explain yourself to me."

"No, I do. I should have told you, I should have been honest with you, especially after you told me about your wife."

He wipes away my tears with his thumb and looks at me with that tender, blue stare. "You don't owe me an explanation, or an apology. But you do need to forgive yourself. You need to let it go and stop torturing yourself, otherwise it will eat at you. Trust me, I know." For a moment his expression darkens and once again I glimpse that other version of Daniel, the things he saw, the places his mind took him.

"Would you have said that if you were still alive?" I ask him.

"Would you have been so accepting then, if there'd been any chance for us?"

He shrugs, his shoulders slumping in a gesture of defeat so clear that I know his answer before he utters it. "Perhaps not."

I nod, deciding to say no more. After all, there's no point dwelling on the hypothetical. "You're right." I glance around at my empty house. "I need to move on with my life."

"You're planning on leaving soon?" The sadness which creeps into his voice is almost too much to bear.

"Yes. The more I find out about my family, the more I realise that the best thing I can do for myself is to leave all this behind." Daniel shrinks further as his melancholy grows and my determination begins to waver. "I don't mean you," I add. "I don't want to leave you. I – I love you, too. I don't think I realised it until it was too late."

"Until you knew there couldn't be any future for us." His words hang in the air, part-statement, part-question. All truth. I don't answer him. I can't bring myself to answer him.

"What did my mum tell you? About Bert?" he asks in the end.

I frown, half-expecting him to know already. My experience of talking to the dead so far has led me to think of them as these all-seeing, all-knowing entities who drift around unseen, listening to any conversation they please. I realise then that it must be different for Daniel. He is, unlike Bert, visible, somehow more tethered to the earth. Maybe that's because he's not long since departed; maybe as time goes on he will become like Bert and disappear and simply drift away whenever it suits him. I shudder at the thought. There's a lot about being dead that I don't understand but then, given that I'm still alive, I suppose that's the point.

We go through to the living room, taking a seat as I launch into the list of revelations which Emma had in store for me during yesterday's conversation. Daniel sits close to me, his hand resting on top of mine, his expression somewhere between curious and thoughtful as he listens. I talk and talk, uninterrupted and unquestioned, and I remember how good it is to have someone there who is just willing to hear you, to understand you. I remember what it was that drew me to this man in the first place; I remember how much I enjoyed talking to him on that first evening he came round, and while we stripped wallpaper and revealed Eleanor's murals, and while we had dinner and on every occasion since. I allow myself to remember, just for the briefest moment, what it was like when I thought he was alive. Then I realise that the feeling hurts me and I pack it away, burying it deep along with the rest of the pain that I feel.

"Not that any of the information your mum gave me actually helps," I finish, sounding as defeated as I feel. "To be honest, knowing the truth about Bert just makes me feel even worse. And as for Mum, knowing that she came back here after she left me leaves me with more questions than answers. I don't think I'll ever really know what was going on with her, or where she went after she presumably left Kirtlebeck again, or why she never came back for me."

Daniel gives my hand a squeeze as he releases it, and I realise my fingers have been frozen by his touch. "How do you know it's the truth about Bert? Have you asked him?"

I shake my head, rubbing my cold hand absentmindedly. "I tried. He didn't answer me, which I think says it all."

"Perhaps not. Maybe you should give him the benefit of the doubt, at least until you talk to him."

"Well I know for a fact that at least some of it is true," I bite back, my hackles rising inexplicably in the face of his reasoned tone. "He did have an affair, he told me that himself. It happened when they lived in Manchester. That was why they moved to Kirtlebeck."

Daniel stares at me for a moment as though he has several questions on the tip of his tongue and he's trying to decide which one to pursue. In the end, he doesn't ask me anything. "Even so," he says, "it's quite a leap from adulterer to murderer."

The sincerity of his assertion strikes me and I find myself wondering again about his own experience of infidelity. What must he have gone through? What depths must he have plumbed? Did he ever think about murdering his wife? Her lover? No, Daniel isn't that sort of man; he would never even contemplate such a heinous act.

He wasn't that sort of man. He's gone now, and yet he's still here. Why is he still here? Why is he drawn to me?

"How did you know that I knew the truth about you?" I find myself asking, the words slipping out before I can stop them, before I can formulate and analyse the question in my mind. "You knew about that without me telling you and yet you didn't know what your mum had told me about my family.

He frowns. "It's hard to explain. I just – I seem to understand you, almost intuitively. I knew how you were feeling before I even arrived at the front door. I've known before, too. That day you were terrified in the house by that spirit, the one you think is Eleanor, I knew you needed my help. It's like sometimes you send out a distress signal and I'm called to answer it. But that doesn't mean I know the details of every conversation you've ever had."

"So you're telling me you're my guardian angel?" I tease.

He grins at me, and for a moment the old Daniel, the one I first met, comes alive again. "I don't know about that, but I do think I'm here to help you."

"Help me with what?"

He shrugs. "You tell me. Before you leave this house, Harry, what is it that you really want?"

I look down, folding my hands in my lap, feeling suddenly agitated as all my questions, my deep, burning, unanswered questions, whir around in my mind. "I want to know the truth," I say. "I want to know my family's truth. All of it. I don't want to be in the dark anymore. I want to know where I came from, who I am, no matter how bad it is."

Daniel pulls me close to him and places a kiss on my cheek. His touch and his lips make me shiver but I don't care. I don't care as long as he is with me. As long as we are doing this together. As long as I don't have to be alone.

"Your wish is my command." He salutes me and pulls a funny face, but his brief moment of silliness quickly fades into that seriousness and intensity which has become so familiar in him of late. "But, Harry?"

"Yes?" My reply is tentative and instinctively I hold my breath.

"Be ready for what you might discover. Knowledge doesn't always lift you from the darkness. Sometimes it only plunges you further into its depths."

I nod, looking around me, realising that he's right, and realising that deep down I've known that all along. This house, this empty place, still has a story to tell and secrets to reveal. Answers lurk in every corner, in every room and in every box contained within these walls but I know now that the house won't give them up easily. It doesn't owe me closure. It doesn't owe me satisfaction. It doesn't owe me anything at all.

It certainly doesn't owe me a happy ending.

30

Eleanor
October 1972

The journey back to Kirtlebeck is a blur of vomit and tears. I manage to hold it together at the gallery just long enough to feign some sudden illness and to claim that I'm going to find my friend who, I agree, must have gone outside, and ask her to take me home. Once I get out into the street, however, it doesn't take long for me to fall apart. Raw, agonising emotion attacks me from every angle, taunting me, torturing me, its knives piercing my skin just like I did when I drained the life from that woman. Images of that night return to me; her blood on the floor, her horrified face, her eyes as they dulled, the life in them finally extinguished. All that time I thought I had an accomplice; I thought I had someone there with me, guiding me, helping me to purge my anger, to release my thirst for revenge, to do what was right and just. Now I realise it was just me. Now I know that I am a cold-blooded killer, and a delusional one at that.

I throw up in the gutter. Some passers-by moan with disgust. Others giggle, but no one stops to check if I am alright. I am grateful for their indifference; I want to be left alone. After all, it turns out I have been alone all along. It is this thought which makes me begin to sob first; not remorse nor regret for what I've done since I still feel neither of those, but the pure pain of grief. I got to know Meg. We became friends. She helped me through the hardest time of my life, picking me up from my descent to rock bottom and showing me another path. I loved her. I still love her. But now she must be dead to me. Now she doesn't exist at all.

I catch the bus home in a daze, staring out the window so that the other passengers can't see my tear-stained face. All the way back to the village my mind reels, my thoughts not settling on the earth-shattering events of today but whirring with images of my time in Kirtlebeck, my time spent with Meg. I remember the day we first met, when she came to my home and we drank tea. I recall her beauty, her air of mystery, the insightful way she read me like a book and turned her enthusiasm for decorating into the first of many lessons she taught me. Don't forget about yourself – those were her words, words which I heeded and acted upon, words which scraped me off the ground of the darkest place and told me to stop being lost, to find my way again. And yet, what a fool I have been! The way she always looked the same, the way she always turned up when I needed her, the way the lights of her cottage were always on for me – all of it should have told me something, if only I'd been paying attention. All of it should have told me that she was nothing more than an imaginary friend, a personality created by my fevered, unhinged mind. All of it should have told me that the only voice I was hearing was my own.

I get off the bus, breathing a brisk 'thank you' to the driver. My legs feel weak and it takes all my resolve to force myself up the lane towards Kirtlebeck End. When I reach the thick trees surrounding Thistle Cottage my pace slows almost to a standstill. Initially I turn my head away, unable to bring myself to look, frightened of what I might see. Is there even a cottage there, or did I invent that too? In the end, however, morbid curiosity gets the better of me and I force myself to confront the reality which was, for a time, clouded by the power of my raving, deluded brain. I catch my breath; Meg's cottage is indeed not how I had imagined it to be. Where mere hours ago I had glimpsed a warm, rustic home now sits an empty shell, its windows little more than barren cavities, its roof half-collapsed and exposing the masonry to the elements. The only aspect which remains of my fantasy cottage is its white walls, but even these bear scars, charred by the black soot of a fire long ago. Thistle Cottage is nothing more than a bleak, derelict carcass, uninhabited and long forgotten. It isn't Meg's home; it's no one's home. And yet I went there, I sat in its cosy sitting room and drank tea. I admired its Persian rug and the little landscapes hung on the wall, Meg's keepsakes from the lost love my mind invented. Where was I really, all that time? Sitting in the midst of the rubble, indulging in a waking dream?

"Eleanor, you've lost your mind," I mutter. With a shudder I give Thistle Cottage a final glance, and then I keep on walking.

When I open the front door of my home Anna is standing on the stairs, an empty dinner plate and glass in her hand. She stops mid-descent and stares at me, a strange, strained expression fixed on her pretty young face. I look back at her and feel my own face begin to crumple. Not now, I tell myself. Not in front of Anna. I have to hold myself together for her sake, if nothing else.

"Mum? You're back early." Her voice sounds odd, her words clipped as though she is restraining a few emotions of her own.

"Yes. It was over quicker than I expected." I slip off my coat and shoes and walk towards her. She comes down to the bottom step, meeting me halfway but bowing her head in such a way that I can't get a closer look at her. I frown, my motherly instincts heightened. Something about her is amiss. "Everything alright? How did you and Alison get on with your studying?"

"Good. Yeah, good." She makes eye contact for the briefest second, but it's long enough for me to see that her eyes are a little swollen.

"Anna, have you been crying?"

She doesn't answer me, but instead flings herself into my arms, lying her head on my shoulder just as she did when she was a little girl with grazed knees and bruised pride. Softly I stroke her hair, feeling stunned by this sudden outpouring of emotion as she sobs against me.

"What is it, sweetheart?" I ask. "What's wrong?"

"It's Dad," she begins. "He came home, and…something's wrong, he…"

Before she can say anything else, an enormous thud reverberates through the ceiling, startling both of us. I release Anna from my embrace and look her directly in the eye. Her tears have dried up now, replaced by something far worse – fear. All the confusion, all the trauma of my earlier discovery dissipates as I am brought sharply into the present. "Don't worry," I try to reassure her. "Whatever is going on, I will sort this out. You stay down here, maybe get yourself another drink and put some music on the record player."

"But Mum," she protests. "I tried to talk to him, I really tried, I…"

"This isn't for you to fix, Anna. You haven't done anything wrong."

My daughter nods, giving me a meek smile before heading through to the kitchen. I take a deep breath, looking up the stairs towards the source of the commotion. "Well then, Bert," I mutter to myself. "I think it's time for you and I to talk."

I creep up the stairs and along the landing, partly due to some inexplicable wish to maintain the element of surprise, and partly because of the sense of trepidation I suddenly feel. I hear him moving around in my bedroom, raking through cupboards and removing items with hurried force. My heart thuds hard in my chest as I remember the knife, stowed away in a shoebox. Could that be what he's looking for?

"Bert," I say softly as I stand in the doorway, my eyes surveying the chaotic scene before me. "What are you doing? Why are my things all over the room?"

"Eleanor! Where the hell have you been? Anna said you'd gone out but she'd no idea where. I thought something had happened to you."

Downstairs I hear the distinctive vocals of David Bowie as Anna puts some music on. My daughter's obedience and loyalty to me brings a smile to my lips but the sight of Bert's stern face soon wipes it away. I recall Anna's tears and wonder what sort of tirade she had to endure from him concerning my whereabouts. "I'm surprised you care," I snap.

"Oh don't start all that again! We don't have time for this; we have to leave."

"Leave?" I walk further into the room, dodging the piles of my clothes which Bert has left strewn all over the floor. "And go where? And why?"

"Jesus, Eleanor! You're as bad as your daughter! I don't have time for your questions right now – just do as I say and start packing your things. I want us to be out of here within the next hour." He looks around the room then rubs his hands down his face. "Oh God! I can't believe it has come to this, I can't believe I…" His voice breaks and I realise that he has begun to cry.

"Bert, I'm sorry, but you need to explain to me what is going on." I speak as calmly as I can manage, but inside my heart is singing. I know what's going on; of course I do. I know that he's found her.

He looks at me, his face red and crumpled with emotion, and slumps down on the corner of the bed. "You're right, Eleanor. Of course you're right. You're my wife and I owe you an explanation. In fact, that's the very least of what I owe you."

He hesitates for a moment, a pained expression fixed on his face. "Go on," I prompt him.

"You've thought for months now that the reason we moved here was so that we could have a fresh start, so that we could get away from my…my affair, and that's partly true, but it's not the whole story. The thing is, back in Manchester I got mixed up with some bad people. Moving here was about putting some distance between me and them too."

I narrow my eyes at him. "What sort of people?"

Bert rakes his hands through his hair and lets out a heavy sigh. "The Bevans."

I flinch as I hear that name spoken aloud. Her name. "Is that supposed to mean something to me? Who are the Bevans?" I ask, feigning indifference.

"For God's sake Eleanor, do you walk around with your eyes and ears closed? I know you don't know many people but I would have thought you'd have heard that name before. Put it this way, they are a powerful family. I did a lot of work for them back in Manchester, put a lot of their vehicles through the garage, no questions asked. Do you understand what I mean?"

"They're criminals?"

He snorts at the innocence of my question. "They're the sort of people who turn up with cars covered in blood and bullet holes and you valet them and patch them up without hesitation."

My mouth falls open. "You concealed crimes, you cleaned up evidence? And I take it they paid you handsomely for those services?"

He nods. "Naturally. Money for the work and money for my silence."

"So what went wrong?"

His face falls again, tears welling up in his eyes. "I met her, didn't I? Barbara Bevan. The beautiful Barbara Bevan – Gabe Bevan's long-suffering wife. I fell for her, and she for me. We wanted to run away together but I had you, and Anna, and the business, and I hesitated. But then you found out about us, and Barbara was worried that Gabe was beginning to suspect something was going on. We both knew what he was capable of, and we knew that we had to get away. So, I brought you and Anna here, and Barbara went to stay with her sister before slipping away to Kirtlebeck a few weeks later. We thought that somewhere like this, somewhere quiet and far away, would be enough. We thought we could be happy, make a real go of things."

"What, with your wife and mistress both installed in a tiny village? Sounds like a real fine plan," I mutter.

Bert's face reddens at my mocking tone. "The plan was to keep our heads down and wait until it all blew over. That's why I couldn't have you getting involved in that damn exhibition! The last thing I needed was your photo in the local paper while I was being hunted by the Manchester mafia. I had to protect us, all of us. But it wasn't enough. All I wanted was to love her, to rescue her from it all. And now she's dead. I thought I could save her but I couldn't and now she's gone, she's…"

"Lying in a pool of blood on her kitchen floor." I finish his sentence for him, a triumphant smile creeping on to my lips.

Bert looks up at me, his mouth falling open. For a few moments he says nothing, he just stares at me, his eyes growing wider as the implications of what I'm saying finally hit home.

"You knew?" he says in the end. "All this time, you knew she was here?"

I nod. "Seems you're not the only one with secrets after all, doesn't it?"

"So you found her before I did?" He asks me, his confusion growing. "When? I went to see her today, to apologise. The last time we were together we argued really badly and she threw me out, said she never wanted to see me again. So I steered clear, waited for it to blow over like it normally did. She would always call me in the end; I knew I just had to be patient. But when more than a week passed without a word from her I began to worry, so I went over to the house to check on her, to make amends…" his voice breaks again. "I never got the chance to say I was sorry."

"Very touching." The tone of my voice is brutal but I don't care.

"Heartless bitch!" He shakes his head at me. "I've known for long enough about your madness, but I never realised just how sick you are. What sort of person finds a woman dead and just walks away and leaves her there?"

At that I begin to laugh, a low, primitive cackle rising from deep within my gut. "Oh Bert you've no idea, have you? I didn't find her – it was me! I killed her!" I wander over to my cupboard and pull out the shoebox. I lift the lid and carefully unwrap the gruesome contents, waving it victoriously at my husband. "You see this? This is what I used to cut that woman's throat. The Bevans haven't been here; they haven't found you – it was me! It was me and I don't regret it for a second."

For a moment Bert just stares at me, an awful groan emerging from between his lips. His expression is contorted, his eyes burning with rage, with hatred and the agony of fresh grief. Before I can comprehend what is happening he runs at me, overpowering me with his sheer strength and tackling me to the ground. Dazed, I let go of the knife, letting it fall somewhere behind me as we tussle on the floor, Bert holding me down as I try hopelessly to get free, landing glancing blows on any part of him I can get my hands on.

"You bastard! I hate you!" I yell.

Bert presses down hard on my chest, suppressing my screams and forcing calm into my flailing hands. "You hate me? You murdered Barbara, you took away the woman I loved more than anything in the world, and you have the audacity to hate me?" He grabs the knife from behind my head and pushes it under my chin. "I should cut your throat for what you've done."

"Do it." I issue my challenge through gritted teeth, tears of fear and fury streaming unabated down my cheeks. "You've taken everything from me: my pride, my happiness, my sanity. You might as well take my life too."

"We've taken everything from each other." His tears mirror my own, only wetter and more regretful, accompanied by great heaving sobs. I swallow hard, the knife trembling against my throat as Bert loses all composure. He looks deep into my eyes, showing me so much pain and anguish that I wish I could turn my head away. "It would have been better for both of us if we'd never married, if we'd never met at all."

"But then we'd never have had our daughter. We'd never have had our Anna," I reply, wincing at the desperation in my voice as I offer up the only positive thing to emerge from our union as evidence of its value.

"Your daughter, you mean." The hatred returns to his eyes and he presses the knife down hard. "She's always been yours more than mine. She despises me, you know. She told me so today. You've poisoned her against me."

"If she hates you then that is your own doing. Your affair has ruined our family!"

"Then I've not a bit of her love to lose by killing her mother, have I?"

Bert grits his teeth, his whole body rigid and inflamed as he becomes intent upon his mission. I close my eyes, squeezing them shut as I feel the sharp agony of the knife as it begins to pierce my skin. I don't want to watch myself die. I don't want to watch the expression on his face as he kills me. I think of Anna, sitting downstairs and listening to songs of star-men and space oddities, ignorant of her father's crime, helplessly facing a future stuck with him alone. The bleak prospect of my daughter's situation tempts me to fight back, but I know that it is hopeless. I do not have the strength. I do not have the power. For a time, I thought that I did have power, that I could do anything, that I could paint bold images, make new friends, forge my own path and kill without consequence. Now I know that it was all an illusion, just like Meg. Now I know that everything I have cherished was a fantasy.

From within my darkened world, I hear a sudden, dull thud. The knife halts its deadly task; I feel it fall away from my neck, to be swiftly replaced by another uncomfortable pressure, the feeling of a man's head against me, his full unsupported weight pressed hard against my body. Carefully I open my eyes, dreading the scene which awaits me. Light floods in and I struggle for breath as I am confronted by three truths: I am disorientated, I am crushed, and I am covered in the blood.

In front of me Anna stands, a shocked look fixed upon her face as she clutches a heavy brass ornament in her hand. She is as pale as a ghost, her eyes wide and her hands trembling. For a long moment both of us are silent.

"Anna," I cry out, my voice little more than a rasp from

underneath the lifeless body of my husband. More blood seeps from the gaping wound in his head. I have seen blood like this before, when it spurted forth from the neck of my enemy. I felt nothing then, but now the sight of his blood makes me sick, a horrified, deep churning feeling possessing my gut. He was my enemy too, but I loved him once. I loved him dearly. Perhaps deep down I hoped one day to love him once more. Repulsed by my momentary weakness, I cry out again: "Anna, sweetheart!"

The urgency of my tone startles my daughter; her white face grows red and tears begin to fall. She looks straight at me, and it seems in that moment as though all the sadness, horror and regret in the world are contained within those eyes, sapping their youth, obscuring their brightness. I realise then that a light has gone out, one which I fear will never shine again.

"Oh Mum," she cries. "Mum, what have I done?"

31

Harry
February 2018

We spend the whole day in Mum's bedroom, sifting through the boxes of photos, of artwork, of trinkets, looking for any clues I might have missed after I first found these things in the attic. It's an effort to bring all those boxes back upstairs from the living room, but I do it anyway. Ever since that day when Eleanor made her presence known I have felt uncomfortable downstairs, illogically worried that spending too much time down there will provoke her return. If Daniel finds it nonsensical he doesn't comment; he seems to understand my disquiet, my wish to find comfort in the one room which makes me feel connected to my mother.

Part way through our exploration I tell him about my mum's stories. His expression is grave as I summarise their content, as though, like me, he appreciates the glimpse they provide of her state of mind. Beyond that I tell him that they're of little use; works of fiction rather than memoir, horror stories constructed in beautiful prose.

"My mum was a talented storyteller," I remark sadly. "As dark as her stories are, I think I will treasure them forever."

I admit that the stories frighten me, that after reading most of them I am struggling to bring myself to look at what is left. Daniel gives me a small smile, gently squeezing my shoulder in a gesture of empathy. Then he picks up the pile of papers, sifting through them with care.

"Where did you get up to?" he asks.

"Margaret Gets Revenge," I reply with a shudder. It's not a title I'm likely to forget any time soon.

"Then there's only one more story to read," he says, taking a handful of pages out of the pile. "Why don't we read it together?"

So we do. We curl up on the bed, his cool arm cast over my shoulder as we study the final instalment of Margaret's story, written down in Mum's flowing script. Intriguingly entitled Margaret Returns, we discover that the end of this sorry tale is in fact a new beginning when, instead of getting her wish for eternal life with her beloved, Margaret returns to the earth alone. Finding herself tethered to the place in which she committed that final atrocity, Margaret initially despairs of her fate, locking herself away and waiting for the stories of her now infamous act to fade from memory.

"Everyone talked about her," my mum writes. "No one knew her but everyone knew her story; everyone knew what she had done. Margaret had no choice but to hide, to make herself invisible from the world, to hope that one day soon they would all forget."

I shiver as I read those words aloud, drawing Daniel's attention to them. He nods, knowing what I'm thinking, seeing the parallel my mind is drawing between Margaret's tale and Eleanor's experience of the relentless gossip which I feel sure pushed her into self-imposed solitude. I wonder too about the trick death played on Margaret, sending her back instead of allowing her to move on. Is that what happened to Bert, too? Is that why he is still here, even after all this time? Like Margaret, is his existence here some sort of eternal punishment for what he did? Then I remind myself that this is just a story; it isn't reality, and it isn't truth. The only truth I should be looking for is the one which tells me why my mother sat down and wrote these stories at all.

"Time passed, and as it transpired, all was not lost. For on one fine summer's day a stranger arrived, an artist who harboured such talent, such passion and torment that Margaret was immediately reminded of him. Except this wasn't him; this was a woman, a woman who was lost, a woman who was scorned. A woman who, like her, had been betrayed. A woman who needed her help. Finally, Margaret came to understand why she had returned. Her purpose now was to guide this wretched creature; to lift her from the depths, to teach her about hope, about power, about destiny. To teach her about revenge."

My eyes linger on that final sentence, and I find myself drawing closer to Daniel. He places a tender kiss on top of my head, his fingers caressing my arm as I turn the last page over in frustration.

"That's it," I say. "That's the last story. That's how it ends."

"What are you thinking?" he asks me.

I shake my head in bewilderment. "Honestly? I don't know what to make of it. I mean, Mum was obviously blessed with a vivid imagination."

"Do you think that's all it is?"

I look at him, trying to read his expression, trying to understand what he's getting at. "What else could it be? I mean, the whole premise – the cheating men, the scorned women – I assume the inspiration for that came from the painful experience of watching her parents. But the rest? It's a ghost story. A good one, and a creepy one, but just a ghost story."

Daniel raises an eyebrow at that last remark, and a shiver runs down my spine as I am reminded again of what he is now. "So the stories weren't any use, then?"

I sigh and rub my eyes, now tired after a day of searching for clues which simply aren't there. "They tell me that my mum had issues," I reply, "which given what I've discovered about Bert, isn't really surprising. I think they're some sort of extended metaphor, some creative way of dealing with all the shit which had happened in her life. And in that respect, they give some context to her disappearance from my life. Perhaps having a child of her own brought all her demons back to the fore, and she simply couldn't cope? Perhaps she thought she was doing the right thing by leaving me? I think I have to accept that I'll never know for sure."

Daniel pulls himself upright and turns to face me. "But what if those stories aren't just metaphors. What if they contain some truth?"

I start to speak, to counter his question with a dose of cold rationality, but he puts up his hand to stop me.

"Suspend disbelief for just a moment and imagine that these stories your mum wrote really did happen. What are they telling you then? Come on Harry, you're sitting here talking to a dead man about this! Is it really so hard to believe? Is anything that hard to believe in this place?"

The old house creeks in indignation at his jibe and another shiver runs through me. "No, I suppose not."

"Right. So?"

I throw my arms up in exasperation. "So, what? Who is Margaret, then? Is she Mum? Is she Eleanor? How could she be? No one set a fire here and burned Bert to death!"

"That wasn't what I was thinking." Daniel's tone is serious, contemplative.

"What were you thinking?"

"At the end of the story your mum writes that Margaret makes it her mission to help someone, an artist who had been betrayed. Doesn't that sound familiar?"

I put my hand over my mouth, half in shock as the pieces fall unexpectedly into place, and half in embarrassment at not seeing what was right in front of me. "Eleanor," I whisper through my fingers.

Daniel gives a slow nod. "Yes. And think about those photos my mum showed you, with the strange lights all around Eleanor."

"Your mum suggested she had a guardian angel."

Daniel's eyes darken. "Maybe it wasn't an angel, after all."

My mind races, constructing this alarming jigsaw into some

semblance of logic. "Mum says that Margaret planned to teach this woman about revenge. Do you think it's possible that she helped Eleanor to kill Bert?" My stomach churns at the dark turn my thoughts have taken.

"I think it's entirely possible, yes."

"But what about that other woman, the one who was found dead, the one the police connected to Bert? Where does she fit into all this?"

He shrugs. "Maybe Bert did kill her. Maybe she tracked him down and he didn't take kindly to the reminder of the past."

"Or maybe Eleanor killed them both." The words fall reluctantly from my lips and I glance nervously around me. I don't like speaking ill of the dead, especially when I suspect they're here, listening to every word I say. "That would be the ultimate revenge, wouldn't it? Both lovers – dead."

"Yes," he replies quietly. "Yes, it would."

"Poor Mum," I say, shaking my head in disbelief. "If even half of this is true, then it's no wonder she went to pieces. The things she must have heard, the things she must have seen, it just doesn't bear thinking about."

Daniel strokes my arm, but the ice in his fingertips chills rather than soothes me. Apparently sensing my discomfort, he lets me go and we sit together for some time in silence, both contemplating the things we have learned. Or rather, I correct myself, the things we have speculated upon. There is still no proof of any of this; there is nothing in these stories, or in the family photographs, or in Eleanor's artwork which moves any of my family's sorry tale beyond the point of conjecture. All I know is that Bert disappeared, my mum ran away from me, and Eleanor died and left me this house. The rest is rumour and theory, and I have to accept that it may never be anything more than that. The story of the Murray family is little more than a Rubik's cube, passed down to me to solve. But what if I can't do it; what if I can't get all the colours to fall neatly into place. What then?

"You feel so cold all the time," I remark after a while, breaking the silence even though that wasn't really what was on my mind.

He shrugs. "Maybe that's because you know about me now."

I rub my forehead, a wave of weariness passing through me once again. "I wish I didn't know. I wish I still felt your warmth."

"You wish I was still lying to you?"

"No…yes…I…I wish you were still here."

He gives me a sheepish grin. "I am here."

"You know what I mean. I wish you were still alive."

His smile fades and he pushes a strand of my hair back from my face. "I know. God, there's nothing I want more than to be with you, Harry."

I take hold of his hands. "Then stay with me. Stay here." I can hear the desperation ringing in my voice but I don't care. I don't have anyone or anything left in this world. What would it matter if I chose to shut myself away, to live among the dead rather than the living? What would it matter if I spent the rest of my life with a ghost?

"But you're leaving." Daniel's eyes search mine, and for the first time I notice that they are less blue now, more opaque, less intense.

"I don't have to, I…" My words falter for a moment. Since the moment I came here I've been so focussed on clearing this place, on unravelling secrets and mysteries, on moving on. I hadn't even considered staying as an option until now, when the idea began to fall clumsily from my lips. "I could stay. I could live at Kirtlebeck End. I could live with you."

Hope brightens his face, simultaneously making my heart leap and ache. But almost as soon as it appears his expression dampens, and he pulls his hands back from mine. "No. You have to move on. You have to get away from here and live your life. I'm already dead and gone. You can't let me hold you back. You can't let any of this hold you back."

"But why must I leave?" I ask him. I feel argumentative now, my idealism about a life spent with Daniel overtaken by my irritation at being told what to do. "Perhaps I need to stay here. Perhaps that's the only way to ever find out what happened to

Bert, to my mum. Perhaps I have to keep searching for answers. Perhaps I can't leave until I find them."

"No, Harry. Please, listen to me…"

"No!" I jump up from the bed, startled by the determination ringing in my own voice. "Please listen to me, Daniel. You've no idea what it's like to have nothing and no one left in this world! All I have is this house, a load of photos, some paintings, a couple of murals and some creepy horror stories penned by my mum. Oh, and this empty, unused diary I found when I first got here." I pick it up off the dressing table where I'd left it and wave it at him. Tears gather in the corners of my eyes and I swipe at them angrily. "It's from 1990 which, thinking about it now, probably means it was my mum's. Of course, she hasn't written anything in it. She could have left me a note inside; something, anything telling me why she left, that she was sorry, that she loved me. But no, nothing. It's empty. It's empty, just like me."

Daniel gets off the bed and walks over to me, enveloping me in his loving embrace. The gesture is too much to take and all the emotion, all the pain and all the sorrow I've been holding back bursts free. My words give way to heavy, ugly sobs, my tears running unabated down my face as I cry into his arms. I can't hold it in anymore; I just can't. All the grief and anguish I brought with me about Mum, about Dad, about the terrible decisions I've made in my life, all of it has been compounded by everything I've discovered since, everything I suspect but cannot know for certain. To arrive in this place hoping for answers, hoping for comfort, hoping for closure and to find only mystery and darkness is soul-destroying. To be forced to contemplate that one or both of my grandparents was a murderer and my mother was driven insane is too much to bear.

There is no good to be found in this house. No good at all.

"You're right," I whisper. "I should leave."

He runs his fingers through my hair and my skin tingles in response to his eerie offering of solace. "As soon as possible," he replies. "It isn't safe for you here."

Before I can pull away, before I can ask him what he means, the first loud bang reverberates through the house. Before I can give him that look which tells him I realise now what I should have always suspected, that he understands far more than he's telling me, the noises start. The clatters, the creaks, the groans. The hisses. The whispers. Instinctively I hold on to him, my eyes darting warily around the room as my subconscious registers that he doesn't seem startled at all. He's not surprised. He was expecting this.

"Daniel," I croak, my throat suddenly dry. "What's going on? Do you think it's Eleanor? Is she back?"

I yelp as the bedroom door flies open, forced almost off its hinges by an ethereal rage. Terrified, I try to cling tighter to Daniel but find that I can't. I look back at him, mystified to see that he's still there, right next to me, but somehow out of my grasp. I notice that his arms are still around me, just as they were moments before, but now I can't feel them. I can't even feel the cold. I can feel nothing.

"You can't leave me," I say. "Not now."

I watch as a tear runs down his face, his skin growing ever more translucent right before my eyes. "I'm not leaving you," he replies, his jaw set hard. "Not until this is over."

"Until what is over?" I wince as another loud bang drowns out my question.

Behind me the bedroom door slams shut once more, making my heart pound in my chest and my blood run cold in my veins. I turn around slowly, willing myself to face whatever is there.

"Hello?" I try to call out, alarmed at how small, how timid my voice suddenly sounds. "Who's there? What do you want?"

"Harriet, it's me." A familiar voice comes at me and I almost breathe a sigh of relief. Almost, until I remember who he might be and what he might have done.

"Bert?" I say. "Where've you been? What's going on?"

Bert says something but I struggle to hear it over the noises which have grown ever louder and incessant.

"What? What are you saying?"

"You need to get out of here now, Harriet," he repeats. I can tell by his tone that he is trying to shout but his voice sounds so quiet, so distant, as though he isn't quite here with me.

"Why? You're not making any sense." I glance at Daniel helplessly. "Can you see him?" I ask. "Can you see Bert?"

Daniel narrows his eyes. "No," he replies. "I don't think he's really here."

"Then where the hell is he? Bert? Bert! What do you mean? Why do I need to leave?"

"You're in danger." His voice comes at me again but it is ever weaker, ever more faint. "Get out of there, please. Please, trust me."

I want to scoff; I want to throw his talk of trust back at him and ask why I should ever trust him when he never tells me the truth. When he disappears and avoids my questions. When he might be a cold-bloodied killer. But as the noises around me begin their ascent to a crescendo, I realise that now is not the right time.

"Alright," I concede. "I'm going. But just tell me why. You owe me that much."

Bert is silent for a second, and in that brief moment I despair of getting a response. But then I hear his voice again, louder this time, closer and more forceful, as though he is putting every ounce of his cold, dead being into delivering his warning. As though my life might depend upon his words.

"Because she's coming," is all he tells me. "She's coming for you."

32

Eleanor
October 1972

Before today, the advantage of living a quiet life at the dead end of a village never really struck me. As I'm digging my husband's grave at the bottom of my large, secluded garden, liberated from all fear of being spied by a nosy neighbour or passer-by, it occurs to me that this is the definition of splendid isolation. The evening draws in, forcing me to work faster against the darkness which promises to come. My back and arms protest at the exertion, every part of me aches and sweat pours from me, but I keep on going. I have to do this, I tell myself. I have to see this through, for Anna's sake as well as my own.

My daughter sits on the ground beside me, gripped by a stunned silence. I can only imagine what she's going through, the trauma she must be feeling. "It'll be alright," I keep telling her. "You did the right thing. You had no choice. He was going to kill me." I convince myself that this is true, that he was going to cut my throat. But of course, I will never know for sure.

Anna says nothing, but as the hole in the ground reaches about half the required depth, she picks up a shovel and starts to dig. Quietly I admire her bravery as she sets about her work, removing great chunks of earth with a steely determination and a strength which I didn't know she possessed. In spite of everything that has happened and all the things we have both had to do, I am immensely proud of her. I know now that I would do anything for her, and she for me. She is my world and I am hers. Struck by this powerful thought, I am compelled to drop my shovel and wrap my arms around her. She collapses into me, her body shaking with emotion as I stroke her hair and wonder how on earth I'm going to mend my broken child.

We finish our task before night falls, glad of the dusk to conceal us as we drag Bert's body from the house to the garden, wrapped in a bedsheet made to serve as a makeshift shroud. Hurriedly we drop him into his grave along with the knife and the ornament which, if found, would surely serve as damning evidence against us both. Anna doesn't comment on the knife or ask why I'm burying it, a fact which surprises me and which I attribute to her shocked state. I think about saying something but in the end I don't elaborate. She has suffered enough, I think. It is a story for another time.

Finally, we set about burying Bert, a mercifully quicker task than grave-digging. The end of the garden I chose as his final resting place is little more than an area of rough ground and bare soil, uncultivated and unloved. It is unsightly, but as a result it is not obvious that the ground has been disturbed. From time to time I have been taken with the notion of tending to the area, planting shrubs, trees and perhaps raising one or two flower beds. Now I find that the idea appeals to me even more. I imagine the prettiness of a grand tree, marking the spot whilst concealing what lies beneath, its strong roots wrapped around him like tentacles, trapping him down there just as he had always trapped me. Yes, I think, a large tree will do very well indeed.

When our work is complete we don't hurry inside, instead standing together, our eyes fixed on his illicit grave. Anna reaches out for my hand and grasps it tightly. For a few moments we are silent in our solidarity, united in the numbness of feeling which precedes grief, sorrow and acceptance. I know that Anna will mourn him; her anger, however acute, will eventually dissolve into sadness, into bitter regret. I wonder then if she will grow to hate me. I wonder if I will grow to hate myself.

"Mum, shouldn't we have called the police?" Anna asks, her mind beginning to stir. "Maybe I could have explained, told them what he was going to do…"

"No, sweetheart," I interrupt her. My tone is harsh but I can't help it. The gruesome imagery of the recent past races through my mind: Barbara Bevan's bloodied corpse, the abandoned carcass of Thistle Cottage, the sadness in Meg's eyes as I learned the truth of my own insanity. "It's better this way," I soften my voice, trying to reassure her. "The last thing we need is the police poking around in our business. They might take you away from me and I couldn't bear for that to happen."

Anna's eyes widen with fright. "Take me away? Where? Oh no Mum, I couldn't, I couldn't leave you, I…"

"It's not going to happen," I assure her, pulling her towards me and taking her in my arms once again. "Not if you leave everything to me." I pause, barely able to contemplate the things I'm going to have to do in the coming days. The missing person's report I'll have to file. The lies I'll have to tell. The role of grief-stricken wife I'll have to play. "I promise you, I will make this right, my darling. I will make a better life for both of us."

"I'd listen to your mother."

A voice comes at us from behind, startling me. I turn around, my mouth falling open as Meg emerges from the shadows. Instantly my heart begins to race, my skin breaking out in a cold, clammy sweat. I thought she'd gone; I thought the knowledge of my delusional state had been enough to banish her from my twisted imagination. And yet, here she is, standing before me, those deep dark eyes resting on me with their inquisitive gaze, the hint of an amused smile teasing at her lips. She is a vision made flesh, so real that I could almost reach out and touch her, just as I have so many times before. Instead I keep my hands at my sides and my mouth shut. I will not allow myself to unravel again, for Anna's sake and for my own.

I begin to turn away, to ignore my delusion. Then I realise that Anna has turned around to face her too.

"You've both done very well," Meg says. "You've been through a lot but it's over now. You've had your revenge and those who have wronged you both have paid for it. I'd say this whole adventure has been an enormous success, wouldn't you?"

Anna nods, and I look in horror as her pained expression gives way to a smile. "Thank you, Meg," she says.

"Anna," I hiss. "Anna! You know who this is?"

"Of course I do, Mum. It's Meg, our neighbour."

"No sweetheart, you don't understand," I begin, my voice growing desperate, my mind racing, trying to understand, to rationalise all of this. "She's not real, she's not really there, she's…she's my delusion, my imaginary friend. I thought she was real, she seemed so real, but then I took her to that exhibition today and I tried to introduce her to other people and no one could see her. Anna, darling, listen to me – no one could see her apart from me!"

"But I can see her." Anna walks over to Meg and stands by her side. I shudder as Meg drapes a slender arm over my daughter's shoulder. "I've seen her every day on the lane, ever since we've lived here. I think you're mistaken, Mum. Maybe you're tired, or stressed after everything that happened today…"

"No!" My voice echoes in the evening silence. "I know what I saw at the gallery, Anna. She disappeared right in front of me, just faded away into nothingness. That's when I knew I had dreamt her. I've been so alone since we moved here that I think my mind created a friend for me."

"I've not been lonely though, have I? And yet she's become my friend too. Honestly Mum she's been brilliant, we've had so many long chats, and she gives such good advice."

"You see," Meg interjects. "I've been a big help to both of you. I daresay that without my guidance, neither of you would be standing here right now." Her voice is soft but her words seem deliberate; teasing, almost mocking me. I feel a shiver creep over me as the penny finally begins to drop.

"Anna," I begin, "come here sweetheart. I think we need to go inside. I think we need to get away from whoever or whatever that is."

"But Mum, why? Meg's not done anything wrong!"

"I beg to differ," I snap. "I'd say she's done us a great deal of harm. Please Anna, come here, come away from her."

"What do you mean she's harmed us?"

"Anna!"

"What?" A look of teenage defiance greets me.

"What did she tell you to do?" I ask, my voice shaking in anticipation of the answer.

Anna glances at Meg, who gives a brief nod of approval. "She told me to look after you. She told me you needed a lot of love and support, that it would help you work on your murals, cope with living here, with Dad, and…" Anna's voice weakens to a whisper.

"And?" I prompt her. "What else did Meg tell you to do, Anna?"

Anna gathers her resolve, looking at me with a steely gaze, quite unlike any expression I have ever seen on my daughter's face, her mouth rigid, her eyes like ice. It is then that I see it: everything she has borne, everything she has felt she had to do, writ large on her corrupted little face. When she finally speaks the words they are not a surprise but a confirmation of the truths which I ought to have known: her great burden, her loss of innocence, her complete liberation from all sense of morality. Her time here, her journey to this point, has been not unlike my own. I should have seen it, if I had been any sort of mother at all.

"I did it for you, Mum," she says.

"Did what, Anna?" I ask, although I already know the answer. "What did she tell you to do?"

The determined look on her face never falters. "She told me that I had to kill him," she replies. "She told me to murder my father."

33

Harry
February 2018

Daniel and I make it downstairs as the noise around us seems to reach fever pitch. It is as though the house has come alive; as though it is talking to me, with every creak, every moan, every straining sound an expression of all it has seen and heard. Every growl alerting me to its anger. Every sob giving voice to its despair. Yes, I think; the house at Kirtlebeck End has finally abandoned its silence. It has finally decided to tell its story. It has finally decided to let the world know how it feels about all that was said and done within its walls.

I glance over my shoulder at Daniel. His face is grave, his eyes afraid; everything about him seems shrunken, reduced. Faded. Disappearing. I know he reassured me that he will stay, that he's not finished yet, but something about the way he stands there, like he's losing his grip, like he hasn't got the strength to hang on, worries me. He might want to stay, but what if he doesn't have a choice? What if it is time for him to leave, just when I need him the most?

"Are you ready?" I ask.

He nods. I take a deep breath and grab the old door handle.

Immediately I let out a squeal; it is freezing cold, so cold that I can't bring myself to hold on, to turn it. I retract my hand, rubbing it, trying to summon some warmth back into my frost-bitten fingers. "What the hell is going on?" I ask. "Who is doing this?"

Daniel leans forward and tries to grasp the handle. My heart lurches for him as I watch him struggle; he is too weak now, earthly objects have grown beyond his reach. I feel despair stir in the pit of my stomach as I realise that means he will never be able to hold me again. He won't be warm or cold for me anymore; he will be nothing. He will be gone.

"I...I can't," he stammers. "Bloody hell, I'm not ready for this yet." He places his head in his hands, the sound of his angry, desperate sobs joining the wailing chorus which echoes through the house. I want to comfort him, to tell him that it'll be alright, but I can't. It won't be alright. I'm alive. He's dead. There's no coming back from that.

Feeling frustration and rage building within me I pull my sleeve down over my hand and try the handle again. I ignore the cold as it seeps through the fabric of my jumper, pulling hard on the handle. When the handle moves but the door doesn't budge I try again, and again, and again. I try relentlessly. I try as though my life depends upon it.

"It won't move!" I scream as I start to kick the door, over and over. The sound of my trainer-clad foot thudding against the old solid wood can barely be heard over the rest of the commotion in this enchanted, ghost-riddled house but I don't care. For a moment I lose complete control of myself. For a moment I think about nothing other than how to break free.

Then in an instant, all the noise in the house stops.

I look back at Daniel, and he at me. We are both at a loss for words, joining the house in its sudden silence. I try the door again, relieved to find that the handle is no longer cold. But still the door remains stuck fast. I jump as the old heating system creaks into life, reminding me that evening is drawing near, bringing more cold, more darkness. I shiver and try the handle again. The door still doesn't move, but this time I'm alarmed to notice that the handle has grown warm.

"We're never getting out of here," I whisper, partly to Daniel, partly to myself. "She's making sure of that."

"Who?" Daniel asks me. His tears have dried but now he just looks withered, exhausted.

"Eleanor," I hiss back. "Who else could it be?"

Daniel looks as though he is about to answer me, as though perhaps he wants to argue with my assumption, but our frantic, whispered words are interrupted by another sound, a new sound. The sound of someone outside, knocking on the door.

"Oh thank God!" I exclaim. "Someone is here. Someone who can help. Maybe it's your mum, or maybe that mechanic from your garage, finally coming to look at my car." The words pour clumsily from my mouth in time with the wave of relief as it washes over me, calming my racing heart. "Someone is here, Daniel. Someone who can help."

But Daniel only frowns. "But we can't get out. The door won't move."

"Then we'll break it down," I insist. "We'll shout and scream and let whoever is out there know that we need their help."

The sound comes again. Three gentle taps. I peer through the stained glass at the side of the door, but the pretty colours obscure my view. I can see someone is there, though; I can see the shape of them as they hover there, waiting. Desperate to be free from this place I try the handle again. It's so hot now that it burns my hand, but it turns, and with it, the door begins to move.

"Oh thank you God," I begin as I pull it open, ready to greet the friendly face on the other side. Ready to get away from this house. Ready to be saved from it. Ready to be gone for good.

But the face which greets me isn't Emma. It isn't the mechanic either.

Horrified I stumble backwards, falling into Daniel. Or rather, through Daniel. My heart sinks as I realise that any semblance of a corporeal form has finally left him. "You," I squeak, pointing. "It's you. You're…"

The woman walks inside, tossing her long black hair over her shoulders as she examines me with her deep, raven eyes. "Yes," she says, knowingly, as though she's read my mind, as though she understands what I was about to say. "Hello, Harriet."

"You're the woman in the mural." I say it anyway, even though it doesn't need to be said. Even though saying it doesn't make it any less bizarre, any more rational. "But that was painted in the seventies. You haven't aged a day."

She gives me a seductive, mesmerising smile. "It's nice to meet you finally, Harriet. My name is Meg Roberts. Or at least, that's the name by which your mother and grandmother called me. The name my mother gave me was Margaret. Sounds rather old-fashioned nowadays, doesn't it?"

I gasp, backing away further as she comes towards me. I stumble as my foot hits the stairs. She looks from me to Daniel and I watch as her face changes from forced friendliness to downright disapproval. The weight of her gaze is too much for my poor, dead friend.

"Harry," he says, his voice small and helpless. "Harry, I…"

But he doesn't get to finish his sentence, and I can only look on in horror as he fades away before my eyes.

"Daniel." I whisper his name, but it does no good. I don't have the power to summon him from wherever he is now.

"Good," Meg says, clapping her hands together. "Now we're alone."

"I know what you did," I say to her through gritted teeth. "I know that you murdered your lover, that you burnt down his cottage and killed yourself in the fire. My mum wrote about you. She told your story."

"Meg laughs. "I know that, silly girl. It was me who encouraged her to write it, to put those creative talents of hers to good use. I liked your mum – she was very good at doing as she was told."

"Was?" I question her. Of course, deep down I know the truth. I've always known somewhere in my heart that my mum is gone, that she is dead, that I will never see her again. Nonetheless, I grab on to Meg's use of the past tense, desperate to know, desperate for confirmation.

"Yes, Harriet. We're all in the past now – your mum, Eleanor, me. Dead and gone." The way she sings the words makes me shudder.

"But you came back." My voice is a dreadful, hoarse whisper. "Did she? Did she come back like you did?" I look around me, my eyes seeking out otherworldly signs, my mind immediately going back to that day with the noise, the ice, the expression of grave disappointment sung into my ear. Was I wrong to assume that was Eleanor? Was it, in fact, my mum?

"No," Meg snaps, and I realise I've hit a nerve. "They left me, you know. Your mum and your grandmother; selfish, ungrateful wretches! After everything I'd done for them! You've no idea how lonely I've been, stuck in this house. When Eleanor died I tried to go back to that special place, to my beloved Thistle Cottage, only to find that the bastard you've been batting your eyelashes at had knocked it down! I had half a mind to stay there and torment him for it, until I realised your grandfather was still here."

"Bert?" I seek confirmation almost instinctively, although deep down I know it's futile. What other grandfather could she possibly mean?

She nods, examining her nails as though distracted. "It's been wonderful listening to your little chats, it really has. He worms his way around you, he manipulates you, just like he did to Eleanor. Even though you knew he wasn't being honest, you still listened to him, you still gave him the benefit of the doubt." She looks straight at me then, and I feel the heat of her hatred emanating from her eyes. "But then, you're not much different from Bert, are you? You're as bad as him, in fact."

You're as bad as him. Those words ring in my ears, and another piece of the puzzle falls into place. That day when someone or something made its presence known, freezing me, scaring me half to death. It was her. Every eerie moment here, every strange noise, every ethereal breeze comes racing into my mind. How many other times has it been her?

"It's been very satisfying, getting to know Bert," she continues, a tawdry sickness consuming her voice. "Turns out that he really crumbles when faced with a powerful woman."

"What did you do to him?" Despite my fear, I feel my hackles begin to rise.

"Nothing he wasn't willing to do to himself. Death hasn't come easy for Bert. I suppose that was inevitable, given how he died. Over time he's become more than willing to have someone else call the shots around here."

"Poor Bert," I mutter, forgetting, for a moment at least, that none of this changes what he might have done, who he might have killed. That none of this changes the lies and half-truths he told me. It all makes sense to me now: all those times he couldn't reach me, all those times he disappeared. It was her. It was all down to her. Meg is at the centre of all of this.

"You're evil," I begin, getting up and walking towards her. My fear departs as anger rushes through me; anger for Bert, anger for Eleanor, anger for my mum. They were just people. They were just a family. They had their foibles, their problems, their imperfections, but they didn't deserve any of this. They didn't deserve Meg. I draw close to her, staring into those deep, dark eyes. It strikes me then that they are like chasms, like black lagoons peering down into an infected soul. Their depth isn't beauty; it's pure horror. "Why did you seek out my family? Why couldn't you just leave them alone?"

"I've only ever done what was necessary," she spits back at me. "Vengeance is the only way to salve a broken heart. I helped Eleanor to see that. I gave her hope. I was her inspiration. She came alive again after she met me. If I'd left her alone, if I'd never come to her door all those summers ago, she'd have withered and died like an untended flower."

"You don't know that," I protest.

She laughs at me again, a short, sharp cackle. "Trust me, Harriet – I know. I know what it's like to suffer betrayal, to be neglected, to be cast aside. I know how it feels to be so bereft of love that you no longer know who you are. I'll know those feelings for all eternity. They're what drives me. They're what gives me strength."

Standing inches away from her, I realise that it's impossible to know what she is. Like Daniel when I first met him, she appears so alive, so present, so human. A wave of nausea passes through me as I catch the scent of her floral perfume. I wonder why it's so strong, so sickly sweet. I wonder what it's masking.

"Don't you want to know what happened?" she taunts me. "Don't you want to know your family's story? It's all you've thought about since you've been here, isn't it?"

I nod, realising that there's no point in denying it. Whatever happens today, however this ends, we both understand that I have to know the truth. "Go on," I urge her, my voice heavy with resignation.

She reaches into the pocket of her long, flowing skirt, that wicked smile growing again on her lips as she produces a single piece of paper, neatly folded. "A gift for you," she says. "From your mother."

Speechlessly I take the note, clutching it in my shaking hand. A note from my mum. A note to me, in her own words. The note that I've always dreamed about. The note that I've always dreaded. With trepidation I unfold the delicate, yellowing paper and begin to read the words Mum wrote to me in her now-familiar script.

My beautiful Harriet,

I am sorry I had to leave you, my sweet little girl. I have spent so many years trying to suppress my demons, to bury my past, to forget it all and be happy. I tried so hard to be the mother you deserved, but every time I looked at your loving, innocent face it was like a knife in my heart. I had to leave. I had to come back and face up to what I'd done. I had to give you and your father the peace you deserve. You didn't need my guilt, my darkness weighing you down.

When I was a girl, I killed my father. I struck him over the head with a brass ornament and I helped my mother to bury him in the garden. Together we concealed my crime; we left him to rot in the ground, cultivating a beautiful garden above him, planting a great tree over him to always mark the spot. Together we convinced the world that we were the bereaved, the victims of a strange disappearance. Together we tried to move on. For a long time, I believed that what I had done was right and just. I believed that the person who led me there had my best interests at heart. Even when she told me her harrowing story I wasn't horrified; in fact, I was inspired by it, inspired enough to write it down. Inspired just like my mum had been during that fateful summer when she painted those murals.

But now, all these years later, I have discovered that those who helped me back then weren't who I thought they were.

Today my mother confessed that she, too, is a killer. She told me that she murdered my father's lover in cold blood. All these years I spent hating him, believing the stories others told about him, believing that he had been the one with blood on his hands. Now I know that none of it was true, that although he wasn't an innocent, he was more innocent than we are.

I know now that my mum has been living in fear. Ever since that day in the garden when we stood with our shovels and finally grasped what that woman had done for us, she has been terrified of the evil which inhabits our house. I should have realised that sooner; when she burned all her old clothes in the garden, when she took down every photograph in the house, or when she papered over her beloved murals. I should have understood then what she was trying to hide from, what she was trying to forget. Sadly, this is a reality which it has, to my shame, taken me far longer to grasp. But now, my darling child, I understand. I understand and I cannot live with myself any more.

Goodbye my precious girl. If this letter ever finds you, it means you have been to the house at Kirtlebeck End. Please know that there is nothing good for you there. Please understand that you must get as far away from that house as possible.

I love you.

Mum x

I look up from the note and stare at Meg, aghast. I think about the first time I walked into the garden here, all those weeks ago, and how I gasped in delight at that enormous tree. How impressed, how delighted, how spellbound I was. How horrified I would have been if I'd known that my grandfather lay beneath it. How horrified I am now; so horrified that I can't even bring myself to cry. My mum and my grandmother were both murderers; my mother when she was little more than a child. Part of me wants to reject these words, to attribute them to some sordid game conducted by Meg's malevolent hand. But another part, a bigger part, knows that they are true, that these are the facts on which everything pivots. These are the two events in my family's story which mean that everything else makes sense.

"It was you, wasn't it?" I rasp, my throat desert dry. "You made them do these terrible things?"

Meg shrugs, a smirk twitching at the corners of her mouth. "I can't make anyone do anything, Harriet. I only helped them to travel a road they were already on."

I shake my head, recalling Mum's stories, knowing there was far more to it than that. "Where did this note come from? How do I know my mum really wrote this?"

Meg laughs, and I bristle at how much my pain is amusing her. "Surely you recognise the handwriting? Anna tucked that inside that little diary you found in her room, right before she took matters into her own hands. Eleanor found it and I suggested that she should give it to me for safekeeping. The last thing we wanted was for her dear granddaughter to find out the awful truth."

"What do you mean?" The tears begin to fall now; tears of frustration, tears of anger. Tears of grief. I look down at the note again, trying to make sense of it all. The writing is more controlled, more mature than the script from Mum's stories, but it would be hard to deny that both were written in the same hand. "What do you mean, she took matters into her own hands? What happened to my mum?"

Meg looks straight at me, and I see her nostrils flare as her eyes burn. "She left me. She took a bottle of pills and left me, just like she left you. I remember the morning Eleanor found her, cold and dead in that bed you've been sleeping in. What was left of her heart broke that day."

I sink to my knees, the strength of my sobs overtaking me. "Oh, God! Mum!"

"God has nothing to do with this," Meg growls, her voice sinking several octaves. "He wasn't there when Anna died. He wasn't there when Eleanor buried her daughter in the garden, just like she'd buried Anna's father all those years ago. Only I was there. I was always there for them."

"You ruined their lives! You tormented them!"

"I helped them."

I look up at her, my vision blurred. "And what now, now that they're both gone? Is it me you've come to help?"

That sick grin spreads across her face like a disease. "Oh no, sweet Harriet. I can't help you, not after what you've done."

My heart thuds hard in my chest as I try to get to my feet. "What do you mean, what I've done?"

"I think you know. I think you know it became impossible for us to be friends once I heard all about your dirty little secret, your filthy little affair. You might have managed to work your charms on poor Daniel, but they won't work on me."

Her smile is gone now, her jaw set hard and angry as she corners me at the bottom of the stairs. Instinctively I press myself against the wall, as though I could disappear into it, as though it could swallow me whole. As though it could rescue me. But it can't; this house can't save me, it never could. It's Meg's now, part of her story to do with as she pleases. I was only ever a visitor. I was only ever passing through.

I startle as every door in the house slams shut. Meg laughs, an insidious, dreadful laugh, and I look on in horror as she twirls around in front of me, warm air emanating from her every movement as the house grows hot, so hot. The creaking and groaning begins again, and I can't decide whether the house is objecting to this new disruption, or embracing it. All the weeks I've spent here believing this place was my shelter, my refuge from the things I'd done, the people I'd left behind. Now I know that it was nothing of the sort. Now I know that there has never been anything good for me to find here.

Meg's laughter grows louder as I look down at my feet, startled to see smoke rising from the floor. Coughing, I take a step up on to the stairs just as the entire hallway is suddenly consumed by flames. Through the fire and the smoke, I realise I can no longer see the front door. I can no longer see anything. Except Meg, standing in the midst of it all. Meg and her deranged smile. Meg and her flowing skirt and her dancing.

Realising I've no means of escape, I run upstairs. The fire seems to follow me, obstructing my path, obscuring my way. I try to flee into Mum's room, to seek sanctuary in the one room which has felt like home over these past weeks. The room which, I now know, my mum died in. It crosses my mind that if I'm to die today, it would be fitting for me to die in there, too.

But Meg isn't having any of it. I try to turn the handle but it is so hot that it burns my hand.

"There's nowhere to go now, Harriet!" she screams from below.

Choking on the fume-filled air I try another door, then another, whimpering as each handle singes my skin. Then finally, I reach Eleanor's room at the end of the hall. The room with the mural. The room which unnerves me. The room which I have, so often, skilfully avoided. Behind me the fire approaches. There's no way back from here, I realise; I either find my way into Eleanor's room or I burn on this spot. Covering my burnt hand with my sleeve I brace myself for another scolding rejection and try to open the door.

To my surprise, although the handle is hot, the door opens.

I run inside, slamming the door shut behind me. The mural casts its cosmic gaze down upon me as I frantically pile sheets up at the base of the door, hoping to stem the tide of the smoke, desperate to buy myself some time, any time. My mum might have given up, and Eleanor might have succumbed to old age, but I'm not done living yet. I even try to open the window, wincing as I grip it with my injured hand. Of course, it is stuck fast, obeying Meg's command to keep me in here. To make me choke. To let me die.

"I'm sorry," comes a voice. A small voice, far away but just about here. For a moment I think the mural is talking to me, that now that I am trapped in here and forced to listen, it has decided to share its story. I look up at it, taking in its now familiar swirls of colour and edges of darkness. If it did speak, what would it say? What would it say about its creator?

"I'm sorry." The voice comes again, and this time I realise who it is. I sink down against the mural and put my head in my hands.

"Sometimes little places like this are the worst for things not being as they seem," I say, resignation hanging heavily in my voice as I quote his words from an earlier conversation. Words I didn't understand then. Words I understand all too well now. "You knew everything all along, didn't you, Bert?"

"Yes. I'm sorry Harriet, I truly am. I couldn't tell you and I couldn't stop her. I'm nothing in this world, and I'm nothing in the next, either. I'm stuck here, with her."

A tear slips down my cheek as the first smoke creeps under the door. "You're not nothing. You're here. That has to mean something."

"It's been wonderful talking to you, Harriet. You'll never know how much it has meant to me." His voice is faded but rings with emotion.

"I can't believe you knew that Anna killed you. All those times we spoke and you never said anything," I whisper. "And you must have known what Eleanor did to your lover, too. How could you keep that to yourself? How could you let me think that it was you who'd killed her?"

"Enough lives have been destroyed by what happened in this house. What possible good could have come from you knowing? And besides," he adds, his voice tight with emotion, "I wasn't perfect. I made Eleanor's life a misery. I lied and I cheated; I was cruel and I was unkind. I would have killed Eleanor that day, if

Anna hadn't killed me. I was beside myself with rage when I found out that she had murdered Barbara. She wasn't just my lover. She was my everything."

"Oh, God." I put my head in my hands, unable to listen to any more. So much pain. So much darkness. So much death.

"Meg is wrong about one thing," Bert says. "Anna – your mum – has been back here. She's the one who left you that note on the door, telling you that she loves you, asking for your forgiveness. Your mum hasn't abandoned you, Harriet."

I want to ask him how he knows this, if he saw her, if she's still here. But I can't. I can't bring myself to utter the words. I can't bear to hear his answers, if he has any. I've learnt the hard way that questions about my family only ever bring me heartache and death.

The smoke is pouring into the room now, thickening the air with its toxicity. I cover my face with my sleeve but it is futile; within moments the air becomes hazy and the poison fills my lungs. I feel the heat of flames surging at me from every direction as the house succumbs to Meg's wrath. Downstairs I can still hear her giggles and her taunts, even though I don't care to listen; I don't want her voice to be the last thing I hear. I press my back harder against the mural and find myself imagining what will happen when the flames reach Eleanor's prized work, my fume-addled brain visualising the paint melting, the bright colours running free, only to be consumed by the endless black of the cosmos, of flame, of ash. It occurs to me then that everything gets consumed by the dark in the end.

"Smash the glass, Harriet. Jump out the window," Bert urges me, but I only shake my head as I slump wearily on to the ground. The glass won't break, and even if it did, the fall will kill me. Whatever I do now, it will kill me. I realise now that there was only ever one way that this was going to end.

"Do you think everyone remembers how they died, Bert?" I ask, wheezing out the whispered words.

"I don't know," he replies. "Probably."

I give a small smile. "Then I'd better close my eyes." I think the words but I'm not sure if I say them. I'm not sure of anything anymore, other than some remote awareness that my mind, my body, all of me is slipping away. Going on a journey. Travelling somewhere new. I think about what that place might be, what it might look like, who I might see.

I think about whether I'll see Eleanor there. I think about whether I'll see Mum.

I think about anything, apart from the house at Kirtlebeck End. Apart from Meg, apart from the fire and the smoke, apart from the breath as it is squeezed from my chest. I don't want to think about this. I don't want to remember any of this.

I don't want to remember that this is how I died.

Epilogue

Harry
April 2019

I grab a seat at the bar and make myself comfortable. It is early on a Friday evening but already this place is busy, filled to the brim with the laughter and clinking glasses of weekend revellers. I settle further into my seat, enjoying the hum of other people's lives as they carry on around me. Listening to the chatter, the banter exchanged in that rapid, increasingly familiar accent. Appreciating being in the midst of it all, yet still being satisfyingly detached, reassuringly anonymous. A grain of sand in the Sahara. A tiny fish in the ocean. The relative newcomer in this huge, sprawling place I now call home. I smile to myself, letting those words sink in. Glasgow is my home now. A city just like Manchester, and cities never quieten, not even for a moment. Cities never stand still. Cities are always alive. I think that's why I like them so much.

I nurse my glass of sauvignon blanc as I wait for Roisin to arrive. This is always how we end our working week; a glass of wine in our favourite pub before grabbing a pizza and heading back to the flat we share. We do a 'straightfae', as Roisin calls it, using one of the many puzzling expressions I've come across here which sound so clumsy when they roll off my Mancunian tongue. I glance at my watch. It's a little after five; I'm usually here first as my office is nearer, but I know she'll only keep me waiting ten minutes or so. That's what I like about Roisin; she's reliable and straightforward. No secrets, no hidden agendas. No ghosts, no skeletons.

Exactly the sort of person I need in my life.

I sip my drink, recalling the day we met just a few short months ago. She'd placed an advert online for a flatmate and I, new to the city and keen to escape the grotty bed and breakfast I was living in, had answered. We'd arranged to meet in a café; a public place, so that she could check that I wasn't a weirdo (her word, not mine). Once she'd satisfied herself that Harriet James was, in fact, a real person and not a pseudonym for a sociopath, we'd relaxed over our coffees and got to know each other a little better. I remember feeling stuck between a rock and a hard place, unwilling to share too much about my recent life, but worried that if I didn't tell her enough she might think I was hiding something. Which I was, of course. I could hardly tell her about the time I'd spent buried deep in the south Scotland countryside, talking to ghosts and digging up my family's awful past. I could hardly tell her that I came here because my whole world had burned down around me.

I could hardly tell her that my grandmother's house had almost killed me.

An involuntary shudder passes through me as I glance down at the scar on my arm. It's still astonishing to me that given what happened, I suffered so few physical injuries. By the time the fire brigade reached me I was unconscious from smoke inhalation, but other than my arm I wasn't burned, a fact which seems nothing short of a miracle, given the ferocity of Meg's fire. The mental scars run deep, of course, and I'm still grappling with those. I'm still taking things one day at a time. Moving to Glasgow has been a huge part of my recovery; starting again, somewhere new, has given me a sense of distance, of closure. Frankly, it's been utterly liberating to come here, to get a new job, to have a flatmate. To not be alone. I take another sip of my drink and try not to think about who I have to thank for that, who first put the idea about Glasgow in my head when he told me he once lived here. I find it hard to think about him now that he's gone. Now that I know I'll never see him again.

Now that I know he was the one who saved my life.

It was weeks before Emma would tell me the truth. In the days after the house burned down she was my rock, taking me in after I was discharged from hospital and nursing me back to health. Listening to me with compassion and understanding as the whole sorry tale of what happened poured forth from me. Sitting with me while I told the police I believed my grandfather and mother were buried in the garden. Squeezing my hand gently when I was forced to lie to them, forced to invent a confession note Eleanor had left but which had been lost in the fire as a way to explain how I knew what I knew. Standing by my side while their bodies were finally laid to rest properly, with a priest's blessing in the same cemetery as Eleanor was interred. Visiting each of their graves with me, handing me tissues as I tried futilely to make my peace with my family's sordid tale. Holding me in the night when the nightmares about Meg became too much.

There were times when I felt like I was dying all over again. Perhaps Emma realised that; perhaps she sensed that there were some things I just wasn't ready to hear.

It wasn't until the fire investigation reached its conclusion that I finally learned everything that had happened. I sat on the floor and wept that day, spilling tears over the report's findings: fire caused by electrical fault due to outdated wiring. Nothing about Meg, nothing about vengeful spirits conjuring fire out of thin air. Nothing about what actually happened to me. Although I knew it was impossible, I think I wanted the investigation to find some shred of evidence of Meg's presence there, or at least something they couldn't explain, something to cast doubt over any rational explanations. Instead of putting me at ease, the fact that they had found a cause made me feel like I was going mad, like I was delusional. Like I imagined it all.

"I need to tell you something," Emma had said, wrapping her

arms around my shoulders after I'd sobbed out all my worries, all my fears for my sanity. "The day of the fire, I saw Daniel."

"So did I," I replied, telling her what I'd told her so many times. "He was trying to help me, but then he disappeared and I never saw him again."

She drew a hesitant breath and I knew then that there was more to this story than she'd told me.

"After he left you, he came to see me. He came to tell me what was happening, to warn me that you were in danger, that there was a woman in the house, a spirit, and she meant you harm. I couldn't make sense of it, of course, but then we both saw the smoke billowing from the house and I knew that whatever he was trying to tell me, it was true. I called the fire brigade then, and well, you know the rest."

"Daniel saved my life," I whispered. "Why didn't you tell me before?"

She gave me the gentlest look, the empathy so heavy in her tired, lined eyes that I felt I could start crying all over again. "I thought it would be too hard for you to hear, so soon after it happened. I know how much you cared about him, and he about you."

I gave her a watery smile. "I loved him. But he's gone now, hasn't he?"

She nodded, and her own tears began to fall. "Yes," she replied. "I believe he has."

I stayed with Emma for several more months, until my arm had healed fully and the land where my house once stood was sold. With nothing left to keep me in Kirtlebeck, I decided to leave then, just as I'd always planned. I decided to go somewhere new, somewhere no one would know about me, my family, or our story.

Somewhere I could start again.

"Guess who?" Delicately fragranced hands cover my eyes and a smile creeps over my face as I realise my friend has arrived.

"A total pain in the arse," I retort.

"Charming." Roisin pulls up a seat beside me and orders a glass of wine to match mine. Always sauvignon blanc. Always large. "Good day?"

I nod. "Uneventful. Just how I like it."

She grins, waving a mock-dismissive hand in my direction. "Oh come on, Harriet James, you need to live dangerously sometimes!"

"I really don't. Danger isn't all it's cracked up to be, trust me."

Roisin puts her wide green gaze level with mine. "And there she goes again with her cryptic remarks. I'll get to the truth of it all, you know." She glances down and places a light, caring touch on the puckered skin of my arm. "Like, what happened here. You'll tell me, when you're ready."

I take another sip of my drink. Around us the bar grows busier, the evening draws in, night falls. Life goes on. Thank you, Daniel, I think to myself. Thank you for making sure that I am still here to enjoy it.

"Yes," I agree, mirroring her smile. "Yes, I will. One day."

The End

ABOUT THE AUTHOR

Sarah L King lives in West Lothian, Scotland, with her husband and children. Born in Nottingham and raised in Lancashire, her books include the historical fiction novels, *The Gisburn Witch* (2015), *A Woman Named Sellers* (2016) and *The Pendle Witch Girl* (2018), all set during the Lancashire witch trials in the seventeenth century. In 2017 she published a contemporary novel, *Ethersay*, a mystery/women's fiction/political fiction hybrid set during the Scottish independence referendum in 2014. *The House at Kirtlebeck End* is her fifth novel.

When she's not writing Sarah loves long country walks, romantic ruins, Thai food and spending time with her family.

For further information please visit her website & blog at http://www.sarahlking.com/